FERRETT STEINMETZ

Flex

WITHDRAWN

ANGRY
ROBOT

ANGRY ROBOT
An imprint of Watkins Media Ltd

Lace Market House,
54-56 High Pavement,
Nottingham,
NG1 1HW
UK

angryrobotbooks.com
twitter.com/angryrobotbooks.com
Your flexible friend

An Angry Robot paperback original 2015

Copyright © Ferrett Steinmetz 2015

Cover by Stephen Meyer-Rassow
Set in Meridien by Argh! Nottingham

Distributed in the United States by Random House, Inc., New York.

ISBN 978 0 85766 460 0
Ebook ISBN 978 0 85766 461 7

Printed in the United States of America

9 8 7 6 5 4 3 2 1

FLEX

"*Flex* is hot, inventive, and exciting. A real joyride of a story… a whole new kind of magic and a whole new ballgame. Totally recommended."
Seanan McGuire

"Amazing. I have literally never read a book like this. Read this NOW, if only to be forced to turn the page wondering what the hell Steinmetz is going to come up with next."
Mur Lafferty, John W Campbell Award-winning author of The Shambling Guide to New York

"Featuring one of the most original magic systems ever devised and a pair of likable, layered protagonists, *Flex* is a fast-paced, imaginative, and emotionally engaging adventure."
Ken Liu, winner of the Nebula, Hugo, and World Fantasy Awards

"*Flex* is a breath of magical, drug-addled, emotionally tortured fresh air, with one of the most unique and fascinating main characters I've read in ages. With great characters, evocative writing, and boundless creativity, *Flex* is one of the strongest debut novels I've ever seen, and one of my favorite novels of the year."
Dan Wells, author of I Am Not a Serial Killer

"Half part *Breaking Bad* and half part urban fantasy, *Flex* is an enthusiastic romp through a world of ingenious magic accessed by geeky, obsessive projection. Tremendously entertaining rule-tinkering and loophole-hunts abound. A terrific read."
Robert Jackson Bennett, author of City of Stairs

"Big ideas, epic thrills, and an unlikely paper-pushing hero you'll never forget. Just when you think you know what's next, the book levels up spectacularly."

John Scott Tynes, author of Delta Green: Strange Authorities

"Not since Philip K Dick started toying with reality for fun and profit has there been a novel so enjoyably hallucinatory as *Flex*. A heady mix of the surreal and the mundane, it will appeal to fans of video games, donuts, insurance, bureaucracy and crime families. Oh, and modern day mage wars. Yet for all of its wild plot, this is a story about the tender bond between parents and children, the loyalty of friends and how the odd among us find their places in the world. Ferrett Steinmetz has written a page turner!"

James Patrick Kelly, winner of the Hugo, Nebula and Locus Awards

For Uncle Tommy, who made me want to write

*And for Rebecca, who gave me the spark to
finally do it well*

You kids play nice together

PROLOGUE
The Flex and the Flux

Julian knew the exact price of everyone's pants in this nightclub. His own pants were a shabby APO Jeans knockoff ($17), purchased in a muddy alley from a toothless Chinese man, that Julian had hand-stitched with needle and thread ($2) until they'd pass casual inspection.

On any other night, Julian would feel like a fraud in this glamorous world of $275 jackets and $180 jeans – *fake it 'til you make it* – but he'd smile like he was a rich businessman's kid, not the son of an $18,000-a-year drycleaner who was dealing coke to pay his tuition ($38,439 per semester). Any other night, he'd be discreetly swapping out his water ($6 a bottle, plus a splashy-generous tip) with a smuggled flask of Popov vodka ($16.99 per gallon), drinking to muffle this horrid idea that maybe – just maybe – being rich was something in the blood, and you could never ever buy success no matter how many deals you cut.

But tonight, he'd snorted Flex. And Julian saw numbers *everywhere*.

Hot lights flickered over bodybuilders draped in velvet, each flexing into new hypermasculine poses at set intervals – an experimental art exhibit he and Anathema had stumbled into, lured by tumbling streams of statistics. The gallery patrons plucked toothpicked pieces of brie ($1.50 apiece) off of silver trays ($49.95 from Williams-Sonoma). Each tray had wasplike blurs of probabilities hovering over them – the secret knots that tied the future together.

Magic. He had snorted crystallized magic.

"I can't believe you got me *Flex*," Julian told Anathema, grinning dreamily. He rubbed the gritty residue from his nostrils, then licked his knuckle clean. It was a cloudy G-46 – supposedly low-grade by 'mancer-standards. It still made his tongue spark like electricity coursing through a fresh piercing.

Anathema had yet to name her price. If she could set him up as a Flex dealer at Addison Prep, Julian would never worry about tuition again. His father had believed in the value of hard work, spending fourteen-hour days scrubbing soup stains off of rich men's ties at his dry cleaning store, proud that he owned it. His dad had also eaten nothing but chicken broth and vitamins to make ends meet, and eventually the bank had seized his business anyway. The lesson: become a banker.

But how? Julian had applied to hundreds of scholarships to wrangle his first semester at Addison Prep – but the Addison Prep crowd was infamously sharklike, cliquish. That was Addison's strength; those who survived the boarding school's humiliating rituals emerged wreathed in that nouveau-riche scent, Wall Street's Chosen Ones. To his fellow students, as to Julian, poverty was the sign of a character flaw: his Dad's simple faith in mankind's goodness had doomed him.

And so Julian hid his poverty, shamefully stirring crackers, ketchup packets, and hot water together in his closet to make Poverty Soup, knowing that if anyone caught him, he'd be lucky to get a job dry cleaning.

If Julian could convince Anathema to be his supplier, then his $38,439 tuition was a given. His *future* was a given. His *flaws* would be *forgiven*.

Anathema unpeeled a vulpine smile. Her teeth were yellowed with meth-mouth – but unlike most meth-heads, she'd filed them sharp. Was Anathema a model turned junkie? That would explain her wild, middle-aged ex-beauty-queen look, half starved and disdainful.

Nothing explained the tiny rat bones sewn into her dreadlocked hair, though.

She elbowed him hard enough to bruise. "Which useless socialite will you cull from the herd?"

"…what?"

She jerked her chin toward the bodybuilders. "You think this art display is as stupid as I do. See their muscles trembling as they maintain those poses? The artist's trying to represent strength wrapped in velvet. Bah. Imagine wolves bursting past the bouncers, yellowed teeth slicked with saliva; they'd corner these soft, steroid-fed prey in the bathroom, tear those swollen biceps off the bone. *That's* strength. No. You don't want art. The Flex led you here to complete your obsession."

Anathema made Julian feel like a drycleaner's kid. How the hell did you *respond* to that? Was this how people spoke when they tripped balls on Flex?

Flex was beyond him. Flex was distilled magic, gifted to ordinary people by 'mancers. And no one understood magic.

Julian could handle the local dealers: twenty-something burnouts who sat in cat-piss-stained apartments, lording it over the ignorant teenagers who begged them for coke. But Anathema had crept through his dorm window at night, claiming she had supplies for the right kind of dealer.

That offended him. Julian wasn't a dealer. He only sold to friends. So what if he made friends by selling dope?

Still, he had to suck up to her. She had Flex, and edible 'mancy was nearly a rumor. Most 'mancers went crazy, got Unified, or blew a hole into the demon dimensions… and the survivors rarely felt like bottling 'mancy for sale. All 'mancers had an obsessive-compulsive fixation so strong, their desire bent the universe around them. The one in a thousand crazy cat ladies who tipped over the edge into felimancy didn't want steady incomes. They wanted housefuls of cats.

Julian finally understood why 'mancers didn't care about money. Anathema was right: this art was bullshit. Yet a noseful of magic had changed tedious pretention into dazzling flitter-blurs of statistics. All the patrons here were wreathed in mesmerizing flickers of potential futures, interlocking rings shrinking as their decisions contracted to a single point of action.

"Come on, little lamb." Anathema smiled, then smiled wider when she saw Julian flinch. "The wolves must feast. Choose your devourer."

"…what?"

"You know," Anathema purred. This reassured Julian not at all; Anathema was so comfortable with this Flex high, it made him wonder how many times Anathema had 'mancy-tripped before. 'Mancy was illegal, a terrorist attack upon the laws of physics.

Julian started to protest that no, he did *not* know what Anathema was talking about, when he noticed the woman his eyes thirsted for.

She was a brunette in her late thirties, a lush body housed in a provocative green cocktail dress – but sagging slightly in that MILF way that Julian found so cock-achingly appealing. She sipped a martini ($14) with a staid grace, so thoroughly bored by the exhibit's pretentiousness that she was ignoring it all to read an eight-dollar book of Margo Lanagan poetry.

Julian's heart was devoured.

All-male Addison held mixers – but the school supervisors treated women like they were nitroglycerin, packing everyone in tight so no one could react; strictly slow-dance affairs. Oh, Julian had gotten laid thanks to the coke, but it had been a sorry thing: fevered orgasms in broom closets. And the women? Sad, yelping inheritance kittens who waggled their asses to Flo Rida and giggled at Tosh.0.

This statuesque beauty laughed at only the cleverest of jokes. The odds swirling around Green Dress told Julian exactly how unlikely he was to impress her.

She'd been hit on by callow boys all her life; her affections could only be won by a man of intellect, spirituality, confidence. The sort of man who genuinely deserved Wall Street.

Why hadn't he read *The Great Gatsby* instead of *The 7 Habits of Highly Effective People*?

Anathema clutched his shoulder, her meat-flecked breath hot in his ear. "Even in this artificial hellhole, the laws of nature still apply: to fuck is to conquer. You want to ejaculate her full of your hollow desperation. And for one night, I've given a little lamb the teeth of a *great – big – wolf*." She flicked calloused fingers towards the opal brooch on Green Dress's chest. "'Ware her protection."

'Ware? Julian thought. *Who speaks like that?* But Anathema was right: the opal ($6,999 at Tiffany's) signaled both caution and wealth – real opals were rare, as most shattered black in the presence of 'mancy. Julian loved Green Dress's willingness to protect herself.

Julian grabbed the bartender's arm. "Two of your best." ($36, plus tip.)

The bartender dropped the drinks on the table, did not push them over. The risk of him asking for Julian's ID contracted to a certainty. Enwebbed in those potential futures were the probability fields of the bouncers, the patrons, the musclemen–

– the musclemen–

–*Flex*–

Julian squeezed probabilities; a muscleman shifted into a straight-armed lunge, accidentally punching a waitress. Expensive drinks flew into the air.

The bartender moved to see who was hurt.

Julian snagged a martini and headed over. Green Dress looked up with a grimace.

"This is the tough part," Julian stammered, trying to remember the Pick-Up Artist books he'd read. Her cool gaze squeegeed them from his mind.

"What is?" she asked.

He swallowed. "Breaking the ice."

Green Dress put down the book. Her opal brooch danced upon on her pale cleavage. "Look, kid, I'm flattered, but I've got a boyfriend."

"You did, yes."

–Flex–

Distracting the bartender was one thing. This change flexed *back*, a shark thrashing on the end of a fishing line.

Julian needed this. He needed *her*. He bore down, strangling uncountable odds until they condensed into one necessary future.

The opal cracked from shimmering silver into jagged black.

The woman's cell phone rang ($499 plus a twelve-month Verizon contract). She plucked it off the table. "Why are you calling me here, Kenneth?" she asked, then paled. "You – you slept with *who*?"

Anathema pulled Julian away as he reached out to comfort Green Dress. Anathema's grip was stronger than the bodybuilders; he was being hauled back to the bathroom by hungry wolves...

"You don't have enough Flex left to break *those* odds." She pushed Julian into a cushioned seat. "A full-scale breakup? On command? That's a frontal assault." She batted him on the nose. "Why waste precious energy going for the throat when you can dig traps?"

Julian flushed. He hated the way Anathema made him feel... well, as naïve as he *was*. "...So?"

"With the Flex comes the *flux*. Your desire, lent might by this reality-corroding poison, pushed some serious probabilities around. Now the universe pushes back. You need to let bad things happen to bleed off the good." She sized him up, green eyes glittering. "Can you? Can you let the bad things happen for me, little lamb?"

The numbers flew backwards now, a countdown to a bomb, offering horrible outcomes. The headmaster's wife chatted in the corner; she could suspend him for being out on a school night. A chicken croquette crawled with salmonella.

And behind it all, swelling like a blister, the biggest, baddest possibility: *she could notice her opal is broken.*

"Give me more Flex," Julian moaned. "I need 'mancy or she'll leave..."

Anathema scowled. "You *want* to do 'mancy?"

Julian scrambled to placate her. "Is that a bad thing? I, I... don't know how 'mancers act. I've never met one... I don't think I've met anyone who *has* met one..."

She bared those sharp meth-teeth again. "'Mancers are scum. Sinkholes in the universe. They're going to destroy the world as you know it."

She clapped a calloused palm over her mouth to smother her laughter.

Julian was near panic when Anathema shoved a paper sack into his hand. The cloudy Flex crystals glowed faintly, covered with tiny, rippling hairs. Flex wasn't true 'mancy – only a 'mancer could wear a hole in the universe through their obsessions – but a 'mancer could distill their magic, gift it in bastardized formats to mundanes. Julian crammed the crystals into his mouth, crunching them to powder; by the time he'd choked down the Flex, Anathema had slipped through the crowd, exiting with a fluid grace.

Green Dress grabbed him. Her languid beauty had transformed into haughty fury.

"Still wanna break the ice, preppie?"

"Y-yes."

"Then let's do this."

She assaulted him in the cab, kissing him like she was dispensing revenge. He felt her breasts, palming the broken opal, ditching it under the cab driver's seat.

It should have been his life's climax, getting head in the back of the cab. But horrid potential futures squeezed his temples: the taxi's front tire could blow. A cop could pull them over. A traffic jam could bring her to her senses.

Julian used the new Flex to push the old flux away. It was like trying to pay off credit cards with other credit cards; debt accrued.

Did it matter? He was kissing a woman who never would have noticed some pimpled kid working at a dry cleaners.

She hauled him up to her apartment. He wanted lovemaking; she fucked him angrily, like a porn star. At her instructions, he came all over her beautiful face, then sent her ex-boyfriend photos of her smeared cheeks.

"Can I sleep here?" he asked.

"Whatever." She rolled over.

He'd fucked her, and she'd barely noticed him. He slid his arms underneath her in supplication... and when she sighed and settled reluctantly back, acknowledging him, Julian shivered in unknowable bliss.

What he'd done was wrong. He knew that. But her tolerating his presence felt like a benediction, a sign he deserved *some* place among the wealthy and beautiful, and oh God, he'd lied and was going to Hell.

And as Julian thought about Hell, the thought swelled in his head like a blister. Something popped, and all those terrible possibilities flooded in.

The gas main beneath them exploded.

A million-to-one chance, the inspectors later said. But that was no consolation as the flame filled the apartment, fusing his skin to hers, her shrieking in pain, him shrieking as he realized what he'd done. The last thing Julian saw was the numbers fading, returning to zero, burning up along with his flesh.

Julian had been good at counting costs.

Just not good enough.

PART I

Burning Down the House

ONE
Missing Things

Paul Tsabo woke to discover that once again, his six year-old daughter had stolen his right foot.

"Aliyah!" He half-rose from the La-Z-Boy he'd drifted off in, then realized hopping about the apartment on one foot would be more likely to make Aliyah giggle than repent. Not that Aliyah was much on repentance, anyway. He wondered what he'd do if she didn't come; without Imani to help corral her, Aliyah might realize exactly how much leverage she had at Daddy's new apartment.

But no, his daughter appeared in her bedroom doorway, clad in her pink-and-green Kermit-hearts-Piggy nightgown. She clutched the prosthesis protectively against her chest. She had her best pouty face on, somehow adorable beneath her mop of tangled black curls – a messiness Imani would have combed flat, but Paul liked to see his daughter's wildness made manifest. Against his daughter's soft brown body, his artificial foot's sharp carbon-and-titanium profile looked like a blade.

"You know the rules, Daddy! You fall asleep before bedtime, I take your foot!"

"We made no such rule, Aliyah. Bring my foot here."

She stayed put. Despite his irritation, Paul felt pride at his daughter's cleverness. She'd never once asked how he removed his foot; she'd just watched him press the pin-lock button that let him take it off before bedtime. And she moved deftly enough that despite the sores on the inside of his prosthetic socket, she'd managed to spirit his prosthesis away.

We're gonna have to bar the windows on that one before she turns thirteen, Imani had once laughed... and for the first time, Paul was concerned that Aliyah's bedroom window led straight out to the fire escape.

"I said bring it here, Aliyah."

"I only get two days with you now, Daddy! It's no fun if you fall asleep." That was almost heartwarming, but then she added, "You don't even have good TV."

Paul felt guilty about the lack of kids' entertainment. The handful of Dora the Explorer DVDs he'd brought were stacked in boxes along the living room walls, packed up along with the TV. Back at Imani's house, Aliyah had all the toys in the world, but Paul had been sufficiently stunned by the affair-and-divorce that he hadn't even thought to get some stuffed animals for Aliyah's room.

"I'm sorry, sweetie," he said, rubbing grit from his eyes. "I'll unpack the DVDs tomorrow."

"I don't *want* DVDs!" she yelled. "I want to play with *you*."

Ironically, Paul had nodded off because he'd been up too late playing. Paul remembered experimenting with the manila envelopes last night; they'd crumpled and expanded, breathing like living creatures, as he filled out forms asking for CIA surveillance data. To his delight, the envelopes had unfolded themselves shyly, like a bride lifting her veil, to reveal classified reports meant for the President's eyes only...

Paul was just an insurance claims investigator.

That was when Paul realized he was able to do 'mancy.

"You're sleeping *and it's not even bedtime!*" Aliyah hugged Paul's foot and retreated farther into her bedroom. "I had a jigsaw puzzle saved for us to do! But you worked late again and now you're sleepy!"

Aliyah had inherited her mother's ability to target his weak spots. "Sweetie, I *have* to work late; that's how I help people–"

"Help me with puzzles!"

He winced. Imani had yelled at Paul for similar reasons – *Why do you spend all your free time at that damned insurance company?* And Paul had shot back, *Maybe because nobody yells at me in my office.* But that wasn't quite true. When his marriage had deteriorated to the point when the most innocent remark risked inciting hour-long arguments, arguments he refused to have in front of Aliyah, Paul could have retreated to the bar for safety.

Instead, he went to the office, because he loved filling out forms.

"Aliyah, I–" he started to say, then foundered.

It was ludicrous, losing an argument with a six year-old girl. Paul remembered something his co-worker

Lenny had told him once, back on the force: *You'd be a damned fine cop, Paul, if only you had any people instincts.*

And it was true. Whenever he asked how she felt about the divorce, Aliyah pursed her lips as if to say *None of your business*, falling silent until Daddy changed the subject. He'd tried everything to get her to open up, but Aliyah kept her secrets tight. Not that he'd have been able to explain why Mommy and Daddy's marriage had ended anyway; he'd naively thought that they were going through a bad patch, albeit a long one, and things would clear up once he just figured out how to explain to Imani what had *really* upset him about that 'mancer crushing his foot.

But even when he was baffled as to why his marriage was crumbling, Paul knew his day was done once he'd checked every box on his Samaritan Mutual case files. He was *effective* there, quietly correcting clients' mistakes, ensuring Samaritan's notoriously stingy claims department couldn't refuse them. If he couldn't fix his marriage, at least he could fix *other* people's problems.

Paul loved the *justice* of paperwork. Bureaucracy knitted humanity together – imperfectly, perhaps, but it was mankind's rough attempt at a hive mind. When human memory failed and you needed to know where your neighbor's property ended or how much money was in the bank, where did you turn? The paperwork. People were sloppy, forgetful, occasionally evil; good records kept the corrupt from lying, arm-wrestled tight-pursed bureaucracies into handing out cash, left trails to track down stolen goods.

So Paul had holed up late at the office to avoid fights, devising increasingly elaborate rituals for his paperwork, pretending he needed to fill out each form in perfect order to feed an imaginary guardian Beast.

Then, shortly after Imani had filed for divorce, his rituals had begun to *work*...

This bureaucratic marvel he'd assembled in his office – it now ran on its own, fuelled by what he knew, objectively, to be his 'mancy. He'd tracked down enough 'mancers as part of his job to know how things worked: 'mancers believed so thoroughly in their obsessions that their belief wore a hole through the laws of physics.

But the Beast hovering over his desk didn't feel like obsession; whenever he commanded fountains of folders to erupt from his file cabinets, the act felt *freeing*, wild, as though the universe was using him as an excuse to go on a beautiful bender.

He envisioned the octopoid shape of the Beast: a floating origami construction of forms and certificates, inhaling addresses and exhaling information. Last night, after pulling the CIA reports, Paul had realized the Beast could access anything that used paperwork – he'd flipped through its infinite file cabinets to fetch data from Hollywood agents, from the IRS, from the United Nations...

...so lost in this new toy that he'd forgotten his daughter was staying over tomorrow night...

Paul felt like a terrible parent.

"Come here." Something in his tone must have changed, for Aliyah hopped in his lap. She hugged him, and the world grew a little kinder. He put the artificial foot down on the table with a clatter, getting a painful glimpse of the divorce papers Imani had sent over with Aliyah.

"Sweetie, I'm sorry," he told her. "I shouldn't fall asleep when you're here. But you can't keep stealing my foot."

"I can. You never notice."

He stifled a chuckle. "Okay, you *can*. But you won't, or you'll get in trouble. Daddy–"

What should he tell her? That he'd spank her? That only bad girls were criminals? Those sorts of things were likely to appeal to Aliyah, who seemed to feed on rebellion.

Might as well try the truth.

"Daddy's very ashamed of not having a foot," he admitted. "It makes him feel stupid and sad when you take it from him. How would you like it if I took your foot?"

She hid her face; someone less familiar might have thought she was covering her smirk, but Paul knew Aliyah well enough to understand she was hiding shame. "You take my nose sometimes."

"Never permanently. And never for reals."

"But Mommy says you lost the foot for good reasons! You were fighting 'mancers. You shot them and stopped them from making drugs. She said you got a badge."

"She said it *is* a badge. Of pride. That's... not quite the same, sweetie."

He rubbed his forehead. Aliyah was technically correct; he *had* gotten a medal for shooting that illustromancer. But he'd never felt *good* about that. The illustromancer had made Flex because the poor girl had become convinced she could buy Titian's paintings from the Metropolitan Museum with enough cash.

Paul had tracked down rumors of a scrawny girl who lurked around the museum every day until closing time, ragged, breathless, gazing at Titian's portrait of Emperor Charles for hours. His fellow cops ribbed Paul for his weak interrogation skills – but no one doubted his courage and resourcefulness. His boss had once told the department, proudly, that Paul could track a cockroach through a garbage dump.

Paul had been so desperate to stop her. 'Mancers ripped holes in reality – if you ripped too many holes, you wound up like Europe, a demon-haunted ruin of melted physics. So he'd tracked her to her lair, a tarp-covered alleyway festooned with reproductions...

...and it was beautiful.

The paintings loved her so much they performed for her; the illustromancer sat rapt, watching the show as a naked Venus whispered sweet nothings in Adonis's impassive ear. A lute player sat attentively at Venus's feet, playing music so beautiful, Paul blinked away tears at the memory. The Virgin Mary, robed in bright crimson, endlessly cast off her body to ascend into an angel-filled heaven vaulted with radiant yellow.

Paul had always been told 'mancy was a violation of natural order. But standing before the illustromancer, he felt like the world had been robbed of something precious – and only here could it be regained.

Then the illustromancer had seen Paul, and Paul's police uniform, and screamed. Before Paul could explain that no, he was in love too, Emperor Charles had thundered out of the frame to protect her, a lantern-jawed brute on a black steed, crushing Paul's right foot beneath one massive hoof.

Paul, panicked, had blown off the top of the illustromancer's head. As she died, the great steed crumpled into old newspaper. The remaining posters had sagged away from the walls, bowing like mourners before collapsing into her blood.

The papers touted the triumph – *Mundane Kills 'Mancer!* He was an unlikely hero, scrawny and stammering, but his superiors had offered Paul a promotion.

Yet every time he thought about moving up the ladder, he'd remember those grieving paintings. After a few months, he'd quit the force to take a job with Samaritan Mutual. The world wanted to reward him for murdering miracles?

Why would he fight for a place like that?

So he resigned himself to investigating insurance claims and – on those rare occasions his supervisors deemed it necessary – looked into potential magical interference.

Until last week, when he had *become* potential magical interference…

"Not all 'mancers are bad, sweetie." He envisioned the churn of paperwork in his office, pulsing, growing. "The 'mancers in the army protect us."

"But the one you killed was wandering *around*!" She started to climb up on his shoulders, a strange habit she'd developed whenever she got agitated. "They should all be in the army! Or dead!"

He froze. Aliyah was right; he was a criminal.

"When I grow up," Aliyah announced proudly, "I'm going to hunt 'mancers. Like you."

"I don't hunt them, sweetie. I find them. The cops and the military capture them." *That is, when I don't overlook evidence to let them get away.* "And I'm not quite sure why you woke me up when it's already half an hour past your bedtime."

"Because I was boooooored."

"Bored girls need their sleep. Go on, brush your teeth."

"But I *have*!"

She put her hands on her hips in mock outrage, but a gentle swat on Aliyah's butt as he set her down sent her scurrying with a giggle. Paul smiled, watching her go – then winced as he pulled his prosthetic foot over the transtibial stump jutting out below his right knee.

The foot clicked into place, but his stump no longer fit into the cupped receptacle that held foot to body; it had shed muscle over time, as stumps do. The looseness caused blisters as the remains of his shin rubbed against the silicone sheath – a pain he'd learned to live with, since Paul's insurance only covered a new prosthetic fitting every two years.

He limped into the bathroom to check in on Aliyah. Good thing he'd lost the foot back on his cop's insurance plan, or else he'd be walking on a wooden peg leg. Government insurance had gifted him with a battery-operated top-of-the-line model, one with a motor that adjusted to his gait. His friends all thought he had great insurance thanks to his employer, but Samaritan had hired Paul so they could argue – whether it was true or not – that any expensive claim was 'mancy and, hence, Samaritan Mutual could cut you off without a damn cent. His continued employment was proof of Samaritan's craptastic coverage.

Imani had accused him of taking the job as punishment. Paul couldn't argue.

He limped to the bathroom. Sure enough, Aliyah had neither brushed her teeth nor washed her face. He abluted her, then tucked her into bed – she needed no night-light – and watched her until she fell asleep. She drifted off quickly. For all her rebellions, she was a good kid.

But it felt so strange, putting Aliyah to bed without Imani's help.

Paul walked into the living room, wide awake despite the hour. All his books were still packed away in boxes, waiting for him like Christmas presents. He'd been relishing the meticulous work of filling bookshelves, of separating that jumble of hastily packed history books by era, then sorting them down into alphabetical order. There would be oversized books, books with two authors, new rules needed to handle these exceptions. When it was complete, he'd have an orderly book-garden, filed in clear structures and hierarchies: a comprehensive history of mankind's attempts to better itself through written structure, from the first cuneiform attempts to track grain storage, all the way up to analyses of the Affordable Care Act.

All of which would be a welcome distraction from signing the divorce papers.

He picked them up. Imani had written on the envelope in her neat, calligraphic handwriting: "I hope you find what you're looking for." Punctuated by a tiny, cracked heart.

He frowned. *She'd* cheated on *him*. *She'd* filed for divorce.

This separation was unbearable because they still loved each other. Love was plentiful, endlessly renewable. What wore thin, Paul had come to understand, was *like*. And Imani had never understood why the illustromancer's death had bothered Paul, never understood why Paul didn't take the promotions offered him at the NYPD, never understood why anything felt *wrong* to Paul. "Why can't you accept the world for what it is?" she'd cried.

Because he'd seen what the world could be. And he'd shot the woman who'd shown him.

Paul couldn't explain that, not to himself, not to anyone, so he'd buried himself at work. Exasperated, Imani had fled to another man, Paul's opposite: ambitious, a member of the mayor's cabinet, muscular and passionate. Reality fit David Giabatta as tightly as David's custom-tailored suit.

That was the trick, wasn't it? Reality. It felt wrong without 'mancy. It had always felt wrong.

He stumbled into his bedroom. As he bent to sign the divorce papers, they flowered open in a spontaneous generation of 'mancy, unfolding into a thousand different pieces of paperwork that would also occur as a result of this action: Imani's name change form, the removal of his name from their mortgage, her separate cable bills.

It seemed cruel at first, all these reminders of things they used to do together… and then Paul realized the forms were trying to reassure him in the only language they knew how:

There will still be a future.

His 'mancy, this love, was illegal. If anyone at work unlocked the door to Paul's office, they'd find the evidence for the military to press-gang him into the Unimancy squad. They'd brain-burn him, take his daughter away. Because 'mancy was evil, it had annihilated Europe, it was the ultimate crime.

But he loved magic. And here was proof it loved him back.

"I'm a bureaucromancer," he whispered. He'd never said that out loud before. Yet as he spoke the words, he felt their correctness; after years of numbness, he'd found his way back to beauty. His daughter, his magic, all this inexplicable joy knitting together into one seamless whole.

That's when the gas main blew up in the apartment below him, and Paul's world caught fire.

TWO
Teach You to Burn

Aliyah was screaming.

Paul shoved the dresser away with both hands. Something had blown it across the room, knocking him down and landing on him. The hardwood floor's polished surface had buckled into splintered hillocks, with blue-white flames jetting up between them.

"*Baby, stay calm!*" he said. "*Daddy's coming to get you!*"

But what could he do? The boxes he'd packed his books in were ablaze, the wallpaper blackening. This place was going up fast, so what was his best bet? He'd never been a fireman. Hell, scrawny as he was, he *couldn't* have been; he'd only passed the NYPD physicals thanks to sheer tenacity, running wind sprints until his lungs burned.

"*Sweetie! Are you okay? Are you hurt?*"

"*I can't see, Daddy! I can't see!*"

Paul lurched towards the living room, then stumbled back; his body rejected the act of walking into those flames before his conscious mind could intervene. His hair crinkled, singeing from the heat, his temples

31

blistered from just poking his head in. The doorway smoked, a billowing blackness shot through with orange flame.

What the hell had happened? Why weren't the sprinklers kicking in? Below him, he heard a man and a woman shrieking, dying slowly.

At least Aliyah was uninjured.

Or in so much shock she didn't realize how burnt she was.

He had to get her out of here.

But how? Paul could see shards of his La-Z-Boy embedded in the ceiling. Ragged bits of burning rug fluttered upwards, carried aloft by air rushing in through the gaps created by the explosion. The black smoke roiled, shimmering – was that gas? Aliyah's Dora the Explorer DVDs had been blown across the room, Dora's face chewed by ashen blackness.

"Crawl to the fire escape, baby!" Each breath was like inhaling a carton of cigarettes. *"Scream! Get someone's attention!"*

She didn't reply.

The smart bet would be to creep out the fire escape of his own bedroom, on the tenement's back side. There was no way he could make it through that conflagration. Just abandon your child to her burning bedroom and hope the firemen would get there.

No. He had to take the chance.

Paul crouched down, hunting for cooler, breathable air, and looked for patterns in the roiling smoke and flames. He needed to find a rhythm to the burning, some safe pathway he might travel to Aliyah. Pyromancers were the first known 'mancers – scarred cavemen with melted cheeks, brutes who set forests ablaze to watch how the flames danced through the trees.

He was a bureaucromancer, for Christ's sake. What the hell could he do to an inferno?

Paul thought of the Beast in his office. Bureaucracy never did anything in haste. The flames rushed in, devouring, consuming. What form could deal with that?

As if by answer, the charred remains of his divorce paperwork fluttered down neatly into his palms.

It wasn't about forms, he realized. Ancient man had cut throats, making sacrifices to fill their cities with potency – fuelling the nameless powers that watched over them. Bureaucracy was a slower, safer process: surrendering a morning to the DMV, devoting your brainpower to complete your taxes. But the goal remained the same: take *these* actions to donate your life's force to the collective might, do these *other* actions to bleed that energy back.

There was raw power in the paper. He just had to unlock it.

Paul leaned against the wall, his world spinning; hot ashes blistered his lips, flames devoured the oxygen. The divorce lawyer had filled out most of the paperwork – all that was left was a space for his signature – but Paul pressed his divorce papers against the smoking wall and began to annotate.

He scrawled in new boxes, added new fields. And as he did, the paper extended underneath his flattened palm, unfolding like a kite to become the size of a newspaper, and then wallpaper, and then something even larger, a patchwork mural of stapled forms. Paul scribbled new checkboxes in the corners, and his ragged block printing condensed into crisp 8-point Times New Roman. He corralled the words into different boxes, which cloned themselves into different shades – puce copies, canary yellow copies, smudged gray Xerox.

He endlessly repeated the same words: *Request for refile. Extension. More information is needed.*

"*Aliyah!*" he gurgled, wringing the last good air from his lungs.

No answer.

Right, he thought, and did the one thing that activated every act of bureaucratic magic:

He signed his name.

The paperwork peeled away from the wall, a flock of origami cranes flinging themselves towards the fire. They wrapped paper wings around the flame in loving, suicidal embraces before crumpling into charcoal husks. But a storm of further correspondence rocketed through the doorway, etching Paul's skin with paper cuts as a hail of forms hurtled towards the blaze, driving it back, clearing a thin pathway towards Aliyah's bedroom.

Bureaucracy did not move quickly. But it *could* delay the inevitable.

Despite everything, Paul laughed, a gleeful howl, because he'd finally done what the illustromancer had done – raised something magical from a mundane world, then used this glory to beat back horrors. It felt insanely good, *literally* insanely good, that rush of shoving backwards off the bridge and trusting the bungee cord to catch you.

Paul crawled down the path underneath a canopy of black smoke, his good foot blistering, his artificial leg sparking with jittering electricity. He'd never done 'mancy this intense; until now, he'd just swiped the phone numbers of aging Hollywood starlets from old Rolodexes. He tried to ride that surge of triumph – but instead, he felt like he'd been shoved into a room full of balloons, the swelling, ear-popping pressure before the storm.

The flux, he thought, panicked. You could bend reality only so much before it bent back. Experienced 'mancers could juggle their karmic debts for weeks, but that was a training Paul didn't have…

Get to your daughter now, he thought. *Pay it off later*.

Aliyah's room scrubbed his eyes with cinders, sucked the clean air from his lungs. He dropped to the floor, sucking in the scant remnants of oxygen trapped in her pink shag rug, feeling for Aliyah. He patted the bedspread, making his way towards the window…

…and touched her bare arm.

He had a moment – a moment he would remember for the rest of his life – where he realized her arm was moving up and down in time with her lungs. She was breathing, raggedly, with great effort. Aliyah had passed out from the smoke before she'd figured out how to undo the latches on this new window.

She was alive.

Then the flux hit.

"*No!*" Paul screamed as the universe flexed back,

pouring all the fire his paperwork had consumed into his daughter. Aliyah's tangled hair burst into a bonfire; her skin peeling, she roasted so badly that even unconscious, she began screaming. Paul kicked open the window, hauled her out to the night air, yelled to the paramedics below *Please, save my daughter*.

Which they did.

Most of her, anyway.

THREE
Acts of God and Magic

Bureaucracy had burned Aliyah. Now bureaucracy saved her.

–*Paul's lungs were shriveled like wet cotton balls from the smoke damage; the ER technicians face-fucked him with a breathing tube, strapping him down to irrigate the soot from his larynx with squirts of cold water. He heard Aliyah wheezing next to him, the paramedics saying this girl's lungs were badly burnt, maybe too burnt to survive–*

–*they kept her sedated. They planed off Aliyah's dead skin until they hit bleeding, living flesh. They changed her tubes, sucking pus from her lungs. Aliyah shook her head as if to deny this was happening, gargling like she was drowning–*

But through this body-ripping cruelty, Paul felt bureaucracy guiding the hands of the medics. Her bandages, peeled off every eight hours, the task checked off by nurses and verified by supervisors. Aliyah's allergies to antibiotics, dutifully drawn from medical files and posted by her bed. Her blood, carried away in vials, broken down into clean numbers.

Though the nurses sagged with exhaustion, the actions that kept Aliyah's heart beating were converted into simple steps.

Paul loved the regularity of the hospital and hated his love of it.

His devotion to bureaucracy had stolen time from Aliyah. He'd stayed late at the office for months now to avoid fights with Imani, silently mastering Samaritan Mutual's baroque paperwork systems.

Why hadn't he spent that time with Aliyah? Why hadn't he quit his job to cuddle her in his arms, appreciate the miracle of the rise and fall of her tiny chest?

Why had he burned her?

My 'mancy saved her, he reminded himself. Aliyah had been lucky, the doctors had told him and Imani over and over, to have survived the smoke for as long as she had. She would have suffocated if Paul hadn't gotten there when he did. Paul remembered the exhilaration of files hurtling over his shoulders in an administrative hailstorm, of commanding burning wood to step aside so he could rescue his daughter...

—Aliyah's skin crisping beneath his fingertips, the flames taking revenge—

"I saved you," he muttered. "I *saved* you."

Paul tried to memorize what was left of Aliyah's beautiful face. Aliyah's remaining skin pulled tight into new formations as the burns puckered; the doctors shoved splints into her mouth to ensure her shrinking cheeks didn't tug her lips shut. Her old smile disappeared, lost in scars.

Maybe he'd saved her from death, but... he'd done that. It had been an accident, but apologies didn't heal her blisters.

And still, she might die.

Paul paced the burn ward. It was a hallway-sized terrarium, a jungled warmth designed to keep heat trapped inside skinless patients. They kept the lights dimmed to shield the children's eyes, cloaking Aliyah's bed in a funereal dusk.

You couldn't look your own child's death in the eye, he discovered. Exhausted, he fluttered between desperate hope that Aliyah would make it and bracing himself in case she didn't...

Aliyah groaned, shifting beneath disposable cotton pads.

They're late with her painkillers again, he thought. *You know why, don't you? The nurse's charts are too complex, their schedules strained. You could optimize their night shifts, cull their unnecessary paperwork–*

His hand paused as it reached for the nurse's button. Paul couldn't heal his daughter. He could imagine no document that would regraft her skin

But what use was all this new power if he couldn't use it to help someone?

Paul felt the hospital vibrating around him, a strained web of bureaucracy aching for solutions. He reached out, sick with guilt over what he'd done, desperate for escape.

The bureaucracy reached back.

The schedules of every nurse poured into his brain, their hourly wages and the department's budget – comforting, beautiful numbers, a puzzle of people.

The schedules melted at his touch, eager to be reshaped by compassionate hands. He sank into this unearthly joy, layering vacation requests over union rules. Aliyah twitched, her sedatives wearing off. Paul smiled: under his loving watch, every child would be soothed on schedule.

This would be a place of healing, a magic to counteract the damage he'd done.

And when he'd settled upon the proper configuration, Paul searched Aliyah's bedside for a form. Energy hummed in his fingertips; he had to sign something to enact this magic. His breakfast menu would do. As he reached out, fingers trembling from the painkillers for his own burns, the bold lists of "egg-white omelet" and "orange juice" shrank to tiny ribbons of overlapping schedules – a paradise of the best nurses, working according to their circadian rhythms–

It felt *so good*, doing this, so natural, like kicking off too-tight shoes at the end of a long business day.

Paul signed. The schedules contracted. The orderlies frowned, sensing next week's plans had changed…

…Flux squeezed his temples.

A nurse headed for Aliyah, a fresh bag of Fentanyl in his hands. The ward's efficiency was improving already. But the laws of physics jostled close, demanding restitution: Paul had fixed things, and now something had to go wrong.

Cold reality flooded in. Had he been doing 'mancy in a children's ward? Next to *Aliyah*? He'd chased enough 'mancers to know what flux blowback did – hell, he'd hunted most of them down only because their 'mancy rebounded. He had to get out before anyone got hurt—

The children—

The flux leapt from his body, darting into the janitor's closet. Paul lurched forward, unsteady on his artificial leg – too late. There was a gurgle, a hiss, then a choked shriek as one of the orderlies stumbled out, wreathed in green smoke, blisters bubbling on his lips. A bleach bottle tumbled from the orderly's hands as Paul's eyes watered, the children's ward filling with the hot scent of chlorine gas...

He must not sign a form.

Paul tended to Aliyah: he ensured that her saline bags never went dry, her dead tissue was debrided twice a day, her sleeping form was flipped every four hours to keep clots from forming. He brought every change in Aliyah's symptoms to the doctors so nothing would go overlooked.

Aliyah's charts offered to grade the doctors' performances. He didn't dare accept their help.

No one blamed him for the orderly's mistake. They called it an accident: a clogged drain full of ammonia that had reacted with a bucketful of discarded mop bleach. A freak event that had created a cloud of deadly poison and sickened eight kids.

Only Paul knew how close he'd come to killing children.

He'd been trying to *help*. But he'd flipped competencies: once a master of red tape, now a fumbling 'mancer. Worse, the world wanted magic. The letters fidgeted under his gaze as he glanced at insurance forms, eager to act at his behest – and yes, the burn ward ran more efficiently, but he remembered the children coughing as the nurses clapped oxygen masks over them and he *must not let that out–*

If he focused on Aliyah, he could do no 'mancy. He'd hurt her too much already. But magic, he discovered, now squirmed effortlessly out of his daydreams...

Imani sat next to him.

She frowned, looking him up and down. Paul felt suddenly shabby – his suit, once crisp, was stained brown with sweat. Whereas Imani, stylish as always, wore a long tan coat with seven onyx-black buttons, splitting at mid-calf to reveal a black skirt. It looked both businesslike and regal, which suited her – an Egyptian princess's stiff bearing.

Imani reached out to place her palm against her daughter's ankle, a perfunctory but firm touch, enough to let Aliyah know she was here. Then she brushed a greasy lock of hair away from Paul's forehead.

He froze at her touch, as always. There was something so transcendently beautiful about her that he'd always believed she might vanish with the dawn.

"You stink, Paul." Her voice was blandly factual. "Have you been home since Aliyah got here?"

He smiled ruefully.

"I haven't had a home since the fire."

She sighed. "Don't tell me Samaritan Mutual is refusing you replacement housing..."

"No, Kit found me a place." His boss and best friend Kit had pressured Samaritan Mutual's notoriously stingy claims department until they had grudgingly checked Paul into a no-tell motel. "It's just... easier to sleep here."

Imani's face went slack; she picked out appropriate expressions for every occasion but had never quite mastered polite regret.

"Paul." She placed her palm against his ankle in what she'd meant to be a caring gesture, but her hands touched cold metal. She flinched back, wiping her fingers on the hem of her dress.

"You'd better learn to quash that reaction," Paul snapped.

She blushed. "It's just – just still a surprise, that's all."

He jerked his chin towards Aliyah's bandaged face. "That's what *they'll* say." People always winced when his pants leg fell open to reveal his black carbon shin... then their faces softened into sickening pity. Bad enough enduring that sympathy with a deformity you could hide under a pair of slacks – but a face?

You saved her, he told himself, for the thousandth time. *She'd be dead without you.* But scarred as she was, her future would be a hard, hard thing.

"Paul, look – you've been in lockdown mode for two weeks. That's understandable. Kit tells me it's a pretty standard response to trauma. But now she's stabilized, you – you have to start helping her."

"I'm doing everything I can to help."

Except 'mancy. Not 'mancy.

She arched one perfectly plucked brow. She'd always seen through him. "Everything?"

"...yes."

She tossed an envelope onto his lap. Paul recoiled – *the Beast!* – and it tumbled off, sailing underneath the bed. Imani sighed, slid one high-heeled foot underneath to retrieve it, then pressed the paper into his palm.

Paul squeezed his eyes shut: *if I don't look at it, I can't hurt her–*

"Just tell me what it is," he hissed.

"Oh, for Christ's – they're refusing her reconstructive surgery," Imani said hotly.

Shocked, he looked. The clauses twitched under his fingertips, shamed: Samaritan rejected a perfectly good claim because the treatment would cost half a million dollars, and the surgery wasn't "necessary to life-sustaining functions."

The clauses wriggled invitingly: *But we could make them fund it…*

He shoved the thought aside, smelling chlorine. "How did you get this?"

"While you've been bathing Aliyah in pity, *I've* been bombarding Samaritan with requests," she shot back. "With Kit's help, I've got four world-class plastic surgeons willing to testify this technique is the only way to repair Aliyah's features. Half a million dollars. Yet your employers think 'a face' is an *unnecessary expenditure*. And the man who Kit tells me is the best in all of Samaritan Mutual at pushing claims forms through? The man every cop on the NYPD came to when a bureaucratic obstruction needed to vanish? *That* man has been treating every piece of paperwork like it's a rattlesnake."

Paul imagined how he'd force a claim through Samaritan Mutual's layers of tight-pursed bureaucrats – and as he did, he felt the universe Flex invitingly...

"No," he muttered, quashing the urge.

"*No?*"

"No, no, I mean, of course I'll–"

"I tried to do the right thing when you lost your foot, Paul. I played the good wife, dispensing sympathy. I thought you'd come *back* to me. But you didn't. You *gave up.*"

"I'm sorry – it's not your–"

"I won't let you give up on Aliyah. You work for an *insurance agency. Her* insurance agency. And by God, you'll pull every string or I'll fight you for sole custody."

You want her to be safe, yet you're asking me to use magic I don't know how to control!

"That's not fair – you don't–"

"I don't care, Paul," Imani snapped, exhausted. Then her face softened; half the reason their marriage had chugged along for as long as it did was they could never stay mad at each other.

She leaned in. "...is it the 'mancy, Paul?"

Paul stiffened.

"I know that..." Imani wrung her hands. "...that killing that 'mancer broke something inside you. And your apartment must have been ablaze with magic – if you saw things in the fire, it's okay to talk. I've asked Kit, he says he can get Samaritan Mutual to pay for PTSD treatment–"

If she knew I was a 'mancer, I'd be locked up in the Refactor, Paul realized. *It must be something else...*

Paul shook his head, stupefied by the facts. "...They think a 'mancer was responsible for the fire?"

"Someone's dosing people with fatal levels of Flex and setting them loose. We were lucky Aliyah survived the attack – Kit thinks it may be a terrorist 'mancer at work. But... you've tracked down 'mancers. For Samaritan. So, you know how they think. Is that..." Imani swallowed. "Is that why Samaritan is refusing Aliyah's treatments, Paul? Acts of God and magic?"

That was the line of most insurance companies, who loathed 'mancers. Insurance companies profited by making bets on nice, predictable averages; magic's unpredictability bent their bell curves in half.

Oh, you could get insurance against magic, but that was expensive, since no actuarial table could predict 'mancer strikes. And 'mancer claims were insanely variable; rebuilding a burnt house was a fixed cost, but 'mancers could turn apartment complexes into fried chicken.

So most folks opted for the cheaper "Acts of God and magic" coverage. Samaritan could deny any claim, no matter how expensive, if Paul or his boss Kit could ferret out evidence of 'mancy. That was Paul's whole job, tracking down 'mancers to save Samaritan some dough.

"Magic doesn't matter in health insurance claims." Paul's voice was taut with fury as he tried to comprehend what Imani had just told him. All of Aliyah's pain had been part of some crazy asshole's *plan*? Someone had almost killed his daughter *intentionally*?

"So... they're not rejecting her because this is 'mancy?"

"Samaritan Mutual has to cover any injury, regardless of source. They just have to think it's a worthy treatment."

Imani sighed with relief. "Then make her worthy, Paul."

She squeezed the back of Paul's neck affectionately – a cruel touch that reminded him of the intimacy they'd once shared – before withdrawing.

Paul slumped by Aliyah's bed, trembling with rage. He knew Imani was right: he needed to help Aliyah. Aliyah's treatments would probably cost half a million before this was done; 'mancy or no, it'd take all his skills to wrestle that kind of funding out of Samaritan. He had to *focus*.

But... someone had burned his daughter. On *purpose*. Back when he'd thought Aliyah's pain had been an accident, Paul had wished that God had existed, just so he could punch Him in the face. Now someone was responsible – if Kit thought the fire had been started by a 'mancer, then it was a 'mancer – and Paul's job was hunting down evidence of 'mancy.

He couldn't abandon Aliyah to chase a criminal, that would be irresponsible, but... was there a way he could use bureaucromancy to find this bastard? Or would his flux backfire and destroy the evidence that might help track this murderer down?

Paul had no clue. He knew how to *find* 'mancers, not how to *be* one...

"...Daddy?"

It was the first time she'd spoken since the fire. Her breath was paper-thin, her voice thick in her misshapen mouth.

"Yeah, love?"

"…Is it true, what Mommy said?"

Oh, God. What could he tell her? That he'd lost faith after killing the illustromancer? That he'd taken a shit job as penance, and now she might be burned forever, thanks to Daddy's bad choices?

"What did Mommy say?"

"That a 'mancer burned me."

He thought of the Beast in his office. He couldn't control his magic. If he pushed through approval for Aliyah's work, her anesthesia might malfunction. Maybe Aliyah's funding would rob the medicine from a hundred sick toddlers. Experimenting with lives at stake was irresponsible, reckless, mad.

It was the only way to save her.

"Yes, sweetie." He squeezed her toes. "A 'mancer burned you."

"They're bad." Her eyes were cold and clear. "All the 'mancers. Bad men."

"Yes," he agreed, settling into the role. "Yes, they are."

FOUR
Samaritans at Samaritan

On the subway, riding to work, Paul went over the police reports one more time. It had been a risk, extracting the information – he'd sat in his hotel room, scribbling information requests on the Herald Square complimentary notepads until they'd expanded into full case files. He watched, delighted, as report by report, his 'mancy brought him everything the government knew about the person who'd set his home on fire.

Then the flux had hit, and the ceiling collapsed on him. Not the whole ceiling, just a posterboard-sized chunk of termite-infested plaster, but enough to remind Paul that maybe he shouldn't fuck around.

But he hadn't been able to squash his need to read up on the person who'd hurt Allyah. Paul reread the reports on the commute over to Samaritan, double-checking that he hadn't missed anything.

He hadn't. The information was just terrifyingly incomplete.

Paul ignored the pair of overly affectionate college students squeezing into the subway seat next to him and checked the facts again: two people had burned to death when that gas main had exploded – some young kid brimming with Flex, and the unlucky business executive who'd bedded him. Someone had fed that poor college kid Flex until the world had exploded.

Four people had died of brain aneurysms when a forty-six year-old stockbroker, desperate to see her senile mother speak again, had OD'd on Flex. The nurses on the old-age ward claimed the mother had jolted upright, wailing in tongues about the anathema of civilization collapsing – then her eyes bled. Then her daughter's eyes bled. When two orderlies moved in to help, all four of them stroked out.

Eight people in a Drake's Cakes plant died when an obese man on Flex, desperate to have the snack cakes he'd been starving for since his favorite sweets producer went bankrupt, burst in and made a plaintive plea for the good old days. By an astounding coincidence, seven of the plant's employees had been ex-employees of the now-defunct snack cake manufacturer, and each recalled working there as the happiest days of their lives. As their foremen protested, all eight men set out to replicate the recipe – but in retooling the equipment, a freak accident drowned them in a tide of boiling corn syrup.

Sixteen people waiting in a plastic surgeon's office had died of a rare allergic reaction to anesthesia when a one-in-a-million canister leak hissed sevoflurane into the air conditioning. Which of the patients had overdosed on Flex had yet to be determined, but nobody doubted that Anathema had struck again.

"Anathema" was merely a code name, a placeholder designation stolen from a weird word the babbling victims at the old-age home had been unable to stop repeating as they died. The only people who'd had direct contact with Anathema had been Anathema's victims, none of whom had survived to tell the tale. Paul had scoured every file from the FBI, the NYPD, and SMASH, hunting for possible motivations: all anyone knew for certain was that a 'mancer was luring people to their deaths by feeding massive amounts of Flex to desperate people. Was Anathema white? Gay? Indonesian? Genderqueer?

Nobody knew. Not one living soul had seen him, her, or it.

The only thing people *were* certain of was that if Anathema was not stopped, thirty-two more people would die a strange and hideous death in the next few days. Each of these horrific catastrophes had killed twice the number of the one before. Which was a terrifying thought, as 'mancers' obsessions were normally self-contained: for all their power, they were usually dangerous only by accident, happy to interact with their own world. Most died to their own flux blowback.

But when a 'mancer set out to kill as part of his obsession...

Paul crumpled the report angrily; the college kids stopped nuzzling each others' necks to give him a puzzled look. He ignored them. Aliyah had been scarred *on purpose*. All her future pain, traceable to one person.

He squeezed his metal ankle absently. He'd get Aliyah her reconstructive surgery so that she'd never endure the pain of people giving her pity-filled looks on crowded subways. But he also wanted to punish the man who'd inflicted her anguish. Two separate goals, each insanely dangerous – but skimming the case files, Paul thought he might have figured out a way to have one hand wash the other. Revenge and healing, wrapped in one dangerous little package.

The question is, could he trust his boss Kit to help him?

Paul had pulled up Samaritan's case files as part of his research, and had discovered one unsettling fact: Kit had to know Aliyah's injury was from a terrorist attack. Kit had investigated Paul's apartment personally, as well as the other attack sites. And Kit was far from dumb.

So why hadn't Kit told Paul about the Flex overdoses when Kit had visited Aliyah at the hospital? Why had Kit kept Paul purposely ignorant?

Come to think of it, Kit had only visited a few times. Odd behavior for a best friend. Odder still for Aliyah's godfather.

What on Earth was Kit hiding?

A realization: Paul could trace Kit's movements if he had to. Each of Kit's E-ZPass toll payments left a bureaucratic record somewhere, Kit's expense reports marked where Kit had eaten his allotted meals, Kit's credit card records would reveal where Kit had stopped to fill up on gas...

The FBI reports uncurled beneath his fingertips, the

letters on the page marching like ants, helpfully reforming into authorization request forms at Samaritan Mutual.

Paul wadded the report tight again. He'd always been a quick reader, reading people's emails over their shoulders before he realized what he was doing – his eyes absorbing the words before his conscious mind could shut it down. 'Mancy was like that: reflexive, unconscious.

Had anyone on the subway seen the newspaper change? Thankfully, the smooching couple was self-absorbed, and everyone else was staring down at their phones. Paul looked up at the advertisements lining the ceiling, featuring teams of black-armored SMASH agents: "*Physics: not just a good idea, it's the law. Report all 'mancy! Call 1-800-SMASHEM!*"

There were a hundred mundanes on this car. If one person saw him doing 'mancy, SMASH would haul him to the Refactor.

No. He had to research in the safety of his office. His plan was good, he thought, but… he was too inexperienced. This plan needed a real 'mancer.

That's why he planned to find a mentor.

He got off at the next stop, butterflies vomiting in his stomach. And yet for all his nervousness, his arrival was somehow reassuring: he was at Samaritan again, the safe place Paul always retreated to when everything went wrong.

As Paul walked through the lobby, he ached to pretend nothing had happened, to spend the day completing forms. That was how he relaxed;

sometimes, he'd ask his co-workers if they had anything they wanted filled out. Samaritan's forms were notoriously impenetrable; it was satisfying, resolving the departments' conflicting requirements into one perfect claim.

The only forms he'd be signing today would be magical ones.

Samaritan Mutual's Claims Adjustment department had all the charm of a community college: rows of battered industrial desks from the 1960s, flickering fluorescents, permanently grimed tile floors. People walked back and forth to talk to each other, since Samaritan's CEO, Lawrence Payne, infamously disdained email. "Email makes men waste time writing thoughts that should be spoken," he claimed – and so most forms were still filled out with typewriters, and the phones never stopped ringing.

The office was Payne-free today, which made Paul grateful. Mr. Payne, an octogenarian ex-Marine, descended periodically from his penthouse suite to sit in on random calls. He called them his "snap inspections", keeping the office in a tizzy of busywork.

Still, all conversation came to a stop as Paul pushed his way through the frosted glass doors. His co-workers' faces turned towards him like flowers towards the sun, angling to offer him pity.

Please, don't, he thought. He envisioned himself as an ocean wave, moving inexorably toward the shore. If anyone interrupted him, he'd smash against them in a spray of salt tears. Aliyah filled his every waking hour with regret, a regret that threatened to unman him; he needed to ride this swell of hatred, scouring grief with vengeance.

Kit intercepted Paul, ushering him into his office, closing the door behind them. "Imani said you might show today."

Kit was an elderly New York widower in a rumpled suit and hat – a man who looked perfectly at ease sharking chess games with the other old Jews down under the arch. Under Kit's cool gaze, Paul never felt crippled; he felt like a man with problems – a small distinction, but invaluable to an amputee like Paul.

"Let's see if you put your money where your mouth is." Paul opened up the greasy donut box that invariably rested on Kit's desk, feigning jocularity.

Sure enough, there was a lonely cruller buried among the sugar-coated and glazed donuts. Paul lifted it out, took a healthy bite.

"I rather think I put my money where *your* mouth is," Kit said, matching Paul's pseudo-friendly wariness. "I only buy crullers on days I know you're showing up. No one else here will eat them, which is proof of their good judgment. Only you would covet these dry, éclair-shaped wannabes, flavorless unless dunked in a superior material... Evidence of a deep character defect..."

Kit maintained that the donut a man chose told you much about his personality, often going off on tangents about the borderline sociopathy of the Boston Kreme aficionado, which led many at the office to jokingly call Kit "The Dunkinmancer."

"So how'd you know the fire was 'mancy, Kit?"

Kit didn't play the bullshit game of saying *Oh, I didn't* ***not*** *mention the case to you*. Instead, he crossed his arms and gave Paul an unapologetic stare, as if to acknowledge *Yes, kid, I played you*.

"I was sent to investigate because we thought it was arson. I was motivated because of Aliyah. And when I met the boyfriend of the woman who'd died in the fire, he seemed shocked that he'd cheated on her. He told me how everything had fallen into place with unbelievable coincidences – an old flame who showed up when he'd been drinking, an apartment door left unlocked at the right time, the usual magical horror show. So I correlated taxi GPS timestamps from the art show she'd attended, then fished *this* out from underneath the driver's seat." He produced a shattered black opal from his vest pocket. "*Et voilà*. Proof of another physics-bending menace to society."

Kit's work never failed to impress. Paul tipped his coffee to Kit in salute. "Due diligence."

"I try twice as hard and it takes me four times as long to find those goddamned 'mancers," Kit said. "You? You're a magical dowsing rod. If every cop had your instincts, we'd clean the town of these maniacs."

Paul winced. Kit's loathing of 'mancers had been a constant undertow of discomfort in an otherwise comfortable friendship. But Kit's hatred was a common failing.

"If I'm so good," Paul asked, "why'd you hide the case from me?"

Kit blew air through pursed lips. "…let's talk about your paperwork, kid."

What did Kit know? Paul stiffened. If Paul left evidence of his 'mancy at the apartment, Kit would have found it.

"I haven't been here in two weeks, Kit," Paul said, keeping a lean smile plastered to his face. "I haven't done any paperwork."

"That's... not quite true. Why don't we go to your office?"

Where the Beast lives.

'Mancy had a *feel* to it. Paul had chased magic for so long, he could sense a 'mancer's presence. Kit had never quite gotten the knack of 'mancy – possibly because he despised its existence – but he wasn't prone to overlooking evidence, either.

Kit steered Paul across the hallway to Paul's office. He fumbled out a key to unlock the frosted glass door with "Paul Tsabo" stenciled on the front. Kit looked harried, jerking his head from side to side as if Mr Payne might interrupt at any moment.

Paul heard papers rustling inside. Kit knew. He *had* to know. He was just applying pressure to see if Paul would admit to his crimes – and if Kit knew, then this would be the last stop before Kit turned Paul into SMASH, sent him off to be Refactored and brain-wiped.

Kit was toying with him. Had to be.

Should he instruct the Beast to attack Kit when the door opened? *Could* he? He could cut Kit's electricity off, destroy his credit line – but could the Beast *murder*?

Could *Paul* murder?

"Look, Paul," Kit said. "You didn't get the time off."

"You said I had caregiver leave to take care of Aliyah."

"I said you could *have* caregiver leave. Come on, bubeleh, this is Samaritan Mutual – you think they'd give you unscheduled days off, even for a child as sick as Aliyah? No, we covered for you."

Kit unlocked the door. Paul braced himself for the blizzard of paperwork that would come flying out, Kit's cry of horror as he was engulfed in a whirlwind of claims forms–

But no. The door swung open to reveal Paul's office: a cramped space with statute books lining the walls, a gray IBM computer with a sputtering Internet connection, piles of computer printouts. The Beast lay dormant across the shelves, sleeping piled in black plastic trays.

Yet they weren't *his* piles. Paul stacked his forms to crisp perfection – a ritual to feed the Beast. Someone had replaced his stacks with *heaps*.

He picked up a few forms, marked with angry red errors. His signature was on the bottom... or a reasonable facsimile thereof.

Kit wrung his hat. "...we've been doing your work for you."

Paul was stunned. Paperwork took up a disproportionate part of Paul's day, but he still had to leave the office to investigate crumbled buildings, crashed cars, vandalized shipments. His co-workers had all taken extra shifts to cover for him.

"Seventeen cases," Kit admitted. "Everyone pitched in so you could look after Aliyah. So if a customer thinks you're an Asian woman, just run with it, okay?"

"That's…" Paul relaxed, suddenly ashamed – had he seriously considered killing Kit? His best friend? That was crazy. *He* was crazy. 'Mancers were lunatics by definition – Paul's bureaucromancy was *proof* that he was unhinged. Knowing that everyone in New York wanted him locked up and brainwashed just added "paranoia" to a stack of existing mental issues.

He wasn't thinking clearly. He should drop everything to go live out in the woods as a hermit, living out where there were no forms or paperwork or bureaucracy to tempt him into 'mancy…

No. Even if he wanted to abandon the magic, he could never abandon Aliyah.

"Why didn't you tell me?" Paul asked.

"About Anathema?"

"That it wasn't an *accident* that had burned my daughter, but a *person*."

"Because you're obsessive, Paul. We all remember the way you took off after that Illustromancer – she wasn't even your case. Then once you decided to quit the force, nothing could stop you – not your friends, not your co-workers, not your marriage. We were all terrified you'd take off after this madman."

Paul was shocked. "You think I'd have left Aliyah alone in the hospital to – to go get *revenge*?"

Kit shrugged, guiltless. "I know you love your kid. But you wouldn't be human if you didn't want a little payback. And you've got that smart-guy trick of thinking up good reasons to justify the things you wanted to do anyway. Maybe I should have told you, but…" He waggled his hand. "Anyway, I pulled some strings to keep your name out of the news – who knows what you'd have done if the reporters had come sniffing around, asking what Mr Shot-A-Mancer intended to do about this Anathema problem. God forbid you lose your job on some unauthorized wild goose chase – what happens to Aliyah without insurance?"

"Samaritan wouldn't fire me. Not for going after a *terrorist*…"

"Oh, yeah?" Kit picked up an S-1071 Claims Reporting Form between forefinger and thumb, as though it were a used Kleenex. "The home office sent it back."

"Back? They don't send stuff back unless it's unusable, Kit. This is…" Paul examined the form, wrinkling his nose at the careless errors: a failure to add the "list of property damage TS-234 form" when the claims ran over five lines, a mistallied subtotal. "…acceptable. Barely."

"It's acceptable *from me*. From a bureaucratic standpoint, you're this department's bright spot – you cross every T and dot every I. When your work slipped… they noticed."

Paul was flattered. "Don't be ridiculous, Kit… They're not *that* meticulous…"

"This is Samaritan Mutual. If a penny rolls under a desk here, accounting asks for it a week later. And yesterday, I got a query, passed down from high up, asking if your daughter's injury was affecting your work. They're already hunting for reasons."

"Kit, they have to know I'll sue if they fire me."

Kit squeezed Paul's shoulders. "Settling that lawsuit would *still* be cheaper than paying your daughter's claims. Aliyah's an expensive case already, Paul. Fire you, they save a lifetime of treating her."

"That's… inhuman."

Kit shrugged. "That's Samaritan."

Paul shivered at the thought of getting fired. He wondered if he could use bureaucromancy without insurance to pay for Aliyah's reconstructive surgery. He didn't think he could. Bureaucracy didn't materialize things out of thin air. You had to have a reason. Lacking insurance might be game over.

"I wouldn't have abandoned Aliyah," Paul said. "She's my number-one priority. I won't deny that I want to track down this bastard, but… I wouldn't do anything that endangers her."

Kit's age-spotted face was suffused with relief. "That's good to hear."

"Now you're going to assign me to the Anathema case."

Kit did a double take. "You need to fly straight, my friend. They're on the hunt to fire you already, and I will not give them more ammunition. Besides, there is no 'Anathema case'."

"What about yesterday's rain of frogs?"

Kit paled. "…how do you know about that?"

From the Samaritan case files I conjured up in my hotel room yesterday, Paul thought. "I have my sources. You're assigned to investigate a highway pileup in Staten Island, which we both know is a Flex lab overspill. And what are the odds *two* 'mancers are brewing Flex in New York?"

"I'd be hard-pressed to risk your life, my friend. I'm not risking Aliyah's. That girl is my goddaughter."

"You're Jewish. You don't have goddaughters."

"For her, I'll make an exception."

Paul laughed despite himself. "You want me to prove myself invaluable? There's at least $75,000 in outstanding claims, with more incoming. That's $75k in savings once I prove those dinged fenders are due to 'mancy. And that's just a start of all the money I'm going to save them. I'm not putting myself in danger – I'm making so much profit for the company that they don't dare fire me, no matter *how* expensive Aliyah's claims get."

"You think you can save them a million?"

"I can try. And if a humble insurance agent happens to track down a terrorist in the process, well... you think they'd fire me with my face all over the *New York Post*?"

"God damn it, Paul." Kit rubbed his temples, then looked around for a donut. "If you were just an insurance agent, I'd handcuff you to Aliyah's bed. But you know how many mundanes have killed an active 'mancer, by themselves, in the last decade?"

"One."

"Yes." Kit slumped into Paul's chair. "And to be honest, Paul? *I* want revenge. The rage I feel when I see Aliyah – God, I can't imagine how it is for you. The cops are clueless. SMASH is asking *us* if we have leads. But you, Paul... you have a gift, tracking these lunatics down. If you can stop this son of a-bitch, well..."

"So you'll give me the case?"

"You call in SMASH when you find him," Kit said sternly. "The SMASH agents, they're all 'mancers. Let this Anathema and these SMASH maniacs kill each other, as God intended."

I'm a 'mancer, Paul thought. *Would you kill me?*

Then he remembered contemplating murder when he'd thought Kit might expose him, and knew the answer: *yes. Yes, Kit would.*

Kit shoved a card into Paul's breast pocket. "Here's the address. Make this case ironclad."

Kit withdrew solicitously, closing the door behind him.

"All right," Paul said. "You can come out now."

The papers lifted off the desk, straightening themselves prissily into fine stacks. Then they spread apart. The Beast rose up before Paul, forming an octopoid shape, papers curling in to form crumpled tentacles.

An elaborate dance began. The errors on each form were whited-over, erased, re-inked. But not all at once; the papers brushed by each other in a careful pattern, like commuters getting on a crowded subway. The pens didn't always correct a flaw right away; sometimes they floated over thoughtfully enough that Paul could envision an invisible caretaker chewing their other end, contemplating the change.

He watched it mark and erase, debating what to do next. His bureaucromancy was beautiful. For the first time since the fire, he felt a calmness pervade him.

After weeks of running scared, he'd found the peace to think things through.

"I can't trust you," he whispered.

The Beast halted, upturning the forms so the printed-side pages faced Paul. It looked confused, a dog that wasn't quite sure what it had done.

"I can't trust *me*," Paul clarified. "I barely know what I'm doing. With Aliyah's life on the line and a crazy 'mancer out for blood, any mistake could blow up in my face. And if I hurt her again, I couldn't live with myself. I... I need someone to show me how to do this."

Paul took out the card Kit had given him, held it out for the Beast to sniff. "Somewhere out there is the man who made the Flex that burned my daughter. He's clearly experienced. Most new 'mancers either kill themselves with accidents or fall right into SMASH's hands. He knows how to bank the flux."

The Beast nuzzled the card with a folded manila envelope nose. *So?*

"I'm going to make him train me in 'mancy."

The Beast shivered, a porcupine of straightened paperclips.

"Yes. Yes, it's... dangerous. But this Anathema... if I can play my cards right, I can convince him I know enough to help him. Then he'll teach me. The only way I can save Aliyah is to get Samaritan to pay out, and the only way to do that is to master my bureaucromancy and the only way to do that is to convince Anathema that I should be his student."

The Beast shook its head doubtfully.

"I know. I'm not much of an actor. Or a fighter. But I can do this. I *have* to. And once I've learned everything there is to learn… I'll kill him."

The Beast formed hands from paper, flexed them nervously. Then it whispered one word:

Revenge.

FIVE
Sexing Chickens

On August 14th at 3pm, the clouds overhead turned a pestilent green, then rained thousands of frogs down onto Father Capodanno Boulevard. The National Weather Service estimated the frogs – later determined to be square-spotted pickerels – had been catapulted high into the air by a freak tornado that had touched down in a nearby pond.

This was not the weird part.

The weird part was the way the frogs were deposited by the side of Father Capodanno Boulevard; they dropped into place approximately twelve inches apart from each other in a row that stretched on for half a mile, cushioned by a fluke gust of wind before they would have splattered into the glass-strewn culvert by the side of the freeway. They all faced the opposite side of the road. It was as though the frogs had been deposited by a meticulous and eccentric storm in preparation for a race.

Which was exactly the case.

After standing stock-still for precisely six seconds, the

frogs all leapt into the rush hour traffic in an amphibian ballet. Bleary truck drivers blatted their horns in surprise, skidding to one side; moms in minivans crushed frogs underwheel as their children screamed.

The frogs darted back and forth in vain attempts to reach the other side, in what should have caused an instant traffic jam. No one slowed down, though they stomped on the brakes; every on-board computer in every car on that rush hour road went haywire simultaneously, accelerating to an even fifty miles an hour. Drivers panicked. Some careened into the ditch, driving until their car smashed into the bordering wood of pollution-starved pine trees; others veered into the guardrails.

At first blush, the amphibious fatality rate shouldn't have been high; the frogs were the size of a man's palm and should have been safe unless squashed directly underneath a tire.

Except whenever any automobile passed over them, even a truck with what was later measured to be a twelve-inch ride height, the frogs were squashed into wet red heaps. Their shattered bones emerged arranged into rough skull and-crossbones shapes.

This was still not the strangest thing. The strangest thing, recorded dutifully on police security tapes, was how the frogs all leapt in straight lines until they turned right or left – rotating at perfect ninety-degree angles.

Stapleton was a perfect neighborhood for a little covert 'mancy, Paul thought. What 'mancers wanted for Flex labs was cheap housing with big backyards for penning in the sacrifices.

And Stapleton had been a rising star back in the 1960s. The houses, painted in sunny colors, had been built to hold huge futures: sprawling porches to hold cocktail parties, chicken-wire-bounded gardens to grow tomatoes for hearty family meals, a big backyard for big golden retrievers to run in.

But the industry in Stapleton had dried up. The gardens were choked by weeds, the porches warped by years of rain, the sunny yellows reduced to peeling grays. Half the houses here had been repossessed; their unmowed lawns were now wild thatches choked with rusting Coors cans. The children of Stapleton wisely stayed inside, the bright pixelated worlds of their Wiis superior to anything this dismal exterior could offer.

Any dogs on those lawns are coming to bad ends, Paul thought, limping along the road. *Someone's using their Wii for more than gaming*.

Paul limped down the road, feeling lucky to be out on the case. His stump rubbed blisters inside the misfit cup, and though the motor in his ankle helped steady his gait, he'd be lucky to get four hours of walking from a full charge. Yet there was only one real way to track down a Flex lab: on foot.

He always thought of chickens when he hunted 'mancers. Mainly because of how he'd explained it to Aliyah.

"It's… hard to explain," he'd told her. "Finding magic is kind of like sexing chickens."

"What?" Imani had grinned, shoving her latest case aside to kick her feet up on the desk. "*This*, I gotta hear."

"What's a sex chicken, Daddy?" Imani and Paul had both cracked up – a good, clean laughter, one that had probably added two months to their marriage.

"Not a sex chicken, sweetie," Paul had explained, calming Aliyah's laughter-inspired outrage. "You know there are boy chickens and girl chickens, right?"

"Technically, 'boy chickens' are roosters, sweetie."

"I am aware, my sweet wife. Anyway, when chickens are born, they're small fluffy bundles that are – well, about the size of an egg. So you know how people tell which chickens are girls?"

"No…" Aliyah sat still, attentive. She loved learning new things.

"Well, you get a job as a chicken sexer. And on your first day on the job, an experienced chicken sexer sits behind you. And with a magnifying glass, you look at the tiny fuzzy chick-butt."

Aliyah burst out into giggles. "Chick-butt."

"Yup. And you look. And the chicken sexer behind you says, 'Girl.' And you pick up another chick, which looks *exactly the same,* and the chicken sexer says, 'That's a boy.'"

"But how does the chick sexer *know*?" Aliyah asked.

"That's the trick! Even the chicken sexer can't explain how he knows. But sit with the chicken sexer for a week, and after a while, *you* start being able to tell! Eventually, you'll look at a chicken butt and think, 'That's a girl.' And you'll have no way of knowing *why* you know that. But after seeing enough boy chick-butts and enough girl chick-butts, the back of your mind knows how to tell the difference, even if the front of your mind can't explain it."

"I'm pretty sure you're telling her this story just so you can use the word 'chick-butt'," Imani said, leaning back on her elbow, radiating bemusement.

"No, this is completely true," Paul shot back.

"Don't *make* me go to Snopes.com, my love."

"Go to Snopes. Go to Wikipedia. Go to the American Organization of Chicken Sexers, if you like. They'll tell you the same." He knelt before Aliyah, quashing the irritation that Imani was contradicting him in front of their daughter. "But that's what magic's like, sweetie. 'Mancers are rare – I've hunted them for almost a decade, and met maybe thirty – but see enough magic, and you get its feel."

It was a partial truth. Kit hadn't been able to see 'mancy, no matter how many cases they'd investigated. Still, Paul chuckled; for months afterwards, Aliyah solemnly told everyone she met that "My daddy uses magic to sex chickens."

Paul looked along the row of gambreled roofs, the dry yards pinned with forlorn "FOR SALE" signs. After yesterday's frog shower, there was some chicken-sexing going on around here, for sure. The cops were looking everywhere within a five-mile radius, but they didn't know what to look for. You had to feel the 'mancy.

He quashed a concern: *What if Anathema had moved on?* Maybe. But 'mancers down on their luck enough to need a Flex lab usually found it difficult to move all their accoutrements. And Anathema–

–there.

That house set his chicken sense a-tingling.

Paul strolled by a three-story house with a sagging porch, trying to figure out what had set off his alarms.

The first evidence was simple police work: though there was a "For Sale" sign in the front yard, the first-floor windows were propped open to let in a breeze.

A 'mancer called this place home. Paul was sure of it. The same 'mancer who'd made the Flex that had burned his daughter. The rain of frogs came when this sonuvabitch had lost control trying to freeze his magic within hematite, and flung the damaging weirdness as far away as possible.

That's what this 'mancer would teach him: to master flux.

He popped open the Pepsi bottle he'd brought along, as if he was an old cripple who needed to cool off. He sipped the lukewarm soda, checking for obvious 'mancy signs: the glint of a copper wire running around the perimeter of the yard, a large pile of rust.

No such luck. But the yellowed grass in the yard…

…Paul squinted over the decaying picket fence. The uneven grass sprouted in thatchy clumps. But those three dandelions over here, bobbing in the breeze? They had three identical dandelions five feet to the left, their fuzzy white heads bouncing to the same rhythm. That mounded anthill over there? The exact same anthill existed five feet over, the ants running in the same direction.

The entire yard was one five-foot square of bad lawn that had been copied and pasted. A side effect of the magic this 'mancer was trying, inefficiently, to distill.

He reached down to flick a stem of wheatgrass; the

others quivered in time. Paul marveled; he'd never seen a cloned landscape before. Then again, he'd never seen most magics. Only the army had standardized magic into Unimancy; everyone else fixated on unique hobbies, blossoming pastimes into power.

Inside was the 'mancer who had harmed his daughter. A man ramping towards mass killing. A man not afraid to murder.

I should call the cops.

His job existed because people disliked being told their Mercedes wasn't covered for frog-related weather accidents. They tended to sue, claiming mundanity. Samaritan Mutual's legal shark tank had found you could pay amphibian experts and meteorologists to argue exactly how unlikely an event this had been…

…or they could send Paul out to tip the cops toward a 'mancer bust. Which gave Samaritan massive good will with local judges to boot.

That was what Paul was *supposed* to do: get the location, point the local authorities there, oversee the capture.

But following orders would not get Aliyah's face fixed.

So, instead, he looked at the house and saw it not as a structure of wooden beams and plaster but a piece of property – purchased from a bank, subject to a thousand regulatory codes. The house generated bills from electrical companies, water companies, sewage companies, mortgages, every expenditure dutifully recorded…

… Paul felt the Beast shift back at his office. It felt like flexing a muscle in another city.

Paul envisioned filling out the forms. In dusty rooms, the forms materialized, words appearing on them as though via invisible typewriters. Then he took out a small pad of paper and signed it, activating the magic.

Complete house blueprints materialized in Paul's mind – both the original plans and the attic addition authorized in 1974. Based on that layout, the basement would be the best place to make Flex.

Could he sneak into the basement?

His prosthetic foot's motorized whir broke the silence as he opened the front door. The living room revealed a stained carpet with a couple of old Burger King cups toppled over in the corner, a scattering of pennies where a couch used to be.

He had to verify this 'mancer's skills first. No sense learning from a man who knew less than he did.

Paul slipped through a grimy kitchen and down the narrow stairwell to the basement. The only noise was his stupid foot, whirring as it repositioned his ankle joints on each step. It seemed louder than ever, as if trying to speak: *Hey, remember what happened the last time you went head-to-head with a 'mancer? That's right; you got me!*

It didn't matter. He needed to see the magic. Partially to verify, and partially because... well, he'd been lured to the magic's beauty ever since meeting the illustromancer, a moth to the fire–

–Aliyah's face melting in a caul of flame–

The basement had once been a 1970s-style man-cave, complete with faux wood paneling and a tiki bar.

The liquor bottles had been removed from the glass shelves, replaced by neat stacks of plastic boxes.

It was a wall of videogames: gray Nintendo cartridges, white Sega Dreamcast games, green Xbox games...

It had the jumbled love of a child's bedroom, each game battered from being shoved into its console a thousand times. This wasn't just a game collection; it was an altar to gaming itself.

The murky basement windows turned sunlight into shadow. Paul used his cell phone as an impromptu flashlight.

A sixty-inch flatscreen had been mounted on the wall. Several consoles were wired into a connection box, ready to switch channel input from the GameCube to the PlayStation 4 at the touch of a button. A comfortable leather chair rested before this altar, the leather cracked with the indentation of a meaty ass. Crumpled Red Bull cans lay scattered around the chair.

Paul felt the echoes of his own obsession in this place. The entire room revolved around this one interaction: a man, in a seat, and the game before him.

And the Flex-making equipment in the corner.

Paul had seen it all before... but now he could potentially *make* Flex, that equipment was laden with uncomfortable possibilities. There were sacks of crushed industrial-grade hematite, spilling their glittery brown treasure into the shag – illicit merchandise worth thousands.

Did this 'mancer know what he was doing? The Flex tools laid in heaps along the floor – the bingo machine, the alembic, the blood-letting knife–

But where were the siphon's copper wires? If Anathema didn't have a way to whisk excess bad luck away, then he was an amateur. Call in the SMASH team.

No, Anathema *had* to have a siphon. These were old games, from a man who'd gamemancered for decades. And judging by the raw force he'd channeled with yesterday's live-action Frogger recreation, his flux was fatal.

Come on, man, Paul thought, searching for wires, *you wouldn't risk the house collapsing on your head. You'd lay in something preplanned to go wrong if the distillation got out of control.*

That's why most flux-brewers had pets. For the bad luck to be truly bad, it had to happen to something you loved. Get a dog, put it in the back yard, run the copper wire so when the freak accident hit, the flux flowed along the path of least resistance.

Didn't have to be your dog. Just something you loved. Some 'mancers used their mothers.

Then Paul found it: a thin loop of copper wire running from underneath the chair, where the proper sigils had been engraved, leading to the videogame shelves.

That's what you love most, Paul thought. *Your collection.* He filed that knowledge away, trying to reconcile "a love of videogames" with "a love of mass murder." He peered in – were they *violent* videogames? Was he–

The crunch of tires on gravel.

A door, slamming.

Paul brought the plans to mind, hunting for another escape route. None. Stupidly, he'd holed himself up in this basement. Now he'd have to face down a more experienced 'mancer–

–with his foot. His stupid, missing foot.

A cheerful burp. A rattle of cans, shoved into the fridge. Then footsteps, skipping down the stairs. The 'mancer whistled the Super Mario tune.

A strange sense of clarity stole over Paul. All his other options had sublimed away, leaving nothing but a bold con. If it failed, he died.

He plunged his hands into his pockets, standing as dramatically as he could in the far shadows. He was glad he'd worn his suit today – it made him more imposing.

The 'mancer hit the lights. Fluorescents flickered on.

She gazed at Paul with mascaraed eyes.

SIX
Samus Removes Her Helmet

The girl who burned Aliyah shouldn't look that... sunny, Paul thought, dazed. *Or that young.* A 'mancer in her mid-twenties indicated abundant talent.

The gamemancer's pudgy face held a pixie-like mischief – even as she sized Paul up with storm-gray eyes. She looked like she'd stepped out of a Final Fantasy game, all black ribbons and buckles; her ironed hair had been pulled back into pigtails, emitting a playful gothiness.

She was fifty pounds overweight, but rather than hiding her figure, she displayed her ample tattooed skin in a cleavage-baring crinoline dress. It was bold, iconoclastic, appealing. Maybe even sexy, if she hadn't been flexing her purple-nailed fingers around an imaginary controller.

The tingle of magic filled the basement, a summer storm pregnant with lightning.

"I don't like killing," she whispered. Which surprised him. She'd killed thirty people in calculated murders – how could she have regrets?

If Paul responded immediately, she'd set the tone for this encounter. So he matched her glare for glare, hands trembling inside his pockets.

"The problem is, you know where I operate," she continued. Paul's phone sizzled and popped. "I'm betting from your cheap government suit that you know what I'm doing, and I'm not in a position to relocate. That doesn't leave us many options." She looked mournful. "I *really* don't like killing."

As she moved her fingers in preset patterns, summoning gamefire down upon him, Paul said, "What if I told you that you had only ten minutes before the cops arrived?"

She paused – literally paused, thumbing an imaginary stop button. "Why would you tell me that?"

"Just enough time to get out with your videogames," Paul continued. "Your tilt the other day – it caused a rain of frogs not two miles from here. They're hunting for you. Hunting *hard*."

Her eyes slid to one side, looking for an escape. He slipped in the biggest lie of all: "I came to warn you."

"Who the hell *are* you?"

"You can ask questions. Or you can get those games out. You might make it out with your skin intact once the SMASH team arrives, but those videogames? Shot to shards."

"How do you know?"

He flexed that muscle back at the office. It had been a lie when he started… But now, fluttering into an inbox in the Stapleton police department, was a notification of an all-points reality hazard at 672

Tompkins Avenue. He'd faxed it into the cops two hours ago.

Normally, he'd need to sign something to activate the 'mancy. But having seen this gamemancer Flex imaginary fingers, he imagined a pen in his hand, signed *symbolic* paper.

A helicopter's rotors echoed across the rooftops.

See? Paul thought, dizzied by the accomplishment. *She's already teaching you.*

She ran her fingernails along the bright orange Bowser tattoo on her forearm, arm hairs raised from Paul's 'mancy. Her wariness slackened into wonderment, that pixie-like face lighting up with a silly grin, and Paul felt the spark leap between them: *You do this, too.*

Though if she was experienced enough to tell what he was doing – if other 'mancers *could* tell what other 'mancers did – then he was dead.

"Oh. My. God." Her voice rose to a fanboy squee – a cheerful gushing that sounded nothing like a murderer. "What's *your* obsession?"

"Questions, or safety." Paul sounded more confident than he felt. "Choose."

She flinched, then broke towards the shelves. Paul felt bad; she was panicked. He emptied out a sack of crushed hematite onto the rug, puffs of smoky green spiraling upwards, and tossed it to her. She hurled her cartridges in.

"Aww, *dammit*." She stroked the beat-up chair as though it were a cat she had to put to sleep. "I'm gonna miss you, boy. But I can't carry you."

"Better than the Army," he said. "Now run. We'll be in touch." *We?* he thought, amazed at his ability to manufacture bullshit.

She gave him a guarded look. Already, she hated being in his debt. Or, perhaps, for being responsible when she wanted to play.

"Your name," she commanded. Paul chuckled, trying to preserve the mystery; she stood, Doc Martined feet planted far apart, implacable.

"I said *your name*," she repeated.

He should have despised her. She was a terrorist. She'd hurt Aliyah. She also didn't bullshit, didn't try to pretend this was anything other than a Flex lab, didn't try to pretend she hadn't intended to murder him. She held an *honesty*.

And she loved magic. Just like him.

"...Paul," he told her.

"You're good, Paul." She heaved the bag of videogames over one shoulder, the hematite bag over the other. "But you're no Cigarette-Smoking Man."

And she was gone.

SEVEN
How to Take Down a 'Mancer

Paul slumped back against the tiki bar, feeling the exhilaration shiver through his muscles. He'd done it. The first step towards saving Aliyah.

Now he just had to track that 'mancer down again, convince her there was usefulness in an alliance... and she'd teach him how to tame The Beast.

The thought had a strange eagerness he didn't care for, a dog yanking on the leash. The training was necessary, but he also had an addictive urge to share his secret. He'd hidden his love of magic all these years, but with the girl's company came the ability to *enthuse*.

He felt no enthusiasm now. His skull was clogged with pressure: flux.

He limped up the stairs, feeling a new hitch in his artificial foot; she'd done splash damage, frying his phone. Could *he* do 'mancy that blatant? He doubted it; bureaucromancy worked subtly and slow. Then again, he'd cleared a path through the fire...

He emerged from the basement just as a SMASH team fired tear gas in through the kitchen windows. Four canisters punched through simultaneously, spraying green smoke, fired by four separate men combined into a single Unimantic weapon.

"*I'm from Samaritan Mutual!*" Paul yelled. "*Don't–*"

He doubled over, vomiting. Paul thought his hands had trembled before, but now they rattled like branches in a windstorm–

–*nerve agents*, he thought. *They're taking no chances with a 'mancer–*

As Paul's knees gave out, four gunmetal-black cylinders sailed through the shattered window, rolling on the tile floor–

–*flashbangs*–

–they exploded, a supernova that obliterated Paul's thoughts.

Rough gloves grabbed his shoulders, smacked his head until his hair stopped burning. They tugged a hood over his head, bound his wrists with plastic strips.

I'm not a 'mancer, Paul tried to say, but his words turned into fountains of puke.

They hauled him outside. Paul's foot caught on something; they yanked so hard, Paul thought his artificial leg would pop off. They slammed him against a police car.

"*Nerf him*!" Someone jabbed a needle into his neck, and the remainder of the world spun away.

Being awakened by your own projectile vomiting was not a good way to come to. A young Unimancer in a gray camo SMASH uniform tugged Paul's head back, wiped off his chest.

"...Death Metal?" Paul asked.

The kid cocked his head in a mechanical, birdlike way, trying to recognize Paul. Paul remembered busting this kid for making a new brand of Flex called "Death Metal". Anyone who took it got musical powers of a distinctly rocking flavor, spewing hellfire and shattering windows. It hadn't taken Paul long to compile a list of obsessed Death Metal fans.

The kid's long black locks had been shaved to a crew cut, his tribal neck tattoos laser-removed to pale scars.

"Do I know you, sir?" His stare was robotic.

Paul remembered Death's Metal's Flex as chaotic energy, mostly harmless – whereas actual death metal was guttural, horrific growls, Death Metal's Flex was cartoonish. People who used Death Metal's drugs filled the air with wild fountains of goggle-eyed skulls and skeleton guitars and gyrating groupies...

"You..." Death Metal offered him water, which Paul drank gratefully. Two people screamed at each other, their arguments cutting into Paul's ears like buzz saws. "I tracked you down. For making Flex. In Duff's Bar in Brooklyn? In the pit?"

Death Metal blinked, as if that was a long time ago. Except it hadn't been; it'd been maybe a year since Paul had pointed SMASH at him. Now all of that glorious 'mancy had been squashed out of him, reduced to a sad telepathy so he could join the military hive mind.

"Do you still rock out?"

Death Metal's impassive face hitched in a half smile, but then became distracted by something Paul could

not see: his Unimanced allies. Two other soldiers placed
a loving palm on each of his shoulders.

"No, sir," Death Metal said, shaking off the memory.
"I think as one, now."

Then the three soldiers looked, their faces wrinkling
with simultaneous concern, over at the argument
between a beat cop and their commander.

"...*I'm* overriding your authority!" That voice grated
on Paul in familiar ways. "You think Paul Tsabo – the
guy who's put away more 'mancers than anyone else –
is a 'mancer? No. You're not taking him to the
Refactor."

The Refactor? Paul thought muzzily, legs twitching.
*They can't bring me to the Refactor; I barely survived police
training...*

"Procedure is to bring every suspect captured within
a non-Euclidean zone back for testing," a stern female
voice replied. "'Mancers have no look. I personally
Refactored each man on this team; they all looked
ordinary when they arrived. That's why we leave
detection to the *professionals*."

The three Unimancers kept their gazes on their
mundane commander, muttering her words as she
spoke them, nakedly adoring her.

"The man's a cop," insisted the grating voice.

"He's an insurance claims agent."

"You never stop wearing the badge. He stays."

Paul rubbed his eyes. There were four other SMASH
members in black armor, shotguns slung across their
backs, each wearing prominent white opals on their left
shoulder: expensive, precise 'mancy detectors. They

stood obediently behind a slim woman with a curt buzz cut and a bulldog face.

The woman glared at the ten Stapleton cops who had surrounded Paul. She shifted stances, ready to fight all ten at once... but she had the wariness of a woman who no longer relished kicking ass.

Paul could see she was tempted, though. Anyone would be. The guy standing before her was almost as scrawny as Paul, but he carried himself with a bodybuilder's world-taunting swagger. A wispy mustache floated over an annoying smirk, a pube-style mustache you had to have either an insane amount of self-confidence or an insane amount of self-denial to think was at all attractive.

Lenny Pirrazzini, unfortunately, had both.

Lenny was a man of firm habits: you put in your shift, you went to the bar for a beer, then tucked your kids into bed. Where Paul saw beauty in the way 'mancy changed the rules, Lenny saw threats to tradition.

Still, he'd idolized Paul for all the wrong reasons, and so Paul was never more grateful to see him. He stood before the SMASH team leader, thumping his chest with both hands, detailing the many and varied reasons he didn't have to hand *shit* over to you brainwashed Gandalfs.

The Unimancy leader eyed the cops again. They were doughy officers but steadfast in their resolve: no one hauled away an ex-cop on their watch.

"Your bosses asked us along on this milk run to educate you," the woman said, sneering. "Mr Tsabo has *been* bagged, he's gonna *get* tagged, and that's the end of it."

One cop stepped between the SMASH agents surrounding Paul to put a protective hand on Paul's shoulder – an unconscious echo of the Unimancers protecting their own. Paul was glad – he'd seen what happened to mundanes who'd been shipped to the Refactor. The government ran tests for weeks, stressing you both physically and psychologically until you broke and retreated to using 'mancy. But if you weren't a 'mancer, sometimes you just broke...

Paul couldn't hide his power there. And when they found out, they'd brainwash him into Unimancy.

"So hand him over," the SMASH team leader snapped. "Or this cooperative exercise is ended."

"Hey, we *got* this." Lenny flicked her the finger. "Tear gas, flashbangs, boom. Fuckin' 'mancers collapse like every other dumbass criminal when you bushwhack 'em. Big surprise! Call *me* in! I'll do your job for you, fishtits!"

...*fishtits?* Paul thought.

She smirked. "You've got a terrorist in your midst, and you're throwing away valuable training?"

Lenny's grin wilted. But he never changed his mind, once he made a decision.

The SMASH team gathered up their equipment and tromped into the onyx-black helicopter with the gold logo emblazoned on the side: Special 'Mancer Apprehension, Suppression, and Hauling. The words ringed around a hand closed into a single fist, each finger from a different person: one black, one white, one painted female nail, one yellow, one red.

The cops watched the SMASH team evacuate, ringing around Paul protectively until the helicopter's flashing red lights vanished over the horizon.

Then Lenny punched Paul in the shoulder.

"The man is *back*!" Lenny gave Paul a horse-toothed grin. "Of *course* you wanna pop that daughter-burning sonuvabitch yourself!"

Well, I guess New York's Finest know about Aliyah, Paul thought.

"Got a little eager," Paul demurred. Lenny leaned down to sponge the vomit from Paul's tie. "Didn't think you'd ever transfer out of Manhattan, Lenny. You loved the street…"

"They needed a sergeant here to show 'em how it's done. But what the fuck are *you* doing, huh?" He rapped his knuckles against Paul's artificial foot. "This means you can't just run in and shoot bitches. You gotta get wise. *Sneaky*." He cuffed Paul in the head.

"I wanted to see his lair," Paul lied. "See how he thinks…"

"Yeah, well, their infrared picked up your body heat, and wham, you're puking up next week's lunch. You almost got carted to fuckin' Nevada."

Paul hung his head. An experienced SMASH team had taken him down easily. All his 'mancy hadn't helped.

"Get him up, get him up." Two officers pulled Paul to his feet. Paul groaned as he saw the Channel 5 news crew filming eagerly. Of *course* the press was here. This was a PR exercise. And Paul had just made the nightly news.

The cops intercepted the reporters, but the flashbulbs dazzled Paul's nerve-gas-addled eyes. Lenny escorted Paul over to the police car, whispering in Paul's ear.

"Look, I know you wanna kill after what happened to your kid." He thumped Paul on the shoulder. "The government can wipe those freaks' brains, put us normal folks in command of 'em, but still... one day, that shit will backlash and bam! New York's the next Europe.

"Still," he continued. "You can't fuck with those guys head-on. Work underground, my friend. They bring us ordinaries to the Refactor to make sure we're out of the *way*, man. Remember, we're all in this together."

Then Lenny thumped the hood of the car; a thumpy man was Lenny Pirrazzini. "Hey, Freddy, get our hero home safe, a'ight? Because we need at least *one* competent sonuvabitch to take down this Anathema bastard. Paul, visit me; we'll go hunting. Like old times."

We never hunted before, Paul thought – then the car drove away. Paul lolled back. The nerve gas made his vision wander helplessly towards every movement.

"There's a Thermos under the seat," the driver – Freddy – said. Paul unscrewed the cap, grateful for a swig of milky Dunkin' Donuts coffee. Easy on the stomach. He felt a little more like a cop with each sip.

Today was a bad beat. Not all bad; he'd found his 'mancer. But SMASH now had suspicions. And the reporters...

...he remembered how he'd made the front page after killing the illustromancer. People had sent shredded Titian prints, sent long emails detailing the bloody tortures Paul should have inflicted upon her before she died, held his most shameful moment up as exemplary. The press overlooked him as Aliyah's father because as a child, she'd been kept out of the reports – but now?

The headlines would reflect Lenny Pirazzinni's interpretation of events: Paul Tsabo, 'mancer killer, was on the hunt.

As the cop car zoomed back towards Manhattan's bright towers, Paul wondered: had the SMASH team even been involved before he'd altered the flow of time? Would they have even shown up if he had called it in from his cell phone?

He knew so little about magic. His hands trembled from the nerve agent, his eyes dry as raisins. Yet that strange stuffiness had lifted. Were tonight's events flux or ordinary bad luck?

The gamemancer. The gamemancer would teach him how to master flux.

She had to.

EIGHT
"If I Have to Die, It Should be by Magic."

Over the next three days, Paul replayed one conversation in his head, over and over again.

"Your name?"

"Paul," he told her.

Why in God's name, Paul wondered, hadn't he thought to ask, "What's *your* name?"

All bureaucracy started with an identifier: the name, the social security number, the case ID. You couldn't look people up by "the heavyset girl with the Bowser tattoo". You needed to place a hook in the Beast.

He sat in his office, his wastepaper basket overflowing with crumpled forms. He'd had the Beast slither through the police department's paperwork, searching for distinguishing marks – but if his gamemancer had a police record, it had been before her tattoo.

Even if she had given him a fake name, that would have worked. But the paperwork resisted finding her by a name *he* had assigned.

He had problems thinking of her as "Anathema". Anathema was a murderer. This girl had been friendly, even cordial. She'd treated him like a colleague. Deep down, he didn't want to believe someone who shared his enthusiasm for 'mancy could kill someone.

Even though she'd been about to kill him.

He holed up in his office, ignoring the phone. Reporters were calling. They asked whether Paul was hunting the 'mancer who'd hurt his daughter, begging for confirmation of evil magic at work. He'd taken to yelling, "Why don't you tell people to donate to my daughter's charity fund instead?" before slamming the phone down.

That worked, to some extent. Folks had donated eight thousand dollars – enough to pay the deductibles.

If he'd asked people to donate to a fund dedicated to slaughtering 'mancers, he'd have a million already.

Paul tried to relax by filling out the other paperwork – the counterclaim forms on Aliyah's treatment. Samaritan Mutual was mustering its resources, compiling its in-network doctors to explain why Aliyah's reconstructive surgery wasn't life-saving, and therefore not covered. Paul knew how to play that game. He doubted he could win without using 'mancy, but he could keep the ball in play long enough to satisfy Imani he was doing something.

Still. The clock was ticking. Any day, Anathema would engineer her next accident. This time, it would be thirty-two innocents dead.

What if Paul had to kill that pretty, pudgy girl before she killed again?

The Beast slept fitfully. The stacks of forms rose into the air whenever Paul thought he had a lead, like cats confirming this new noise was indeed the can opener. But as soon as Paul realized *No, this won't work either*, they collapsed back into place.

The frustrating thing was, there were magics that tracked down strangers; the mob had twin huntomancers (and as a cop, Paul had once been told to look the other way after they'd helped the department corner a particularly messy serial killer). Collectomancers sometimes developed powers that led them to the action hero they needed to complete their set. A junkomancer in Queens was an open secret on the force, a harmless kook unaware he was a 'mancer – but he could find anything, literally *anything*, in his junkyard.

Bureaucromancy needed things to be filled out in order. He could not skip that first step: identification.

"Maybe I chose the wrong magic," Paul muttered, kicking the wastebasket.

The crumpled paper balls rolled towards Paul, lining up in neat rows before his feet, forlorn children looking up to a teacher. He felt guilty.

Paul knelt down, patting the tops of the discarded paper tentatively, not quite wanting to commit to the action lest he look foolish. They rubbed up against his fingertips, rustling as they fought to be touched.

"It's not you," he told them, smiling. It wasn't. The Beast was a force multiplier, a way for a messy humanity to store information no one man could remember. If Paul had to bend his will to its needs, then so what? That was its beauty. The worst anarchist still filled out forms to buy a house. The richest driver still had to renew his license. Bureaucracy treated everyone alike.

No, he thought. You did not break the rules. You made them work for you.

The wadded papers purred at his feet. Paul basked in their trust.

After banging his head against the Anathema issue, Paul needed to see Aliyah.

He'd have liked to say she missed him, but they kept her sedated much of the time to speed healing. Still, his visitations were like going to church. It didn't matter if nobody heard you; it mattered that you went.

Paul stopped by the bathroom, splashing water over his face and straightening his tie, before he went in to see her. Not that Aliyah cared what Daddy looked like – but if he ran into Imani, he wanted to look energized, a man going toe-to-toe with Samaritan Mutual.

"Got a hot date, Paul?" a voice purred.

Paul whirled. The gamemancer emerged from the bathroom stall. She now wore a cut-off black T-shirt that exposed a doughy midriff, accentuated by a bandolier of brass bullets slung around her hips. She wore a supremely satisfied look.

"Paul *Tsabo*," she added, nodding.

Paul ran.

Her fingers twitched. The bathroom door vanished, replaced by an image of a door. In desperation, Paul kicked the wall, but it had become impregnable. A bazooka shot at close range, Paul realized, would leave only a dark smudge, to fade harmlessly a few moments later.

Why had he chosen bureaucromancy when other 'mancers could do this? *Why*?

He hoped Imani would get Aliyah the treatment she needed. This would be a messy, mysterious death.

But he would not die sobbing.

He turned to face her, his back to the wall; all he needed was a blindfold and last cigarette. The other walls in the room had turned flat and two-dimensional, the bathroom mirror a rectangle of blue shading.

She nibbled a peeling purple fingernail, looking curiously wicked.

"You're pretty calm about this," she said.

"If I have to die, it should be by magic."

"Hmm." She glanced back towards the bathroom stall. "How long did you wait for me to show up, Paul? In that basement?"

"...I dunno. Ten, fifteen minutes?"

"You're lucky." She pulled herself up on the bathroom counter, waving a Wii controller at the stalls. "I've been in there all *day*. Listening to guys pinching loaves next to me... It got boring after the batteries ran down on my DS. But I didn't wanna leave lest I missed you, Paul."

Paul wasn't quite sure what to say to that.

"I should have figured you'd find me. You can track down anyone, I suppose. Just... turn the world into videogame radar, make me your mission point."

She arched plucked eyebrows. "Really, Paul? After I just told you I've been waiting in the bathroom all day? ...Though, yeah, actually, I *should* have done that."

"What magic did you use?"

"Googlemancy. Do an image search for 'Paul policeman artificial foot mancy' and you get Paul Tsabo. Next time this happens, Paul, give yourself a fake name. A *cool* one. I mean, 'Paul'? You could have said, 'Call me the Whisperer in the Darkness.' 'My friends call me Agent Steel.' 'I'm Batman.' *Anything*. It sort of breaks the mystique when you finally get your lurker and he's named *Paul*."

The words "next time" gave Paul a small, wavering elation he might live.

"So, you think I should have been… *lurkier*."

She pulled her fists to her chest, then crossed her fingers, as if betting on a lucky horse. "Come on, Paul! The lurking? It's totally badass. You think I played videogames twenty hours a day because I *liked* the real world? Crap, I've been waiting all my life for some mysterious stranger to show up and involve me in an Adventure. What'd I get? Minimum wage jobs. Community college. Zero bearded guys showing up to tell me I'm a wizard now, zero droids arriving asking me to rescue hot princes.

"Then I'm in the basement, brewing. And there is – *the stranger*!" She framed the scene with her hands. "A little wimpy, no James Marsden, but *official*. A government-agent suit. An offer of aid. Ties to a secret organization! Even a missing limb pointing at a mysterious past! Booo-*nus*!

"For the first time in *years*," she said, licking her lips, "I went to bed excited. If you existed, maybe there was a sword in a stone somewhere. The world had let me down for so long – but for the first time in a long time, *anything* could happen."

"So, what happened?" Paul asked.

"Got bored." She sucked air between her teeth. "If you'd showed up the next day, Paul, my life woulda been a wonderland. Next day, I was jittery. Today, I thought, 'Wait, will he show up again? What's the Paul-signal?' So I started doing research. And what'd I find?"

Paul shifted his weight to his good foot. "…a gimpy insurance agent?"

"With a burned daughter. So, seriously, Paul. What are you up to?"

NINE
Unthinkable Team-Ups

They stood at the foot of Aliyah's bed.

This was the hour the parents came to visit, seeing their burned children off to sleep. Their happiness was stretched thin as Saran Wrap. You couldn't cry around your children; that would scare them. So the parents all acted like they were interviewing their kids for TV shows, receiving each piece of news with high-eyebrowed, cajoling grins.

Only the gamemancer looked grim.

She turned her Nintendo DS over and over in her hands, blinking back tears. She scrutinized Aliyah solemnly, as if searching for the cheat code to heal these blisters.

"...So, how much do you need?"

"Too much," Paul whispered, then added: "Half a million."

"Jesus."

"I mean, to do it proper. They're doing what they can here. But..."

"...You don't want to take a chance with your

daughter's face," she finished. "Five hundred thousand dollars." Paul could see her weighing the figures in her head. "I don't have that kind of money."

"I wasn't asking you for *money*!" Paul snapped.

"Then what the fuck are we doing, Paul? Hiding in Flex labs and surprising 'mancers doesn't seem like the best way of providing medical coverage."

Don't mock me! You made me do this! he almost shouted, then realized: *She didn't know.* Plenty of little girls got burned in New York. She hadn't drawn the connection. She probably didn't even understand that Paul had burned Aliyah, trying to save her.

Then: *She said "we."*

One glimpse of Aliyah's burns, and this 'mancer wanted to help. He could see the determination on her face; she was being sarcastic because already, she cared too much.

Were those the emotions of a murderer? Maybe. He'd seen too many weeping killers in his time on the force to think taking a life robbed you of empathy. Kit cheered at 'mancer's deaths, but he'd have taken a bullet for a stranger. Paul had wanted to strangle the girl who'd burned his daughter... until he'd met her. And whoever Anathema hated enough that she was killing for, well...

...maybe she was a weird mixture of callousness and caring, like every other human.

"I need a teacher," Paul said. "I can work the system; I can't handle the flux. Last thing I want to do is to – to make it worse for her." He flexed his fingers, always feeling Aliyah burning.

The gamemancer made an aborted gesture with her hands, an arc-like movement that tried to encompass too much and failed. "We don't *teach* each other, Paul. 'Mancy's as specific as thumbprints. The Konami code's not gonna do the same thing for you that it does for me."

"...the Konami code?"

Her fingers twitched, tapping it out. "Point is, flux is... it's trial and error. Like... walking. Eventually, you fall down enough times that you figure out when to stick out your leg." She glanced down at his metal ankle, wincing. "...too soon?"

"I don't have *time* for trial and error! If I flux myself into the Army, or hurt anyone else, then... No. *Unacceptable*. I need to do this on the down-low."

"'Down-low.' That word sounds foreign when you use it, Paul. Like a lozenge in your throat. I'd stay away from street slang if I were you."

"Don't mock me. I need your help."

The gamemancer flung her hands in the air. "What do you want me to do, Paul?"

This hadn't gone the way Paul thought it would. He thought he'd hate her; her grief had melted his anger. He thought he'd have to blackmail her; she was all too willing to assist. He thought she'd have wisdom to share; she had none.

He looked at the other parents, loving caretakers. If this was their only option, wouldn't they take it?

"...Teach me to make Flex," he whispered.

She stepped back. "Why the hell would I do that?"

"Flex is the only thing that every 'mancer I've ever known can do," he said, so low his voice hurt. "Maybe you can't train me to play videogames, but I know 'mancers of violently different persuasions have taught each other how to brew Flex successfully. We can all do it. It's as close to ritual magic as we come."

"So I break out the alembics and run you through the crystal. What's that teach you?"

"When you make Flex," Paul said thickly, "You offload the flux into something else. The ritual is practically all about channeling bad luck away from you. And managing flux is really the most critical skill a 'mancer *can* learn. If I can..." He swallowed.

"Flex isn't easy money, Paul. Trust me on that one."

"This isn't about money!" Paul swallowed back revulsion at the idea of inflicting more flux backlash on the world. "If I can get good at this, then money's never an issue. It's just that–" He sighed. "If I can make Flex, then I can probably get a grip on my backlash."

"...*if* you make Flex," she echoed scornfully. "Did you not notice my rain of frogs, Paul? That wasn't my first time on tilt, either. So what makes you think *I'm* the great Flex expert?"

"You know more than I do."

She chewed her lip, nodding, not liking where his logic led but unable to argue with it. "You know I know where your daughter lives, right?"

"What's that supposed to mean?"

"It means if this is a sting operation, I'm gonna be pissed. You're a – well, you're not a cop. But you're a bloodhound *for* cops. And I–" Her tears mixed with mascara. "If it turns out that you trotted out this poor girl as some emotional con to get me jailed, you are the worst fucking human being in the world."

"I'm not." He was stunned, wounded, confused; he *did* intend to kill her, but Aliyah wasn't part of that. "I'm not."

She saw the hurt on his face. She turned away to squeeze Aliyah's toes – a mother's instinct, loving and kind. Then she yanked her fingers away.

"...I can't believe I'm involving someone else..." She cracked her knuckles. "All right, I'm in. We'll start tomorrow."

Aliyah shifted beneath Vaselined dressings, woken by the 'mancer's touch. "...Daddy?"

"Don't move, sweetie." He knelt down. "You have to stay still for the skin grafts to take root."

"But the staples *itch*." Paul smiled; it was the first time since Aliyah's burning that she'd felt feisty enough to whine. "And the TV is bad."

"You – you have Uncle Kit's Dora DVDs, don't you?"

"The nurses forget to press play."

"Know what *you* need?" a new voice said. Paul was startled to see the gamemancer kneeling next to Aliyah; he'd forgotten she was here. "Distraction. Take this." She booted up Super Mario on her Nintendo DS, then handed it over. "When I was a little, lonely girl, that's what my parents gave me. It opened up new worlds."

Aliyah took the black plastic case reverently. Her fingers were stiff and clumsy, knotted with scar tissue. But her *smile*...

"Mommy says videogames rot your brain."

The 'mancer snorted. "I could show you some things

that'd make your Momma's brain spin like a spun penny."

Paul chuckled. He'd never thought of doing 'mancy in front of Imani. It'd be nice to see her reaction when she realized why he'd hidden his emotions. Well, not nice, but... *fitting*.

"You have cartoons on your skin," Aliyah asked. "Does it hurt? I want some."

"After all you've been through, sweetie, a few needles would be a cakewalk."

Aliyah smiled. "What's your name?"

The 'mancer reached out to caress what was left of Aliyah's hair. "Valentine," she said. "Valentine DiGriz."

TEN
Three Scenes Before the Flex Gets Made

Reporters lurked in the lobby, hoping to photograph Paul Tsabo. Give them the slightest confirmation he was on the hunt again, and they'd do what they'd done after he'd killed the illustromancer: turn him into a symbol of their own lust for killing.

Paul thanked God they hadn't tracked down the motel Samaritan had put him up in. So the reporters milled around like they did at the hospital these days, low-level freelancers hoping to catch a scoop. If the story caught fire, they'd assign full-time reporters to follow Paul; that had happened for one dreadful week after he'd murdered the illustromancer, cameras thrust into his windows.

He slunk around to the back, feeling guilty. Kit was right: in the wake of Paul's tear-gassing and arrest, people were starting to wonder what Paul was up to. Which was why Kit had ordered Paul to take a mandatory vacation, making Paul spend a few days out of sight to let the heat fade. Paul shouldn't even be at Samaritan.

Yet when he got to his office, he found not a reporter, but Kit, poking around.

"Maybe I'm getting old," Kit said, pushing a collection of statutes aside to peer behind Paul's desk. "But... do you have a rat problem here?"

He knows, Paul thought. *He's sensing the magic.*

"...No. I mean, maybe there's a nest in there somewhere, but Mickey Mouse hasn't bit me yet."

Kit looked embarrassed, thrusting forth his usual box of donuts. His ritual Dunkin's offering usually was half gift, half personality test, but this was a particularly flimsy excuse to get inside Paul's office.

Paul's fingers hesitated over a vanilla kreme donut, then plucked his usual cruller from the pile.

"You almost took a different flavor," Kit said. "That means you're reevaluating your priorities. I see that a lot after major life trauma – divorces, sudden losses..."

"It's a *donut*, Kit."

"You are what you eat." He set the donuts down, looking grave. "I hear rustling, Paul. Something knocking papers off your desk. My secretary doesn't hear it. I figure she's got better ears than I do, but..."

"Kit." Paul grinned wide, a friend indulging his old buddy's craziness. He did not want Kit looking too closely, or he'd stumble upon Paul's stockpile of top-secret SMASH case files. "I just turned down a vanilla kreme because I didn't want powdered sugar all over my desk. You think I'd tolerate mouse turds?"

"Heh. No." He frowned, as if to say, *Maybe*.

"If it bothers you, get the exterminator."

"I don't want to run the expense by Lou."

"So get a dead rat and throw it under my chair," Paul said. "Lou's a cheap bastard, but filthy rats scurrying around Samaritan? Management doesn't want the competition."

Kit gave Paul an admiring grin. "Pretty cagey for a paper pusher."

"That's what paper-pushing is, Paul. Leveraging white-collars until they *have* to act for you." Paul socked Kit gently on the shoulder, an artificial gesture all the more embarrassing when he realized he was emulating Lenny Pirrazzini. "Did you want to talk to me, or would you like a conference call with my rats?"

"That's probably how you get all your paperwork done. Your rats fill it out for you. Like shoemaker's elves." A nervous laugh.

He's kidding but not kidding, Paul thought. *That image is taking root in his mind.*

Then: *So what are you going to do about it when he finds out?*

"I wouldn't let an elf *touch* my paperwork." Paul reached into his cabinets, taking deep satisfaction in the perfect alphabetization, and plucked out six thick Samaritan forms. "That's *my* fun time. Hell, you ordered me to get out of the office, and what am I doing? Going to a nice lake, putting the pole in the water, then filling out reports for that 'mancy bust."

"...there's a hitch."

"No way. That bust is *perfect*. I got proof positive those frogs were 'mancy. We can deny every claim."

"Yeah. But the government's requesting records on you. They claim you were inside the house. Were you?"

Paul froze.

"...Paul, Paul," Kit said sympathetically. "What the fuck were you thinking?"

"I was taking pictures of the lab," Paul lied. "You said we needed a solid case..."

"You needed *two hours* to take photos?"

Crap. He'd forgotten about his little temporal exchange. For him, he'd waited five minutes for SMASH to arrive... but to the mundane world, he'd faxed in the report two hours before.

His only way out involved playing to Kit's most loathsome assumptions... so he caressed the gun underneath his vest.

"...I was hiding. Hoping *she'd* show back up."

Kit pulled Paul against him in a manly hug.

"...You fuckin' idiot." Kit sighed with relief. "I know you want revenge, Paul. But the government's claiming Anathema sensed you there. They say you blew the case."

"She wasn't there when I got there!"

"...you think this Anathema is a she?" Kit asked suspiciously. "On what evidence?"

...*shit*. Paul had gotten incautious. "...just a gut feeling. She's crazy dedicated. You know what they say about terrorists – if you see a woman terrorist, shoot her first, because she's more committed than her male buddies."

Kit grunted, not quite satisfied. "Sounds crazy, but... you understand 'mancers. Or maybe you're just crazy. The government thinks you are. They say the two 'mancer-induced traumas have made you psychologically unstable. They're offering a free trip to the Refactor for counseling."

The government billed the Refactor as a grand healing center, a spa to cleanse 'mancers and help mundanes.

"The only help I need is tracking this bastard down." *Bastard*. Use male names.

Kit rolled his eyes. "Was there ever a cop who went to counseling voluntarily? All right, do your thing. But if you'd been a civilian, you'd be under the white lights now. As an employee, well... Initially, having an honored cop on the team seemed like a smart PR move. Now your presence gets people asking why we refuse 'mancy claims. The upper floors are discussing whether you're bringing more heat than you're worth."

Paul shuddered. He couldn't lose his insurance. "Okay."

"The next time you get a wild hair to crawl into some 'mancer's hobbit hole, *call* me. We're navigating tricky waters. Reporters have been calling me all day. I should write you up just for showing your face here, my friend."

"I'll stay low. You know what *you* should do?"

"What?"

"...call the exterminator, you rat-hallucinating old bastard." Paul grabbed the forms and strutted out, followed by Kit's laughter.

"Daddy will be back in two days."

Aliyah grunted a vague affirmation.

She moved the Nintendo DS's joypad, her left hand

comparatively nimble, her contorted right hand stabbing the buttons convulsively as she hopped Mario over another set of barriers. She barely looked up when anyone entered, retreating into this bright world of bricks.

But what were her alternatives? She was bedbound. Games were better than more TV, weren't they? And... didn't he owe her some fun times, anyway? After what he'd done to her?

She took comfort in his presence, complained when he left. Still, he prodded her into interacting; he wanted to have some good memories of her to take with him when he was off in a cabin, becoming a magical drug dealer. He needed to remember her voice to remind him that failure wasn't an option.

"And *why* is Daddy going to be gone?"

"You're hunting 'mancers."

"No, no, not quite." Paul wasn't sure how to deal with Aliyah's sudden obsession with hurting 'mancers. "Just an out-of-town claim, sweetie. I'll probably never see a 'mancer."

"You'll kill them the next time you see one."

Her offhanded certainty chilled him. "You like that game, don't you?"

"It's full of hiddens."

"...hiddens?"

"Vallumtime showed me." She waved the screen at him, not quite so Paul could see it; at six, Aliyah hadn't quite mastered the concept that just because she could see it didn't mean everyone could. "These pipes lead to a new level, but you have to squat in them. If you break this brick, then a vine goes up, and *that's* a new level. That's why Vallumtime fell in love with videogames. She wants the world filled with hidden doors."

Paul frowned. He didn't remember Valentine saying that the last and only time he'd been here with her. Yet somehow, Valentine's words resonated with him.

"There should be something unpredictable around every corner, shouldn't there?" Paul tried the thought on for size, adored it.

"I like it when you visit. Mommy makes me put the Nintendo away."

It was petty, Paul knew, but he loved any indication that Aliyah's affection for him was greater. Eventually, Aliyah would start playing them off each other; his little manipulator. Already, she'd figured out that as the sick girl, she could charm the nurses into bringing her fresh batteries because – in a phrase that Aliyah had memorized word-for-word, though Paul doubt she understood it – "the fine motor control these games requires is a form of physical therapy."

"I like watching you explore," Paul allowed. "So, what are you doing?"

"Mario wears costumes. Now he's a 'nukey." Paul craned his neck to see a tiny Mario, bouncing around in a raccoon suit. "He flies, see?" Mario bopped a turtle with his tail; the turtle's shell went flying. He bounced off, landing on a bright orange flower, taking on its color.

"*No!*" she yelled. "*Not the blossom!*"

"What's the matter, sweetie?"

"He's a stupid 'mancer now. See?" She jabbed the B

button; Mario spat fireballs that bounced across the screen. Then she hopped Mario into a chasm. "So I have to kill him."

Paul ambled down the rows of vans in the Avis parking lot; checking a pink sheet, he looked for its matching license plate. The roar of ascending airplanes rattled the cheap tin roofs that kept the rain off the cars; rain-slickered employees huddled inside shacks, looking miserable.

Paul squeezed his temples. The flux made his head feel like a balloon animal, with a small child squooshing him. The distraction vexed him, because he wasn't sure the car he was looking for even existed.

Sure enough, there was the plate: ENF 106. A white Dodge Grand Caravan, as promised.

He piled the equipment into the back, sure the security guards would come running. But no; nobody cared he was stacking alchemical glassware into a van he'd never signed for. Paul started it up, pulling out to the big orange SEVERE TIRE DAMAGE – DO NOT BACK UP sign.

An old black man with a pleasant grin leaned out into the rain, hand extended.

Holding his breath, Paul handed over the pink slip that was proof he'd rented the car. Well, not him. The car was in someone else's name. And he'd never actually gone to the front desk; as he'd envisioned all the steps involved in renting a car – the insurance signoffs, the gas contracts, the car inspection – the blank white paper he'd scribbled on had blushed pink, the vehicle ID numbers indenting the page to the meaty *chunk* of invisible dot matrix stamps.

He was about to rent a car he'd conjured from blank paper.

The attendant noted his concern. "Rough flight?"

"Family business."

The attendant nodded. "They'll get you every time." He licked his fingers and thumbed through the paperwork. He took the green sheet that had appeared underneath the pink sheet sometime in between the time Paul had handed it to him and the time he'd thumbed through it, then handed the pink sheet back.

The attendant waved him through with a smile.

Paul was certain the van would dissipate as he turned onto the freeway, dumping him onto the asphalt. But no; the hard pleather of the steering wheel was underneath his hands, its wheels hummed on the freeway, the sleek USB ports were ready for use. Paul turned the Sirius radio on full blast, only to be greeted with a gentle Viennese waltz.

The genteel strings seemed inappropriate. He'd done magic. *Real* magic.

Paul flipped the station over to a classic rap station; "Gin and Juice" blared out. Imani had despised rap, preferred soft, formless R&B that was all whispers and "hey, girl". And he'd always caved, because was music *that* important?

Now he knew the answer. Yes. Music. Music was everything.

He had his mind on his 'mancy and his 'mancy on his mind.

Paul's luck held as he found a parking space in front of Valentine's apartment on the East Side. Her apartment complex was run-down but colorful, painted in blood red with white trim. The people inside styled themselves bohemians... yet Paul knew from experience everyone inside dealt with 1930s plumbing.

She buzzed him up. He massaged his temples and pushed through the door, feeling the jittery nervousness of a man on his first date. It wasn't quite a date – she was a kid, for Christ's sake – but he still wanted to impress her.

She's a killer, he told himself.

He got to the top of the stairs to find Valentine's door open, her room in chaos.

It was a studio apartment with practically no furniture; a dirty mattress had been heaved into the middle of the floor, an oasis among piles of junk. There were piles of dirty T-shirts and panties, old videogames, Styrofoam take-out boxes, DVD cases of hentai films, Master Chief action figures, old Amazon boxes, everything layered with a sprinkling of packing peanuts.

A cardboard box next to her bed served as a bedside table; it contained a small plastic Pac-Man lamp and a black plastic tub of something called ANAL LUBE.

There was a slightly less cluttered spot before her television, which Paul guessed was where her gaming chair had once sat. It now contained one very illegal bag of crushed hematite.

This is the lair of New York's subtlest terrorist?

Valentine rooted through the piles, not bothering to

look up as Paul came in. Today's outfit was an embroidered black shirt with glittery red hearts, and V-shaped knee-high boots.

"Can't find my Flex bra," she muttered, tossing a petrified McRib over her shoulder.

"...Does the right bra help with magic?"

She laughed. "No, you silly! But making Flex stinks. I'm not bringing that smell with me to the club. Oh, *there* you are."

She bent over to pick up a large-cupped foam bra, then yanked off her shirt. Paul saw her ample breasts plop out before he averted his gaze. He watched from the corner of his eye as she hooked the bra in front, rotated it around her body, then stuck her arms through the straps.

There was nothing seductive about it. Valentine simply didn't care who saw her naked.

As Valentine tugged her shirt back on, she knocked over the tub of ANAL LUBE, which rolled toward Paul's feet.

"Oh! Sorry." She balanced it back on the box, noting Paul's shocked expression. "That's not for me, you know." She slapped her butt. "I'm an exit-only kinda girl."

"Then why..." He looked, baffled, from the large tub to her and back. "Why's it there?"

She gave him a wry look. "I don't think you really wanna know."

"...maybe I don't."

"Your comfort level is mine, my man. My 'man*cer*." She mock-punched him on the chin, then stuffed the hematite sack into a black garbage bag. "You pick up the stuff we needed?"

"Yeah. I got a bingo machine, the copper wire, the–"

"You have the air of responsibility about you, Paul. Let us not sully that with details."

They wrestled the sack downstairs. Between the flux pressure in his head and the heavy lifting, Paul worried he'd pop a vein before they wrestled the equipment into the van.

Valentine whistled as she slid into the passenger's seat, resting a huge Dunkin' Donuts bag in her lap. "*Nice.* I can see I'm going places with you. You didn't put this car in your own name, did you?"

"Conjured it from blank paper." Paul plugged his leg into the USB port to charge it, feeling supremely cocky.

"Dude!" She offered the high five, then frowned, scrutinizing him. "What *is* your school?"

Paul froze, caught in a tug-of-war; he wanted to share all his secrets with Valentine, exchange 'mancy tips, geek out over this amazing thing they shared – but then he thought of her future targets. Secluding her for the weekend meant she couldn't kill innocents today, but… that was just delaying the inevitable.

She didn't *feel* like a killer. But Imani hadn't felt like a cheater. And Paul had been a mediocre cop, his dogged attention to detail offset by his eagerness to look for the good in people.

He remembered her first words to him, words that defined the 'mancer lifestyle: *I don't like killing.* He didn't like killing, either. The one time he'd shot someone had almost destroyed him, and he'd barely known the illustromancer. Killing Valentine would be destroying the only person who understood him...

Could he kill a 'mancer again? Even for Aliyah?

"That's... hard to explain."

She looked hurt. She reached down into the Dunkin' bag to bring out a box, a cruller in the center.

"...donut?" she asked.

He craved sweetness. He went with a glazed.

"You struck me as a cruller guy," she said, leaning back. "Instead, you went with the donut that's *almost* interesting. Glazed is the donut for people who don't know what donut they like."

"You sound like my friend Kit," he chuckled. "He does Dunkin' prognostications."

"That guy is one wise dude. Never trust a man who doesn't like a donut." She swigged her coffee, eyeing Paul guardedly. Then: "Is that something you... *can* do?"

"Can do what?"

"Getting vans. Is it part of your *raison d'être*? How bad's your flux level? I got a backseat full of hematite; I don't wanna get pulled over."

"I don't know how bad it is. I haven't done this enough to compare, remember?"

"And you're not sharing enough for me to tell." She crossed her arms, fuming; it reminded Paul of Aliyah holding her breath until she got what she wanted.

Paul ate his donut.

"...*be* that way." She blew a lock of hair away from her forehead. "Flux is all about the SFX."

"The what?"

"*Special effects*." She huffed a perfectly teenaged "Ghod" under her breath. "If the stuff I do is related to videogames? Low flux. If I get a van, they either fade away like a power-up after fifteen minutes, or arrive with a squad of cops in pursuit."

Paul remembered the forms, flying like falcons at the apartment's flames. He'd pushed his bureaucromancy to save his daughter, but… even then, it felt like cheating. No wonder it had rebounded so terribly.

"It's a balance between 'how difficult would it be to do without 'mancy' and 'how in-flavor is it,'" Valentine continued. "Turning the bathroom door into something you couldn't kick open woulda taken me ten minutes with a hammer, so… final blowback? I chipped a nail." She displayed a nasty blood blister.

"So," Valentine concluded. "How big a stretch is 'getting a van' for you, O Mystery 'Mancer?"

"I'm a…" He trailed off. "I've got some juice for this."

"Tell me, *tell* me!" She bounced up and down like a kid waiting for her birthday cake. "You're only the third mage I've ever met. You know *my* juice. It's only fair; give it up!"

Her excitement buoyed him up; he couldn't remember finding someone who *wanted* to talk about 'mancy. "…only the third?"

"Hey, it's not like there are support groups. I read somewhere just one in ten thousand people fit the psychological profile to become 'mancers."

"It's one in fifty thousand," Paul corrected her. Her eyes narrowed, and Paul realized he was still part cop to her.

"You *would* know."

"Most don't survive," Paul said. "Many are institutionalized, tranked quiet. The rest, well, most get their first flux blowback and wind up Refactored or dead."

"Worst game show ever: Refactored or Dead!"

"You're right. There *aren't* a lot of us."

She settled back into the seat, looking out over the morning traffic. It occurred to Paul how lonely a life she must lead; playing games twelve hours a day to feed her obsessions, with no one to talk to. He thought about the tub of ANAL LUBE, and Valentine's bubbly charm suddenly seemed saturated with isolation – a happy welcoming into her parlor because you could never see the rest of her house.

"…It's not that crazy," Paul admitted.

"Finding a third mage?"

"Getting a van."

"Okay." He liked that she respected his mystery, pathetic as it was. "You feel it squidging around you? Like a bad masseuse kneading your forehead?"

"Absolutely."

"That's the universe playing debt collector. If you're not careful, your subconscious guides it; that's where the disaster happens. If you wanna blow it off, shape the charge."

"How?"

"Been thinking about this. Me, *I* imagine something bad. If it's close to the amount I owe, it'll flow through. But I had to be careful, because it's like learning to pee. First time you open up your pee-hole, you can't stop.

Once you build up the muscles, you can dole it out."

Paul chewed his lip. "I can't pee like that. I don't think guys can."

She hid a smile behind her coffee. "Face it, Paul. Our genitalia is superior in *every* way." Her face fell, looking pensive. "Shame I'm addicted to cock."

These did not seem like the words of a mass murderer. "So when I'm starting," Paul said, "I should envision bad things on a par with the weirdness I've committed, right? Nothing too bad? And then – let it flow?"

"Yup."

"All right. Buckle in."

He squeezed his eyes shut and pulled over to the right lane. A bang and a flapping sound, and Paul cruised to a stop with two flat front tires.

"*That's* the spirit!" Valentine cheered.

ELEVEN
How to Make Flex

Five hours and two Dunkin' Donuts stops later, they pulled up next to Paul's safe house.

"Is there a word that means 'pretty' and 'dumpy' at the same time?" Valentine asked, then: "Hope not. Somebody'd use it to describe me."

Paul stepped out of the car, delighting in his power as he viewed the house. It was *real*.

The house he'd procured was a ramshackle thing nestled in deep woods, twenty-five minutes away from the nearest grocery store. It had been an earnest living space where a family had once dreamed of living out in the country, then discovered the reality of isolation.

Still, the place had a beautiful view – perched on the edge of a rough promontory that sloped down into a river. The backyard had a crescent curve at its edge, marking the drop-off into the wooded valley. He listened to the green branches rustling in the wind, a great contented sigh.

He patted the house like a baby's bottom, in part to verify its reality; yesterday, he'd used his 'mancy to purchase it under an assumed name in a sheriff's sale several weeks back, all for five hundred dollars.

"...A rental?" Valentine squinted at the house's dilapidated wood shingles. She was probing around the edges, trying to dope out what 'mancy Paul commanded.

"Nope. I own it. Or someone with a name very much like mine, anyway."

She considered. "You're not a doppelmancer, are you?"

"...*is* there such a thing?"

"I dunno. But you sure are buying a lot of things and not paying for them."

"Oh, I'm paying for them." Paul tossed a glass alembic at her.

She pondered that, then grinned and gave him fingerguns. "Ah, Paul. You're keeping me on my toes."

It was a convivial moment, soaked in that fluttering teenaged anticipation you got before putting on a play. He sensed the hours of hard work ahead, hauling in the equipment and setting it up... but it was a fine labor, a skilled thing meant to fuel their dreams. The sweat brought an ardent satisfaction; each heavy box carried into the house fit another piece into some clockwork construction. The ritual alembics and chalk diagrams would be assembled not just into a lab but a lifestyle. Paul's brain thrummed with elation as he realized, shit, yes, he was going to do something he'd dreamed all his life:

They were going to go into this house and make magic.

That cheer was incinerated by his follow-up thought: *magic that will brew illegal drugs. Which she will use to kill people.*

"Come on." He fished the key out from his pocket. "Let's get this over with."

Valentine twirled the handle on the bingo machine they'd set up in the moldy living room. She plucked out five wooden balls with fading letters, laid them into a tray. She frowned, a fortune-teller reading tea leaves.

She kept whirling the handle until the balls ricocheted inside the metal cage, then removed five balls to stare at them. It could have been cautious preparation, were it not for the way she bit her lip and avoided his gaze.

"No patterns *this* time?" Paul asked.

"Nothing obvious." Valentine drained another Red Bull, her hands shaking from more than caffeine. "I've been told sometimes the balls come out spelling arcane mathematical patterns, so you'd never know it wasn't random without a PhD... but if that's the case, we're doomed anyway."

"I haven't done 'mancy since we got here. Neither have you. We should be at perfectly normal odds now, unless you know something I don't."

Paul sat at the kitchen table they'd moved into the living room, wanting to get this over with. He'd spread his forms out before him, perfectly aligned, flanked by three new Bic pens. Valentine had eyed his equipment with interest but said nothing.

Beyond the paperwork were long-stemmed alembics,

ultra-slim watering cans of smooth glass. Copper tubes corkscrewed in and out of inscribed distillation devices that would, theoretically, condense Paul's raw 'mancy. Valentine had set a silver knife, its blade scabbed with blood, next to the Bics.

He drew aimless patterns in the cookie sheet heaped with brown hematite, which looked like a huge container of eye shadow. Paul swallowed back anxiety; it was like waiting in front of a rollercoaster, standing in line while you looked over the drop and imagined the fall.

Valentine glanced at the unused loops of copper wire in the corner. "Are you sure we can't use the siphon?"

Paul flattened his palms against the table. "There's nothing that would make me endanger Aliyah again. My job is the only other thing I value – and if I lose that, I lose the insurance, I lose Aliyah. So tell me: what do I have that's big enough to ground loose flux?"

"Nothing," she whispered. "If this goes wrong, the worst luck will hit everything in the area. Billion-to-one long shots that will cripple me in all the ways I fear most." Valentine closed her eyes, hyperventilating.

"You promised you'd help."

"I did. You realize you're taking your life in your hands, right?"

"I do."

"And that you could take me with you?"

"Yes."

"I started with that first part because I thought it'd be more motivating, but you realize it's the second part I care about."

He whipped out his phone to brandish a picture at her: Aliyah in better days.

Valentine nodded. Then she held up her fist and waggled it in the air, as if deciding whether to throw rock, paper, or scissors.

She extended her finger, pointing at him.

"Do magic," she commanded.

Paul stared blankly.

"...how?"

"'Mancy isn't rituals, Paul. It's love. When you started, I'll bet dimes to dollars you didn't fire up 'mancy to *do* anything. You just... did it. And the 'mancy flowed from that love."

Paul thought back to his nighttime shifts at Samaritan Mutual, trying to conceive of the Universal Unified Form – the single form that, once created, would be so comprehensive, it would obviate the need for any other form ever again. Just silly daydreams to distract him from his impending divorce – but, in Paul's mind, the form was sprawling, large enough to lie across mountains like a napkin thrown over a dinner plate.

But there had been something reassuring about cataloguing every activity a human being could ever request of someone, then devising a set of flexible fields to cover that eventuality. The Universal Unified Form omitted nothing. No matter what trouble you encountered, the Universal Unified Form had a place for you.

Paul scribbled on the blank papers, starting where he always did: *First Name. Middle Name. Last Name. Sex. Date of Birth. Address 1. Address 2. City...*

Alembics rattled on the table. The blank paper expanded to the size of a kite as Paul scribbled upon it, drawing boxes and underlines and scores to handle the automobile purchases, then any repair work that had to be done upon the automobiles, then the lists of parts the shop might order to repair the automobiles...

He half-heard Valentine's voice: "N-46! I-26! B-7! G-54. No pattern."

The automobiles had factories that needed parts. The parts required bills of lading, tax statements, tracking numbers. The people who delivered the parts would have insurance claims, expense reports, OSHA forms...

...the Beast. The Beast that touches every civilized human...

"B-15!" Valentine's voice rose in excitement. "I-30! N-45! G...52! O... 68! Keep going, Paul; keep going!"

Paul imagined the tax forms for the parts and felt that distant muscle Flex. Back at Samaritan, his office was a blur of dancing paperwork. If Kit was there, he heard the cheerleader pom-pom shake of all the forms cheering Paul on...

"B-10! I-20! N-30! G..." She swallowed. "G-10,456,243? O-£? X-marks-the-spot? Paul, you're... you're doing something very strange here!"

Paul didn't stop. He was on to the international treaties, the trade agreements, the currency exchanges. Valentine waded through waist-deep piles of paper, trying to grab the rolls as they shot out in freshly inked streams, wrestling them like a snake. She got a grasp, hugged them and hauled them back to the alembic.

She looked terrified, elated, orgasmic. She was literally hip-deep in the magic, flush with a wild thrill.

Paul recognized the feeling from when he spied on other 'mancers, that happiness of watching the universe dance to someone else's tune...

Valentine wept.

She folded the forms into crisp edges, squeezing droplets of pure sunshine into the alembic. As the drops tumbled off the edge of the forms, the forms turned gray and dull. They crumbled into ash as she extracted the raw magic into the alembic.

It was like watching his dreams die.

Valentine turned to grab another handful. Paul yanked her back.

She slapped him.

"*You can't leave your love in this, Paul!*" she yelled, barely audible over the tumult of thrashing confetti. "*It has to be clean!*"

Paul knew why. Death Metal and his cartoonish Flex, so easy to trace back to a music lover: that would be him, if he didn't flense his personality from the magic. How long would it take Kit to track bureaucratic-flavored Flex back to Paul? Especially with Kit wondering about the rats?

"*Help me!*" Valentine was drowning in paper.

He strangled his magic, squeezing his personality out, poured the sad, strained remnants into that damned glass cup. He'd never thought of Flex as a mockery of 'mancy, but it was; all that passion, all that individual beauty, stripped clean so boring people could fulfill mundane dreams.

"I know," Valentine whispered, her tears falling into the dead ash piling up at their feet. "I *know*."

He understood now why Valentine had gone on tilt. She'd turned that basement into a kinetic joy of whizzing hedgehogs and diving starfighters… and she couldn't bring herself to kill that beauty. Freed, her magic had surged forth in a wild cascade, following its own bliss…

The sun-fluid, raw magic, boiled out of the alembic, turned the copper tubes molten red, tumbling into sigilled boxes and out again, becoming less him with every step. It was a magic slaughterhouse, a place where you shoved in bright-plumed birds and vomited out shredded pink meat.

Paul felt nauseated from this destruction, sick from the flux smashing down on him like a mattress, making each breath a struggle.

The fluid boiled out. The magic danced like water tossed on a red-hot pan, squirming on a cookie sheet heaped with hematite.

"You have to force them in," Valentine told him. "You have to bond them." She took his hands, pressed them against the tray, trapping the raw magic between Paul's palms and the gritty hematite. "I can't do it. It belongs to you."

Paul scooped up great handfuls of hematite and magic alike, mashing them together like eggs into cake mix. The power thrummed up his arms, trying to flow back into his body. He forced it back. The gritty dirt clumped together, condensing into cold chunks of crystal as he rooted the magic inside. Pounds of hematite shrank into pebbles of glowing Flex.

His arms ached. The congestions of stray luck, the flux, pressed his eyelids against his eyeballs. But opaque white stones of Flex rested in a nest of damp hematite.

"Okay." Valentine spoke with the low hush of someone about to defuse a bomb. "Now. Shove the flux in there, too."

Paul thought of some stupid freshman, unable to handle the flux blowback, scarring Aliyah forever. Of all the other innocents killed in horrid accidents, all for the crime of being near some asshole riding high on stolen magic.

He couldn't let that happen to anyone else.

"...No."

"We're not making this shit for friends, Paul." *Who are you making this for, Valentine?* "You're carrying a cataclysmic load of bad luck. If you don't bind the flux with the magic, all that is gonna rain down on your head." She licked her lips, pleading. "And mine."

The flux snaked in around him. He thought of crippled Aliyah. Maybe that was Valentine's goal – she needed Flex brimming with bad luck to get desperate people to shred themselves and everyone around them. And Paul – he'd pass these deadly coincidences on to the people least fit to handle them...

"I can't." The room sparked in colors the human eye could not name, the excess magic straining against the bonds of reality. "I know it'll kill us, Valentine. But I can't... I can't let this go..."

"That's the *deal*, Paul! You wanted to learn magic! You wanted me to teach you! So *put the fucking flux in the stones before it backlashes!*"

"I will not!"

She flexed her fingers, an old-style gunslinger hovering her hand over her holster. "I'm too close to the center. Even if I ran, I'd still get zapped. So don't make me try something stupid." She swallowed, then added: "Please. Paul. *Put the fucking flux in.*"

Something rustled beneath Paul's fingertips. The last living bit of the Universal Unified Form heaved itself up weakly; the remnants of a transfer form.

Of course.

"*Get back!*" As he shoved Valentine away, a huge gout of that color-that-was-not-a-color surged from his fingers, catapulting her across the room. He knelt before the half-dead form, scrawling the relevant words across the top:

Hazardous waste transfer.

What was bureaucracy best at, if not transferring blame from one department to another?

Valentine fought to get at Paul as he scrawled magic sigils across the page: *Generator's name and mailing address. EPA ID number. Waste codes.* And then the critical portion:

Assigned Material Transfer Site.

"Woods outside of cabin," he wrote, and scribbled his name just as Valentine grabbed the silver dagger to stab him.

The house slid left.

The earth shook with a bowel-loosening rumble, glassware flying in every direction. Paul saw the woods sliding downward, massive tree trunks toppling, long-buried roots spraying dirt into the air.

An earthquake, Paul thought, so amazed he couldn't quite fit the thought inside his head. *In upstate New York*.

He stumbled to the window to watch the outlook in the backyard break free. Trees in the shallow soil on the mountain's slope tumbled downwards into the river below. The water would be choked with dead wood, the surviving animals waking to a whole new environment.

Valentine grasped the windowsill, smiling in crazed wonderment – at him, at the last rumbles of dirt cascading down the hill, of the trees shaking like thrash-metal fans in the pit.

There was no pressure.

He'd rerouted the flux somewhere else.

Valentine scrabbled on the floor, grabbed a clear chunk of Flex between two fingers, peered through it. Paul could see a distorted ripple of Valentine's eye, the Flex transparent as water.

"This is clear," she said in a hushed tone. She shook the crystal to verify its existence. "*Clear*, Paul. B1-grade. I'm no expert, but… this is legendary. Top quality. Nobody's made this since the 1950s." She scrubbed tears from her eyes. "This will fix all my problems."

"You could have done it yourself …"

She did a double take. "Are you kidding? I've never made Flex, Paul. Failed every time. But you! That was *awesome*!"

He couldn't have heard her right. She was responsible for his daughter's condition. She was the murderer. That's why he'd sought her out. But she…

"…you've never made Flex?"

…you're not Anathema?

Valentine capered around the room joyously, pumping her fist, the dance of the innocent. "I told you I was no expert, Paul. But you? You're the Flex-fucking-*master*! Clear Flex is the holy grail of 'mancy. And you can keep making it for as long as you want because *you can redirect the blowback*!"

She shook his shoulders. "Do you understand, Paul? *You are the King of Flex*!"

Paul stared at her for a few moments, uncomprehending. Then he thought about Imani and Kit, thirsting for 'mancers' blood. He thought about SMASH, reducing all this glorious variety to a single grim purpose. He thought about Samaritan Mutual, hunting 'mancers to remove this glory from the world.

This is what I was born for, he thought dizzily, and his laughter was wild as magic.

INTERLUDE #1
Three Weeks From Now

Jimmy sat in the Starbucks, an Adidas bag stuffed full of handguns at his feet. He finished his hot cocoa, wiped whipped cream off of his bristled mustache, then craned his neck around in hopes of seeing the woman who'd answered his ad.

He looked down at the note that had appeared in his PO box this morning – no stamp, no return address. Written in dried blood was an encouraging message:

You want to know if you can do it. I know you never have. Meet me at the Starbucks around the corner.

Bring your guns.

His hands shook in anticipation, so he used one to squeeze the other, then realized he was holding hands with himself. Jimmy usually touched his boys when he got nervous. He had a Colt stashed under the mattress, a Desert Eagle on top of the fridge, a Barrett semiautomatic duct-taped under the kitchen table. Whenever he got jittery, he'd take them out and clean them. There was something soothing about their weight filling his hand.

It's not that Jimmy Lutz wanted to shoot a burglar, mind you; he just wanted to know he could *do* it if he had to. He spent all his free evenings down at the Bullet Hole Shooting Range, a rusted tin shack that had been cited on numerous occasions for negligent discharges. He bought the custom targets, the old ones with Osama bin Laden's face – and each time he squeezed off a shot, he wondered: *Could I look a terrorist in the eyes and kill him*?

He wasn't willing to *start* a fight. That would have been dishonorable. The only person who'd ever swung at him was his Dad, and Jimmy wouldn't have *touched* a medaled Gulf War veteran like Dad, nossir. But Dad had all those tales of knifing Iraqis in the desert, leaving Jimmy feeling… untested. Fallow, like the wilted lettuce at Whole Foods he cleared out – a big wad of rotting potential.

The guys at the Bullet Hole were burly men in leather vests. All of *them* had a tale about kicking some guy's ass, and that reality swelled within them, filled them with something indefinable. People *noticed* them. People didn't interrupt when they told stories. Whereas Jimmy had been waving at the waitress for fifteen minutes, wanting another cup of cocoa.

"Excuse me," Jimmy coughed–

"When you kill," said a low female voice, "you become more real."

The woman's face was haggard, ex-military for sure, a gaunt beauty ravaged by harsh truths. She had dreadlocked hair with tiny bones knotted in it. She slid into the seat across from him with a rangy grace, a compelling confidence that Jimmy envied.

"You wrote this," she said, sliding across a *Soldier of Fortune* magazine folded open to his ad:

MERCENARY FOR HIRE
15 yrs. shooting experience.
Low costs, high reliability.
Interesting jobs our specialty.
PO Box 356

"You no longer masturbate," the woman said matter-of-factly. "Instead, you read the replies. Over and over again."

Jimmy swallowed back shame. He'd run that ad for a year now – and stored the responses in a shoebox underneath his bed, next to his favorite Glock. He'd memorized them all – rebel-killing in Argentina, bodyguarding services in Kuwait, a cryptic invitation to resolve "a situation" in Ontario. Even though the window to reply was long past, he kept rereading them, imagining what would happen if he'd said yes, then jetted off to a foreign country to finally put his Desert Eagle to use.

His fantasies were long, involved, and bloody. Sometimes, he died. Sometimes, he killed. But in every case, he knew exactly who he was by the end of it, a fate better than this cowardly tension.

Jimmy swallowed the last of his cocoa to calm himself, coughed up gritty dregs. "It's okay," she said, squeezing his hand. "I have a situation. You're the man it calls for."

She smiled, revealing rotted teeth – no, not rotted. *Filed.* A primal savagery radiated off that smile, a woman who'd clawed raw hearts from still-warm rib cages.

"What you need," she said, pushing a paper sack across the table towards him, "is ancient rituals."

He looked in the bag. It held a smoky crystalline mass, dull green like jade, bristling with flylike hairs.

"Peyote." Her eyes gleamed like a cat's. "A proper warrior's ritual. In the days of old, when boys were not sure they could be men, and when tribes could not afford to let a boy live, they gave them this. It keyed them into the universe's flow – and when they ventured out to kill for the first time, their spears were *sure*. As will yours be."

"I – I don't have spears…"

A sneer. "No. You have those. Talentless tools that erase the distinction between a warrior and a wet-eared child."

"So… I shouldn't use my…" He swallowed, not quite willing to say it in public, then nudged the bag at his feet. "Those?"

"Go into the bathroom. Eat the peyote. You'll see."

Jimmy almost fainted when he got up, the room spinning as he realized he might know what he'd be capable of when people tried to kill him. Even if that was just crying and shitting his pants, well, the question would still be answered.

He looked down at the bag. He'd always thought peyote was a mushroom or something, not a crystal, but… he'd never done drugs. He'd never done anything wild. He'd barely lived.

He gulped the peyote.

By the time he emerged, his fingers jittered. The woman stood by the bathroom, his bag in her hands – and he felt a fierce possessiveness until she draped it around his shoulders like a queen giving her prince a boon.

"I'm–" His tongue was gummy. The world was reforming around him, changing into pathways and potentials. He remembered the guys at the Bullet Hole talking about the Perfect Action, that one pristine karate chop you strove for in every practice session and got maybe twice in a life time.

Every step he took was the perfect action.

He walked across the coffee shop, amazed; each step fell exactly where it *should* be. He danced between the waitresses, his body flowing along the ley lines in the air…

If he drew his gun, he would shoot pure; the very universe itself would wrap fingers around his wrists to guide his aim. "It has to be someone who has it coming," he told her.

The woman cocked her head. "Can you not feel it?"

It was as though she'd twisted a radio dial, bringing a broadcast into focus. Jimmy fought to keep his hot cocoa down; this ominous dread was like being forced to stay paralytically still while a knife-wielding maniac built a house of ten thousand cards on your belly. It was like suffocating beneath a million butterflies – a snowstorm of tiny infractions.

The wrongness saturated New York, emanating from that direction.

"You feel it, don't you? You must kill him. Or he will chain us with paper…"

This peyote promised freedom, meat, blood – promised a world where the clever survived and the incapable died…

"Of all my weapons, you come closest to understanding why he must die," she whispered. But Jimmy was already running, each step perfect, chasing this awfulness to its source…

Jimmy cruised to a halt before a bunch of shabby tenements and shuttered liquor stores. A chain link fence protected a mostly vacant lot with a couple of rusting cars balanced on piles of old brick.

What interested him was the sidewalk.

The sidewalk stretched before a cracked stoop, though the three surly teenaged Hispanic kids noticed nothing untoward about it. They drank forties in crumpled paper bags, escaping the summer heat. Their guns were jammed into baggy jeans.

Their guns were of no interest. They could not touch him. What was fascinating, like a dissected toad pinned to the street, was the sidewalk etchings.

Most sidewalks had scratches; you noticed that when you hung your head as often as Jimmy did. But the scratches here, concealed beneath layers of gum and piss stains…

…they were inscriptions. In old-fashioned script. Like the Constitution.

Fine, miniscule words, spelled out in cracks, surrounded the building – enclosing the tenement in that death-by-papercut sickness the girl had tuned him into. Jimmy got on his knees to scrutinize it…

"Fuckin' drunk." One of the kids flicked a cigarette towards him; the rest laughed. The paper trail enclosed them, too. They guarded this strange power, coveting it.

Jimmy brushed the still-lit cigarette butt out of the way to read what he could:

… the seller hereby confirms the goods failed to conform to the implied contract, and the buyer went to great lengths to shield the seller from the true consequences of selling for the first time, leading to the definition of this hematite-trapped non-Euclidean warping potency as a nonconforming good. Whereas also that the original protectorate clause was voided…

His eyes skidded away in revulsion. The sickness was pent inside like a demon in a circle–

He tugged the Desert Eagle out and fired. The kid's head exploded.

Jimmy felt no surprise. That bullet had been traveling to its target since the beginning of time, all the heavy elements in a cloud of hydrogen condensing into metals mixed in the earth to be drawn out by factories and carried to him by trucks then delivered to him by the woman at Starbucks. His trigger pull was merely the last stage of an exotic bullet-delivery scheme that had been set in motion with the first vibration of the universe.

The second and third bullets were *even more* perfect, one clipping the second kid's carotid artery, the other plunging through the third's eye.

He examined the dying men as though they were a

strange art; a calm feeling of perfection pervaded his body. Though a weird congestion tickled his temples.

Jimmy felt a strong urge to step aside. A fusillade of bullets from above ricocheted off the pavement where he'd stood. More kids, enthralled by the magic, firing out of the windows at him.

He scooped up the bag and danced into the building. Entering the tenement felt like pushing into a pile of shredded documents; red tape bound his reflexes. Jimmy could feel the building saturated with this—

—*bureaucromancy*. The word floated through his head as if someone had gently pushed it in – and the mail here always arrived on time, bills were paid dutifully, a leakage of laws filtering through the building like a prism. Things were more *orderly* here.

Which made it hard to lose himself in the violence. The shots came easy; it was as though the bullets told him where to fire. The bullets punched through doors, exploded into bodyguards rousing themselves to action. Men charged out of doorways and straight into his muzzle; he slaughtered ten, twenty, thirty of these penny-ante thugs.

But each death squeezed itching guilt into his brain: the legal struggles as family members squabbled over possessions, grim coroners signing death certificates, shutoff notifications to cell phones. Jimmy wanted to lose himself in the carnage – some number kept ticking in his head, telling him he needed to kill two hundred and fifty-six people or this was worth *nothing*—

No. That was too many. The peyote demonstrated how easy killing was: fire through that door, and the bullet would cut down an innocent man whose biggest crime was rising from his couch to get another beer.

Those people didn't deserve to die. He fired only in self-defense, pulling back. And the more he resisted, the more that strange pressure closed in around him.

Jimmy loped up to the third floor in a carnage daze, fighting to retain his grace; this odd pressure clogged his reflexes. Was it guilt? Guilt over the dead men?

The blood on him itched as it congealed. So did this bureaucromancy. It saddled him with responsibility.

He had to cut this unnatural order off at the source.

He kicked in a door. Inside a grimy apartment was the source of all this paper potency: a scrawny white guy handcuffed to a radiator.

The white guy looked up slowly, as if afraid to hope. His leg stump was stark against the stained tile floor, his wrist bloody from escape attempts.

Wait, it wasn't his wrist – the dude's left arm had a thin wound that looked like it'd been bleeding forever. He sat in a pool of crusted blood.

The source of all this horror sported a haggard castaway's beard, a button-down shirt stained with weeks of sweat. Not much of a threat.

Jimmy paused. Was the irritation the man... or the green Rubbermaid bin on the table, heaped with clear crystal? The crystals shivered like Mexican jumping beans. He reached out to pick one up.

A spotted brown hand grabbed his wrist.

His interceptor was an ugly, dark-skinned sonuvabitch with a big nose and weird pockmarks all over his face – but he wore a perfect cream-colored suit, as if he hoped an excess of style would distract from his deformities.

The dude grinned. As if to confirm Jimmy's suspicions about style, the man's teeth were sapphire-plated. They still looked moldy.

"I am Gunza," he said, cocking his head, a terrible green light flashing in those teeth. He popped a crystal from the Rubbermaid bin into his mouth and chewed it; the crystals sparked between Gunza's teeth, like Wint-O-Green mints in the dark. His teeth glowed with green malice.

Jimmy lifted the gun, hunting for the perfect shot––except it wasn't there. Just the congestion.

Gunza took the barrel of Jimmy's Colt .45 between his palms and placed it lovingly against his forehead, a prayer begging for bullets. "You can shoot when you're filled with 'mancy." His voice drove the surety from Jimmy's heart. "But can you shoot when it's just me and you? Can you look me in the eye and fire, Jimmy Lutz?"

How did he know my name? Jimmy thought, panicked. The legless guy on the floor gestured for Jimmy to get out, but Jimmy barely noticed: those teeth, those crystalline glowing teeth.

Jimmy's mouth dried up. The peyote's potency dribbled away between his legs. Those teeth belonged to someone who *could* murder trivially. They terrified Jimmy, because he'd never wanted to be like that.

When it was clear Jimmy could not shoot, Gunza slapped the barrel away with a scornful laugh.

"An empty sperm," Gunza said. "A genetic sinkhole." He turned away, and Jimmy felt himself fading from

view as Gunza took a red plastic canister of gasoline and
splashed it around the room.

"We're gonna die in a fire," Gunza told the guy on
the floor. "Then we're gonna go somewhere remote.
No inspectors. No SMASH. And I'm gonna set up a lab,
and you'll be my Flex bitch."

"Listen to me," Jimmy whispered. The gun, which
seemed to have aimed itself a few moments ago,
quivered in his hand.

"I'm not doing that." The man on the floor retreated,
pressing his back against the radiator. "That's not
happening."

"I said *listen to me*!" Jimmy screamed.

Gunza set the room ablaze.

Jimmy pulled the trigger, feeling like he shouldn't
shoot someone in the back, his Dad would never have
shot an Iraqi in the back – so he pulled the gun to the
side at the last minute, because the truth was he *couldn't*
kill, not without the peyote. He imagined all the
families weeping at funerals; he'd murdered men in
cold blood and it hadn't made him real, it made him
pathetic, terrible, soulless–

–he'd never considered what would happen if he
killed someone and it turned out he wasn't a killer–

The gun exploded in Jimmy's hands, a catastrophic
misfire, the bullet spiraling up and back to punch
through his forehead.

The last sight Jimmy Lutz saw was Gunza stepping
forward to do something unspeakable to the poor
bastard chained to the radiator.

TWELVE
New and More Dangerous Connections

"There is no reason on earth you should meet my connection," Valentine explained. "You're *famous*, Paul. I mean, you're an E-lister, below Kathy Griffin, but... you hunt 'mancers, and this is a Flex deal. If anyone recognizes you, I don't have a lot of experience using my 'mancy to deflect *bullets*."

Paul stood amidst the detritus of Valentine's apartment, adjusting his New York Mets baseball cap. A coffee can of Flex now sat on the box that served for a nightstand, right next to the tub of ANAL LUBE. The contents of that coffee can were worth more than the apartment building.

"You don't understand," Paul put on his sunglasses. He'd applied a pair of artificial muttonchops to his cheeks. "I'm not Paul Tsabo. I'm your uncle Revenna – well, not your uncle by blood; your mother met me a long time ago in college, and I've been there for every one of your birthday parties. I got you your first copy of Super Mario Paint, and you told me about your 'mancy when your powers first manifested, because..."

Valentine's nervousness showed in today's outfit. Instead of her normal cleavage-baring extravaganzas, today she wore a white Che Guevara T-shirt and purple jacket over a pair of clean blue jeans. For Valentine, that was practically dressed for an interview.

"Jesus, Paul," she said, cutting him off. "When you got a fake ID, did you memorize the license number?"

"I *still* have it memorized."

"Yeah, well… you look different enough from a distance. The Destiny 2 shirt is a nice touch. And maybe I'd go with your overly elaborate backstory, even though if I'd had a relative that helpful, I never would've blossomed." She tapped his artificial right ankle with her foot. "But that?"

"That's not… nobody notices. I'm not going to jog…"

"Face it, Paul – scrawny, missing a foot, big old limp? You could dress up in a gorilla suit and I'd still pick you out. You can't come along."

Paul crossed his arms. "I need to see what we're into."

"It's not 'us', Paul, it's *me*. I'm the person who's supposed to *make* it for him. The less he knows about you, the better."

"Valentine DiGriz." Calling her full name got her attention; a tiny bit of parent magic. "I have to follow every lead. If he deals in Flex, maybe he knows about… Anathema."

Paul hated to say the name, because it meant failure. While he'd spent the weekend brewing glorious drugs with Valentine, there'd been another killing – and sure enough, thirty-two models had been crushed at a beauty contest by a set of unsecured overhead lights.

"He doesn't," she said, exhausted. "If he had real Flex in the pipeline, he wouldn't be using *me*."

"Even so. It's a lead. And then there's..." He pushed back his cap, hating to have to say this. "I want to make sure my magic is going to the right place. I'm not a... a drug dealer. That Flex is clear because I didn't want anyone else *hurt*. If we just hand the Flex to some other maniac, then..."

She rubbed her eyebrow piercing. "Don't fucking *guilt* me, Paul. I had someone I needed a favor from."

"Do you trust them?"

"Oh, yes, Paul. We all know drug dealers run kitten farms where they raise sunshine and love."

"Some dealers sell to their friends."

"Didn't you used to be a cop? You know Flex doesn't attract pot dealers – or, at least, not for long. This guy who needs it, he's... he's got something to prove. That's why he wants this. Flex is a name-maker."

"So... He's not going to sell to a guy who might set an apartment complex on fire?"

"Oh, *fuck you*, Paul!" She punted a cartridge across the room. "You come in here, begging for my expertise, then question me? It's a drug dealer. He's *not nice*. What he does with this stuff probably won't make you happy."

Paul crossed his arms. "Will it make *you* happy?"

She punched her thigh. "Get in the fucking closet, Paul."

"What?"

"I said get in the *fucking closet*!" She outweighed him by a hundred pounds, and Paul had the distinct feeling she'd seen more fights than he had. The closet door

swung open, revealing stark blackness. 'Mancy rose
from her fingertips, a cold electron flow.

"Hey, wait–" he protested. "I didn't–"

"In." She shoved him in and slammed the door.

His flesh peeled off. It was painless, like someone
lifting a sticker off a sheet. Paul couldn't see what lay
underneath but felt his physical essence exposed – not
bones, not muscle, but a mathematical equation that
contained the expression of all his movements.

Some other skin slid down over him, fitting snugly
over him. He reached for the doorknob and stepped
out, limping as he always had – the same sore filled
pain, the same gait.

Valentine held up a marker-scrawled mirror so Paul
could see his reflection:

He was a twenty-year old punk kid.

His arms, now exposed in a wifebeater shirt, were
muscular and spiraled with tribal tattoos; he touched
them experimentally. He could feel his own skin sliding
underneath artificial layers.

Paul explored his new face with his fingers. His lips
were lush and pouty; his fingers lingered on his new lip
ring. His hair was dyed a spiky blonde, hidden beneath
a black watch cap.

This new reflection offended him. He looked like an
idiot who grunted more than he spoke, shrugging at
everything he didn't understand.

Then he realized: his leg. His leg was whole.

Hoping against hope, he reached down: he felt foamy
meat underneath the jeans, like padding. He squeezed
hard; there was no feeling, just a hard titanium core.

"Good enough." Valentine made a flicking gesture with her thumb, pushing an imaginary button to accept the change. "I reskinned you. If anyone asks, you're my new boyfriend tagging along to protect me. The disguise won't last long, but it should get your dumb ass through this meeting. You'll do nothing but listen – and if *that* doesn't satisfy your curiosity we're doing the right thing, I will take this coffee can of Flex and fucking walk. Are we clear?"

"Is this the kind of guy you *date*? This… dim-witted prettyboy?"

"Yeah, well," she huffed, "*Clearly,* I don't hang around men for their intellect." She grabbed the coffee can full of Flex.

"You sure you want to hand all that to Gunza sight unseen?"

Valentine thought better of it, emptied a single crystal into a crumpled McDonald's bag, leaving the bulk of the drugs behind. "Come on; let's get this over with."

As she shut the door behind them, Paul took one last glimpse at the ANAL LUBE can, beginning to understand just what Valentine liked to do with pretty, incoherent boys.

As Paul struggled to limp after Valentine through the subway tunnels – she pushed ahead at a rapid clip, pointedly not looking back – he had to admit: he felt more alive than he had in years.

Samaritan Mutual had promised him an exciting career, a cross between a private detective and CSI, but what he actually did was spend his time sifting through wreckage for subtle clues, then testifying in court. It was tedium – and discovering he was *good* at tedium had encouraged him to settle into a numbing routine.

Now he was on the beat again, sneaking into a drug dealer's lair.

He would quiz this dealer for potential magical connections, sure. He would ensure his Flex – yes, *his* Flex – got to the right place, sure. But it was also that he needed to witness the changes in the world he'd wrought.

He'd help Aliyah, of course. He'd stop Anathema. But he couldn't deny the joy of rising to new challenges.

And there *were* challenges. Now that he had a coffee can full of guilt-free 'mancy, what the hell would he do with it? He could sell it to get money, he guessed… but he didn't know who he'd sell it to, and in any case, the idea of becoming a drug dealer sickened him. He'd seen the harm done when idiots couldn't handle the flux; inflicting that on innocents would make him no better than Anathema.

Maybe he could use the Flex to get lucky himself, stumbling across the right loophole to force Samaritan Mutual's hand… but there was still the operation, the most critical part of the process.

The problem was, *he* didn't need to get lucky; he needed Aliyah's *surgeon* to be lucky.

He'd envisioned walking up to the doctor before the operation with a handful of the world's most illegal drug, saying, "Here. Sniff this." That plan didn't end well. Nor did it work out well if the doctor decided that Aliyah was not his top priority and so instead decided to intuitively burn his gifted luck on scoring with some pretty nurse. And so Paul had spent most of the day plotting, angling for ways he could use his Flex to secretly dose an operating room and have them all focused on the most important thing of all: Aliyah.

Even Valentine's rage could not daunt him. She sat next to him, playing a Game Boy, until she got up wordlessly at their stop. Paul read the newspapers over other people's shoulders; he noted with a dim pride that the Buffalo earthquake had made the third page. *I did that.*

Still, he fretted every time a commuter bumped into him; the skin shifted around him, threatening to rub away. He restrained a maddening urge to itch his tattoos off.

The subway exit emerged in a cramped metropolitan area doing its best imitation of a suburb; rows of cheap, tiny houses with stamp-sized lawns. The locals had planted greenery in an attempt to liven up the place, but the wage slaves who lived here got home too late to mow the lawn and couldn't afford hired help... so the nooks between the houses had wild thatches sticking out in areas no lawnmower could reach. Stray cats darted in and out everywhere.

Valentine tapped the McDonald's bag against her leg, getting her bearings. Then she headed towards a white house with narrow, shuttered windows. The bay windows looked slit-eyed, suspicious.

Valentine knocked. The door cracked open, a reedy voice piping up from within. "Who is it?"

"Valentine." She rattled the bag. "Got a delivery for Gunza."

A whistle of doubt. "Has the placebomancer come through at last? And who's with you?"

She sighed. "My boyfriend."

"Wait."

An exchange of voices from inside. Valentine danced from leg to leg nervously, like she had to go to the bathroom. Paul realized he'd been so caught up in mastering his own magic that he'd never asked why Valentine needed the Flex.

The door opened. Two young Hispanic kids, maybe fifteen, waved them inside. They wore striped brown shirts with popped collars, pink baseball caps, looking like extras from Jersey Shore. Paul noted the guns jammed underneath their shirts, though.

Paul froze when they patted down his calves, but the reskinning held up to their perfunctory frisk. Their message was clear: *You're not actually a threat.*

The two guards escorted them upstairs to what had once been a grand bedroom, refashioned with a large desk, a safe, and a wide-screen television mounted on the wall. The TV blared out *Teen Mom.*

Behind the desk sat a young man with sapphire teeth.

"Valentine, baby!" Gunza got up from behind the desk, swaggering as he moved to hug Valentine, dressed in a black suit with a Chinese collar. He might have looked a little like Neo from the Matrix, except Gunza was toad-ugly. His pockmarked, mole-flecked skin could have been either a leathery suntan or a light Negroid complexion – but his smile inspired an instant dislike in Paul. It was a smile designed to intimidate, all bared gums and shocking jewels.

The sapphires looked like discolored rocks at the bottom of a dirty aquarium.

The two thugs closed the door behind them. Gunza cocked his head towards Paul.

"Who's this?"

"My boyfriend."

Gunza's body language dismissed Paul instantly. "Hope you don't place bets on this one."

"I didn't *bet*," Valentine retorted. "Raphael bet on himself, with his money. I told him I wouldn't help him win. But he entered anyway."

Gunza spread his hands in oily sympathy. "Black opals galore at the tournament. You get anything worth a decent prize, you bet your ass they're gonna scope for 'mancy. Even a Halo tournament. So you couldn't help him, and your boy came in… what, 503rd out of 512 players?"

Valentine's face fell. "I let him win when we played head-to-head."

"You made him think he was badass. The badass was *you*." He poked her in the breastbone, a gesture that both respected her power and dismissed it. Then he gestured to two cheap wooden seats, inviting them to sit down. He eased back into a leather chair as though it were a throne.

"I'm surprised to see you coming back with new boy here." Gunza tapped his teeth in curiosity. "You hated those Flex factories we built you. I thought you stayed only cause Raphael would get the chop if you didn't produce. Now you with fresh meat here, and still ready to brew?"

"I still don't want Raph *dead*," Valentine said, surprised.

"Won't kill him. Not over ten large. But we'd sure mess up his hands. Make sure he never clutched a controller again."

Gunza searched Valentine's face for a reaction. She gave him nothing.

Gunza let out a hissing noise of derision, then turned to Paul. "Bitches, right? She's in your bed, but she's thinking about Raphael."

Paul's cheeks went flush with anger; Valentine had done this for love, to protect a boyfriend who clearly didn't even care about her.

Paul feigned a shrug. "...She's good in bed."

Gunza brayed laughter, giving him a thumbs-up. "Not my style, backdoor man. But you get yours, friend." He returned to Valentine. "Anyway, I'm twenty large into you. I set up Flex labs for you; you burned two, the third got raided. My family's questioning my investment, so I was gonna send some birdies to your crib... Your timing's good. What you got?"

"Enough." She pushed the bag across the desk.

"This better be a hell of a Big Mac."

He peered in the bag. His eyes widened.

"...This is not what I think it is, is it?"

Valentine jutted her chin out, pleased to have the drop on him. "What do you think it is?"

Gunza rolled a smooth crystal between his fingers. "I *think* this is B-1 grade Flex..."

"Don't you know for sure?" Paul asked. Valentine kicked him hard enough that a chunk of skin peeled off his titanium foot.

Gunza focused on Paul, as if really seeing him for the first time.

"...Flex ain't exactly common." Paul heard the effort it took for Gunza to be magnanimous. "Everyone claims they had a piece, once, but maybe one in a hundred ain't liars. Ninety-nine percent of the shit people say is Flex is E or bath salts – people just think they're 'mancing. Go on. Ask me if I've done Flex."

"...have you?"

"No." That feral grin. "But I am *dying* to."

"What do you want it for?"

Gunza scratched his chin, taking pleasure in Valentine's distress. "If I want coke? I get what my family gives. E? They got their own labs and don't want me involved. Not much room for expansion... but if I can rope in Flex, then I can ensure nothing breaks again."

"So, no murders?" Paul swallowed. "Nothing... nothing stupid."

Paul frowned into Gunza's intense, almost palpable scrutiny. Valentine cursed underneath her breath.

"If this was N-31 grade, or even I-15," said Gunza evenly, "I'd sell it to whoever asked. Flux is a toxin for dealers; our bad luck is good luck for cops. But if this is B-1, then is all upside, yes? We have errands that can't afford snarls. If I'm banking Flex, I can guarantee my family's operations. No killing needed."

A weight lifted from Paul's shoulders.

"Try it." Valentine spoke loud, trying to draw attention away from Paul. "It's the best."

"A question." He rested the Flex on the desk between them, steepled his fingers. "You, Valentine, are a grade-A fuckup. Date all the wrong boys. Can't keep a job. Won't kill. As a 'mancer, you play fuckin' Guitar Hero twelve hours straight and forget to make Flex."

He held the Flex up to the light. They'd brought him one single crystal, a small one, nothing compared to the coffee can back at Valentine's apartment. Paul admired his handiwork; the Flex was flawless, like a drop of distilled water.

"So, how does little fuckup Valentine break three cribs and then devise perfect Flex on the fourth? I was gonna call myself lucky if I got G-46 outta your ass, but B-1?"

Valentine refused to show fear. "I just didn't... didn't want to before."

"No. You found an ace." Gunza flicked a glance towards Paul. "A new sweetie, perhaps?"

Valentine gripped the arms of her chair. "Does it matter?"

Gunza licked his finger, drew it down in the air before him, marking off a point in her favor. "Doesn't."

He crushed the crystal underneath his palm messily, spraying Flex everywhere. "But I gotta test this. So here's the question: how can I tell if this is real? I put my brain into this question. Because if I track a source of Flex, then I am the luckiest man in New York. So I have devised a test."

Gunza peered down at the Flex with deep gravitas, then chopped the small pile into a fine line with a razor. He chuckled, an embarrassment he chose to reveal.

"I don't even know how much I'm supposed to take," he said, then snorted it all.

His head rocked back in surprise, his wide nostrils blowing the remnants across the desk. Paul saw the radiant glow of Flex disappearing into Gunza's wide nostrils and felt violated; his magic was being smothered inside a stupid drug dealer. He wanted to call it back but could feel the 'mancy knotting inside Gunza, the odds flexing to Gunza's will.

Valentine grabbed his hand. She felt it, too.

"*Whoo!*" Gunza's head snapped forward, glowing tears streaming from his eyes. His emerald teeth looked like they'd been lit by lasers. "*That – is–*" He shook his head from side to side like a dog shaking off water. "Is that what you feel, Valentine? Is that what you feel *all the time*?"

"When I'm lost in it," Valentine said sadly.

"This…" He rose from his chair like a preacher addressing his congregation. "…is the *greatest thing ever*. I am the luckiest man alive to find you, Valentine DiGriz, and your new theoretical boyfriend. And if I *am* that lucky–"

He pulled out an automatic rifle, spraying bullets in an arc across the room. The TV exploded, the sheet rock disintegrated.

As the muzzle swung across Valentine's face, the gun jammed with a dry click.

"*Ha!*" Gunza shoved a .22 into Paul's cheekbone and pulled the trigger; another misfire. He tossed both guns across the room triumphantly, pulled Paul and Valentine into a close hug. They froze like scared rabbits.

"You're so lucky." He wept happily, as if he hadn't tried to murder them. "Because *I'm* so lucky. Oh, my friends, this Flex will *change our world*."

THIRTEEN
New and Exciting Job Descriptions

"I don't want to go back to work," Paul told Valentine back at the motel he'd been living at since his apartment had caught fire. He'd offered her the bed, but she'd curled up on the floor in Invader Zim pajamas, arms wrapped around the coffee can full of Flex. "I don't want to leave you alone. But if I don't get back there today, they'll think something's wrong with me. Before this, I hadn't taken a vacation in seven years."

"It's not your fault, Paul." Valentine stirred her coffee endlessly but never drank it.

"It *is*. If you hadn't met me, you wouldn't have had any Flex. Now he's going to come after you to get more. He has to – to have you…"

Paul remembered the Uzi jamming just in time to save Valentine's life. He shuddered because Gunza had seemed – well, not nice, but reasonable before then. Gunza had already shown he was willing to kill. With an unlimited supply of B-1 Flex on the hook, he'd do anything.

Thank God he'd made Valentine leave the coffee can full of Flex at her apartment. Thank God Gunza had been dumb enough to blow his tiny sample of Flex on proving its potency – though Paul'd had nightmares about the gun not jamming and Valentine's head blowing off. If Gunza had been more conservative, more cunning, Lord knows what he might have done with a 'mancer in his grip...

"I will get you a new ID and a nice home in California." He wrapped a hotel blanket over Valentine's shoulders. "This evening, I will book you on a first-class flight to San Francisco, where Gunza cannot find you."

"He'll find me." Valentine cuddled her Dunkin' Donuts coffee for warmth. "He has to."

"We're *safe*. Gunza doesn't know where you are or what I look like. I'll get you out."

He kissed her on the forehead, feeling a strange ache: the only 'mancer he'd ever known, and he was sending her away.

It took him a moment to identify this ache's familiarity: it was similar to what he felt for Aliyah. This fierce protectiveness. This anger that anything might want to hurt her.

This pain at separation.

He charged into Samaritan Mutual, vowing to get her out of town before midnight. At least the reporters had dissipated. Which was good, because he was infuriated at making Valentine vulnerable to Gunza, at wasting time not finding Anathema. If someone had shoved a microphone in his face, he might have said something very unwise.

Paul hadn't made it five steps in before Kit pounced on him.

"Come on, bubeleh," Kit said, grabbing Paul's elbow to steer him back towards the elevator. "No time to explain. Just agree with everything I say. You–" Kit pushed his porkpie hat up on his bald head, noticing how Paul's face was covered with scratch marks. "What the hell happened to you?"

"Allergic reaction to mosquitoes."

It had nothing to do with bugs; it had everything to do with Flex and Valentine's reskinning.

He'd sat on the hotel bed last night while Valentine was showering, scooping up handfuls of Flex crystals and letting them rain back into the coffee can, wondering how to use this unadulterated 'mancy to help Aliyah. Then it occurred to him that he was being stupid: *wish for more wishes*, the old genie loophole. If he took some Flex and then used that artificial luck to stumble across the perfect plan to save Aliyah...

He'd popped a crystal into his mouth and crunched it like an aspirin.

His fake layer of dudebro had sloughed off.

The pain struck with no warning; Paul's reskinned flesh had stung like a swarm of bees. He'd clawed at his face, strips of artificial skin clogging his fingernails.

He tried to summon his 'mancy for help, envisioning insurance coverage and calamine lotion – but something bright ping-ponged inside his skull, destroying his ability to concentrate, like a group of hyperactive toddlers rushing across an opera stage.

The Flex. It was desperate to find its way back home inside him, like a moth battering against a lamp, but he and Valentine had squeezed all of the personality out of it. It wasn't a part of him any more.

He envisioned the new Flex as a shiny iPod, sleek and impersonal and dedicated to a single task. His own personal 'mancy was a hoary, 1950s-style punch card computer system, a dusty arcanum assembled by hand, with paper-punch snippets of logic stored in a hundred shoebox files stuffed underneath desks. He could retrieve the punch cards one by one, piece them together to crank out deeply personal programs that no one but he could possibly make sense of.

The simplified 'mancy of the Flex held a primal, salmon-like urge to return home; it thrashed around in his head, causing Paul migraines as it vainly attempted to insinuate itself back into Paul's complex and personal mythology.

Valentine had emerged from the shower to find Paul rolling in agony next to a pile of dead skin. She'd apologized profusely: "Christ, Paul, after we went to so much trouble to yank our personalities out of this stuff, I thought it was obvious we'd turned it into a different kind of magic. If I'd known you were gonna try to tank up on it, I woulda *said* something."

Eventually, she explained, Paul would have walked into a closet and emerged restored to his original look, as characters did in videogames. But the Flex had jangled her 'mancy, too. She didn't know how to fix this weird transitory state.

She'd gotten him Solarcaine. It hadn't helped.

Paul reached underneath his suit to scratch his forearms. They were bumpy, an amalgamation of tribal tattoos and Paul's hairy Greek skin. He'd had to scrub his face with a loofah until he was recognizable enough to return to work – and even now, as Kit looked him over, Paul realized his cheeks were swollen and hived.

"Christ," Kit spat, pushing Paul into the elevator. "This was tricky enough without you looking like Frankenstein's monster. Anyway, keep your mouth shut and don't contradict me."

"What's going on? Why are we–" Then Paul noticed which button Kit had pressed.

They were headed to the managerial floor.

"Have you been trying to get Aliyah some new treatments?" Kit whispered the question like it was a sin. "Claiming that what we're authorizing isn't enough for her?"

"Well, yeah. I had to–"

"They're on the warpath now. Between that and the reporters and SMASH, they're hunting for an excuse to fire you. But don't worry; I've got a plan."

Kit shoved him, blinking and terrified, onto the managers' floor.

The managers' floor wasn't much different than Paul's floor, but there were subtle signs of status: glass barriers between certain cubicles, pricier artwork on the walls, the secretaries wore more fashionable dresses. Unless you'd worked for Samaritan, you'd never know just how dangerous being here was.

Samaritan's management only noticed expenses it could cut.

Kit steered Paul into a meeting room just big enough for six people to sit around a large round table. Kit's boss, Lou, a fat toad, sat there. As did Lou's manager, an emaciated ice queen called Rita.

Then Paul saw Mr Payne sitting in the corner and felt the same shock of fear as when Gunza had shoved the gun in his face.

Payne's stiff white hair was cropped in a buzz cut, giving his head a bullet-like shape; his eyes were chips of glacial ice. He wore a crisp funeral director's suit over his broad ex-Marine frame, which was appropriate; most of Payne's meetings ended in terminations.

"Sit down, Mr Tsabo," Lou said. Everyone knew Lou did all of Rita's hatchet work. Plus, with Payne in the room, she didn't dare utter one more word than necessary.

Lou and Rita both looked towards Mr Payne. He nodded.

"We're getting questions from the government about last week's Flex bust," Lou said. "Reports are you were inside the building when the SMASH team neutralized the location, despite having called them in an hour earlier."

"So?"

Lou did a little high dive with his index finger, arcing it up high in the air to land on a folder containing Paul's employee records. "Scouting locations is outside your job description, Mr Tsabo. You are not currently, despite your past history, a policeman. Your job description states clearly that if there is any danger of harm, you are to remove yourself from the premises. So, the company is now wondering whether you're trying to play hero on our dime."

They were laying the groundwork for Paul as a loose cannon, preparing for a firing. Just as Paul was about to go after Anathema…

Kit cleared his throat. "If I may…" He reached underneath the table to haul out a box of donuts. "Sorry. I can't call it a meeting unless there's refreshments, you know?"

"Chocolate Kreme," said Lou. "My favorite!"

"There's also a dry cinnamon in there for Rita." Rita took the donut daintily.

Payne shooed the donuts away with a flick of his fingers. Paul remembered Valentine's words: *Never trust a man who doesn't like a donut.* Reluctantly, Lou and Rita took their uneaten donuts off the table and secreted them in their laps.

"Uh, anyway," Kit continued. "The, uh, danger you're speaking of is nonexistent. The reason Mr Tsabo was in the Flex lab is that he'd ascertained – correctly – the 'mancer had long fled. Paul was merely looking for clues we could use to verify that the rain of frogs was connected to this lab."

"The government claims he's interfering."

"The government was two hours late," Kit riposted. "The records show Paul called in the 'mancer's location at 10.08am that morning. Google Maps" – he slid a paper across the table toward them – "shows a car was in the driveway at the time Paul reported it. The government responded too slowly – they know it, you know it, and now they're making a big stink about Paul to distract people from the fact that they let Anathema slip through their fingers."

Lou coughed, uncomfortable. "There's still the matter of Mr Tsabo entering the 'mancer's den – a violation of company policy – "

"That's instincts." Kit leaned forward. "Look, the reason Paul and I are your top claims investigators is because we leave no angle unturned. I'll be honest: I've walked into my share of 'mancer dens."

Oh, God, Kit, Paul thought. *You're putting your job on the line for me.* Kit had just dared Payne to fire them both, leaving the New York branch without a 'mancy investigative unit during an outbreak of 'mancer terrorism.

"That's against *policy*," Lou said.

"Is that the official line?" Kit asked. Lou and Rita exchanged discomforted glances; they sensed the trap but didn't know how to avoid springing it. And they wanted no surprises in front of Payne.

"...It is."

"Then I guess you don't want this." Kit tossed a Ziploc bag onto the table. Paul recognized it:

His Flex.

"That breach of policy right there," Kit said, "just saved you a *million* in claims from every house within Buffalo's tremor range. I sent Paul up there myself, asking him to investigate on his day off because he was closer." Lou and Rita were focused on the Flex, so only Paul noticed the sly wink Kit threw him.

Kit. Kit had driven six hours on a hunch.

The man was relentless.

"The local yokels had checked a cabin near the epicenter," Kit said. "Predictably, they found nothing. But Paul found this lodged in a ventilator grille."

Paul's arms itched, but he didn't dare scratch. Payne plucked the baggie from Lou's hands, then examined the crystal with the concentration of a pawn shop owner appraising a diamond.

"This is B-1 grade Flex." Payne's voice sounded like a cockroach's legs rubbing together. "Nobody's made anything of this quality since the 1950s."

"What this means, my friends, is we have a new Flex manufacturer. Someone who causes *earthquakes* when he dumps his flux." Kit crossed his arms. "Now. Do you want someone like Paul on the case, or the cops who overlooked the key piece of evidence? Because if you value procedure, then I guess you can pay out those claims. And pay the next batch when this guy starts knocking down buildings. But, hey, *you're* the ones who answer to our stockholders…"

Payne scowled at the bag, then scowled at Kit. "Are you telling us you've assigned Mr Tsabo to head up this investigation?"

"I'm telling you Paul here is your best chance at corralling Anathema."

"My God, Kit. You risked your job for me? You have the bills from your wife's funeral, Kit – a pension–"

–a best friend who's brewing Flex–

"You have a daughter," Kit replied. "Look, Payne wants you gone. But put away a terrorist and they don't dare fire you. That's why I'm putting you in charge. I can't promise our bosses will pay for Aliyah, but I can damn well give you cover."

"Kit..."

"You hate calling in markers, Paul. But I'd be a terrible, donutless human being if I didn't help you out." Kit patted Paul's shoulder. "Now get some calamine lotion."

Paul felt plastic, artificial, trapped in Valentine's reskin, lying to his friends, having to track down *himself* to save his daughter.

He locked the bathroom door behind him, tugged up his sleeve. His forearm was still sheathed in a fake layer of tattooed muscle.

He wanted out.

He clawed at the pseudoskin, desperate to obliterate the snakelike loops of ink that wound around his wrist. Paul didn't hear the toilet flushing behind him. Nor did he see the ugly man stepping out of the stall with a serene grace, nostrils flecked with Flex.

He glanced over at Paul with the incurious calmness of a man who expected the universe to provide him with what he needed. He noted the artificial skin clogging the sink drain.

Paul, focused on scrubbing, leaned forward; Valentine's driver's license tumbled from his breast pocket, falling onto the tile floor. Cursing, Paul knelt to pick it up.

The man covered the license with the tip of his snakeskin boot. As Paul looked up, Gunza bared glittering emerald teeth.

FOURTEEN
The Hammers Come Out

Paul tumbled backward, cracking his head against the sink bottom. Gunza picked Paul up off the floor to engulf him in a hug.

Paul trembled in Gunza's grip, a baby bird in the palm of a six year-old.

"Genius." Gunza kissed Paul on the forehead. "*Master*. I was worried I'd never find you again. The moment I lit up, *you* lit up. We were linked. You couldn't send a girl to do your job; no, you had to *witness*. How could you not? You were the Flex. You *are* this Flex."

Gunza's fawning respect was more unsettling than any gun.

"How did you find me?" Paul asked, stunned. "We gave you a sample. A *tiny* sample."

"Crawled the carpets," Gunza replied dreamily. "Picked through each loop, sorting dust from Flex, spending all night plucking each stray crystal off the floor. By morning, I'd reassembled a spoonful. Enough to find the master."

Paul had underestimated Gunza's determination. So *stupid*.

"What do you want?"

"To show you who I am, sir." Gunza reached into his vest, pulled out a roll of fifties. "To show you what I can do."

Paul clenched his fists. Gunza riffled the stack, extended it towards him. "Go ahead," Gunza urged him. "Take it. It's *nothing*."

Paul tried mightily to be unimpressed, but Gunza's nothing would have paid Paul's rent for a year. He imagined peeling off twenties for Aliyah's surgeons until the hospital accountants told him to stop.

"Not worth it," Paul said. Which was a lie. He burned to. But selling to men like Gunza? Never.

Gunza sucked air between his bejeweled teeth. "You sure?"

This was the friendly portion of negotiations. Every thug was a reasonable man at first. But once bribes failed, the hammers came out.

He should probably reap the rewards, get on Gunza's good side while he could... But making Flex was excruciating; it was like strangling a part of his soul even when he wasn't selling the end product.

Paul had swallowed his instincts before, burying himself in work over guilt at killing the illustromancer. That had done enough damage to Aliyah. He'd do horrible things to save her, but he had to retain his self-respect – otherwise, he'd be no father.

"Positive."

Gunza turned to leave.

"No threats?" Paul asked.

"What shall I do, sir?" Gunza asked. "Could call in the military, but that wouldn't get me more Flex. Could kidnap you, but you're a 'mancer. Eventually, all guns misfire around you. Could tell your boss; maybe he rains cops down on my head." He bared those sapphire teeth again. "No. On you, I have no grip. Find me if you change your mind."

"That's... oddly reasonable."

"I'm as reasonable as my options." The door swung shut.

What did Valentine look like now?

He glanced at Valentine's new driver's license on the way back to the hotel. He'd spent three hours envisioning all the errors that would have to occur for a genuine driver's license to be created with wrong information, and the Beast had spat out a California ID. On it was Valentine, looking sullen beneath a tangle of bleached-blond hair.

Had he changed her? As she'd changed him during the reskin? There was so much he didn't understand about his power... but for the first time, he felt as though he might master it.

Squeezing the cash from Samaritan Mutual would be a challenge. Paul could set Aliyah's treatment to approved, but someone would notice. Ironically, of all the places he could work for, Samaritan Mutual was most resistant to his powers...

He unlocked the hotel room door, only to find the room maid-clean. Valentine's cell phone was no longer plugged into the wall, nor was her PlayStation wired to the hotel television.

The sole sign of Valentine's presence was an empty coffee can on the bed. Paul peered inside to find a note in Valentine's handwriting:

They have my boyfriend.

FIFTEEN
Stupid Acts of Heroism

Paul paced around the room, listing all the reasons he shouldn't go after Valentine. Gunza was expecting it; that's why he'd let him go. Valentine shouldn't have cared about a boy who hadn't so much as texted her since Paul met her.

"She's in her twenties," he whispered. "She's *supposed* to do dumb things for love."

He clutched the coffee can, feeling guilt. She'd told Paul to put the flux in the Flex. She'd told him to stay at home. She'd told him to keep his mouth shut. If he'd just listened, she would have handed over a can of substandard Flex, and Gunza might have let her go.

She'd been treading water, and he'd pushed her under.

If he'd been thinking with his old brain, his Samaritan Mutual planning brain, he would have thought this through – anticipated Gunza's next moves, then hauled them both out of the line of fire. Instead, entranced by the Beast's power, fixating on how to save Aliyah, he'd thought 'mancy could handle the details.

Now he knew: magic was no replacement for common sense.

Time to turn on detective mode: what would Gunza do next, knowing that Paul was the *real* source of Flex? Knowing Gunza had assumed, correctly, that Paul would come after Valentine and her idiot lover to save them?

Paul left a message at Kit's office, explaining that he'd be investigating deep for a couple of days.

Then he flipped through a folder thick with forms – his generic stockpile he'd taken to keeping with him, a modern grimoire. He pulled out a change of address form. As he scrawled, Valentine's generic white California's license faded to the engraved baby blue of a New York license. He checked the address. After that, it was a matter of figuring out which departments had jurisdiction.

This would get bloody before it was done. But he could at least free Valentine.

The burn ward's lights had been turned way down, leaving sleeping children wreathed in dim shadow. Aliyah had fallen asleep in mid-game, her Nintendo DS in her hands. She hugged it, dreaming.

Paul squeezed Aliyah's foot. She woke with a start: "What is it, Daddy? Do they have to do something bad?"

Of course, Paul thought. He showed up for all her debridements to hold her hand, so arriving at two in the morning meant something awful was about to happen.

He'd burned her. He'd done this. He'd done so much wrong to her already.

He was about to do more.

"No, no, sweetie. But Daddy has to... he has to go away for a while."

She cocked her head in curiosity. She wasn't dumb; Dad didn't show up this late if it was ordinary. "Is it an emergency 'vestigation? 'Mancers gone bad?"

Yes. "No. Can you keep a secret? A big one? You can't tell anyone."

"Yes."

"Even Kit. Even Mommy."

"Yes."

He believed her. Aliyah had always locked her emotions tight.

"Aunt Valentine is in trouble. Big trouble. And I have to go get her out of it."

Her face steeled. "Is it killing trouble?"

What the fuck am I doing? Paul thought. *I should be lying.* Yet he had promised himself that if Aliyah was old enough to ask the questions, she deserved honest answers from now on.

"Yes," he whispered. "It's killing trouble."

Aliyah looked concerned but not surprised. She turned her Nintendo DS over and over in her hands, drawing strength from it. Imani would have preferred Aliyah retreat into books, but Super Mario World was Aliyah's bolthole when the world became unmaintainable... and Aliyah never forgot who gave her gifts.

She reached out to touch Paul's cheek, her fingers

still slippery from the skin grafts.

"You *save* her," she commanded. "You kill the bad men. You bring Aunt Vallumtime *back*."

Paul found himself crying, absolved by his own daughter.

"I will," he promised. "I will."

Paul pulled up at a respectful distance, still in his rented white van, scoping the factory entrances with binoculars.

He double-checked the address on the license; sure enough, at the Beast's urgings, the address had rewritten itself to reflect where Valentine lived now. According to Google Maps, Gunza had stashed Valentine in an abandoned factory near Queens.

The factory was huge, a testament to some once-mighty industry that had moved elsewhere. The bricks were black with soot; even the graffiti artists had given up on this locale. The windows had been smashed in, a row of knocked-out meth teeth. Pigeons fluttered in and out, the birds having created a messy ecosystem in the building's high rafters.

Occasionally, one of Gunza's thugs swaggered out to take a call on their cell phones. They gave exaggerated "Hey baby's" that Paul could see from across a parking lot, doing unconscious peacock walks as they strutted to impress the women on the phone. No surprises there.

Paul double-checked the taser at his belt and waited for the inspector to arrive.

A blue inspector's van pulled to a stop before the

main entrance – Paul made out the white sticker on the guy's windshield. A potbellied older man got out, holding a clipboard.

Two more Jersey Shore thugs emerged, looking quizzical; they'd clearly been expecting Paul. They patted their waists, unsure whether to brandish their guns or put them away. With them distracted, Paul bolted across the parking lot at top speed, a rolling limp that tried to compensate for his slow right ankle.

The fire exit was open. They weren't worrying about Valentine escaping... or maybe they wanted to lure Paul in. Regardless, the entire place reeked of 'mancy. *His* 'mancy.

Paul crept into the cavernous space; it was shadowy inside, made darker by the vast pieces of iron machinery that squatted on the concrete floor. Paul didn't know what purpose these boilers and racks of rusted sheet metal had once served, but they cut the football-field-sized expanse of concrete into a maze. His foot whirred with every step.

He emerged by a rusted clock and timecard holder next to a set of abandoned offices. Their broken windows looked out over an open area marked with faded spray paint that had once marked the boundaries for forklifts.

There sat Valentine and a young boy who must be her lover.

They sat on fold-up chairs, facing each other, as if they had been dragged out here to have a chat by some psychotic therapist. Between them sat a bingo machine: the makings of a Flex lab.

They were surrounded by three thugs and Gunza, who never took his eye off of Valentine.

Paul slipped over a broken picture-frame window and crouched inside an office as Gunza listened to the thugs reporting back.

"He says you requested the inspection last week." One of the thugs handed over a slip of paper.

Gunza glanced at Valentine, asking for silent confirmation this was Paul's handiwork. She shrugged. Her boyfriend stared up at two pigeons fighting over a twig.

"It says someone wants this place condemned," Gunza said, puzzled. "Who the fuck wants it condemned?"

The thug tapped the paper. "*You* do."

"'Mancy for sure." Gunza reached into his pocket for a small baggie, scooped a dollop of Flex onto his pinkie fingernail, inhaled it. "Put them in the offices, where he can't see them. If he comes near, Flex him a coincidence to leave."

"Yeah, buddy." The thug fist-bumped Gunza. "We gonna *use* this."

Valentine was already on her feet; Paul was glad to see her refusing to be being pushed around like a hostage. "Come on, sweetie," she said, reaching out for her boyfriend's hand. "We gotta move."

Her boyfriend – *his name's Raphael*, Paul remembered – was tall, gawkily beautiful. He hugged a skateboard against his chest as though it was a teddy bear. He either trusted Valentine implicitly or was just used to being told where to go, since he was the only person here who didn't look concerned.

Paul felt the dim pressure of 'mancy as the guard approached. Paul flattened himself against the wall as he realized Valentine's guard would enter the office Paul had chosen. Dumb luck or magic?

Didn't matter. He readied the taser. Maybe the false plan he'd created to lure in Gunza would work and they could run free.

Except as the thug entered the room, Paul saw the Flex residue on the kid's nose.

He gave it a try, reaching out to jam the taser against the kid's neck. Sure enough, the taser caught in the kid's double-popped collar, discharging harmlessly into cotton. The kid turned, his face lighting up as the Flex flowed through him, and punched Paul – a perfect shot to the solar plexus, emptying the wind from Paul's lungs.

By the time Paul came to, Gunza stood over him.

"That's all you got, man? Building inspectors?"

"It's what I had," Paul wheezed.

Gunza patted the bag of Flex in his pocket. "We're flawless now. Wanted the inspector gone. I Flexed, and bam! Next I knew, he was griping about how this was a bullshit assignment. Said if he had his way, he'd go home." Gunza grinned. "He went home."

Gunza knelt before Paul. "Now, you the golden goose. You gonna be fed well, doctors look you over. But don't run. You try, we provide disincentives." He jiggled the bag before Paul's nose. "This is your job now."

Paul jerked his head towards Valentine. "Okay.

Now let her go."

"She's disincentive number one." The thugs roared with laughter. "We set up labs before. My boys are out getting what you need to brew. And when it's all in place, you make the Flex."

"Can we have a pizza?" Raphael asked. "I'm hungry."

Valentine looked pained. Gunza nodded paternally. "We all gotta eat, man. Pizzas all around." Gunza looked at Paul. "You got a preference, man? Deep dish, Domino's?"

"I'm not really hungry."

"I like artichokes." Raphael's voice was wan, the words of a beautiful man who'd grown used to having his every sentence found fascinating. "You put some sun-dried tomatoes and artichokes on a pizza, it's like a work of art."

"California Pizza Kitchen it is. We'll put in the call; I'm sure you got things to talk out. But remember, as long as we got the Flex, you got no options. It's five 'mancers against two."

"I know how it works," Paul said. "It's my 'mancy."

"So, we're clear." A thought occurred to Gunza, and he chuckled, a low purr. "Clear as Flex."

"We're clear." Gunza drank up Paul's submission – then strutted to the factory exit with his crew, handing out high fives.

Valentine grabbed Paul's arm, checking he was okay. "If you *had* to come, did you have to half-ass it? Sending one grumpy inspector? What the hell kind of plan was that?"

Paul held up a single finger, feeling more alive than he had in months. *That was step one*, he mouthed.

SIXTEEN
Confrontations and Lamentations

Paul watched as Gunza's boys returned with sacks of hematite, crates of alembics. They emerged from the vans with childlike grins, eager to brag about their Flex-fueled conquests.

"So I'm killing time at Freddy's place while he tracks me down some hematite…"

The other thugs elbowed each other to get closer to the thug telling the story, piglets fighting to suckle at a teat.

"I'm sittin' there with this nut needing to be busted, and suddenly I feel like I'm in a movie." The ones who'd been outside – Gunza had staggered their missions so they'd all get a turn – grunted in affirmation. "I step into the hallway – elevator's waiting for me. I press a button at random. And when I step out, I hear moaning."

The storyteller closed his eyes, reliving the moment. The thugs moaned in anticipation.

"I follow it to a door that's wide open. Inside, on the bed, her head back, hips pumping, is this gorgeous girl fucking herself."

"Fingers?"

"Dildo." The storyteller exposed chipped teeth. "She's lost her fucking mind, not paying attention to anything except the plastic pumping in her pussy. So I pad up next to her bed, whip it out, and stick it in her mouth.

"Her eyes go wide. I think, shit, Little Elvis is about to get bit off – but then she moans, *Oh, God, yes*, and drops the vibrator."

"Like a fuckin' porn video," one of the thugs muttered. "Unreal."

"Naw, that's *Flex*," a third thug spoke, with jaded experience. "You heard what happened to me, right?"

They had, of course. They'd been exchanging these stories like currency, repeating tales in lieu of repeat performances.

A van pulled up. They stopped talking to haul out a PlayStation 4 still in the box, a crate full of videogames, and a new story for the boys to devour.

"Videogames," Paul muttered. "They don't understand how we work, do they? I keep forgetting; I study 'mancers, but the average man is clueless…"

He turned to see Valentine cradling a white plastic gun in both hands. A space-age thing, like an iPod made deadly.

"They're distracted now."

Raphael groaned. "Valentine…"

"Gotta give it one more shot." She fired the gun at the office wall, which she had spent an hour scrubbing to a dull gray, refusing to answer Paul's questions. A shimmering blue portal irised open.

"Where should I place the orange portal, baby?" she asked Raphael.

Raphael blew his emover out of his eyes, the portrait of irritation. "I don't even know that game."

Valentine blinked twice, then closed her eyes to calm herself.

"Right. You haven't played Portal, either. And that's... *okay*." She fired the gun away from the chattering thugs, angling it tight and low just so it appeared behind a row of plastic sorting bins. Paul whistled despite himself; it was an impressive shot.

An orange oval blossomed open. The blue portal now showed a view of the warehouse from the orange portal's perspective. Valentine stuck her hand through; her hand emerged from the orange portal across the way and waved at them.

A thug grabbed her wrist.

"Where the fuck did you—"

"Had to piss," he replied. Flex radiated off him. "Came back and caught you. Just like we accidentally kicked over the cardboard box you were sneaking under. Just like you tripped and showed off your gothy boots when you skinned yourself like one of us. Just like *all* 'mancy fails when we're Flexed." He shoved her back through the portal. "Back in line."

The portal closed. Valentine crossed her tattooed arms.

"It's all right," Paul assured her. "I didn't think you could get out on your own. Wait for the distraction."

She tapped her toe. "Why the hell did you come back, Paul?"

"I came back for you." He tried to keep the hurt out of his voice.

"You have a *daughter*."

"And you're my friend." Paul extended his index finger to point at her, then simply bounced it up and down, as if his hand stuttered. "I mean, you know, I – I got you into this. I made it worse. You had to protect your boyfriend..."

"I'm not her *boyfriend*." Raphael leaned against the wall, picking dirt from underneath his long, perfect fingernails. "Why does everyone keep saying that?"

"Because she's risking her *life* for you, you idiot. Most would find that a sign of commitment."

"It's *cool*," Raphael said, giving Valentine's sacrifice all the appreciation he'd show someone who bought him a milkshake. "But don't make it big. Gunza wants some shit, she gives it, game over."

"We never dated," Valentine explained quickly. "We just hooked up. A lot. Pretty well, I think."

Raphael's face broke into a surprisingly expressive grin. "Good stuff."

Valentine chuckled at Raphael's praise, a relief Paul found disturbing. She began pacing in nervous circles.

"It's not like either of us has time for commitment. Raph has his modeling career and I'm busy at the GameStop, so... we find time when we can. The trick is, we make that time as good as possible."

"Does that good time include getting Refactored by a SMASH team?" Paul knew he should stay out of it – but he wanted to let this prancing prettyboy know just how much Valentine was doing for him. "Destroying three houses in botched attempts? Taking near-fatal loads of Flex?"

Raphael stopped picking his fingernails to give Paul a disdainful stare. "It's not *dangerous*. It's just *tricky*. It's like she says – with videogame magic, you can always reload the level."

Valentine pleaded silently with Paul: *Please don't correct him.*

"Not every 'mancy is the same," Paul said through gritted teeth.

"Think I'm stupid? *Her* 'mancy gives her, you know, infinite lives. That's why I don't have to worry."

"That's right." Valentine wiped her mouth with the back of her hand, smearing her lipstick. "I'm totally not someone you have to worry about."

"Well, *I* do," Paul said.

"That's sweet, Paul. But, again – what about Aliyah?"

"She told me to get you back."

She shoved him in the chest. Paul fell ass over teakettle.

"What kind of selfish fuck *are* you?" she roared. The thugs looked up, distracted by the scuffle. "So, instead, it's better to have her dad *disappear*? Do you know what it's *like* to have that kind of hole in your life, Paul? To have your parents, just, just–" She slapped her palm to her forehead. "Jesus Christ, you have a daughter with willpower and grace and cleverness – and you're abandoning her to protect – to protect…"

"–someone who deserves it."

Though Valentine pounded Paul's chest when he tried to hug her, she eventually sank into his arms, sobbing. Raphael looked on with a muzzy, wounded confusion, not sure what he might have done wrong. Still, he did not move, shifting from foot to foot as Valentine cried herself out.

"...He's got a daughter?" Raphael asked.

"Yes, Raphael." Valentine shoved Paul away. "A *wounded* daughter. Who he should protect, instead of treating grown women like they're fucking Barbie dolls."

"Well, Mister Say-Bo woulda come here anyway." Raphael shrugged, as if the argument had been settled. "It's not like Gunza wouldn't have found out about his kid. If it wasn't you he came to rescue, woulda been his daughter."

Valentine and Paul both fishmouthed, stunned that Raphael had accurately summarized the situation.

"Not that we need a rescue." Raphael flicked some fingernail dirt away, returning to his impromptu manicure. "Gunza told me he needs enough Flex to keep the cops off his back. Once he gets that, he's cool."

Paul looked over at the thugs, who had returned to their conversation. They were compiling lists of things they wanted to do on Flex – death-defying stunts, coincidental orgies, old scores settled painlessly. They spun fantasies, gesticulating wildly, eager to unleash this new power upon the world.

"Yeah," Paul said, exchanging weary glances with Valentine. "It'll be over after one batch."

SEVENTEEN
Thunder Loves Lightning

Paul pushed the La-Z-Boy through the skim of rust on the floor, shoving the wide-screen television they'd set up for videogames into the corner. He dragged a folding chair in front of the table instead.

Gunza grabbed Paul's shoulder, his fingers tightening hard enough to leave bruises. "Don't think you can stall for time."

This was the confrontation Paul needed to win.

"You think I'm wasting time?" Paul asked.

Gunza was smart enough to hesitate.

"Because I thought you called me the Flex master," Paul continued, stepping up to Gunza's chest. His magic emanated from Gunza's ridiculous pockmarked face, a sickening reflection. "Hey, if you want to instruct me in the ways of magic, I'll listen. In fact, I'll sit in that chair the way you *think* I should and play videogames. But all that'll get you is a high score."

"So, what do you want?"

"What I want," Paul said carefully, "is for you to realize that just because you set up a lab – a *failed* lab

– for a videogamemancer does not make you an expert in *my* style. That when I tend the lab, thunder comes. That you get clear Flex because I *am* the Flex master. And if you start micromanaging *my* magic, you get nothing." He gave Gunza a thump. Then: "We clear?"

Gunza glanced over; his boys held their breath, waiting for Gunza's next move.

He bitch-slapped Paul.

Not the crippling punch Flex could give him – just enough to remind Paul who was in charge. But more importantly, just enough to remind his boys who was in charge.

"Get it done," Gunza ordered.

Paul gave them a bloodied smirk. "I'll need the accordion folder in the white van." He tossed Gunza the keys, took pleasure in noting the way Gunza's aura dimmed as he burned Flex to catch the keys gracefully. "It's underneath the driver's seat."

Gunza flung the keys at one of his henchmen, who scurried off.

Valentine rushed in, putting her hands on Paul's shoulders to steady him. "Are you *insane*?"

"We're all insane." Paul could barely keep from laughing. "We're 'mancers."

Gunza had retreated to his leather reclining chair. He sat beneath a canopy of rusted lifting equipment, tapping his fingers on the armrest: *I'll leave you to it… for now.*

Raphael had been whisked away behind the steel presses… theoretically for his safety, but mostly to remind Valentine not to try anything stupid.

"You gotta get it together, Paul," Valentine whispered sotto voce as she rearranged the glass vials on the desk to make room for Paul's paperwork. "Taunting him does us no good."

"Let me ask you one question," Paul murmured. "Are you any good?"

Her face scrunched up in confusion. "At dating?"

"At 'mancy. My whole plan relies on your talent."

"Oh." She frowned, then gave Paul a bitter smirk. "Okay, fair question. I couldn't work magic for Gunza, right? But maybe that's because I didn't feel like running errands for a guy who'd threatened to smash my boyfriend's fingers. And maybe I couldn't make Flex, but maybe that's because I love my magic too much to cage it.

"I've fucked up a lot of things in my life, Paul. Pretty much all of them, in fact. But 'mancy?" She flexed her fingers, unleashing a smile sharp enough to draw blood. "One skill can redeem a life splintered with flaws. But only if you're very, *very* good at it."

"Good. Because this next act's going to bring down the house."

A boy brought Paul his accordion folder. Paul thanked him politely, began plucking the correct paperwork out from the various compartments to lay them out like tarot cards.

"Why him?" Paul jerked his head towards Raphael. "He's nothing, Valentine. There's no *there* there."

Valentine adjusted the throttles on the pipettes. "I know he's an Atari CPU in a PlayStation 4 casing. But he's pretty." She glanced in his direction and shivered. "*So* fucking pretty. And… he does what I want."

"He doesn't. He uses you."

"It's not as easy for me to date as you'd think, Paul." She squeezed a clamp with a tad more force than necessary. "Not everyone's into my style of kink. And… he's weirdly helpless. He doesn't know a thing about money, because everyone buys him drinks. He thinks he's a brilliant conversationalist because everyone laughs at his jokes. And he… stumbles. He stumbles *so often*, Paul. If someone didn't always pick him up, he'd be homeless by now."

"Letting someone fall isn't a bad idea. Sometimes, they bounce back stronger."

"Yeah, well… if he was stronger, he'd be out of my league." She gave Paul an embarrassed grin. "And I've always been a sucker for clueless men needing help."

"Ow."

She patted him on the cheek. "Truth stings, sweetie."

He felt a swell of affection for her, so intense it was almost painful. "You ready?"

"For what?"

"Thunder. *Big* thunder."

She smacked her lips, and Paul realized she was looking forward to the challenge as much as he. He'd been a 'mancer for less than a month, but he knew the rules of survival: never show off your 'mancy. You spent your life hiding, masking magic under coincidence.

They might die tonight. But they'd go out unashamed, blazing fireworks.

"I'll be your lightning, Paul," she promised. "Proudly."

"I need a pen."

Three of Gunza's thugs rushed forward to thrust pens into Paul's hand, as if hoping to get his autograph. Paul laid them neatly next to his forms. The boys craned their necks, fighting to get a glance.

Rare enough to see 'mancy, Paul knew. Rarer still to see a 'mancer make Flex. With one crystal-clear batch of B-1 Flex, Paul had already become legend.

Anticipation fogged the air. Though Gunza tried his best to glower, everyone's attention settled onto Paul – night had fallen, and the warehouse was ablaze with spotlights aimed at him.

Paul devoured their adoration.

He scrutinized the three pens, dancing his fingertips over each before settling on one. He raised it in the air as though it were a magician's wand; the thugs' eyes followed it in the air, as if they expected the Bic to spray flame.

Paul began to fill out forms.

He envisioned the paperwork that had run this factory back in better days, generic things: maintenance logs for the machines, cap-and-trade pollution permits, certifications for the forklift drivers.

But then he fell into the Beast, that institutional memory that kept record when humanity forgot. It told him what this factory had once been – they'd made windows. The air sizzled, heating as the old machinery groaned to life.

The thugs' cheers died in their throat, caught between exultation and terror. The iron turned dull red, gears began to clank. Paul barely noticed. He was filling out invoices, the forms spilling off the desk, slithering across the floor…

Gunza pressed a gun to Paul's temple.

"You're writing our address down."

Paul blinked – and when he looked at Gunza, his eyes had gone legal pad-yellow, his irises replaced by columns of scrolling numbers. Gunza flinched.

"Of course I'm writing our address down." Paul's voice was as toneless as a banker condemning a house. "This is where we are."

"Don't think you can drop an earthquake on us. Oh, yeah. I read about that. First sign of this building going, I shoot."

"The flux will land miles away. That's a promise."

Gunza inspected Paul; Paul felt the uneven pressure of his own transformed 'mancy washing over him. Gunza was burning Flex to check if Paul was telling the truth – so much so that Paul felt it flicker out. Gunza snorted the last of the baggie.

"I'm watching." Gunza's teeth blazed, as if to match Paul's eyes.

Valentine shouted out the bingo results as the forms expanded to fill the factory, crumpling up against smoldering metal, flowing like an origami river.

"N-37! O-68! B-7! I-21! G-58! N-31! O-75! B-10! I-27! G-50! N-44! O – oh, shit."

"Sounds ordinary," Paul said, slipping in one or two bureaucratic entries he hoped to God Gunza would overlook.

"They're not." Valentine had gone pale. "The letters. They're spelling the same words over and over again – BIG NO BIG NO BIG NO…"

Paul cackled. The thugs pulled out their guns, aiming them at the juddering smelters as though the machinery might rise up and attack them.

"Drain them." Paul began folding the papers, squeezing the 'mancy into the alembics, and Valentine rushed in to help – the factory floor was a jungle of printed forms, so many Paul thought he might drown in them.

Of course bureaucromancy would be so much more powerful in a factory. This was its native environment. Paul and Valentine wrangled the paperwork as it swelled, trying to push back the tide…

Gunza reached forward to help. A 401k form lashed at him and he pulled back, his palm split open with a paper cut. The forms lapped up Gunza's blood.

The 'mancy burbled through the alembics, cracking the glass. It poured out onto the hematite, roiling and rocking on the surface. He'd only intended to make a small batch, but the factory was eager to manufacture again. More 'mancy kept flowing through him until great heaps of Flex piled up beneath his fingers…

Paul shoved the 'mancy into the gritty crystal, trapping it, and he felt the flux boiling up inside – Gunza jammed the gun against Paul's neck, ready to pull the trigger if Paul shaped the blowback–

Paul finalized the hazardous waste material transfer forms, activating them with his signature. The factory floor heaved up – only an inch, but enough to register the displeasure of something powerful that disliked being chained – and then the flux rolled off elsewhere, like a surly child.

The machinery clanked as it cooled down, returning to useless junk. The thugs crept closer, like kids approaching a Halloween house for the first time, unsure of tricks or treats.

Paul lifted the tray, heaped with more Flex than he'd thought he could ever make, and offered it to Gunza. Gunza plucked a crystal from the pile, probing it with his Flex senses – then gobbled it.

He raised his hands in the air, a referee announcing a goal. "This!" he roared. "B-1 Flex! And it's *ours*!"

The boys tumbled forward like puppies, eager to feast. Paul drew back, escorting Valentine to the office as the gang gorged themselves on stolen magic.

"They'll be a while," Paul told her. "They have to feast. Already, they're finding it hard to live without it." Then: "I hope they use it all up in time."

Valentine nibbled a fingernail. "You said there'd be thunder."

"The distraction takes some time to engineer," Paul promised. "Stay ready."

They watched as the gang took superhuman risks, darting between the conveyor belts and steel rollers as they fired live guns at each other. They relied entirely on the Flex for survival; people slipped at the last moment to slide beneath a shot that would have gone through their eye, machinery tumbled from the ceiling just in time to deflect a deadly fusillade, panicked birds flew into bullets.

When they'd burned through the last of their magic, they returned to Gunza, who handed Flex out with the attitude of a lottery winner buying drinks for everyone in the bar.

Raphael giggled, cheering them on, oblivious that the Flex was not protecting him.

His admiration galled Paul. Paul's bureaucromancy was slow, tedious, mundane. It created cargo manifests, not Matrix gunplay. Yet they'd stolen his magic to reshape it into this glorious physical display…and he couldn't even use it. The Flex worked only for the unmagicked.

Valentine tapped his prosthetic foot affectionately. "The ankle's a bitch, isn't it?"

"It's a reminder," Paul said, staring enviously at the young kids showing off.

"Of?"

"It used to tell me what happened to dumb cops who charged in to interfere with 'mancers," Paul sighed. "These days? It reminds me I can do some amazing things, but I'm never gonna be Superman."

"We all have different limits. I can be Superman, but–"

"That's good. We'll need Superman before the evening's done."

"Not a problem. Every person you control in a videogame is superhuman on some level. But I can't–"

Muffled *whoomps* echoed across the warehouse. Then rattling clanks rained down as a hundred metallic objects bounced off machinery.

"*Get down!*" Paul shielded Valentine's eyes as the flashbangs went off. Tear gas hissed into the makeshift corridors. Armored soldiers in black SMASH uniforms rappelled in through the broken windows on every side of the warehouse, so unified they could have been mirror images. They landed as one thanks to their army-inspired Unimancy.

But all of the flashbangs had misfired or bounced into bins where they'd gone off harmlessly. Gunza, recognizing the danger, ran for the Flex, dumping it into a Rubbermaid washtub. His thugs snorted the last of their crystal, eyes glowing as they realized how epic this fight would be.

Valentine had to scream to be heard over the gunfire, the helicopters, the announcements. *"Paul! Where the fuck did you dump the flux?"*

"SMASH headquarters!" he yelled. *"Now. Show me your lightning."*

EIGHTEEN
Thunderstruck

Paul held his breath, knowing what SMASH tear gas did to his motor functions – but as the gas billowed into the factory, a helicopter plowed through the roof.

The 'copter hit the factory's far side at a skewed angle, as if the pilot had jerked it to one side in a frantic attempt to land. Its landing gear punched through the corrugated ceiling by the eastern wall, catching in the steel beams before the wheels tore free, sending a shower of rust and old birds' nests onto the concrete floor. The overhead lights sputtered indignantly and died as the aircraft's insectile frame crashed through the roof, smashing through the wall like a bowling ball. The rotors disintegrated as they tried to Cuisinart themselves free. Paul saw the stumps whirling as the copter tumbled, erratic as a severed head, through the freshly exposed parking lot.

There was a creak as the building wobbled, like a fighter recovering from a punch to the face. Raphael cheered as the warehouse's eastern half lurched downward, sagging in terrifying ways as the beams and walls argued amongst themselves how best to stay upright. The debate settled itself as chunks of roofing pulled free, the walls buckling outward as architecture collapsed into new and semi-stable formations.

Emergency lights flickered on by the doorways, too thin to illuminate the factory's vastness. It was just enough for Paul to see the murky brown tear gas arcing up off the floor, sucked towards the ceiling by the air pressure of the collapsing roof on the other side of the warehouse, then following the helicopter through the destroyed wall.

All this destruction, created for one reason: one of the thugs had wanted that gas gone. And Paul's Flex had made it happen.

Then a barrage of gunfire took down the emergency lights, leaving Paul in shadows.

Bringing SMASH here had been a risk. Time was not on his side – Raphael was correct that if Paul hesitated for too long, then Gunza would hunt for Paul's other weaknesses. Aliyah in Gunza's hands was game over. Paul also knew he couldn't get Valentine out on her own, not with Gunza's team of artificial 'mancers guarding the place – he'd need a distraction. What could pose a serious distraction to Flex-fuelled gangbangers who could engineer coincidence?

A SMASH squadron would take Gunza and company down in short order – too short. But make a small batch of Flex to get Gunza's guard down, dump an earthquake on SMASH's headquarters to reduce their numbers, and it'd be an even battle between the two. Which gave Paul and Valentine a chance to battle their way out in the confusion.

If Valentine was good enough.

He looked around, trying to remember where the exits were; he could see the gaping windows high above, but the ground floor view was blocked by rows of shadowed smelters and crucibles. Paul could feel the low pressure of magic in the air; the messy wash of the thugs burning his stolen 'mancy shoving up against the hard incoming curve of the SMASH team. The SMASH unit was threading their way through the maze, working as one organism, checking corners.

Raphael applauded. "This is *amazing*! Like fuckin', I dunno, movies!" He looked adoringly at Valentine – the closest thing to affection Paul had seen Raphael express. Valentine missed it; she was peering into the maze, feeling the various 'mancies intersect.

She held up her hands, an invisible controller cradled between them. Paul felt her 'mancy, subtle and insidious, thread itself into the flat push of Unimancy.

"They think as one," Valentine said. "And *whoo*, that helps. Follow my lead. Don't do anything I don't do first."

She took off through the maze at a brisk pace, Paul following. Raphael loped behind them both, eager as a kid on his first paintball run. She turned right, left, then shoved them both against a set of supply shelves.

"What one sees, they all see," she hissed.

Paul looked down to where the machinery formed a T-junction. A dull cone of neon green bobbed into view, followed by a SMASH agent in a gas mask and goggles. The green light-cone emanated from the end of his rifle: an infrared projector.

Wait a minute, Paul thought. *Why am I certain that's infrared?*

The agent walked straight ahead, making hand gestures at no one Paul could see, focusing down the center of his field of vision. Paul gripped Valentine's hand; if the agent glanced left, he'd see them.

The guard marched past like clockwork, remaining bizarrely, absurdly focused on the end of the hallway.

"How come I know that's an infrared beam?" Raphael whispered. Then: "How can I *see* infrared?"

The guard froze, then straightened. "*Who's there?*" he said in a mechanical tone, scanning from left to right and back again in clockwork rhythm. Valentine slapped her hand over Raphael's mouth. Paul was certain the guard would investigate – but after staring befuddled for a few moments, he went back to patrolling. Paul peered out to see the guard make it to the end of the hallway, pause dramatically, then pivot on a perfect ninety-degree turn to sweep the next corridor.

Valentine released the breath she'd been holding. "Move forward. He'll loop back around soon."

"Wait, what's going on?"

"We're in a stealth game. They're in patrol mode. Still deadly, but operating on dumber AI."

Paul grinned. "Brilliant."

"It could be better. Everyone here knows the rules, at least on a subconscious level, so the thugs have a chance, too. Plus, I had to expand the factory floor – it was too small for a videogame level..."

Paul realized he could no longer see the hole where the helicopter had crashed through. The factory walls had faded into blank darkness. He tried to wiggle through a gap between two pieces of machinery; an invisible barrier blocked him. Everything had coalesced into impermeable videogame hallways, an unreadable maze.

An alarm blared to their left, revealing a red glow. Paul heard gunfire, yelling, the surprised shouts of combatants – and felt the clash of magics. Then silence. Paul wasn't sure who'd won.

"Use your portal gun," Paul said. "Shoot across the maze and get us out."

A look of purest incredulity. "You can't mix videogames, Paul."

Paul swallowed back a retort. Some other gamemancer might be able to. But if his logic didn't make sense to Valentine, she couldn't make it happen, no more than Paul could use his bureaucromancy to fly.

"This is – this is Metal Gear Solid, right?" Raphael asked. He looked like he'd gotten a free pass to Disneyland. "I was awesome at that game. Even better than I was at Halo."

"This isn't Halo," Valentine said, freaking out. "This is game-plus difficulty."

"Yeah, yeah, that's fine." He shook his head, his whole body rejecting the idea, then lifted his fists in exultation. "This is fucking *unbelievable*!"

Valentine grabbed his face. "They will kill you, Raph. Their guns have bullets. I have spent my life mastering videogames. Do *not* think you can outplay me."

"Yeah, s'cool, whatever. Let's find the boss monster."

Paul frowned. "There's no boss monster, is there?"

A pool of green light bobbed around the corner as the SMASH agent reappeared.

"Go," Valentine said. The guard froze – "*Who's there?*" – as they dashed down another corridor.

"Whatever happens, *do not let them see your face,*" Valentine repeated. "If one of them sees you, all of them will. It's a Unimancer trick. Once they get your face on file, we're Refactored for sure."

They rounded a corner made of an old smelting pot. One of Gunza's thugs was dragging a body out of sight, leaving a sticky trail on the ground; a second SMASH agent lay crushed nearby under collapsed machinery. The kid had slung a stolen SMASH rifle over his shoulder.

"Yo, man," the kid said. "Hook me up with some Flex. I'm low."

Paul held up empty palms. "Can't. Gunza has it."

He poked Paul with the rifle. "Well, *make* some, motherfucker."

"I can't. You saw what it took."

"Fuck!" The kid kicked the SMASH agent so hard, the helmet popped off, revealing a face that had lost all expressivity long before death. Paul recognized the body: Death Metal.

The kid geared back for another kick. Paul grabbed him. "*Don't.*"

"The fuck you care?"

"He is – was – a 'mancer."

"You friends?"

"Not really." Yet Paul felt bizarrely protective of the corpse; this poor bastard had been a 'mancer like him, with hopes and dreams and such a love for music that he'd made magic out of it. The army had wrung that strangeness out of Death Metal, remolding him into a weapon.

Paul swallowed back vomit. He thought he'd been calling in faceless SMASH soldiers to distract Gunza. But now, he realized, he'd called in brain-burned victims to be slaughtered for his convenience.

The kid turned to Valentine for support, but one grim glance from her shut him down. "You fuckin' crazy. He'd kill you if he could."

"That's not him," Valentine said. "They made him a hive mind."

There were no alcoves to drag the kid into, so Paul and Valentine propped Death Metal up against a windowpane cutter, sat him up so he at least looked comfortable. His gray face was drained of humanity, the same as the last time Paul had talked to him.

"You know any death metal?" Paul asked Valentine.

"What?" Valentine bent to tug the helmet off the other agent. "That shit is terrible. Why would I know any of that crap?"

Paul gestured. "It's what he did."

Her eyes widened. "Oh. *Oh*." Then: "Holy crap, you can make 'mancy out of the worst things in the world. Somewhere, there's a fuckin' polkamancer..."

"Yeah, well, you're talking to the guy who turned the DMV into an art."

"That's just *it*, Paul. Magic can make the shittiest things in the world beautiful. I wish… I wish I could have seen him work."

"He was something."

She pushed Death Metal's helmet over Paul's face.

"...What the hell, Valentine?"

"It covers your face!"

Paul ripped it off. "They know I'm here. Their records show I placed a phone call. They think Gunza took me hostage after he caught me snooping around."

"When'd you do that?"

"When I made the Flex."

"*Mastermind*." She turned to pull the helmet over Raphael's face, tightening the straps with the care of a mother putting her infant into a baby seat.

"Like a *helmet's* going to help!" The kid jabbed Paul in the ribs with the gun. "We gotta get out! They're hunting us down!"

A flash of green light. "*Who's there?*"

"*Fuck!*" The kid hoisted his rifle at the incoming guard. The SMASH agent's pace loosened into a terrifying combat readiness as he reached for the taser at his belt. His green glow shifted to a coal red as an alarm began blaring.

What had you been, once? Paul wondered. *What 'mancy had you commanded?*

"Surrender, and you will not be harmed." The agent was male but spoke in a reassuring feminine voice – as though someone else spoke through him. "You will be brought to the Refactor. If you're a mundane, you have nothing to fear."

"Fuck your Refactor!" The kid burned the last of his Flex to get off a lucky shot that punched through the SMASH agent's bulletproof vest.

The agent plunked down face-first into the floor, dying. Valentine shouted *"Run!"* as the kid knelt to grab the taser.

—Flex—

A surge of magic spiraled out of nowhere, roaring past Paul towards the kid. The SMASH agent's last dying twitches activated the taser – which malfunctioned, pumping every watt into the kid's body. The kid's hair caught fire as his heart seized.

Raphael took the whole thing in, horrified, extending his arms towards them. It was as though he wanted to touch the corpses, as if verifying their existence might make sense of this...

He's never been in a fight, Paul thought dizzily. *Someone's always shielded him from the worst of what happens around him – and now he's realizing some of his actions had a cost.*

Valentine shoved Raph down an alcove just as more SMASH agents converged on their downed agent. Paul struggled to keep up on his artificial leg.

"That surge wasn't Unimancy," Valentine said, her voice taking on a Stormtrooper-like echo from inside the helmet.

"Gunza," Paul wheezed, out of breath. Gunza knew any survivors would testify against him. He was hidden in the factory, sniffing Flex, ensuring once they finished their 'mancy, they would meet a horrible end...

"Fuck, he's got a tub of that shit..."

"We can't – can't stop him – he's got all my 'mancy – "

"No. We can fucking fight him. When it was six temp-o-mancers holding Raphael hostage, no, I

couldn't get past them. But one guy? I'll kick his ass."
She cuffed Paul, furious. "Goddammit, Paul, *I told you
to put the fucking flux in*!"

"Should've," Paul huffed apologetically. He'd only
wanted to make a small batch here, just enough to
lengthen the fight. He hadn't known the factory itself
would kick in to help produce – that made this battle
much more dangerous...

"We can get past Gunza and these Unizombies," she
muttered. "We – shit. They're onto me."

The machinery around them shifted, the spaces
between them expanding wide enough for a man to
walk through – then slammed shut. The ceiling above
flickered wildly between pitch black and an ordinary
shadowed darkness, as if two realities were battling for
supremacy.

"Seven of them, one of me," Valentine grunted. "But
they're fighting on two fronts. And don't know how to
fight dirty. And want me alive."

"You gonna be okay?"

"I'm taking a lot of flux. This is... a massive
restructuring of reality, Paul."

"Can you bleed it off?"

"I *have* been. All the easy stuff's been burned off.
Now my apartment's been broken into, my electricity's
been cut off, and I've just contracted herpes. I don't
know how much more flux I can dump without it
affecting our luck *now*..."

Raphael swept her into his arms. She sagged into
him, drawing strength. In that moment, Paul could see
that Raphael wasn't capable of tenderness, exactly...

but he could be someone to cling to, as long as you didn't ask too many questions.

"Are you gonna be okay?" Raphael asked. Paul winced; it was the wrong question. She might admit some troubles to Paul, who at least understood 'mancy's limits, but no way she'd show weakness in front of Raphael.

"Yeah." Valentine let him go. "We'll get out of this."

The warehouse flickered again, shrinking to normal size; Paul saw the exit's dim outline a hundred yards away, visible in slices through a labyrinth of glass-making equipment. SMASH agents guarded the exit. Then Valentine grunted and things solidified again, the formless darkness swallowing them. Paul felt the SMASH team unleashing their 'mancy upon the warehouse, and Valentine pushing back, and Gunza pouring in his own efforts...

A sound like tearing paper.

Something like a claw tip etched a ragged line in the air above them. The rift was colorless. Not clear, not black, but devoid of color in a visual canker sore; it made Paul's retinas ache.

The rift squirmed in vaginal birth spasms.

Broach, Paul thought, backing away.

The 'mancy stopped as they felt the sickness growing above them. The warehouse sprang back to normal. He could see the SMASH team, suddenly bereft of their 'mancy-fueled telepathy, communicating via hand signals.

Paul was exquisitely aware of the rawness of the air around them. Reality had been rubbed thin. It still hung together in a fragile way, like streamers after a hard party… but stray sparks of 'mancy caused a row of old, jagged pipes to smolder with remembered heat.

He stood in dry woods populated by living flamethrowers.

"In case you're not aware, that rift is the first sign of a broach," a voice called out – the same self-assured female voice that had spoken to them through the now-dead SMASH guard. Except her voice now quavered. "If we do not step down, we will be the incursion point for an otherdimensional breach. *Any* 'mancy puts us at risk of a Europe-level catastrophe."

Valentine quivered, trying to regain her strength.

"*She says she won't surrender!*" Paul yelled, trying to sound as scared as a hostage tasked to negotiate with SMASH should be.

"We will stand down." Angry groans echoed around the warehouse. "*We will stand down,*" she repeated. "I understand your frustration, but you newer agents have not lived through a broach. That is because most agents who encounter a broach get no older. The risk to this hemisphere is too large to take revenge."

"She's a *terrorist*!"

"We will allow you to leave if you wish," the leader continued. "But we know 'mancy's danger; we lived it once, like you. You will lose everything you love, sacrificed to magic. Eventually, you wind up with blowback that might as well be suicide.

"We have ways to bleed off flux without personal damage. That's how Unimancy works. We can train you to share the strength of many. We can give you a family that understands what you need. We can give you a life you don't have to tear apart to pay for flux."

Valentine's head turned towards the SMASH leader, wanting to believe her. Paul understood why; how many crappy jobs had she been fired from? How many apartments had she lost? Raphael's sporadic fondness was the closest she dared come to a real relationship – because if she had a true love, her stray flux would seek it out...

With his 'mancy active, Aliyah would be his lightning rod for bad luck...

He pushed the thought away as Raphael tugged Valentine back. Paul wondered if Raphael was starting to understand just what Valentine had done for him. Raph spread his palms open, as if he was ready to let her go–

Valentine shook her head.

"These guys only play Call of Duty." Then she took Raphael's hand in hers, a gruff movement that allowed no tenderness. "Besides, I got the best fuck in New York City with me."

She hugged Raphael, ready to move on–

A SMASH agent leapt down from the rafters, tackling them to the ground.

"–fucking lobotomancies us and thinks she's getting *away* with it?"

Paul whirled as another female SMASH agent clubbed Raphael to the floor with a truncheon. He froze, not sure what to do; he was supposed to be the hostage. Should he help? How? *Fight* them? He was a scrawny guy facing muscular killers...

The first agent whipped off her helmet, revealing a slim, athletic redhead, face flush with anger. "No worries, ma'am! *We got her*!"

The girl knelt on Valentine's chest, grabbing the hypodermic at her waist: "We feel them die. You know that? We feel the bullets in our throats, the knives in our ribs. And *you* turned six of our smartest agents into dimbulbs so these fucking ghetto punks could kill them. Half our team, slaughtered." Paul could see not just the anger, but the terror on the SMASH agent's face: she'd been reduced to a clockwork machine until her commander fought her back to normal. "When you get to the Refactor, they're gonna erase all the parts of you that aren't us. All you'll be left with is our pain. And once we're done, the only reason you won't kill yourself is because you know we'd experience your suicide with you…"

Valentine didn't struggle. Paul remembered her first words to him: *I don't like killing*.

"*No!*"

Raphael thrashed free, grabbing at the SMASH agent's holster. He got the gun halfway out before she shoved him backward.

Raphael flailed, stumbling, then fell on the rusted pipes.

Valentine screamed as the pipes emerged from Raphael's chest. *They can't be that sharp*, Paul thought – then saw the residual magic glimmering through the jagged ends.

Raphael looked down, confused. He fingered the sharp rims of the pipes jutting from his chest, like a musician might fret a strange guitar. Then he looked toward Valentine, as if she might explain this to him.

"Valentine," he whispered – a single word that could have been regret, could have been love, could have been anything. Then he slumped forward.

The first agent plunged the hypodermic towards Valentine's neck.

Valentine caught the hypo in one hand – a hand now blue and scaly, her fingers boneless. There was a popping noise as Valentine's helmet shattered, a flabby mockery of her face spilling out. New tentacles flopped out of fresh body cavities as she swelled to the size of a pony, then a Volkswagen, lifting the first agent in the air with octopoid limbs. She swept the boilers to one side with the strength of a boss monster.

"Bad move," Valentine gurgled.

NINETEEN
Do I Dare Repair the Universe?

"I had my flux under *control!*" Valentine flung the SMASH agent through the ceiling. "But you surprised me, and the worst thing I could imagine fucking *happened!*" She grabbed for the other agent, who dove out of the way; Paul felt the agent magically reconnect with her team. "*You killed him!*"

Valentine threw her head back and wailed, a lamenting sound like a foghorn: *I killed him.* Then she reached down from terrifying heights, her distorted face as big as a water tower.

The commander yelled, "*Do not Unify! We cannot risk broach!*"

A red reticle pulsed over Valentine's left eye. A SMASH member fired, then all of them did, concentrating fire on that one vulnerable spot as the commander screamed at them to stop.

It's a true hive mind, Paul realized, shocked. Unimancy wasn't one person controlling the squad; it was the squad merging into one unit. Angered by Valentine's 'mancy, the 'mancers had ostracized their commander, choosing revenge over mission.

Valentine's left eye punctured and sagged, slopping monstrous pus across the warehouse floor.

Our 'mancy comes with built-in weaknesses, Paul thought. *She exploited their unison, now they're exploiting her rules.*

"*Valentine!*" he shouted. No one heard him over the gunfire and Valentine's bellows of anguish. He pounded her tentacles to get her attention; they were the size of oaks, rooted deep into the factory floor. "*Run!*"

The space around Valentine buckled, filling with tiny rips. A long slit unraveled the air before Paul's nose as he pinwheeled backwards, opening a glimpse into a universe filled with that nauseating no-color. The slit slid straight through a nearby sand bucket.

Instead of sand spilling out, a horde of flylike buzz saws boiled out. They tore into the bucket with a noise like the absence of a hum. The buzzsects ate the bucket's colors, its dimensions, its textures, gobbling its solidity and shitting out formless chaos.

Then, in one convulsing movement, the rip widened to engulf the bucket's remains. Another inverted-hum, and the rift gave birth to a fresh cloud of colorless buzzsects.

"*Open to me!*" the commander yelled, picking her way among the rifts to get to her squadron. "*Let me in! Take my calmness!*" A rift squirmed, bisected her. The buzzsects burrowed under her flesh, her skin glimmering as they chewed the 'mancy out of her body. Then her skull burst open, unleashing a plague of new demons.

They flowed outwards, following the threads of Unimancy that had once linked the commander to her squad...

The agents panicked as the buzzsects multiplied, chewing reality away around them. Debris tumbled in random directions, no longer tethered by gravity. The air between the rifts condensed into a pinkish fluid, wobbling bubbles of uncertain physics...

Jagged rifts slid through Valentine's massive body. She flailed at the buzzsects like she was trying to slap out a fire. All she did was accumulate more rifts, which clung to her, boring deeper. She wailed in horror, the buzzsects lapping up the pus from her destroyed eye.

Paul dodged as the rifts swelled and gave birth, trying to find a safe space. A squad member yelled: *"The commander was right! We have to unite!"*

Rifts boiled out past the warehouse, threading through the parking lot, headed for town...

It's all about bureaucracy, Paul thought, flattening himself against the floor to summon the Beast. He tugged some hazardous waste forms from his pocket. Maybe he could relocate the broaches far over the ocean, where they might burn themselves out – or at least buy the national 'mancy teams time to rein them in–

As he pondered the immensity of his task, the rips converged on him, thin lines curving towards fresh magic. Come on, Paul thought, what sort of bureaucratic hazard does a reality incursion create? There would be reports, filled out by surviving SMASH agents, and the papers under his pen changed to top secret documents.

Paul didn't know how to write the report of how SMASH defeated the incursion. How did you defeat demons? He knew it involved sealing rifts, but only Unimancers knew to do it...

The buzzsects gnawed the form out from underneath his pen tip. His 'mancy dispersed – they fed on 'mancy, they *were* 'mancy. The Beast wanted to nudge reality toward more convenient directions, but the buzzsects – they wanted to erase the known laws of physics, replace them with a more chaotic environment filled with toxic predators...

His 'mancy weakened reality. It made their job easier.

The buzzsects finished off the form, then devoured his artificial leg. "Hey, now..." he muttered, waving at them feebly.

They moved in, plucking at Paul's skin, summoning glimmers of magic to the surface. Lights rippled along Paul's arm; he was filled with 'mancy. Tasty, tasty 'mancy.

They circled, savoring the moment. Then one darted down to excise a chunk from Paul's forearm – leaving no blood, no meat, just a pencil-sized furrow of nothingness. A window to the bone underneath.

Paul looked down, thinking: *That shouldn't happen.*

There were rules. When you cut someone's skin, they *bled*. That was the way things *worked*.

That was the way physics worked. Physics led to chemistry, which led to biology, which led to millions of consistent interactions that kept Paul alive. The smallest atoms followed rules, banded together into molecules, played fair with forces. They all followed the law.

It was like you never, *ever* submitted a Claims Form F-14 without getting it signed off on by your manager.

Or how affidavits weren't acceptable as evidence in court without a notary stamp.

Or the magnificence of requiring two pieces of ID, with photo, to minimize the risk of forgery.

Paul glared at the hole in his arm, recognizing his existence was nothing more than a vast set of interlocking rules, many of which seemed crazy. But taken as a whole, they provided a reliable, understandable, productive environment.

"*My arm is supposed to bleed,*" he said in a stern voice that would have caused any customer service representative to tremble. It was the voice of the irrational customer – the one who knew that he had a receipt, that the gift was still in its protective cellophane wrapping, that the refund policies are posted right on the wall, and he would not leave until the $38.69 he had paid was refunded to his credit card *in full*.

The world, realizing its inadequacy, listened. Chemistry fell back into line, mass rebalanced itself, atoms spun in the right direction. Blood spurted in great gouts from Paul Tsabo's arm.

The buzzsects withdrew.

"That," Paul said, pointing at a deliquescing fog, "should be a bucket of sand." It coalesced into a tin bucket apologetically.

"That," Paul said, focusing his willpower on the floating pinkish bobbles, "should be nitrogen, oxygen, and argon, with trace elements." It puffed back into wisps of air.

"You," Paul said to the buzzsects, "are not aerodynamic." They dropped from the air, twitching helplessness.

Paul turned his attention to the rifts. They were *offensive*. This was not how you created a world that filled out forms. Something greater shifted into place behind him – the universe, perhaps? A larger body of physics and complexity that offered to use Paul as a doorway to step through and reassert itself.

He sat down in a half-lotus position, crossing one leg awkwardly over his stump. His arm pulsed blood, squirting it with each heartbeat onto the concrete floor, but that was good. Blood was proof of commitment.

Paul stitched up the rifts. It took an exhausting amount of energy, but it was as satisfying as completing jigsaw puzzles. He found the blank spaces the rifts had annihilated, investigated until he deduced what law of thermodynamics had been removed, and replaced it. He pulled the rifts towards him in a content daze, analyzing to determine exactly where physics had become knotted, then plucked each knot apart with nimble fingers.

He was unpacking his books. He was filing his forms.

He was in heaven.

By the time he tied off the last knot, the floor was slick with blood and his heart struggled to beat. The remaining SMASH agents called to each other, trying to figure out what was happening, but Paul could not speak.

He fell backward. Someone caught him.
A man with emerald teeth.

TWENTY
Say Uncle

"Who made this?" Gunza held the Flex above the applicant's tongue like a priest dispensing the sacrament. The boy glanced over at Paul chained in the corner, legless.

The kid was hard-muscled, lean, looked good in a fight – but the presence of Gunza's three former guards, alive and hanging from meat hooks, made him visibly nervous.

"You did, Gunza."

"Who grants this to you?"

"You do."

"Who tells you when to use the 'mancy?"

"You do, Gunza."

"God damn right. What happens when you fuck with my 'mancy?"

The kid's eyes flickered towards his old friends. "Terrible things, Gunza." Paul counted the days, realized Gunza had hired the kids on the meat hooks three days ago. Gunza was churning through employees faster and faster.

"God damn right." Gunza lifted the crystal away from the kid's mouth. The kid stretched his neck after the Flex for a moment, extending his tongue like he was trying to catch a snowflake. Disappointed but obedient, he stepped back into line with the other applicants.

Gunza went for the tray of throwing knives.

"Now, I ain't never thrown knives," Gunza murmured, popping the crystal into his mouth. He'd taken to chewing Flex even when he didn't need 'mancy; Paul was beginning to think he just liked the taste. "Seen a circus guy do it once."

He flung a knife towards one of the meat hook boys. It cut off most of an ear, more by chance than skill. The kid screamed into the rag stuffed in his mouth.

"Guess I'm no circus guy," he said.

The other two writhed, moaning apologies.

"Oh, you want luck now?" Gunza slapped them. "You motherfuckers flipped the *lottery* yesterday. All three at once. From the same fuckin' store. Didn't I *tell* them not to use the Flex until I said?"

Gunza addressed that last sentence to Paul, as always. Paul didn't know why Gunza even bothered to talk to him, aside from the fact that Paul had become the sole constant in Gunza's life; he'd spent the last ten days dragging Paul from safe house to safe house, trying to build an empire based on this new drug.

"...you did," Paul said softly, wearily. "You absolutely did."

"So, you dumb fucks blew a triple triple! Think SMASH wouldn't come sniffing after that? When this terrorist bitch has everyone on edge? Place was *swarming* with Five-0. So, we're in a different borough, and you're on meat hooks."

Gunza threw the knives. The results weren't pretty.

But they were educational.

Later, after Gunza made the new recruits clean up the mess of the old recruits, he offered Paul a beer.

"Let me send a postcard," Paul begged.

Gunza swigged the beer, belched in contentment; all of Gunza's beers hit the spot these days. "The SMASH team would dust for… something. Can't chance it."

Paul swallowed back fury. Gunza was a dim prospect, all instinct and no education. If he'd just put the flux in the Flex, like Valentine had said, Gunza would have Fluxed out by now. Instead, Gunza had been moving them from place to place, escaping SMASH traps by engineered luck. He made long, shouting calls to his brothers, telling them he had the Flex, it was time *they* listened to *him*.

He wanted to apologize to Valentine. Was she alive? He kept rubbing the gash in his arm, where the buzzsects had eaten a furrow through his flesh; it bled nonstop, a constant runny-nose ooze, never healing.

Had Valentine recovered from that? Could she?

That thought led to panic. Best to concentrate on Aliyah. Aliyah, he knew, was safe.

"They're Unimancers," Paul said. "They're terrifying when someone points them at a target – but they don't hunt well. All they'd find on the postcard would be my fingerprints. But my daughter would know I'm alive."

"Gotta let go of that life, Paul." Gunza stroked the

Rubbermaid tub of Flex for the ten thousandth time; he kept it parked in his lap, never letting it or Paul out of his sight.

"You can't let go of family."

Gunza gave him an unsettling, clear-eyed stare. "You better hope I do, Paul." He returned to watching television.

Paul leaned back against the radiator, his wrist chafing from the handcuff. The endless string of reality shows Gunza watched bored him stiff.

He thought about Aliyah. Was she okay? With so much of her skin gone, she was prone to infection. Maybe she was dying.

Maybe she was crying for Daddy.

The thought stung so much, he couldn't stare at it straight on, so instead he imagined Aliyah's hospital paperwork – her vital readings, the nurses' charts, the claims submitted to Samaritan–

Gunza pressed a gun to Paul's throat. "Your 'mancy's slow, Mister 'Mancer."

"I didn't–"

"You were changing something. I felt it." Gunza cocked the trigger. Paul trembled. "Valentine's 'mancy is quick. That girl can could do some damage. Wouldn't dare hold a gun to her. But you? You could fuck me up in the long run… but your write-o-mancy, or whatever the fuck it is, won't deflect this bullet. And I will fire, if you don't fucking stop."

"I'm not trying," Paul croaked, his mouth dry. He wasn't. His daydreams caused ripples in reality.

Gunza nodded as if he'd made his point, then

withdrew to watching a rerun of *The Osbournes*.

Paul wanted to dare Gunza to shoot. But Aliyah. He might see Aliyah again.

When Gunza slept, Paul tried to do some 'mancy. But he didn't know the address of this place – and without that vital anchor, it was like trying to find Valentine without her name. Gunza ensured he never had paper or pen; sometimes, he shot at Paul's good foot to break his concentration. He also made sure to keep Paul's head bagged whenever they moved, which was often.

They'd stayed at Gunza's first safe house for two days, with Gunza recruiting new members from his friends, promising as much Flex as they could handle. Sure enough, word had gotten out, and a rival gang made their play. Because Gunza had chosen a small house out in the suburbs – he hadn't even covered the windows or installed bulletproof doors – the battle had been loud and sloppy, won only thanks to wild surges of Flex-inspired luck.

Gunza had gotten into a screaming fight with his brothers after that. Their connections were shit, he told them. Stupid stockbroker wannabes who'd pay, what, two-fifty kay? This shit could make them billions.

Gunza moved to a hotel the next time, trying to play it mysterious, inviting high-wheeling strangers into the room to sell them on the merits of Flex. Except Gunza didn't really know anyone; Paul found out later he'd been taking out ads on Craigslist. He'd gotten a string of sad-sack investors who weren't quite sure why they were there, and they'd had to flee after Gunza had roughed up an elderly man who'd shown up with an insulting $500 – his life's savings – to invest. That man had called 1-800-SMASHEM.

Yet Gunza insisted, loudly and constantly, that he wouldn't settle for his old connections. He'd show his family what *he* could do.

Two days later, his hired guns had turned on him. After that, Gunza had stopped giving it out so freely.

They moved elsewhere. Then he moved again when someone told his brothers where he was staying.

All had been quiet for a few days, until the Lotto winners had forced another move. Now they were in a tenement, surrounded by eager kids – everyone but Gunza had been killed in the factory fight, but the promise of Flex ensured Gunza had no lack of applicants.

Paul felt weary. Gunza was bad enough, and he ached to hold Aliyah, but the maddening bit was how he had to restrain himself from correcting Gunza's mistakes. Had Gunza reinforced this safe house for a fight? No. Had he devised protocols to track who was coming and going? No. Did Gunza have a bolt-hole when things went wrong? No. Based on the previous four moves, Gunza would snort Flex and drive around until he got lucky.

This could have been a magnificent operation. But Gunza had no people skills. Paul wasn't the greatest at glad-handing – Imani or Kit had always handled upper management for him – but Gunza treated his first wave of cohorts like buddies, dispensing Flex without a care in the world. Now he'd taken to surly withdrawal, making them beg and jump for the Flex – sometimes literally – and only for a mission.

It offended Paul. If he was going to be held hostage by a criminal, it should be a mastermind. Gunza was a small thinker with a bloated ego – good enough when spoon-fed tasks but falling apart under his own agenda. Paul bit back suggestions, wanting to needle Gunza into fine-tuning his organization, knowing Gunza would punish anyone who showed him up.

Shouts from outside. Paul looked up.

"I told you, *I got this*!" Gunza said petulantly. "You fuckers are *not welcome*! And who the fuck is this?"

"That's Uncle." Paul recognized the voice from Gunza's many shouted conversations: his brother Hanna.

Gunza's stunned silence told Paul that Uncle didn't show up for casual get-togethers. He spoke in a strangled whisper:

"...why the fuck is *he* here?"

"He doesn't make trips to America," Hanna said. "It's dangerous for him, crossing the border. Show some respect."

"I didn't ask him here."

"We did."

"And I *told* you, I'm gonna make him so much money that–"

"Show me."

The voice was gravelly. Uncle's voice had a weight that leaned on you, like dirt pressing down on a fresh grave.

Gunza quieted. "A'ight," he muttered. "Just a look."

The door opened, the light so bright that Paul squinted. Uncle took up the whole doorframe, a blunt

physique that might have been carved from granite.
Uncle stepped with the delicacy of encroaching old age
but had the sure footing of a killer.

"That him?"

Paul quailed from Uncle's attention. He slid
backward, as if he could fold into the radiator.

"Yeah," Gunza said. Behind him, his brother – a
larger, beefier boy – peered in anxiously, terrified of
making Uncle unhappy.

Uncle's knotted eyebrows raised when he saw the
tub. "That's it?"

"Yeah." Gunza thrust his chin out, daring Uncle to
say anything bad.

Uncle grabbed a piece. He turned glittering Flex back
and forth between thin fingers. It was the largest piece
in the tub, the size of a ping-pong ball. Uncle eyed it
suspiciously, then moved to take a bite.

Gunza grabbed Uncle's wrist.

"You ask first," Gunza said.

You could hear his brother's squeak of terror.

Uncle's craggy face expressed the disdain of a man
who'd discovered a cockroach under his tongue. He
lowered the Flex back to the pile rather than ask
permission.

He shifted his gaze to Paul, his attention as visible as
a lighthouse beam. He took in Paul's stump, the blood-
stained handcuffs, Paul's oozing broach-wound. He
sized up Paul with the attitude of a man trying to
determine how to best stuff a puppy into a USPS
shipping container.

"He goes back," Uncle intoned. "New York's no place

to brew Flex – not with this other 'mancer on the loose. I'll get a U-Haul. We'll transport him to the Mexican border. I know a plane that can take him from there."

Had Paul said he'd rather be in the hands of a mastermind? He was wrong. Through Uncle's gray eyes, Paul saw himself viewed as not a man but a resource. He'd be enslaved, treated like cattle, stuck in a country that ran not on paperwork but on bribes and guns.

"He's mine."

Gunza interposed himself between Uncle and Paul, almost bumping chests. It was ludicrous. He was two thirds Uncle's size.

"You'll be rewarded," Uncle said. "You've done well to bring him to us."

"I didn't bring him to you."

"*You have done well to bring him to us.*" With those words, he offered a chance to rewrite history – to overlook all of Gunza's rebellion, offering him a place not on the throne but certainly within the throne's sight.

Gunza stepped back toward the tub of Flex on the table, fishing through it until he found the exact piece Uncle had dropped. He took one bite, crunching it with sapphire teeth, a wasteful chomp that sprayed thousands of dollars of Flex across the tile.

"*Mine,*" Gunza said.

Uncle's fist shot out, exploding in a spray of hot metal. Shrapnel bounced off the cabinets.

"*My eye!*" Gunza's brother yelled, clawing at his face. "*My fuckin' eye!*" Uncle, never hesitating, punched

Gunza with his good hand; Paul heard the crack of bone shattering as Uncle's arm collapsed, his forearm crumpling.

The chunk of metal dropped to the floor. Paul realized what it was now: a gun that had misfired so badly, the rounds had severed Uncle's fingers from his palm.

What transfixed Paul was Gunza's beatific expression of sorrow. He'd been floating on 'mancy for long enough, he'd lost the concept of being hurt. He stepped away as Uncle tried to kick him – literally *stepped*, with the calmness of a man walking around a fence – and poked Uncle in the throat with his fingers.

Uncle fell to the ground. It was unmanning, seeing that mixture of adulation and fear on that old hit man's face.

Gunza fumbled his own gun out. He wasn't half as efficient as Uncle's gunslinger draw.

"I – I have heard of the Flex," Uncle gurgled. "Seen it twice. But never – never like this–"

"Never will again," Gunza said, bored.

He shot Uncle. Then his brother.

He stood over his brother's body as his guards came running in; Paul could not see Gunza's expression. But Gunza's shoulders heaved, not quite crying, trying to jam too many emotions underneath before his men saw him waver.

Then he jerked his head back as if to stare at the ceiling, sniffing and squeezing his eyes shut. He thrust his hands elbow-deep into the tub, clenched the Flex in his fists as if he was prepared to fight the entire world. He began to snort a fresh batch – then stopped, palm halfway to his mouth.

One final moment of clarity, Paul realized. *If Gunza can walk away from this, here's where he does it.*

Gunza laughed and licked his palm clean.

"Move out," he barked. "We got more company coming."

TWENTY-ONE
Out of the Business

Paul had lots of time to think about Aliyah while he was chained to a radiator.

It had been two weeks, during a critical time in Aliyah's healing process. Maybe she'd been moved to a different hospital. Maybe Imani had wrangled the treatments Aliyah needed. Maybe Aliyah had beaten Super Mario.

Maybe Aliyah had died.

I'm sorry, Aliyah, he thought. *I've killed you.*

No, you didn't. You rescued her. The doctors said she'd inhaled enough smoke to kill her.

He remembered Aliyah shrieking as he put his hands on her, the smell of her roasting flesh. That was what 'mancy did. You changed the world at your loved ones' expense.

Paul was beyond a normal life. Whenever he thought of forms or organization, the Beast stirred. Even though Gunza beat him, shot at him, screamed at him, Paul couldn't stop.

Magic welled up from the core of Paul's being, an

extension of his personality. Paul *believed* organization was how humanity surpassed raw instinct. Mankind needed to keep records for fairness, rules to create level playing fields, laws to punish cheaters. Remembering and enforcing these things improved the world.

If he abandoned those beliefs, what kind of a father would he be?

If he *didn't* abandon them, what would he do to Aliyah?

"It's better this way," he muttered, squeezing his stump. Even if he could slip the handcuffs, the guards outside would catch him crawling to freedom.

Had he ever thought he might catch Anathema? A cripple like him? Hell, he couldn't even tell the difference between a videogamemancer and... whatever the hell Anathema was.

At least he'd saved Valentine. He hoped. She'd been in bad shape the last time he'd seen her, and maybe SMASH had gathered her up after he'd healed the broach, but... he had no way of knowing, so he chose to believe that Valentine was off somewhere, happily playing her Nintendo.

Paul's world had been reduced to Gunza's reality shows, a cut that never healed, and the rusty radiator. Sometimes he nodded off and hit his head on that sharp-edged heater, causing flowing head wounds.

Gunza cleaned Paul's injuries. But no matter how thoroughly Gunza iodined, alcoholed, gauze-taped, or Bactined the broach wound on Paul's forearm, it always drooled blood.

Gunza had stopped feeding Flex to his guards. They hovered about the tenement Gunza had lucked into, attending to Gunza incessantly like overeager birds that plucked scraps from hippos' teeth.

Gunza munched Flex and locked himself inside the apartment, watching endless episodes of *16 and Pregnant*. The sameness drove Paul mad. He'd wake to a pregnant teen from North Carolina and doze off to a pregnant teen from Connecticut. Paul knew Anathema was still attacking – sometimes, when Gunza flipped channels, he caught maddening glimpses of CNN – but how bad were things?

A black girl from Michigan gave a speech about the responsibilities of being a parent, holding up a child who looked so much like Aliyah that it made Paul's heart ache.

"What the *fuck*?" Paul hissed.

Gunza stirred, a cat wondering if it had heard a mouse.

"You killed your brother," Paul said, clambering up onto the radiator. "You killed your enforcer. Now your family, and SMASH, and Lord knows who else are gunning for you. You're keeping me from my child, my daughter who is doubtless *frantic* because she thinks her *daddy* is *dead*...

"...and for what? So you can sit here, getting fat, waiting for the hammer to fall? You're a failure, Gunza. You can't manage an organization without a family to catch your sad ass. You're waiting for someone to take you out. It's pathetic.

"If you're gonna commit suicide," Paul finished, "leave me the fuck out of it."

Gunshots from outside. Gunza glanced in their direction like the kitchen timer had announced his TV dinner was ready. He strapped on his gun holster, then sat before Paul, legs crossed, an old 1960s hippie about to deliver a lecture.

"Been thinking," Gunza said. More gunshots, screams, accompanied by the pressure of a new 'mancy Paul could not name. "I'm out of the business."

"...you are?"

"Naw. Why do you play the game? Money? Pussy? Excitement?" He patted the tub. "That's all in these crystals. That's the error. All the other drugs I sold were an escape from a crappy life. *This* drug *rebuilds* lives."

Gunza padded over to the kitchen table as bullets punched through the kitchen walls, spraying dust and shattered tile into the air; he walked through gunfire like a man in a dream. He bent down to pick up a sloshing gasoline canister, then plunked it on the counter.

"Problem is, they seek me," Gunza continued, as if people weren't dying outside. "You take an eye, my family takes your skull and fucks it. We are factories of retribution. So how do you stop vengeance?"

A pube-mustached sad sack kicked in the door, clutching a Colt .45. It looked ludicrously large in his pasty hands. Behind him, the hallway was piled with bodies; an apartment of gangsters had tried and failed to stop this nebbish with a gun.

This guy? Paul thought. This *guy slaughtered Gunza's bodyguards?*

Then he felt the Flex.

It was a lower-grade Flex that gave him an instant headache – there was something migraine-inducing in that 'mancy, a fingers-on-chalkboard interference pattern that battered Paul's beliefs. Flux boiled around the reedy gun-kid in toxic clouds. He was a thunderhead, ready to explode.

Gunza didn't seem to care. He popped a fresh crystal and leaned into the gun, daring the nebbish to shoot.

The nebbish… broke. It was as though Gunza had woken a sleepwalker. The sad sack sobbed, looking back at the bodies with near-suicidal remorse…

Gunza brushed debris off his shirt, then opened the cap on the gasoline.

"We're gonna die in a fire," Gunza said, splashing gasoline all around the room. "Then we'll go somewhere remote. No inspectors. No SMASH. And I'll set up a lab, and you'll be my Flex bitch."

Paul clambered up farther on the radiator. He wished he could stand on two feet; people who used the saying as a metaphor for manhood never understood how childish hopping around made you feel.

"I'm not doing that." Paul hated the petulance in his voice. "That's not happening."

Gunza flicked a match. The flames curled around Gunza, the Flex pushing them away, but Paul had no such protection. The radiator steamed as the flames snaked across the floor. He yanked at the cuffs, trying to free himself.

The kid screamed something unintelligible and fired. The flux centered on the gun, blew the top of his head

off. The kid tumbled to the burning floor, remains-of-
face-first, blood sizzling into gasoline.

Gunza glanced back, as if surprised that hadn't
happened already, then returned his attention to Paul.

"Then I burn you like a marshmallow," Gunza
reiterated. "And I find your daughter, and I burn her
worse."

"You wouldn't."

"My father always told me, if you got to make
examples, start with kids. Kill a kid, you yank the
parent's heart out." Gunza rubbed the tub, an act akin
to summoning a genie. "Don't think I won't. I'll get
away with it, too."

But what would you do with more Flex? Gunza had
already killed a house full of gangsters, had taken to
torturing subordinates – he'd doubtless find more
exciting ways to kill people. Powered by Flex as he was,
no one could stop him.

It was getting harder to breathe; the flames and the
smoke were starting in earnest now, getting a good bite
on the wood. The air tasted like Aliyah's screams.

"You have to be stopped," Paul gasped.

"Who's gonna stop me?"

That's when the kid – headless, shirt aflame, and still
thoroughly dead – grabbed Gunza with stiffened
fingers.

TWENTY-TWO
Showdown

Gunza let out a shriek that satisfied Paul on levels he had never known he could be satisfied. It was like drinking cold water after days in the desert.

Gunza fired three shots through the dead kid's scrawny chest, which did nothing at all. The dead bodyguards in the hallway moaned, their tattoos crisping as they stumbled through the burning doorway, hands flapping at the end of broken arms, going for Gunza.

"You *fuck*!" Gunza said, frothing, emptying a clip into his former protectors. "You! Die!"

The headless dead kid, unimpressed, slapped the tub of Flex out of Gunza's hands.

Flex spilled everywhere, crystals crackling as they caught fire. They went up like popcorn, bursting into careening pinballs of neon 'mancy. Some entwined with the flame to create bright streaks that erased whatever they touched, eating holes in the floor. Some rolled into the zombies' ankles, who shuddered and healed themselves.

Paul squeezed his eyes shut as he recalled his power to him. The balls veered towards him – but Gunza shoved the dead nebbish aside to grab at them, his hands blistering as he intercepted the rolling balls of 'mancy...

...and they angled away from his fingertips, moving like fighter pilots in formation as they blasted through the kitchen wall, reducing the cabinets to splinters, bursting every last barrier between the kitchen and the apartment next door until only flames remained.

Valentine stood among the flames, brandishing a clipboard.

She wore an eye patch over her left eye, covering the gap where the SMASH agents had shot her. Her gothy prom skirt fluttered around her tattooed ankles as the stray Flex poured into her.

"*I* get all the power-ups in this game," she said.

"*Shoulda known!*" Gunza screamed, going for the biker's shotgun. "Been stockpiling 'mancy for weeks in case you showed. *Bring it on!*"

He brought the shotgun up in Valentine's direction. Paul lunged at Gunza, his wrist nearly breaking as the handcuff hauled him to a halt; with Gunza's Flex neutralizing Valentine's 'mancy, that shot would kill her.

Valentine shrugged. "Every power-up runs out."

She flicked the clipboard in Paul's direction.

Gunza directed his attention at the clipboard. A rain of burning timber tumbled from the ceiling, ready to bury it...

This is my *'mancy*, Paul thought, feeling insanely possessive. *You can steal my magic to dodge bullets, keep me imprisoned, even kill Valentine… But I am the fucking king of paper.*

Paul heard the Beast roar as he held out his hand, a sound like a million dot-matrix printer hammers falling at once, the sound of a billion file drawers slamming shut.

The clipboard sailed underneath the fire, arced around like a Frisbee to land in Paul's grip. And when he saw what Valentine had sent him, he laughed – because the clipboard held an answer so simple that he couldn't believe it hadn't occurred to him: *Revocation of Contract.*

"*What the fuck you laughing for, papermancer?*" Gunza yelled. "*You got no pen! What you gonna fill out, fucker? You dry!*"

"There are commitments far older than pens." Paul held up his bloody arm, as best he could. Then he smacked his dripping hand onto the "signature" portion of the paper.

Contract.

A booming sound. A sparkling firework hiss as the freed 'mancy flew into the air. The former Flex crystals gathered the flame in wispy, ill-formed arms, bringing bouquets of fire to Paul in silent offering.

He lowered his head, dismissing them.

Paul could not have told you why. He could have aimed the magic at Gunza, burning him worse than Aliyah. He could have reabsorbed them into his body, filling up on flux-free 'mancy; freed, they seemed to remember who they'd belonged to.

But his magic had been trapped for weeks in cold

cages of hematite. Putting them to service seemed...
disrespectful.

So he gave thanks and let go.

They bowed in gratitude before dissipating.

Gunza backed away – fearful, not beaten. The
zombies shuffled towards him. He swung the shotgun
towards Valentine.

"Back off," he said. "Or I'll ventilate."

"Really, Gunza?" Valentine glared skeptically from
her good eye. "You're gonna kill me with a shotgun...
in my own videogame?"

Undeterred, Gunza fired. A red life bar blinked into
existence above Valentine's trimmed black bangs, a slim
fraction chipping away as the gunfire ruffled her dress.

She reached behind her, making an audible *clack*.

"I've been thinking," she said conversationally, as the
gangbanger zombies immobilized Gunza. "I blamed
myself for Raphael's death for, like, a week. Then I
realized if you hadn't lent him the money, this would
never have happened. He was a terrible risk. Any
competent loan shark would have seen he'd never pay
you back. You lucked out and got me – but realistically,
all you should have gotten for your trouble was ten lost
large."

When Valentine took her hands out from behind her
back, she held a large, hi-tech bazooka. Her knees
buckled as she balanced it over her shoulder. A
viewfinder popped out, producing a green radar screen
that focused on the spot between Gunza's eyes. Gunza
begged for mercy, yanking at the arms of the kids he'd
killed as he struggled to free himself...

"I hate killing people," she sighed.

Gunza brightened. Then he looked down. His body had morphed into another nameless zombie.

Valentine grinned.

"But I *love* killing monsters."

She fired.

Gunza's organs ricocheted off the ceiling.

The other dead kids sagged, dissolving into pixels. Valentine let out a whoof, tucking the bazooka behind her back where it conveniently vanished, then picked her way through the kitchen's remains. The apartment complex was still aflame – but this was a natural fire, picking up speed but not deadly yet.

"I thought you might not come," Paul said, as she knelt to free him.

She scowled.

"No, I knew you'd come for me if you were alive," he clarified. Valentine untensed. "I never doubted. But I worried that the, you know, broach... or maybe the SMASH team..."

"Oh." She shook her head, grinning. She hiked up her shirt, revealing angry lightning-mark scars across her plump belly and breasts. "That broach will *fuck you up*. We gotta figure that shit out. I don't know what you did, but you keep doing things you shouldn't do. You reknit a broken universe, then get punked by a moron with a gun. You're a paradox, Paul."

"But... the SMASH team..."

"I'm Grand Theft Auto, Paul. They can't catch me." The sound of sirens. "Speaking of which, it's time to go." She tugged him into the hall.

"No." Paul pushed her away, leaning against the wall. "I'm the hostage. When they come, I've gotta be here. I'll tell them... tell them Gunza's sanity dissolved and I finally got my shot at him." He eyed Gunza's gibbets, splattered across the kitchen. "It's not *too* far from the truth."

"All right." Valentine hugged him. "I'm glad you're alive."

He sagged into her arms. "I'm gladder *you're* alive."

She lowered him to the floor, putting him well out of the flames' reach.

"By the way." She paused by the window. "Not a day passed without me stopping by the hospital to tell Aliyah her daddy was still alive."

She leapt outside, grabbing the drain spout and sliding down.

Paul allowed himself one brief sob. Then he crawled down the hall toward the incoming policemen, bracing himself for what would happen once he told the world he'd killed yet another 'mancer.

INTERLUDE #2
Anathema, Wreathed in Blood

Two hundred and fifty-six.

That's how many people *should* have died in the shootout, Anathema thought. She'd carefully architected the progressions, the deaths doubling with each incident, building up to thousands killed with each dosage.

And she'd done everything right, hadn't she? She'd found the perfect sacrificial lamb. She'd fed him the special Flex, which should have honed that fine obsession. Once he'd tasted blood, he should have put bullets through brains until his ammo ran dry.

Yet somehow, the rulemancer had sapped her target's will.

Anathema flattened her palms against her thighs to calm herself, sitting cross-legged before the crackling bonfire. She inhaled warm summer air through her nostrils, the wind infused with animal shit; she exhaled, and felt the stars wheel above her.

The tall grass stretched out all around her, the bonfire made in a small, flattened path of a vast field never once cut by human hands. The night rustled with the sound of beasts making their way across the savannah.

She wanted to hunt. To fill her belly with bleeding meat. Yet even here, in her cave-that-was-the-world, she could smell the rulemancer's stink. His desires, brimming with inked letters and printed contracts, shrank her refuge's boundaries; did he even know he was doing it? Her world shrank all the same, its borders retreating like a lion before the whip.

It was unfair. The rulemancer had the whole city dancing to his tune. She'd grown up strangled by all the restrictions the rulemancer loved: tennis's senseless scoring patterns, court mandated therapy, inheritance taxes. All that structure had made her dull, reliant. She'd barely had the wits to kill her own parents.

She'd birthed 'mancers to *fight* the shape of the world, not enforce it. How could she have spawned such a monstrosity?

And since *that* gestation had spiraled out of control, what else didn't she understand?

Anathema pushed the thought away, gripped her spear. Her harvest glittered at the darkness's edge, a blazing firefly green. *That* was something she could never have done back when others called her Bethany. Nor could she have stalked great beasts, shoving spears into the hearts of lions.

What she knew was that policemen and gardeners and garbage men were extensions of his will, carrying the rulemancer's influence to the heart of her domain. And when she felt his inflexible orders surrounding her, she felt frail as a library-loving teen, tranked to the gills on sadness-dampening medications, as if all this wildness she'd created was just some way of acting out.

She slashed her forearms, smearing blood all over herself. *Acting out*. That was rulemancer terminology, using words to cage emotions. Wild beasts do not think about acting out.

Wild beasts *acted*.

She charged into the veldt, spear held high, knowing tonight she would find the most dangerous animal she could envision. It would try to kill her, and if she wasted a single thought on *acting out* or *self-harm* or *dissociative disorder*, the beast would devour her rebellious, stupid brains.

In this way, Anathema would burn the fetters that restrained her.

If she survived – and she always had – then she would hunt down this rulemancer. Perhaps she had created him. It didn't matter. He irritated her. Did anyone need any more reason than that to swat a fly?

She would hunt, and she would feast, then hunt again. And when she was done, she would peel the flesh from the rulemancer's bones and wear him as a coat.

PART II

Gonna Burst Into Flame

TWENTY-THREE
Rebuild the Facade

When he'd been held hostage, Paul had worried: what if he flinched when he saw Aliyah?

He'd tried to remember Aliyah's burnt face, but that had seemed like a betrayal of the promise he'd made that one day she would be whole again. So instead, he'd envisioned her old, unscarred face... And now, as he was escorted to meet Aliyah for the first time in two weeks, he hoped he wouldn't be shocked by her half-melted eyelids.

Then he saw her, and she was so beautiful, he wept.

The blisters had turned to scabs and scar tissue knotted across her body. She was wrapped in bandages still, to keep the small patches of healthy skin safe just in case by some miracle the plastic surgeries got approved.

But she was, the doctors had told him, safe enough to hug.

After she'd embraced him, she held out a paper chain of colorful cardboard crudely taped together.

"Aunt Vallumtime said if I made a link every day you were away, you'd come back."

She draped the chain around his neck, a hero's welcome. The press snapped photos from a discreet distance, held back by a row of nurses; Paul loathed them, but at this point, you either let the reporters in or they kicked the door down.

"I'll always come back for you," he promised, smelling her little-girl smell, locking away this moment so he'd always carry it with him.

"…did you kill him?" she whispered. "Did you kill the 'mancer who hurt me?"

I didn't shoot myself, no. Then he remembered: he'd told the police Gunza was a 'mancer.

"…no. Not yet."

"That's what Vallumtime told me. But he did 'mancy." She ran her fingertips along the furrow the buzzsects had left in his forearm. She smeared his blood like fingerpaint. "And he hurt you. Did you kill him?"

"He's dead, Aliyah."

She clasped his hands in hers, pressing them against her forehead. For a moment, Paul thought she was praying, then realized she was crying, for the first time since Gunza had taken him.

Aliyah had always hated crying. Even as a baby, she'd never wailed; she'd just given aggravated little hiccups. Her secrecy was genetic, a gift from her mother.

Paul clutched her hands. And when she was done, she gave him a shy and mischievous grin, as if to tell Paul she'd never admit this moment had happened.

"We can both sleep now," she said, then hugged him like she would never let him go.

● ● ●

When Aliyah had passed out and the press had been chased away, Imani and David tiptoed in.

Paul felt a swell of self-loathing at the sight of his ex-wife. Yes, he was the hero of the day, the man who'd killed a 'mancer... but he was also forced to totter around on crutches until they could fit him for a new foot.

He never felt more like a cripple than when Imani looked at him. Except she looked lessened now, weakened. She looked carved by disappointment, her beautiful face harrowed by grief.

She began to say hello – but her politician boyfriend, David, moved to intercept him. Paul hid his embarrassing left arm behind his back; he forever had to wrap it in gauze, the graze left by the buzzsects never healing. It was like having a goddamned maxipad strapped to your arm.

"Glad to have you back, sir!" David said, pumping his hand. Paul had known David could turn on the charm when he had to – but as the ex-husband, he'd never experienced it personally. Paul was glad to see his "hero of the day" aura winning out.

"Good to see you, Paul," Imani said – not quite frosty, but a definite nip of autumn. Which perplexed Paul: *When I was on the force, you begged me to take risks.*

"How's she *really* been doing?" Paul asked, squeezing Aliyah's toe. She slept deeply, the hours of photo ops having taken their toll.

Imani squeezed Aliyah's other toe, a joint parental show of affection. "She never stopped asking about you. Kept acting as though she could trick us into saying you'd be all right, you'd come home."

"She likes knowing what the rules are…"

"…so she can break every last one," Imani finished. Her grin warmed a little, then she bowed her head. "I couldn't promise her you'd come back."

"No." Paul realized the awful position he'd put Imani in. "Of course you couldn't."

"I mean… It's good you're back on your game," Imani continued, blushing. "It's rare anyone survives a one-on-one encounter with one 'mancer, let alone two. I never told Aliyah, but… I thought that painting bitch had taken your leg, and the dealer would take the rest of you."

David had stepped away discreetly to examine the television. Imani kept talking, the words spilling out like water from a cracked water cooler.

"But when we had Aliyah, you'd been off the beat for years. You'd given up. And if I'd thought… you know, you were…"

"…going to put myself in danger?"

"…then maybe, you know, things would have been different."

At first, Paul believed Imani regretted divorcing him, a satisfying thought: *Oh, you would have stuck around if you knew I'd face down 'mancers? What if I was one?*

But then he heard what she was really saying:

If I'd known you were headed back into the line of fire, I wouldn't have had Aliyah.

That idea knotted in Paul's chest like a heart attack. They'd agreed to have a child for the same dumb reason married couples had for generations: *Maybe the baby would bring us closer together.* Of course, it hadn't. Aliyah had consumed the last of their romance, externalizing all their love so it sat in one adorable, rebellious ball between them.

Now he realized: she'd had a child with him because Paul had been *safe*. Like a neutered cat who didn't try to get out any more.

"Why *now*?" Imani asked. "You're excited about work again. That's good. But why *now*?"

"Because there's someone who hurts little girls to make a point?" *And because*, he thought with a shameful teenaged horniness, *I get to do magic to stop him.*

"Something happened when your apartment caught fire." Imani narrowed her eyes. "It's made you driven. Reckless. What happened in there?"

"Nothing happened, Imani. This was what you wanted me to be, wasn't it? Driven?"

"I wanted you *career*-driven. Not chained to a radiator and shot in the *head*!"

"I–"

"I'm not lying for you anymore, Paul. If you get kidnapped again and Aliyah asks me where you are, next time I'll tell her: Daddy's out committing suicide. And I don't know why you–"

"–a word with you, Paul?"

David squeezed his shoulder.

Paul did not slap David's hand away. If he did, he'd start punching David in his good-looking politician's ambitious little weaselface, and if that happened, then he'd keep punching until his knuckles hit the back of David's skull.

Imani tucked her hands in her armpits, plainly furious she'd let her ex-husband under her skin again. The grateful look she gave David for defusing the argument made Paul feel even more inadequate.

"Now's not a good time, David." Paul wrestled his crutches up underneath him, retreating.

"I understand that." David was so agreeable, he'd probably have let Paul pop him one. "I just wanted to suggest perhaps you should hold a press conference."

"I let them in here. That's enough."

"It really isn't." And Paul almost did punch David then, because David's sharp *I-know-politics-better-than-you* tone was like rubbing a salt-rimmed margarita against a cold sore.

"You know Anathema's next attack will kill two hundred and fifty-six people," David said.

"Five hundred and twelve."

"Not unless there's been another assault we're unaware of," David laughed nervously.

Paul said nothing. He'd felt Anathema's hand in the attack on Gunza's stronghold. It must have been her; who else could have made that Flex? And though forty-two people had been shot in the apartment complex battle, Paul had the nagging feeling it would have been far worse without him...

"Regardless, Anathema's still killing people," David continued. "Last night, eight people were murdered on suspicion of 'mancy. Other people are dying because the 911 lines are overloaded. Legitimate calls are crowded out by panicky people reporting 'mancers because they saw pigeons acting weird. And why not? Anything could be 'mancy. We don't even know what kind of 'mancer Anathema is. Eventually, a riot will break out, and then thousands will get hurt."

"That's terrible. But what do you want me to do?"

"You've survived not one 'mancer assault, but two, a modern record. It'd be a help to the city, calming the waters, if you just told the reporters that you think Anathema will be caught soon."

"And *will* he?"

"If the mayor had any good news to report, any leads at all," David asked, "do you think we'd be asking you for PR?"

That news sank in. Paul's stomach squirmed.

"The good news is," David continued, "we've gotten some federal funding to help the victims of Anathema's 'mancy. I've asked Imani; with your permission, we'll name the fund after Aliyah."

Paul tensed. His 'mancy should be fixing his daughter's face, not boosting the career of the man who'd cuckolded him.

"...How much will she get?" Paul asked.

"Donations have been pouring in. As the first injured, and your daughter, Imani thinks we might get enough to repair her face."

"That's good." Paul felt sick. He could help his daughter but only by pretending the government was competent. He'd do it, of course – he'd swallow any indignity for Aliyah – but that didn't mean he had to endure David for longer than he had to. He jabbed his crutches against the hospital floor, hopping away.

David ambled alongside, oblivious to how insulting his easy gait was to a man lacking a foot. "There's a fundraising dinner next Saturday. We can sit you next to the mayor. But publicity has a short half-life, Paul – like Flex. If you don't use it, it drains away."

Paul stumbled into the elevator. "That's not the way Flex works."

"Tell that to the press, not me."

On the way to his office, Paul regretted not getting a temporary wheelchair. But being left with one leg was bad enough. He would not suffer the indignity of having people push him around.

Though after heaving himself out of the hospital, into a taxi, and through Samaritan Mutual's lobby, Paul was reconsidering.

He slumped against a desk, taking a moment to appreciate Samaritan's darkened offices. Offices after closing hours always had a pleasant feeling of camaraderie; anyone on the night shift was your brother. You enjoyed the low-key dimmed lights, the lack of phone calls, the way you could show up in a ragged T-shirt because it was 10pm on a Friday night and you were here; your mere presence was all you needed to impress.

Not that Paul ever dressed down. He *liked* suits. And crisp ties. They were armor for the civilized man. At best, he'd roll up his sleeves, and that only because it looked totally badass.

Only a badass could track down Anathema.

The good news was, bureaucracy excelled at finding

overlooked things. If you were devoted and thorough, you could knit together enough leads to topple a President.

…which, he thought, frowning, was the flaw in his 'mancy. Valentine's magic was flashy – the world now knew the woman who'd brought down the SMASH team was the videogamemancer who'd unleashed the rain of frogs – but once cast, you couldn't trace it back to her.

Whereas when Paul had gotten the home to cook Flex, he'd 'manced it at a sheriff's auction, put it in someone else's name, transferred funds to a forged checking account to pay for it. But if someone like Kit dug in, Paul's name would turn up somewhere.

That was bad for Paul.

Paul would be worse for Anathema.

Paul eyed the paper taped to his office door. An exterminator's notice, listing every kind of infestation that could take place in New York – right down to "mealworms" and "deer ticks" – then certifying there was no evidence of vermin.

A plastic Mickey Mouse doll sat on Paul's desk. It burst into a stiff, arm-flailing rendition of "M-I-C, K-E-Y, M-O-U-S-E" at Paul's entrance. Taped to it was a note from Kit: *Told you there were rats.*

Paul plopped into his chair. He had plenty of work to do… but it was good to be back in his comfort zone.

His file cabinets cracked open. The tops of forms poked out shyly.

"Hello, lads," Paul said, smiling – and the papers leapt out, marching around him in a flapping parade, doing fluttering dances at his return. Then they slid back into their drawers, jittering in anticipation.

Paul pulled open one of two special drawers, the one that would be locked if anyone but him tugged the handle. This was the drawer that contained information – he could reach in and pull out records from anywhere, FBI reports, loan payments, corporate finance records. The first drawer worked as long as he could fill out the internal requests contained in the *other* special drawer, the one that provided him with blank copies of every printed form ever made.

Now he flipped through the request chain, pulling up police reports. Anathema's Flex bombs hadn't hit the same place twice. She–

Paul stopped. Something was lacking.

"Oh, yeah," he muttered, then turned on the radio. NWA's "Straight Outta Compton" flowed into the office. Ridiculous, perhaps, for a bureaucromancer to groove so hard to the thug life... but to hunt Anathema, he'd have to be a dangerous motherfucker who raises hell.

Paul bobbed his head as his paperwork assistants retrieved the SMASH files. Sure enough, Anathema had struck twice while Gunza held him:

Sixty-four people working at an Internet travel agency had died when a wannabe pilot with 20/100 vision had been the only one available on a small prop jet after both pilots had been struck blind. It had been his deepest dream, his wife had said, to fly a real plane... which he did magnificently, for approximately twelve minutes, before both wings sheared off, causing the plane to plow through the roof of the travel agency's office.

One hundred and twenty-eight racetrack watchers had been trampled when a desperate jockey, who'd never had a big win in a decade-long career, had been dosed with Flex. The state-mandated black opals installed at the entry to each stall had shattered, informing the racetrack owners of 'mancy – but by the time they realized the race had been rigged, the other fifteen horses in the race had panicked. Their muzzles foamed as if lions were chasing them, and they leapt in improbably high arcs to trample the spectators. A hundred and nineteen spectators were already dead, as were eight jockeys, as was the dosed jockey who crossed the finish line, saw the carnage behind him, then clutched his chest and died.

Paul looked over the records. Anathema had a knack for finding ignorant people with odd obsessions. She found friendless, isolated people – then fed them low-grade Flex and set them loose.

The targets. They seemed random, but… Paul sensed a pattern.

Also strange: the abundance of survivors. A gas main explosion that violent should have killed everyone in Paul's apartment complex. Likewise, a plane had crashed into a crowded office, wounding hundreds with shrapnel but killing comparatively few. There had been an abundance of broken legs at the Aqueduct – but given the crowd of twelve thousand, a hundred and twenty-eight deaths was slim.

Anathema was injuring far more than she killed.

Was that terrorism? Paul didn't think so. Anathema had made no demands. And as he brought up the FBI's secret files on Anathema, he realized that even though the profilers couldn't detect any clear pattern, he felt one.

She was *building* toward something.

Was his 'mancy trying to tell him something? Or was that his detective's instinct dredging up some message from his subconscious? •

Paul gorged himself on information until SMASH reports piled up in drifts around his feet, inhaling details on every one of Anathema's Fluxsplosions – the nursing ward, the model runway, the cookie factory, the old-age hospital. He submerged himself in data, trying to figure out what linked all these attacks…

A knock on his door. The reports darted back into their folders like startled birds. Who the hell was interrupting him at *this* time of night?

What startled Paul was how bright it was outside. And how scratchy his face was. And how large the bag of donuts was that Kit was carrying.

"*Someone's* worked all night." Kit pushed a hot coffee into Paul's hands. "What, two weeks of torture wasn't enough to get you to take a day off?"

Paul tugged the sticky gauze pad off his left arm; it was soaked. He must have studied for hours.

"It's Anathema." He gulped the coffee gratefully, feeling its warm sweetness fill his stomach.

"What'd you find?" Kit leaned back against a leather-bound set of regulations, grinning. Paul had seen that admiring grin before, in Central Park, where Kit endlessly railbirded chess games. Kit loved watching an opponent doggedly play against a superior talent, losing again and again, refusing to quit until they'd learned *something* from the battle.

"She's an anarchomancer," Paul said.

Kit frowned. "How do you figure?"

Paul fanned the reports across his desk. "Everything she's hitting – it's some aspect that binds us together as a people. The cookie plant? Processed food. The nursing home? People that old die without hospitals. The horse racing? Gross spectacle. The Internet travel agency? The Internet, obvious. The plastic surgery patients and runway models? Helpless femininity. She's hitting targets that are all... *civilizationy*."

That wasn't all, though. Anathema's flux had tangled with his, like two dogs snarling at the end of leashes; her 'mancy opposed his bureaucracy. Anathema was tearing down the things he wanted to raise up...

Kit sucked in his cheeks. "That's... pretty thin, Paul."

"Do I question *your* hunches?"

Kit sighed. "...All right, bubeleh. When you get your reports in for the cops, you can peddle this 'anarchomancer' theory. Then you'll have a nice talk with all those reporters who've been waiting ever so patiently for you. But you can't keep pulling all-nighters. You've got a girlfriend to tend to."

"...I do?"

"Not that you *told* me – hey, I guess you date someone a decade younger, you don't want to mouth it about – but I have to say Imani was *not* thrilled by your new squeeze hanging around Aliyah–"

Paul made the time-out sign. "Wait, wait. Valentine?"

"The cute pudgy goth kid? With the manga turtle tattoo. And the eye patch."

Bowser, Paul almost corrected him – then realized that if Kit thought Valentine's Super Mario tattoo was a manga turtle, that was for the best.

"No, no, no. Not my type. All my crushes are like Imani – thin, willowy, unattainable. I think I get off on being rejected."

"I think you *don't* get off unless it's a challenge," Kit riposted.

"Anyway, Valentine's just a friend."

"A *good* friend. She was there every night for Aliyah. That girl's never had younger siblings – you can tell by the way her shoulders tense around kids – but... whenever Aliyah got upset, she'd talk about how brave you were, then walk her through another Mario level." Kit scratched his temple. "You should tell Imani that you're not dating Valentine. Aliyah's calling her 'Aunt Valentine.' Your kids don't call someone 'Auntie' unless there's a long family history or short, hot sex."

"*Kit!*" There was always something extra naughty about the old Jewish guy talking about fucking. "I don't think of Valentine that way."

Kit waggled bushy gray eyebrows. "Did you have *that* amputated, too?"

"Christ, Kit, she's a *kid*. Show some respect."

"Sorry."

The silence made Paul feel like he'd somehow rebuked Valentine.

"She… she makes me feel like I can *do* things," he clarified. "I mean, does she know my daughter? Hell, no. But she meets the kid once and suddenly they're best friends. I like the way she follows her emotions."

Kit nodded stiffly. Paul recognized the gesture. Kit often said the best way to get people to open up was not to judge… and Kit was conspicuously not judging.

"…and that's good for you?"

"It's different." Paul picked his way through the minefield. "I mean, you know, Imani – if she met a handicapped kid, she'd be asking all sorts of questions like 'What responsibilities will we be taking on here?' Valentine just catapults herself into things. It's… exciting."

And it *was*, Paul realized. He'd just been kidnapped for two weeks, humiliated, near death. The army was sniffing after him. Gunza's superiors were hunting him. He was hunting a terrorist.

Yet he'd never felt more alive.

"There's a fire in your eyes now, kid," Kit said. "The Paul I knew last month would never have charged in after a Flex dealer. And, you know, we're gonna endure some management shakeout from that, but… it's better than depressed, divorced Paul. Where'd you meet her?"

That was a little close for comfort.

"…support group." Paul looked a little shamed. Kit, as planned, let him off the hook.

"Well, let's toast to new friends." He lifted his coffee cup. "Then I take you to my barber."

"What? Why?"

"For a straight-razor shave before your press conference."

"Oh, come *on*, Kit…"

"You will tell them how easily Anathema will be beaten once the heavy hitters weigh in. You will remind them Samaritan Mutual is not just an insurance company but an investigative agency, and that we know how to find 'mancers."

"You want me to *showboat*?"

"I want you to bitch-slap Anathema on the front page of every paper. And do it before our bosses find out I called this press conference. I want you linked with us so they can't fire you."

"Should we really be taunting 'mancers?"

"She's too smart for revenge. Our best profilers have called her out on national television. She hasn't bitten."

"But…"

"*But* we haven't had two 'mancers active in New York since the 1950s," Kit said. "LA? New Orleans? Those hellholes have always been ley lines of activity. New York? We've been clean for *decades*. This influx scares the hell out of us – we thought we were immune. So, play into that. Keep Mr Payne thinking it'd be bad PR to fire a popular figure… and nothing's more popular than the mundane who kills 'mancers."

Paul despaired. He'd been the poster boy for anti-magic hatred back after the illustromancer. Faking that smile had damn near killed him.

"Yet we may have actually learned a lesson from history. We're not dithering like they did after World War II, when all the European refugees flooded in. SMASH is reorganizing after the assault on their headquarters, the mayor's making speeches, and

Samaritan is getting tasked with hunting." Kit took a bite of a glazed donut, closing his eyes in satisfaction. "Every 'mancer in NYC will be dead or in the army before year's end."

"You want them all dead?"

"I want them Refactored." Kit's smile was vulpine, the bared teeth before the checkmate. "That way, they remember what they lost."

As Kit took another donut from the bag, Paul wondered: *How long before Kit figures out the truth?*

TWENTY-FOUR
Important Discussions by Videogame Light

Walking into a home you had conjured out of paperwork was a thrill that only magic could provide.

Finding a good apartment in New York City normally took a month, but real estate agents couldn't work Paul's magic. And so it was that Paul had handed a set of keys to Valentine, along with a Visa gift card loaded with a couple thousand dollars from his savings, and said, "Set our home up with something nice."

It *felt* magical, following his GPS to a new location. He was exhausted from his all-nighter, followed by a long press conference in which the reporters encouraged him to trash-talk, followed by a day-long meeting justifying his kidnapping to Mr Payne. He'd almost fallen asleep on Aliyah during his after-work visit.

Still, as Paul watched the GPS arrow approach this strange address, his hands shook with excitement; what would his new digs look like? He'd purposely not paid attention to the lease, trusting the Beast to find him something nice.

Plus, he'd left the décor to Valentine, a girl with crazy tastes. He'd told her to go nuts decorating, make the place her own. If the apartment was as crazy as her dresses, he might have to tone it down before he could settle in. He pictured his new living room as an explosion of Tim Burton set dressing, all bold colors and skewed angles. What art would she have bought? Would the sofa be one of those crazy ones you could barely sit on?

Imani had preferred staid furniture: frosted glass cabinets, stiff sofas. After years of enduring his wife's ladder-back rocking chairs, the idea of lounging in a bean bag felt like fucking without a condom.

He quivered with potential. The old Paul never would have allowed the universe to choose a home for him.

And his place had a doorman. A doorman! A pleasant Hispanic man in a red coat, smiling wearily as he opened the brass door to welcome Paul in.

The lobby floor's faded marble and faux-gold trim comforted him. Maybe nobody had the energy to scrub hard enough to eradicate the century's worth of cigar smoke that had saturated the walls, but the locals kept the floors swept clean.

This would be so satisfying.

Valentine's garish style might clash with the rent-controlled locals – what if he couldn't live with all those bright colors? – but still, opening up that door was like tearing the gift wrap off a birthday present.

He walked in.

What he got:

- Bare kitchen countertops strewn with crumpled Burger King bags and more crumpled Red Bull cans.
- A stack of unassembled IKEA boxes piled in the corner.
- A wide living room, bare but for a black futon and a wide-screen TV balanced precariously on the futon's box.
- Piles of videogames complete with clumps of cellophane where they'd been ripped open.
- Valentine sitting merrily on the futon, playing *Spyro the Dragon*.

She threw him a happy wave as he entered, not breaking eye contact with the TV. She whipped her head back and forth as she played; it seemed perplexingly hyperkinetic until Paul realized Valentine was compensating for her missing eye.

"Greetings, Herr Paulmeister!" she said cheerfully. "Please hold while I kill this boss monster."

Paul stared at the wreckage of his new place. He should have paid attention to her apartment, not her dress.

Paul started putting trash into a garbage can. She'd at least bought one of those, even if there was nothing in it but the receipt for its purchase.

He wasn't upset. While it would have been nice to come home to, well, a home, there was also a certain satisfaction in building your own space. Maybe Valentine didn't care where the TV was... but Paul would screw in the mounting hardware, set up the surround sound. Which was in itself excitingly transgressive, since Imani disapproved of television and would never have allowed this monstrosity inside her house.

Paul felt a flabby greasiness; he was picking up a used condom. Valentine paused the game.

"Ooh." She winced, plucking it from his fingers. "Sorry 'bout that. Wash your hands."

"You've had this apartment for thirty-six hours!" Paul complained, squirting Purell onto his fingers.

"Been living in my car for two weeks." She stuffed the moist condom into a Burger King bag. "I had a *lot* of pent-up energy."

"You couldn't just go home with someone?"

"Going home with a stranger? That shit's dangerous. And not everyone's so happy once they find out you've got the herp."

Paul made a face. "...So you weren't kidding about that."

"Had my first breakout the day after Gunza took you."

Paul felt miserable: here was Valentine, with a freshly missing eye and a flux-induced STD. Which she'd done to save his ass from the Army and Gunza.

"I'm sorry."

"Hey, chuckalucks." She tapped his chin with her knuckles. "I'd done the research. The world thinks herpes is the Scarlet Letter – but the truth is, you get a couple of breakouts a year, the rest of the time you're totes normal. If periods were a communicable disease, they'd be way worse." She smiled. "Not that I wanted to go viral. But I'll take the hit. For a good cause."

"I'm glad you think I'm a good cause."

She brightened. "Plus, turns out, if you post an ad on Craigslist saying you're a horny girl with herpes, guys will deliver themselves to your door like they were pizza." She pondered. "Pizza that lies about how big it is."

"How many guys have *been* here?"

She looked out the window. "…I had some energy."

"Jesus. You had more sex in one day than I had in my last year of marriage."

"I'd tell you to Craigslist some in, but let's be honest: casual-encounters-mancy doesn't work for the penis-laden. So, how was the paper chase?"

He flopped down on the chair. The last thirty-six hours crashed down around him. "Well, I, uh, called Anathema out in a press conference."

"Really."

"Did you see it on the news?"

She picked up the controller, unpausing the game. "I stopped watching television a week ago. The newscasters kept saying how SMASH was closing in on me. Weirded me out."

"That makes two of us. Did you get any leads on him?"

"I'm just the weapon, Paul. Point me at someone, I'll pulverize 'em with my many violent antics."

"Come on, you can't even do a radar search?"

"He's somewhere in New York; I know that. The minute I zoom in, it fuzzes out."

"You telling me some random mage can blur the screens of Valentine DiGriz? I saw you take down a SMASH team."

Her shoulders tensed. "…Yeah."

Wasn't she eager for adventure? Paul thought, confused. "Come on, Valentine. We need to find Anathema before she–"

She flung the controller to the hardwood floor. "And that's *my* responsibility?"

"I thought you'd want to help." *How much have I taken Valentine for granted?* "I – I'm not sure if I can find her myself…"

"Oh, great. Some nutso bitch decides to take out the city, and *I'm* the only one standing in the way? The person you want to stop this citywide thread is not SMASH, not the cops, not the insurance agents who are paid to fucking do it – but the girl who's been homeless for two fucking weeks, searching for her best friend?"

"No, but – Anathema's killed people. If she strikes again–"

"*Let her!*" Valentine scrubbed tears from her cheeks. "I've done my duty! Don't tell me I don't deserve a, a day off! Don't tell me I don't deserve a few days in a, a really nice apartment, with a bed that's not all itchy, and *blankets*, and…"

She started to cry but squelched her tears in a convulsive effort. Paul moved towards her, then paused in mid-gesture, unsure how to comfort her; a hug seemed too intimate, a pat on the shoulder too callous. All the while, Valentine drew her legs up underneath her, breathing heavily.

"…you don't know," she muttered, reproaching herself. "You don't know."

"Know what?"

She looked up at the ceiling. Paul thought she was trying to avoid crying, but after a moment, he noticed the engraved designs above them. "This is a really nice apartment, Paul. Maybe the nicest I've ever lived in." She sighed. "We're not gonna have it for long."

"The contracts are secure. Even if we're late with the payments, I can stall eviction for months."

She chuckled. "That answer's so *you*, Paul. Such a new fish."

"I've rented apartments before."

She put her hand on his chest. "Stop. You're a kid playing with Christmas toys, all starry-eyed. But... the flux comes and you lose things. This isn't the first time I've lived out of my car. Not the first time I've lost a boyfriend, either... though usually, they just leave. Or cheat. Or both. It's always awful, though. It has to be. The flux has to rip you up..."

Raphael. He'd barely given that poor kid a thought, but of course it was all Valentine thought about.

How could he be such a terrible friend?

"It wasn't your fault," Paul reassured her. "The SMASH team, they pushed when they were supposed to pull back..."

"That's not the point. The point is, this? It all goes away. One day, you'll need some really cool magic, and you'll need a downside. This apartment? Gone. And I'm back on the street. I don't know how I've managed to keep the car. Someday, I'll flux that away and then I'll be sleeping in alleyways. Then what will I do? I'm a videogamemancer. How the hell can I do magic when I'm a bum pushing a fucking shopping cart?"

She barked a humorless laugh.

"You'll find a way. I believe in you."

"It's not about believing. It's about... I want a few days in a nice, warm house with working plumbing and heat and pizza delivery. Because I won't have this after the next hunt. I won't have anything ever."

"That's nonsense. You'll rebuild."

"I'll rebuild it and burn it all. You're new to this, Paul, but... When you're a 'mancer, everything goes away. Because everything comes second to your love of magic. And the magic never loves you back."

Paul pulled away, offended. "The magic never loves you *back*?"

"...no," she said, and began crying in earnest.

He pressed the controller into her hands. "Play."

"I don't want to–"

"No. I mean *play*. Let it loose, Valentine."

"The neighbors – they're old ladies – I've been laying low–"

"Fuck them." Expletives were a delightful new taste on his tongue. "These things? They're childhood friends. They loved you when no one else would. Now *invite them out to play*."

Uncertain, she swapped out consoles, then pressed start. Cartoon cars zoomed to a stop up along a rainbow road, engines rumbling. The road looped out around purple mountains.

Three chimes counted down. Valentine gunned the accelerator.

The apartment lurched.

Rainbows streamed out of the big-screen television

to slide underneath them. A cherry-scented wind whooshed past as the futon was lifted up, tilted from side to side, metamorphosed into a small red buggy. The screen widened as the futon leapt forward, merging with Valentine's car to swerve across the winding roads.

As players, they were immortal; falling into a lava pit only slowed them down. They drove through immense castles, across snowy landscapes, their tires kicking up sand on tropical beaches.

Paul flung his hands in the air rollercoaster-style as burly Bowser zoomed past them, Princess Peach darting between them; it was a friendly race on a friendly day, and Peach waved at Valentine as she plowed the futon through a shimmering box to emerge with a trio of orbiting turtle shells.

Valentine whooped as she rounded the first curve, the wind from the screen drying her tears. She waved back, greeting her oldest buddies before dropping banana peels in front of them. They whooped as they careened off the road, their merry defeat a part of the game.

The garbage can tipped over, tilting with them as Valentine skidded across the finish line. The crowd's cheers vibrated the walls, the other racers pumping their fists in joy as the neighbors pounded on the floor to silence the noise.

The futon dropped to the floor with a clatter, collapsing into a heap of splintered wood.

"First!" Valentine hoisted the controller above her head like a trophy. He hadn't seen a real smile from Valentine since she'd started wearing that pirate's patch, and it did his heart good.

Gold coins poured out from the screen, exploded in fireworks.

"I had a life without magic." Paul ran his fingers reverently through the firework-sparkles, poured glittering remnants into Valentine's hand. "Maybe you get four walls, three meals, and two weeks of vacation. But you give up one thing. And you spend your life wondering what happened to it."

"Pretty slick salesmanship, Paul."

"I'm only selling what I believe. And believe this: as long as I'm slinging spells, I'll 'mance you a home. I won't *let* you sleep in alleyways."

"Pinky promise?"

He held out his pinky solemnly. "Pinky promise."

"If any of my boyfriends made that promise, I'd laugh 'til I cried," she said. "But when you say it, I believe you."

"That's because I don't make promises I don't keep."

"You realize I do, right? All the time. Scandalously. Trivially."

"Good to know."

She shook her head, reached down to tousle Aliyah's paper-chain necklace which, Paul realized, he was still wearing. "You're a good man, Paul Tsabo. Now get some fucking sleep."

And despite the broken futon and his always-bleeding arm, Paul was gone.

TWENTY-FIVE

Lost in Mario Land

Paul didn't visit Aliyah these days so much as he visited Mario Land.

"Go left. *Left*, daddy!" Aliyah told him. She'd shoved the Nintendo into Paul's hands, was making him play again. "See the pipe?"

"It's a green sewer pipe, Aliyah," he said, trying not to show how much he hated playing. He humored her out of guilt, but three days spent maneuvering a stereotypical Italian plumber through endless mazes tried his patience.

He looked over to Valentine for help; she made a *do what you gotta do* face and flicked her pink-nailed fingers towards the screen. Paul felt as though Valentine and Aliyah had formed a secret cabal when he was away; he knew they had long conversations. But in his presence, Valentine clammed up and let Paul take the lead, pretending insouciance but watching from the corner of her eye.

"It's another sewer pipe." He moved to put the DS down. "Why don't we do some puzzles instead?"

"*No!* Go on the pipe. *On* the pipe! Now press down."

Paul obeyed, sighing. Mario hunched down, sliding into the pipe, then dropped into another room with a splash.

"It's a fish level, Daddy! The hidden aquarium. Swim right. Don't hit the fishes."

"That's nice, Aliyah." He placed the Nintendo screen-down at the foot of her bed; Valentine scratched her chin in an *I-wouldn't-do-that* gesture. "Why don't I read to you instead, Aliyah?"

"*No!*" She shoved the game back into his hands. "You have to see!"

"I'm not rewarding temper tantrums, Aliyah," he said sternly. "And I'm tired of playing games."

"They're not games." Aliyah scrubbed her eyes, near tears. "Mommy thinks they're games. Uncle Kit thinks they're games. My stupid fore-friends think they're games. But you know! She showed you!"

Paul had the uncomfortable feeling of tuning into a favorite television show after missing several critical episodes. "Who showed me what, Aliyah?"

She flung the Nintendo on the floor. Valentine shrugged: *Told you.*

"*Aliyah!*" He picked it up. One of its screens had cracked. "There is *no* excuse for breaking Aunt Valentine's gift!"

Aliyah looked at Valentine, then burst into tears. How could children make you feel so guilty for yelling when they were the ones misbehaving? But Paul couldn't help it – Aliyah had been through so much with the burns and his kidnapping that even this seemed to lie under a large umbrella labeled "My Fault."

He swept her into a careful embrace, muttering apologies, unsure what he was apologizing for. She hugged him back immediately, and Paul felt a wave of gratitude; whatever she was mad at, she still needed him so hard it hurt.

"You should know," Aliyah cried. "Valentine told me you were there. But I never found you."

"Found me where?"

"In the castle! She said if the real world became too scary, I could always walk with Mario. Nothing in the castle could hurt me for real. And there were always hidden doors and gold coins, and if I looked hard enough in the hidden places..."

"You can always find what you need," Valentine finished, stroking the strange stubble on Aliyah's scalp.

Paul felt sick. "...and you needed me."

"So, you need to know the *castle*!" Aliyah cried. "Because I couldn't find you last time! I checked every door and every mirror and every pond. So, you – you have to know how to find me. I can't find you. You have to know where to go so we can *meet*."

Paul envisioned his daughter, burned and lonely, endlessly playing Mario levels searching for him. "You told her I was in *there*?" he whispered at Valentine.

She stiffened, bracing for a fight. "It worked for me when I was a kid."

"But what if I'd... I'd..."

He couldn't say *died* in front of Aliyah, but the thought burrowed into his consciousness: his insane daughter, thumbs blistered, trying to find her dead, dead daddy in an imaginary castle.

He realized what a foolish risk he'd taken to rescue Valentine. That was the stupid thing about parenting: the mundane stuff took up so much of your life, you forgot all this pointed towards the future. You spent your days strapping your kids into backseats, reading them bedtime stories, making bowls of cereal for them. That's what you did as a parent: create routines to make the world seem safer.

If you weren't paying attention, you'd forget the tasks were not the job.

Then there would be moments where your kid revealed a surprising complexity. As young as Aliyah was, she still had strange worlds captured within her that she didn't quite have the capacity to share. She'd gotten glimpses outside that safe, padded, Advanced Placement-school cage Paul and Imani had tried to build for her – but ever-suspicious Aliyah knew there were much harder choices and had always sought to find them before they found her.

Aliyah was still so baffled by the *idea* of death that her grief took on the form of an investigation; she was still collecting data on it, like a policeman drawing a chalk outline around a body. Which was good. Because when she'd *really* begun to comprehend the idea of "Daddy being gone forever", instead of breaking down…

…she'd asked Valentine.

What was I supposed to tell her? Valentine asked in a taut frown. *It's not like I had great parental experience. So I taught her my survival skill. And it was fucked up and wrong, but it was all I knew.*

Paul realized why Valentine was so quiet when he was around Aliyah: she was studying him. Taking lessons in case one day she had to do this again.

He buried his face in what was left of Aliyah's hair to stop himself from crying.

I won't leave you again, he promised. *Never*. He squeezed Valentine's hand in forgiveness.

"Why didn't you talk to Mommy, sweetie?"

"...She's a fore, too."

"...A four-two?"

"A 'before','" Valentine clarified. "Like all the kids in her school. They knew her from before."

Aliyah nodded so fiercely, Paul had to yank his head back. "All they ever talk about is my burns. I'm not a burn."

"No," Valentine reassured her, brushing a nonexistent lock of hair away from Aliyah's scarred forehead. "No, you're not."

"Vallumtime's an after-friend. She never talks about this." Aliyah reached out to touch Valentine's eye-patch, as if it was a bond they shared – which, Paul supposed, it was. "She talks about games, and all the fun things I'm gonna do when I get out."

"Be fair. Your mother does that, too."

She straightened herself up – a strangely dignified gesture. "No. I gotta be *strong* for Mom. She looks so sad. I tell her I got a castle. She's got no castle. So I can't ever be sad in front of Mommy." She swallowed. "But I can be sad in front of you, right? The way I'm sad in front of Vallumtime?"

Paul pulled her to his chest so she wouldn't see him burst into tears. "You can be all the sad you want, sweetie."

Aliyah didn't cry, of course. She accepted his hug with a patience that made Paul wonder just who was supporting who in this family. Then she plucked the Nintendo off the bed and shook it; Paul was grateful the crack in the screen wasn't as bad as he'd first thought, a single silver line running off-center. She pushed it back into his hands.

"The coral maze is to the right."

He paused the game. "Aliyah." She refused to look at him, her gaze on the videogame screen. He lifted her chin with his finger. "You know Daddy's not leaving again, right?"

A hooded glare. Aliyah had always been a preternaturally suspicious child, expecting lies in promises of bedtime and dessert. But this look was so cynical, so *scornful*, that Paul felt like a failed parent.

"You can't stay here," Aliyah pronounced. "You fight 'mancers."

As if she'd pronounced a curse on the hospital, the lights went off.

"Give it a second," Valentine said. "The backup generators will come on."

They didn't.

Paul pulled aside the privacy curtain to look around the burn ward, noticing the lack of nurses. Puzzled patients used their cell phones as impromptu flashlights inside the drawn privacy curtains, giving each chamber a lambent jellyfish glow.

"Daddy?" Aliyah asked. "Is everything all right?"

"I can't get a signal," Valentine said, shaking her phone. Judging from the mutters around them, they weren't alone.

"Things are fine, honey," he muttered. "Valentine, is there a– oh, good. Imani's been doing more insurance work. Could you hand me the envelope with Aliyah's hospital records?"

Valentine gave Paul a suspicious glance as she handed it over, her arm hairs stiffening as Paul did the tiniest bit of bureaucromancy. The papers he removed from the envelope were no longer Aliyah's medical records but a transcription of police radio.

"A ballroom explosion?" she asked, wrinkling her nose.

Paul pulled some more papers out, forms to rent a ballroom and the NYC permits for a contest. The envelope sighed at his touch, an unnervingly porn-star sound. "A dancing competition," he said. "They had a halon fire suppression system, it went off, a lot of people suffocated. More were trampled in the rush to escape. There's" – he tallied up – "a hundred and seventeen people incoming? Because we're the closest hospital. They're rerouting to others."

"The nurses must have been called into the ER – are they rerouting again now that the power's out?"

"I don't know. They're not filing reports now."

"Christ, Paul, your–" Valentine looked at Aliyah, realizing she'd almost said "'mancy". "Your, uh, cell phone is so weird. It's got weird limitations."

"She's off the grid. This has her fingerprints all over it, though."

"Whose fingerprints, Daddy?"

Paul did a double take, having forgotten about Aliyah's presence. "The bad 'mancer, sweetie. The one who burned you. She's hurting people again."

Aliyah grabbed his tie. "You're gonna stop her, right?"

Paul laughed, loving her trust: no terror that the bad 'mancer was coming for her again, just an absolute trust her daddy could kick anyone's ass.

"No, sweetie," he said, letting her down gently. "Not this time. But I, uh…" He pondered ways of using his bureaucromancy to restart the hospital generators, but they all involved getting repairmen in sooner.

"I'm on it," Valentine said, headed for the exit doorway.

"Wait!" Paul said. "Can't you just…" He waved his hands in the air. "Can't you rejigger it from here?"

He could have distilled the look she gave him and sold it as pure contempt. "Come on, Paul. I have to fight my way through the maintenance corridors, searching for the switch that turns the power back on. That's how missions *work*."

"…and you think *my* cell phone's weird?"

She shook her head, dismissing him, then raced away in high-top sneakers and crinoline dress, puffing. Valentine wasn't in shape, but she *was* enthusiastic.

"Vallumtime's fixing it?" Aliyah asked.

"Yes." Paul thought of ways to hunt down Anathema. Problem was, anarchomancers weren't big on filing flight plans.

What did she want? She'd injured a room full of dancers this time. If he could figure out what the hell Anathema was trying to do, then he could intercept her–

–movement outside the curtains. Paul looked up, glad to see a nurse had arrived; he felt strangely nauseated, a gut-churning sickness that felt like wild animals had shit down his throat. Maybe he could ask for a prescription. He grabbed his crutches.

The nurse ripped the curtain down, steel rings tumbling from the ceiling. Paul shrieked in surprise, dropping his cell phone. It shone upward, illuminating the woman who stood before him like a monster in a horror movie.

She gripped a hand-carved spear tipped with a chipped obsidian spearhead. Paul saw flecks of dried blood in those hollows.

The woman holding it radiated a scornful strain, a weather-beaten look that Paul associated with old photos of frontierswomen – a pride at having survived situations that would have killed lesser men. Her hair was a dreadlocked snarl of rat's bones.

But her face was bizarrely model-perfect: sculpted nose, collagen-plump lips, plastic surgery residuals. It was like someone had abandoned Miss America on Survivor Island, leaving her to learn how to build shelter from vermin-ridden branches.

She flung the hospital curtain to the floor and scrubbed her free palm against the hem of her dress.

Her dress was made of old camouflage-pattern fabric, crudely lashed together from leather straps and bone.

The stark simplicity of her garb, of her ancient spear, spoke of a 'mancer's lifestyle.

"Anathema?" he whispered.

By way of reply, she stabbed him.

TWENTY-SIX
Nature Has No Mercy

It had taken Paul three attempts to pass his police physicals, back when he'd been fresh out of college. "You're a good kid," the instructor had told him, after he'd washed out for the second time on the wall-climbing exercise. "But you're built like a mosquito."

Paul had done endless pull-ups, trying to build his scrawny muscles into something strong enough to carry the dead weight needed to pass. And when he'd finally vaulted over that wall, he should have felt triumph. All he'd felt was exhaustion.

A natural athlete he was not.

Yet there was one thing Paul was good at, a skill that had carried him through high school when the bullies came knocking: when he had to, he could haul ass.

Which was why, when Anathema stabbed down, Paul whipped his crutch around to knock her spear aside. She radiated sickness, a vulgar death that made it hard to concentrate…

"*Daddy*!" Aliyah screamed as Anathema came at him again, thrusting at his eye – but he smashed the crutch back across her face. Then he used his good leg to launch himself at her.

What the hell am I doing? he thought as he bore her to the ground. But it was the best strategy: he couldn't run with one leg, couldn't hope to outmaneuver her, and so he had to close.

If only she didn't outweigh him by thirty pounds.

Her lean muscles twitched underneath his hands as he struggled to grab the spear. The other parents in the ward moved to help Paul; she roared at them, her neck corded, and suddenly the ward smelled of lion shit and African veldts. The comfortable darkness turned into a vanished sun, a moonless night where any predator could feed on blind, helpless humans...

How do I know that? Paul asked, and then realized: 'mancy. Like Valentine's videogame rules, everyone knew what would happen if they stayed. He heard the football dads scrambling, grabbing their children and fleeing.

How could he fight that with bureaucromancy?

Yet even as he quailed from the way the hospital was hauled back to a darker age, Paul was mesmerized by the beauty of 'mancy. Even though Anathema's land was cold, hostile, and murderous, seeing her reshape the world was like watching a talented artist draw horrible things.

She smashed his smile with her elbow.

"You take the cost away!" she shrieked, snapping at his throat with filed teeth. "You dump it all into nature, onto *objects*, when the point is they *incinerate* themselves once they're done! You're encouraging the spread of our *demise*!"

Is she talking about my flux? he wondered – and then she clocked him hard again, eradicating all thought.

By the time he shook it off, she'd aimed her spear at his throat.

"I should've killed you personally instead of sending one of my obsessed to do the job," she said, trembling with rage. "I thought one hand would wash the other clean – that one flood of ill-gifted 'mancy could erase another. But I forgot how nature works – it doesn't use minions; it encourages *battles*. I created you; I have to kill you."

...*created me?* Paul flung up his hands defensively, seeing the cell phone light split across the sharpness of that obsidian spear tip. It would punch through his fingers and throat alike with one muscle-powered shove.

He looked over at Aliyah, apologetic.

Aliyah flung her Nintendo at Anathema's face.

"*You leave Daddy alone!*" she yelled, looking for something else to throw.

Anathema chuckled, wiping blood from her forehead.

"Your daughter's a better fighter than you are. But I'll teach her that nature has no mercy..."

She drew back the spear again. Aliyah pulled herself free from her IVs, launched herself at Anathema, shouting *no no no*. Anathema, bracing the spear in both hands, ignored Aliyah to aim the spear tip at Paul's heart.

"*Round One*," a deep announcer's voice boomed, tearing the veldt to shreds.

Paul saw Anathema's muscles quivering as she *wanted* to stab down. She'd been frozen in place. Paul felt himself somehow lose focus, shifted from Anathema's opponent to a mere background sprite.

Anathema looked up in fury, involuntarily assuming a fighting position, a red bar appearing over her head. Valentine appeared with an equally feral grin and a full red bar, facing Anathema down. She brandished a glowing sword – which looked absolutely badass when combined with her eye patch.

"Mortal Kombat, motherfuckress," Valentine said, her good eye gleaming.

"*Fight!*" the announcer yelled.

Anathema exploded from her stasis to spear Paul's heart, but her spear tip passed through his body; he wasn't an interactable object. She retreated as Valentine advanced in a looping swirl of attacks, fencing with the bravura moves of a thousand pirate movies. Anathema blocked them all in showers of golden sparks.

"*Daddy!*" Aliyah shrieked, trying to haul him away. Paul was astonished; couldn't Aliyah see how marvelous Valentine was, channeling archetypes to fight?

Meanwhile, Anathema and Valentine battled, their red bars chipping away as each scored hits. Aliyah flinched whenever Valentine's sword sparked; Aliyah didn't see Valentine defending them but rather saw Valentine wielding a wildfire force that threatened to burn her again…

He pulled Aliyah's medical chart off the end of the bed, channeling 'mancy. When he lifted the top form away, the list of medications he needed lay underneath. He ran his finger down the list, searching for familiar names.

"There, Aliyah!" He pointed to a reinforced steel cabinet. "Bring me all the medicines on the second shelf!"

He hated risking his daughter's health to save their lives, but Aliyah did him proud: most six year-olds would have lost their heads, but his daughter merely set her face in the same intense frown she wore whenever she'd set out to beat this level of Mario. Aliyah booked it toward the cabinet, wincing from the pain, retreating from Valentine and Anathema.

Valentine looked triumphant – but her red bar had been chipped away a lot more than Paul would have liked. She'd never been a real fighter, spending most of her life plopped in front of a console, and the loss of her depth perception was a real handicap. Whereas Anathema looked in her environment, fighting with practiced ease. Paul got the uncomfortable feeling that Anathema was toying with Valentine, cataloguing Valentine's moves in preparation for an overwhelming strategic push.

"*Daddy! The cabinet's locked*!"

"*Valentine*?"

Valentine gestured toward the medicine cabinet; it burst open in a spray of sparks just as Anathema punched Valentine in the face hard enough to empty Valentine's red bar, sending her sprawling to the ground.

"Now you die," Anathema said.

Aliyah shrieked when the cabinet burst open, tumbling backward as the magic blew the doors wide.

"Sweetie!" Paul yelled. "Get them!"

Fighting fear that would have unmanned a girl three times her age, Aliyah grabbed a stack of white boxes as though she was snatching fish out of a bear's mouth – and then ran back to Paul, dropping as many as she carried. Anathema brought the spear around, ready to puncture Valentine's heart...

...Valentine staggered back to her feet, the red bar refilling itself. "Round 2," the announcer roared. "Fight!"

"*Useless.*" Anathema waved her hand as though she were swatting flies. Paul felt a surge of 'mancy as the electricity drained away, Valentine's videogamemancy cut off as the room slid back to a time well before circuits had been discovered – before mankind even understood what lightning was.

Back on the veldt, Valentine clawed empty air as her sword faded away, desperately trying to summon back her 'mancy.

Anathema sneered. "You're no fighter," she said. "You're a fat slut."

She stabbed Valentine through the shoulder.

It would have been through the heart, but Valentine dodged – the one trick Anathema, who'd been on the defensive the whole fight, hadn't seen. Valentine shrieked, spear punching through flesh.

Paul jabbed a fistful of needles into Anathema's leg.

Anathema whirled, bringing the spear around to stab Paul, but Paul's "try it" grin was so fierce, she hesitated.

He jerked his chin toward the boxes scattered across the floor.

"The most powerful sedatives civilization has to offer," he said. "You'll be asleep in minutes. How far can you run before you pass out?"

It was a bluff. Paul had no medical knowledge; he'd pulled up the list of restricted drugs the nurses had to sign out for, using the ones that sounded familiar. Plus, he'd jabbed the needles into her thigh, not the best cluster of veins as far as Paul knew; maybe he'd hit muscles, missing her bloodstream entirely.

But he was betting the veldt warrior knew less about medicine than he did.

"I'll kill her first," she snarled, looking at Aliyah. "Just to watch her faith in you die."

Then she ran.

Paul crawled over to Valentine, wondering what the rest of the hospital was doing – but between the chaos in the ER and the fleeing patients, he doubted anyone had witnessed anything coherent. Valentine shivered from her wound. She was bleeding – how badly was badly? Paul wondered, unsure how much damage had been done.

"Brave girl." He pulled Aliyah to him. "Such a brave girl."

"All right," Valentine admitted, slumping onto the floor. "I *probably* should have tried harder to find her."

"You couldn't have," Paul told her. "She's not an anarchomancer. She's a paleomancer."

TWENTY-SEVEN
Going Dark

"We have to get out of here," Paul said. "If the cops ask questions about you–"

"I got it," Valentine said woozily. Her hands trembled with pain as she manipulated her imaginary controller. Paul felt a surge of magic, but Valentine's wound kept bleeding.

"Nothing happened," Paul said, puzzled. "Is she still interfering?"

"No..." Valentine staggered to her feet to peer around the burn ward; she looked pale even by her fishbelly-white standards. "S'around here somewhere..."

Aliyah's grip tightened around Paul's arm. "That curtain," she whispered. "It's glowing, Daddy."

"Oh, yeah. Come to Momma." Valentine whisked open the curtains to reveal a hospital bed; resting on top of stiff sheets was a gleaming white medkit complete with red cross. She grasped it, closing her eyes in gratitude; the medkit dissolved into her, sealing her wound.

"*Daddy!*" Aliyah screamed, drawing back. Paul

swallowed back anger.

"Why didn't you do that for *her*?" he asked.

Valentine blinked owlishly. "Do what for who?"

"Do healing magic. On my *daughter*."

"…this?" She patted her shoulder, pulled taut with new skin. "Toldja, Paul, nothing I do is permanent. This'll last an hour or two, then the wound will break open again. This is just to get me, you know… to the end of the level."

She swayed dangerously. "Aliyah, go help her," he said, crawling towards his crutches.

"You're not – you're not bringing her along, are you?" Valentine's face wrinkled in incredulity.

Kill a kid, you yank the parent's heart out, Gunza had said.

"If Anathema knows who I am, then she knows all she has to do to flush me out is kidnap my child," Paul said, waving towards Aliyah. "We gotta think Next Level, Valentine – we can't just *react*. We've gotta anticipate what Anathema will do next, then get in her way. That means removing Aliyah from the line of fire."

"But Paul, she's still *burned*. What about her medications, her treatments?"

I'll kill her first, Anathema had promised. And without Paul to guard her…

"I'll get Aliyah her treatments," Paul said. "Somehow. But no hospital can protect my daughter from an angry 'mancer – that's my job. Anathema is out for her blood now, too, and – and I promised I'd never leave her. I promise, sweetie," he said, kissing Aliyah's forehead. "You'll never look for Daddy in the maze again."

She grabbed Paul's hand, keeping her distance from Valentine.

The hospital was in chaos; between the 'mancer battle, the blackout, and the influx of patients in tattered tuxedos, nobody had time to pay attention beyond their immediate concerns. Nurses wheeled patients out on beds, navigating by flashlight and cell phones, trying to figure out which functional hospitals they could reroute the dying to.

Paul crutched his way among the crowds. Valentine staggered along; the medkit had dulled her pain, but she was still in shock from being stabbed.

They emerged in the hospital lobby. Aliyah sucked in a breath. It sounded to Paul like a childhood dying.

The lobby was filled with bleeding women in formal gowns, laid out on gurneys, countertops, any flat surface. Paramedics did CPR; nurses straddled screaming patients, trying to staunch the blood flow. Doctors waded through the mess as crying patients grabbed at their ankles, begged for painkillers.

Yet patients and medics alike moved with weary resignation. They knew exactly how many would die today, no matter what miracles they worked: two hundred and fifty-six people.

What made it surreal was the patients' formal wear: the men in tattered tuxedoes, the women in blood-spattered gowns. They'd been ballroom dancing when Anathema's accident struck. The out-of-place decorum lent the lobby the air of a formal gathering, like the dying of some foregone age.

That's what she wanted, Paul thought, shocked to

numbness. *She wanted to destroy their civilization, take it from them whole.*

Aliyah stood silent, taking it all in, collecting more evidence for her growing thesis on unbearable choices.

"We gotta go back," Valentine said.

"*Back*? You can barely walk!"

"These people will never walk again if I don't... I gotta find the..."

Paul followed her into the darkened hallways. He called back to Aliyah, who was mesmerized by the sight of doctors attempting to resuscitate a dapper seventy year-old man in a white tuxedo, his wife weeping by his side.

He tugged her away.

Paul caught up with Valentine, leaning against a supply closet to catch her breath.

"What are you doing?" Paul asked, concerned. Aliyah flattened herself against the opposite wall, eyeing Valentine with suspicion.

"What I set out to do." She pulled the supply closet open, revealing an improbably large, glowing switch on the wall. It danced with blue-white fire, like a bug zapper, but Valentine grabbed it with both hands and levered it up with a grunt.

The emergency lights flickered on; Paul heard the hum of monitors rebooting. Then the sound of blood plopping onto the floor; Valentine looked surprised to find herself bleeding again.

"That soon," she muttered, feverish. "Must be bad." She tapped her imaginary controller, then shifted some blankets to find another medkit at the back of the shelf.

"You gonna last?"

"Have to. If I have to explain why I got stabbed by a 'mancer, with these tattoos, after what happened back at the warehouse? Might as well call SMASH myself." She laughed, a bitter sound. "It's funny. I don't dare ask for help at the hospital…"

"We'll get help."

"Not here, we won't." She limped over to Aliyah. "We good, kid?"

"Are you gonna die now?" Aliyah asked.

"I might. Do you want me to?"

Aliyah held her breath, puffing her cheeks. She looked like the answer was strangling her, a complex emotional mixture no six year-old should ever endure. But here was a 'mancer: her worst enemy, her best friend.

"…no…"

"Vote… of confidence," Valentine wheezed, offering a high five, refusing to put her arm down until Aliyah returned it. Aliyah's response was like a girl sadly pressing her hand against a window to say goodbye.

They left through an emergency exit. Ambulances were lined up and down the block, lights flaring, policemen and firemen barking orders.

A touch of Valentine-provided Grand Theft Automancy made stealing a car a cinch – though that effort required the creation of another medkit, followed by a hunt through the parking lot until they found it. "They're never convenient," Valentine muttered, as though it were a fact of life. "They're hidden, to encourage you to explore."

Paul wouldn't let Valentine drive – her head was nodding – but he had to shuffle through his accordion folder first, finding someplace nearby, vacant, and furnished.

Aliyah switched on her Nintendo. She put in her earphones, ignoring the woozy Valentine lolling in the front seat.

Paul speed-dialed Kit.

"Paul?" Kit asked, concerned. "Something's happening at Aliyah's hospital, news is slim, I'm on my way over…"

"Yeah," Paul said, pulling out of the garage. "Anathema attacked me."

"…She attacked *you*?" Paul heard the guilt in Kit's voice.

"Not your fault. She would have come for me anyway. She's Caucasian, mid-thirties, five-seven, maybe a hundred and thirty pounds. Long dreadlocked hair. She's had plastic surgery, with a button nose, but her teeth are filed."

"Filed? Who the hell files their teeth?"

"That's the thing, Kit: she's not an anarchomancer. She's a paleomancer."

"A paleomancer? I've never heard of a–"

"Okay, fine, a society-hating-mancer. A primitive-mancer? Whatever. The point is, she's been targeting the things she thinks are *fripperies*. She wants us huddled in small groups around a campfire. I was more right than I knew – she's not out to destroy the government, she's out to destroy *civilization*."

"You positive?"

"I just fought the bitch. Trust me."

"Why'd she go after you?"

Because she thinks she created me? Paul thought. *Because our 'mancies are in opposition to each other?*

"No idea," Paul lied. "Listen, I gotta go underground. If I'm in the open, she'll come for me again. She won't stop until I'm dead."

"Paul, no." Kit sounded terrifyingly old. Paul had never thought of Kit as elderly, just well seasoned. But his voice was reedy as he begged Paul to go to the cops, promising they'd protect him.

"Kit, this isn't up for debate. And I'm taking Aliyah."

"...can you take care of her? In her condition?"

Paul glanced in the back seat. Aliyah in her frail hospital gown, IV needle still in her arm, focused on her Nintendo. All the cops in the world couldn't stop Anathema from getting to her – and Anathema *would* go after his daughter, if Paul went to cover. Aliyah would be the only thing guaranteed to draw him out.

"I'll have to."

"You could let SMASH question you – they've got opal-studded safe houses–"

SMASH would love to question me, Paul thought, racing through a gridlocked intersection. *Maybe they'd catch Anathema – but they'd definitely catch me. And Valentine.*

"We're not negotiating, Kit. I'm telling you because you're smart enough to track her down. I'll be in touch. I hope." He shut off his phone, pulling into the parking garage.

The best place he'd been able to afford was a half-built office – one that had paused in mid-construction while the builders negotiated for additional city permits. Even that expenditure sucked wind from his savings account.

He wished he could conjure money. There was a word for that: *embezzlement*. Someone would track back that trail to him. His bureaucromancy was strong leverage for great deals, but free cash would drop a load of flux he could not afford. This place had electricity, running water, locks on the doors. Good enough.

"Valentine," he said, nudging her. "Get *up*, Valentine."

He wondered what he'd do if she didn't – he only had one leg, and Aliyah was too small. Thankfully, Valentine roused herself with the formality of a drunk coming off a bender, as if she was not moving her body but instead conducting it from a distance.

"I don't know what is up," she in a slurred voice. "Normally, those medkits are like five-hour energy drinks…"

Aliyah tagged along behind, never looking up from her Nintendo. Paul reached in his pocket, feeling the flux squeeze tighter, and pulled out the key to this place. He'd rented it for a month. He hoped no one would investigate; if any of the bosses who supposedly signed the rent agreement showed up, this would be tough to explain.

The office itself was under construction, smelling of sawdust; it was halfway to becoming an Art Nouveau workspace, with that clean, white, empty Apple store feel to it. The unfinished ceiling held racks of spotlights to flood the brushed-metal space with glare.

There were completed offices in the back, past a set of stairs that led up to a second floor with a narrow walkway – where, presumably, management would emerge from high-powered meetings to stroll along the rail and look down over the pit of white-collar peons who worked for them. But the peons hadn't arrived yet.

Fortunately, the presidential office was furnished – complete with lush carpeting, a private bathroom, a mahogany bar. The office's premature completion indicated a vanity project where some pointy-headed boss sat above, watching the construction workers assemble his dream... but whatever. It gave Paul a base of operations.

He laid Valentine across the wide executive desk, where she passed out again. He probed her injured shoulder, feeling rubbery pseudo-skin, the kind he'd been wrapped in when he'd pretended to be Valentine's boyfriend. The skin was fever-hot, signaling an abscessing wound.

Aliyah stood solemnly behind him, scrutinizing Valentine. Paul collapsed in a high-tech Aeron chair and patted his lap; Aliyah scrambled up obediently.

"She's gonna die." Aliyah didn't look at Paul, or Valentine, but off to one side, as if Valentine was a blazing summer sun that could not be stared at directly.

"We'll fix Valentine, sweetie. Promise."

She whirled. "You should let her die! It'd be nicer."

"Nicer? Than what?"

The tears flowed, Aliyah's seal broken at last. "Than you shooting her."

"Why would I shoot her?"

"She's a 'mancer. A stupid, stinking 'mancer." She hugged the Nintendo Valentine had given her, clutching it as though she was begging forgiveness from Mario himself. "You gotta kill her, Daddy. You gotta. But you can't make it hurt. It's like Jennifer's cat – they had to kill her cause of cat cancer, but they did it so it didn't hurt. So, please. Don't shoot."

"I'm not going to shoot her, Aliyah."

"I don't know *how* you kill them!" she shrieked. "I know you kill them! I know it's right! She's gonna broach and burn little girls! So, you... you kill her, Daddy. But you can't let her suffer."

Paul didn't think she knew words like *suffer*. Then again, with the way Aliyah's life had gone lately, the word fit exquisitely.

He laughed, feeling shitty for laughing. "Sweetie, I'm not going to kill Valentine."

Confusion. "She's... unstable. Mommy says they're all unstable. That's why you take them down. Sooner or later, every 'mancer hurts somebody."

Like I hurt you, Paul thought, remembering the fire.

"'Mancers are misunderstood, sweetie. They..."

"'Mancers. Hurt. Me." Aliyah scratched at her scalp, where there were only stubbled runnels. "Mommy says I got lucky. *We* got lucky. A lot of people got worse than burned."

"'Mancers aren't all bad, sweetie," he assured her. "Valentine's been your friend, hasn't she?"

"...I guess."

That friendship wasn't enough. How could it be?

When her own mother hated 'mancers, when a
'mancer had kidnapped her father, when a 'mancer had
taken her father's leg, when a 'mancer had burned her?

Paul had seen Valentine defending them against a
crazed Paleomancer. But all Aliyah had seen was deadly
magic that threatened to spiral out of control.

There was only one way to convince Aliyah 'mancers
could be good guys.

"Sweetie," he said gently. "Do you realize Daddy's a
'mancer, too?"

Aliyah's eyes widened. She looked to Valentine as if
searching for confirmation, then stared at her father as
if trying to bring him into focus. He smiled, trying to
tell her that yes, she'd heard him right, and everything
was the same as always.

She leapt off his lap, heading for the door.

"*NO!*" she screamed, the terrible shriek of butchered
pigs. "*NO! NOOOO! NOOOOOO!*" He snatched her back,
wrestling her, and that was terrible, too; she fought
with all her strength and no fear of hurting him, giving
him no choice but to hurt her back.

And still she fought, seeking escape. "*NOOOOO!*"

He couldn't restrain her forever. If she got loose, she
was faster – and where would she go? Out into traffic?
Picked up by some child molester? Lost in New York,
with no one to help her?

…off to tell SMASH what her Daddy really is? asked a
hateful voice.

It was the longest and hardest battle of Paul's life,
wrangling his beloved daughter into that bathroom. He
pushed with his good leg, hauling both across the

carpet, fighting unfairly with police training.

As he shoved her in the bathroom, Nintendo and all, Aliyah sobbed. "I want Mommy!" she yelled, as if her words could change hard reality. "I want *Mommy*! I want Mah-ha-ha-ha-my!"

Paul shut the door on his daughter's weeping. He thought he had known what it was like to be the world's worst father.

Now, as he heard Aliyah wail, he knew.

TWENTY-EIGHT
Sex-Spackle

Aliyah had tried to escape twice since he'd locked her in the executive bathroom. The first time, he'd caught her teetering on the toilet tank... a heart-stopping sight for any parent, doubly so when she saw him coming and jumped for the ventilation grate. The second time, she'd squirmed into the cabinet under the sink, probing for exits – another heart-stopper when he opened the bathroom and couldn't find her.

He cracked the bathroom door open to find Aliyah half-asleep, playing Nintendo. He knew his daughter well enough to recognize exhaustion; once she got her strength back, she'd start screaming for help again.

Or she'd start screaming when her painkillers wore off.

Meanwhile, Valentine had passed out on the desk, breathing shallowly. Paul wasn't sure what was happening underneath her pseudoskin; was the wound worsening?

Then there was his own flux load, a migraine headache. He felt it squirming around him, eager to give him all the worst coincidences, all involving Aliyah; there were a hundred bad things that could happen in there.

The trick, he thought, was not to panic.

He was in this bind because he hadn't considered the future. He'd rushed to help Aliyah, rushed to make Flex, rushed to Gunza's lair.

Paul jotted ideas on a legal pad. He opened the desk drawers to pull out some files from the FBI, wincing at the slight increase in flux, then spread them across the floor to draw it all together.

Two hours later, he woke Valentine. She came to with a groggy surprise.

"What's going on? She attacking?"

"No, we're safe," Paul said. "We need to get you a doctor."

She frowned at the bathroom door. "You can't leave her alone."

"No."

"So where will you find a doctor who'll treat a 'mancer and a screaming girl?"

"Do you think two 'mancers can cast a spell together? I mean, outside of Unimancy?"

She made a pained noise.

"Is that a no?"

"It's an 'I don't know,' Paul. We 'mancers generally don't hang tight, you know? It's not like a pyromancer and, I dunno, a felimancer have a ton to talk about."

"But is it possible?"

"Like I'm a scholar? You've met more 'mancers than I have. How many of them worked together?"

"…None," he admitted. "But that's not to say it's impossible. A lot of knowledge burned in Europe. And the 'mancer panic after made people terrified to investigate. Maybe they used to do it all the time, and we forgot how–"

"But your 'mancy, it's…" She shrugged in perplexity. "It's so *boring*."

"If we can combine 'mancies, I can get you a doctor. And get us a way to lure Anathema in when we're ready. And we…" He swallowed, embarrassed. "We make great Flex together. Whenever we've worked, it's like you left off where I began. And… I know it's weird…"

"It's like a threesome," she said.

Paul didn't know what to say to that.

"You, me, and the magic," she clarified. "You don't strike me as a guy who's had a lotta threesomes, Paul…"

"None, actually."

"…but most are awkward. Really awkward. One guy wants to play monkey in the middle and never leaves, or there's two people who wanna bang and the only way they can do it is to have you in the room, or it's some couple trying to use you as sex spackle to patch up a bad marriage, or…"

"Can we talk less about threesomes?" Paul asked. "I mean, with my daughter in earshot?"

"Birds and bees, man. There's no shame in it."

"You're dying, and you're giving me lectures in *parenting*?"

"I'm sorry, I'm sorry." She wiped her forehead. "I just don't know where I'd begin. I'm all videogames. Not a lot of paperwork there."

"All this starts with one letter. On the desk of a man who probably wants to kill us. Watch me create it." He reached out with his 'mancy, feeling a fresh load of flux clog his sinuses. On a nice desk in Long Island, next to a stack of life insurance claims, a formal summons hived off from the mass of paperwork to slide to the center of the blotter. "There. Can you feel that?"

She squirmed. "…yeah. Good God, is that what it feels like to be you? All that – that responsibility? Your whole world is choked with obligations; it's like – like living deep undersea, where the pressure would kill a normal man…"

He felt her magic seeping into him, too – a selfish spasm of enjoyment, never caring what happened beyond the next level. He wanted to ask her how she *lived* like that. Didn't she realize rents had to be paid, bills had to be set up…

…but, with an effort, he backed away.

"Don't compare," Paul urged her, feeling the foundations of his 'mancy quiver as Valentine's 'mancy infiltrated, their 'mancies jockeying for supremacy. "This isn't about who's right. Remember how lonely you felt when you first did magic? Like no one would ever understand you?"

She held his hand, a sisterly touch. "Yes. I remember."

"This is about us creating something beyond the pale. We couldn't be more different. But we have…" He paused reverently. "We have this."

"Yes." He felt her backing away from his 'mancy; she had decided not to question who he was, instead accepting that she existed parallel to him, different but equal, a tolerance that flooded him with gratitude. She ignored their wildly dissimilar world views to focus on this shared space of adulation.

This magic.

"We can change the world," she whispered, amazed.

"We will," Paul reassured her. "And it starts with you getting his attention…"

TWENTY-NINE
The Most Powerful Practitioner

Valentine talked a lot when she got nervous. She peered out of the frosted glass office window, scanning the construction floor. "How soon until he arrives?"

"...we'll know when he gets here."

"A guy like that knows which side his bread is buttered on," Valentine mused, lent strength by the potential of action. "On the other hand, maybe he doesn't wanna be bossed around. But if he thought we had a really good deal, he'd be here by now. What do you think?"

I think I'd feel better if you shut up, Paul thought, itching in his new leather-and-gas-mask suit layered over pseudoskin. He boiled with nervousness. He didn't know if he could act well enough to make this work. He didn't know whether Oscar would go for his offer. He didn't know what he'd do if Oscar *rejected* his offer.

...he didn't know how to handle Valentine.

He was afraid to look at her now, lest he overflow with emotions. He felt overwhelmed by a bizarre gratitude, almost verging on worship, because – especially after Aliyah – he'd opened his magic up to her. She'd responded with eagerness, entwining her magic with his...

...it was humiliating, how badly he'd needed that release. Ever since he'd discovered that illustromancer, he'd felt this yearning to see the world reshaped by obsession again. And when he discovered he could do magic, that joy was tarnished by having to hide it.

Yet he'd shared. It hadn't been like the Flex, where he'd had to strangle his love. For the first time, he'd cast a spell with someone watching – and she'd not just tolerated his 'mancy, but exulted in his power.

Yet he was certain if he asked too many questions, he'd find that Valentine was secretly horrified by his desires – same as his wife, same as Aliyah, same as everyone he ever knew. Hell, he'd felt her disgust at the compartmentalized way he lived his life; eventually, she'd write him off as another freak.

He needed to keep his illusions for a little while, warm himself by them – the idea that he might be normal to someone.

"...Paul? Why aren't you looking at me? Did I skin your eyes wrong?"

He glanced away, trusting the smoked-glass lens of the gasmask to shield his gaze. She flipped up her eye patch as if she could somehow see out of that cavernous wound.

"Is it Aliyah?"

"...it's fine," Paul said.

"Nope. We're about to face down some mobsters,

maybe eat a firefight. Every time this 'broody secrets before the storm' thing happens in an RPG, it means the next scene's about to go to shit. So, what the hell is eating you?"

"…it's nothing."

She drew in a quick breath, clapped a hand over her mouth to cover her grin. "Oh, my God, Paul. Are you… are you *embarrassed*? About the – the magic?"

He said nothing. Valentine let out a peal of laughter. Paul's face flushed beneath the pseudoskin.

"What the hell are you laughing at?" Paul asked.

"Oh, *sweetie*. You duckling. You adorable duckling. Quack, quack, quack." She laughed again, covering her smile with her fingertips in guilty shame.

"I'm not a duck," he grumbled.

She turned him to face her. "No, come on, Paul, I've done this foie gras rodeo before. You get with someone inexperienced, it's really intense, and then you find out they've imprinted on you. Like a duckling. Then they follow you around, taking all the emotions kicked up by that flood of orgone and trying to tether them to some half-assed construction of you. That spell was great, don't get me wrong, I want to do it again, but… don't try to make it *mean* something."

"I've never done that before," he snapped.

"Well, neither have I! But that's chemistry for you, Paul: primal, unguessable, ephemeral. And oh, my God, if you try to build that randomness into reasons, I will beat the shit out of you."

"I'm not a *child*, Valentine. I'm fifteen years older than you."

"And you frittered away *that* head start. Come on, Paul, you're–"

A clattering from outside. People stepping through the glass and loose nails.

"...Showtime." The false skin on her shoulder sloughed off, plopping to the floor.

Paul felt fake – a skinny BDSM clown in a pathetic gasmask and leather suit. The synthetic leg she'd formed for him had no bones, a floppy sadness that was like trying to walk on a Nerf bat. Valentine hadn't meant to laugh at him, but... The last woman to laugh at him like that was his wife. His *ex*-wife. He didn't need to have those feelings resurfacing.

"You should do this, Valentine." He wobbled on his one-and-a-half good legs. "I don't know this character. I'm not an actor…"

"But you *are* a negotiator." She wriggled her fingers; a rattle shook the nails on the concrete outside. There were yelps, the sound of guns being drawn, the scrapes as sawhorses slid across the floor. "I can't get my landlord to fix my faucet. You're the guy who knows how to forge deals. So, trust me; you gotta channel Mantis, or I'm gonna bleed to death."

"I've never even played the *game*!"

"The character will feed you. You won't really be you; you'll be channeling an avatar. You'll be riding across his personality, like a raft bouncing over whitewater."

"That's supposed to *comfort* me?"

"Get out there before I pass out." She shoved him out the door.

Paul was hauled upward by some shivering force. He jerked back and forth in a series of turbulences, as if the power that held him threatened to shred itself to pieces.

His missing leg no longer mattered; he was gliding out over the second-floor railing, hovering two stories above the office floor, looking down upon it like a God.

The power yanked him along, hauling him high into the air. A mad buzz of pleasure shot through him. His 'mancy was about things stuffed safely into envelopes.

Valentine's 'mancy was about unleashing havoc.

Yet Paul was drawn to it, the secret thrill of watching a car crash. Riding Valentine's power was a violent rush, but there was something beautiful about watching glass buckle and burst into glittering shards.

The four bodyguards had dropped to their knees, clutching at their faces. They stood in a vortex of psychokinetically moved objects – hammers, ladders, cubicles all whirled in a slow-motion cyclone, picking up speed. Everything moved to Paul's tune – a *literal* tune, a slow organ-and-cello waltz.

All except for Oscar Gargunza Ruiz, who stood in the vortex's center – a small dark man in a pristine white suit, planting his cane on the ground as though it rooted him there. He glanced from side to side, sizing up the moving world.

Paul felt a pang of sympathy. He'd felt so small under Gunza's hulking frame, and Oscar was smaller still. What had it been like to be a tiny boy with a violent brother? The FBI had catalogued Oscar's boyhood injuries; the medical records chronicled his repeated trips to the ER...

The thought distracted him, and the avatar-mancy surged forward. Paul's gas mask hissed. His skin pulled taut, emaciated, compressing his body into a gaunt parody of itself.

A low shriek filled the office floor. It took Paul a moment to realize that awful fingers-on-chalkboard noise emanated from him. That he was laughing, a raspy wheeze. The men's fear rose up from below; he drank it down.

Paul had to talk *now*, before he lost himself to this creature Valentine had unleashed. He struggled to remember everything he'd planned to say – but he was flooded with false memories of a man in leather armor and flowing headband, sneaking through hallways underneath a box… Snake? Solid Snake? Was that a name?

What was Metal Gear Solid?

"*Oscar Gargunza Ruiz!*" he rasped, fighting his way back to himself. "Your brother shattered your shoulder in three places when you were twelve, in a fight over chocolate milk. You alone seemed to understand Gunza for what he was: the worst kind of dealer. Not in it for the cash or the power, but the *stardom*."

Oscar looked up at Paul, his placid face registering fear at being so casually unveiled… Or was it revulsion at the memory of his dead brother?

Oh, yes, Paul thought. *There's no love among villains here.*

Oscar's bodyguards readied their guns, made skittish by the potent display of power. No wonder. This vulgar 'mancy had died with Europe.

"You took a different route," Paul shouted down, unable to suppress a tinge of admiration. "When Gunza yelled, you whispered. Where he encouraged sloppiness, you mandated perfection. So, when *you* were granted power years ahead of anyone's expectations, you relegated your brother to the ass end of the business. You handed him just enough power for him to hang himself... and waited for the noose."

Oscar Gargunza Ruiz allowed himself an aw-shucks grin. Then he spoke loudly, with the stiff formality of a man who suspects he may be being recorded. "I confirm nothing. All I know is that my poor brother got himself involved in 'mancy – a business that never pays off. And so I must ask, videogamemancer: who are you?"

"I am–"

One of Oscar's bodyguards fired in panic.

It was not Paul whose telekinesis snatched the bullet from the air before flinging the bodyguard through a glass window, nor Paul who answered Oscar's question.

"*You doubt my power?! Now I will show you why I am the most powerful practitioner of psychokinesis and telepathy in the world!*" Paul/Not-Paul roared, glass shattering in every frame, shards whipping into the whirlwind. "*I am Psycho Mantis!*"

THIRTY
What Stops the Whirlwind?

Aliyah's screaming brought Paul back to reality. Or, rather, Psycho Mantis's reaction to it. Because when Aliyah shrieked as all the mirrors in the bathroom shattered, Psycho Mantis reacted with scorn.

Every living thing on this planet exists to mindlessly pass on their DNA, it thought. *We're designed that way.*

Which, Paul understood, was a quote from a game he'd never played – one sound bite pulled from a limited number of reactions, like an automated voice answering questions on a help line. It *felt* real, thanks to Valentine's 'mancy, but feed it enough unusual situations and the illusion broke down.

You only lived long enough to provide a single boss battle and a set of cut scenes, Paul thought, clawing back to control. *So, you don't get to make the choices. I do.*

He yanked back on the reins just as Psycho Mantis prepared to kill everyone in the room – the one thing boss monsters could always do.

Oscar spoke louder, reassuring his men.

"I was told you were a tattooed girl." He gestured to

his guards: *Put the guns down.* "Or a one-legged man, chained to a radiator."

Paul couldn't decide if the riposte was foolish or bold. It was intended to remind him of the impotence he'd felt at Gunza's hands.

"I am a videogamemancer. I can wear any skin," Paul rasped. "I was never her, and he was never a 'mancer."

"That is not what my brother told us."

"Your brother took the wrong man, then deluded himself," Paul said, struggling to get the words out past the crazed speeches Psycho Mantis wanted to spew. "He died clueless about 'mancy."

"Why would you teach me?" Oscar spread his hands. "What could you possibly desire?"

"Hematite," Paul said. Which was the least of the things he needed right now but what Oscar would be drawn to. "I need to make my own Flex again. Your people had sources."

"Sources that dried up after my brother burned out," Oscar shrugged. "Difficult enough to get mage-grade hematite when it was merely a restricted substance; now that SMASH is combing New York for creatures like you, every manufacturing plant is on the strictest of lockdowns."

"That's not a no."

"Flex was not good for my brother. Nor was it kind to my dead brother Hanna, nor Uncle. My family has long been convinced 'mancers are unprofitable business." He nodded toward his guard bleeding from a hundred deep cuts. "What I see here gives me no reason to change that."

Psycho Mantis didn't like that at all.

"You're not dealing with 'mancers." Paul tried his best to sound calm, reasonable, certainly not like some maniac was sucking the sanity out the back of his head. "You're dealing with *suppliers*. Of Flex. *Pure* Flex."

"My brother told us he had tamed you."

"He was a kidnapper, and a blackmailer, and bad at both. He also needed to bend your family's desires to his, desperate for adulation. He wanted fame. You... you simply want to do business."

It was a shot in the dark, a measured guess. Still, Oscar froze.

"Think of what you could do with perfection, carefully dispensed," Paul continued. "Drug runs guaranteed to work. The cops overlooking all the best evidence. You run a dangerous business. A little surety, dispensed wisely, can go a *long* way."

Oscar's shoulders slumped. "...it seems a little easy."

"I'm a little desperate," Paul acknowledged. "Anathema is breathing down my neck. I need better firepower."

That wasn't true. The Flex drew Anathema to him; something that he instilled in his Flex enraged her. His firepower would be Valentine.

Oscar didn't need to know that.

"...And why should I involve myself in a mage war?"

"You don't," Paul said. "You give me mage-grade hematite, take your cut, and leave. This is a one-time offer."

Oscar pursed his lips. "...you obscure the truth, 'mancer. You left a letter in my house. On my *desk*. It glowed green—so I couldn't miss it; the moment I noticed it, the world halted. Doors stuck shut. All my phones, dead. Everyone in the house repeated the same three sentences, and I realized the sun would refuse to set until I opened your damned invitation."

Valentine's 'mancy, Paul thought proudly. *I put the letter there; she made it a quest item.*

"So, time." Oscar tapped his cane upon the ground. "*Time* was a factor. What do you need so badly that you summoned me here now?"

Dammit. Paul had hoped to slide the most vital item past Oscar. But now it was on the table…

"…I need a doctor. One skilled in surgery and…" He had to make sure Oscar's medics could take care of Aliyah. "…and severe burns. I need him today. Stocked with his own supplies."

Oscar nodded. "I can get that."

"So, we have a deal?"

"If you stop your whirlwind."

Paul stopped Psycho Mantis from snapping Oscar's neck. "What?"

Oscar took off his glasses, cleaned them with his tie. "You are correct about my brother, Mr Mantis. Gunza was a bully. When I heard he had died, I found myself unclenching muscles I didn't realize I had tensed all my life. So, I am suspicious of men who use their power flagrantly and stupidly." He glanced meaningfully over at his bodyguard, the one Paul had flung through a window. "So, I will request: stop your whirlwind. Stop trying to *frighten* me. I've been frightened by professionals, Mr Mantis. People who can instill more

terror with a single nail file than you can with all your
reality-bending. They will all tell you: I reward people
who do business."

That request gave Paul a strange kinship toward
Oscar. He felt shamed. Had he become this violent
lunatic? What happened to his ideals of quiet
commerce?

Psycho Mantis hammered the inside of his skull,
demanding blood; Paul clubbed that hatred back down.
Psycho Mantis retreated sullenly, withdrawing all his
granted power. Wobbling like a badly thrown Frisbee,
Paul heaved himself back over the railing before the
psychic storm broke, sending nails and broken glass
clattering to the ground.

Then he leaned against the railing, his fake leg bending
like a Styrofoam pool noodle. Valentine's 'mancy had
vanished, leaving him with just bureaucromancy to
counter Oscar's next move.

As he looked down at the three angry bodyguards
hauling the injured one away, he thought: *This might be
a mistake.* They put their hands on their holsters and
looked to their boss.

Oscar paid them no mind. Instead, he cocked his
head toward the sound of Aliyah crying hysterically in
the bathroom. He nodded once, as if this confirmed his
suspicions...

... then gestured for his men to leave. The gratitude
that flooded through Paul's body was nearly a carnal
thing.

"My physician will arrive within an hour," Oscar said,
bowing at the waist as if they had completed a ju-jitsu

session. "The hematite, tomorrow."

Paul fought to keep his voice from trembling. "Thank you."

"You may express your gratitude in Flex," Oscar replied.

He left.

THIRTY-ONE
Aliyah, Taught the Truth

Aliyah sobbed. Panicked, Paul pulled the chair out from underneath the bathroom doorknob – not a complex lock, but enough to thwart a six-year-old – and checked in on her.

She was bleeding. The glass from the mirror had cut her.

"Sweetie..." When she saw him, she *shrieked*. It was like she didn't even know him.

Then he realized: she didn't. He was still clad in the Mantis skin, a pallid freak in a gas mask. "It's Daddy, Aliyah; it's Daddy," he said, but she scrambled back across the floor, slicing her hands.

He slammed the bathroom door shut, looking toward Valentine, who was unconscious again. He hoped the doctor would arrive soon. He hoped Oscar wouldn't change his mind and send his thugs in to shoot them. But his daughter, cut by flying glass, that was the worst thing he could imagine–

–the flux.

There was no flux. His head was clear. He'd burned

319

it off, breaking mirrors and terrorizing Aliyah.

Oh, my God, he was the worst parent in the whole world.

"Valentine," he said, shaking her awake.

"Needa sleep."

"No, Valentine. We have a doctor on the way. You have to change skins with me. You have to be Psycho Mantis. Or else, when he gets here, he'll know who you are."

"…Zokay."

"It is *not*. We need to have Oscar and crew believing the videogamemancer switches bodies. Otherwise, Kit and SMASH will come looking for you. You can't be you any more. Not when you do 'mancy."

Valentine roused herself. "Gemme closet…"

She took a step toward the bathroom door; Paul shoved her back. "Not there," he said, envisioning Valentine turning the bathroom into that terrifying skin-swapping void with Aliyah still in it. "We'll use this supply closet. Don't forget to leave your wound open."

The closet opened up into the void, that feeling of being reduced to component geometry. The door flew open and spat Paul out in his own skin.

He landed on his elbow. That missing foot again. Valentine leaned over to pick him up, dressed in full Psycho Mantis garb – except for her right breast and shoulder, which were now exposed. He thought the costume had been disturbing before, but one chubby, blood-soaked tit sticking out on a gaunt male frame was somehow terrifying.

He grabbed for his crutch, hobbling over to Aliyah.

She'd gone quiet, rocking back and forth in a stupor, hugging her Nintendo DS against her chest. She pushed shards of glass around with bloody toes. He had to get her shoes. There hadn't been time to get anything since they'd fled the hospital. That had been, what, three hours ago? Four? He didn't dare check his cell phone; Kit probably had a tracer on his phone's GPS.

He looked at the fresh cuts on her face. He'd done that. But he couldn't afford to have Aliyah see him cry.

"Sweetie," he said. "It's Daddy. *Daddy*."

She pushed the glass shards around some more.

He brought in a broom, swept the glass away, then led her out to the office. Aliyah made a run for it, of course, but he was ready.

"No!" she screamed as he dragged her back, pounding him, smearing him in her blood. "I want Mommy! You cut me! *You cut me*!"

"I didn't cut you," he lied. "That was the mirror."

"You made it explode!"

"…yes." *Didn't you promise not to lie any more, Paul?* "I did, I did. I was trying to scare off some bad men."

"*You're* bad men!"

"You saw me saving Valentine. That bad 'mancer – the one who burned you? – she was trying to kill all three of us. I had to use my 'mancy to save Valentine, and – and she's still hurt. She might die. I had to use my 'mancy to scare some men into getting a doctor who can help her. Not all the 'mancy is bad. Not all the *'mancers* are bad. But the bad 'mancer is forcing our hand…"

Aliyah huffed, hyperventilating in huge whoops that Paul knew would give her a headache later. "Why can't you give it up, Daddy? Just stop it. Don't be... don't be a 'mancer. Be a Daddy. Just... be my Daddy. Be my *Daddy*!"

"Sweetie." He dabbed the blood off her face; thankfully, the cuts were head wounds, bleeding profusely – but nothing that required stitches. "If Daddy could, he would. Being a 'mancer isn't anything you choose to be. It just... happens."

"You're not Daddy! Daddy doesn't have bug eyes! Daddy doesn't blow up mirrors!"

"That mean woman who burned you, she's bad. Remember when you tried to save me from her? She'll come after you if I leave you alone, she's vicious. I need the 'mancy to protect you–"

"I don't care! *Daddy would give it all up*!"

"...Bedtime?" said a deep Russian voice.

Paul was confused until he realized that "bed" was "bad", and it was not a statement but a question from the polite man who had poked his head into the room.

"No," he said, tugging Aliyah back to his lap. "No, no, it's not a bad time."

Aliyah could not take her eyes off of the old man with the drooping white mustache who shuffled into the room. He wore a tweed suit with leather patches on the elbow and carried a large black bag, just like the doctors of old. He eyed the squirming child with bleary gray eyes.

"De child first, or the men in the mesk?" the doctor asked.

"The child. She's in week seven of her burn treatment. She needs debridement–"

"*He's not my Daddy!*" Aliyah yelled, "*He's not my Daddy! Stranger danger! Stranger danger! He's a Don't-Know!*"

She flung her arms around the doctor's legs. "*He – he touches me! He's not my Daddy! He's a toucher, a mean toucher, a 'mancer-toucher!*"

"S'good," the doctor said, plucking her up and plopping her back into Paul's lap. "S'good." Then he waved a beefy finger at her, chiding. "We'll fix de cuts. And look at de burns. The rest, little girl… is none of my bizness."

He got out an iPad and, consulting it for reference, began the process of debriding Aliyah's skin. Aliyah stared straight ahead, doll-like, impervious to the pain. She'd been shown another truth far too soon: there were men who utterly did not care what happened to her.

Paul wished with all his heart that she'd never had to witness that. But she'd doubtless see worse before this was over.

THIRTY-TWO
Why Would You Want a Gift?

The doctor carried four chilled bags of O negative blood in his satchel, two of which went into Valentine. That and a night's rest made Valentine well enough to fetch some Dunkin' Donuts.

She hugged her knees as she sat by the railing, looking down at the Flex-making equipment that Oscar's associates had brought in. "Bleeding to death makes one a little forgetful," she said. "So, *what* made making Flex for drug lords again seem like a good idea?"

"We don't know where Anathema is," Paul replied, flipping through an empty drawer, pulling out medical record after medical record. "And it's a big city. The only reason I found you is because you didn't pull up stakes after blowing a huge load of flux."

"You wouldn't love me if I was a *wise* drug manufacturer," Valentine said loftily.

Paul squinted at Aliyah's records pulled from her doctors' files. The Russian medic had given him printed treatments for Aliyah, but Paul wouldn't rest his daughter's life on some sawbones. So he'd pulled up her planned schedule for the week, pieced together from various computer records and printed out in dot-matrix records, trying to decipher medicalese.

"The point is, we don't know where she is. Nor do we know where she'll strike next. Knowing she's a paleomancer–"

"Really? *That's* the word you chose to describe Captain Caveman?"

"–knowing she's obsessed with bringing down civilization doesn't narrow it down. Who knows what she thinks will pull us back to the Stone Age? Destroying an Apple store? Clogging the sewage system? Shorting the generators? Hell, this is New York: *every* business is devoted to demolishing the natural order."

"Points for plotting," Valentine acknowledged, biting into a Croissan'wich. "Still doesn't get me to why we're brewing again."

"Because the last time I lived next to a big supply of my Flex, she sent in a guy to kill me. He was juiced with something that felt like cockroaches were crawling in my veins – and when she stood next to me, it felt like wolves vomiting in my throat…"

"Whoa!" Valentine said, almost spitting her coffee. "Can you restrain the purple prose until after I fill myself with nutrients?"

"Croissandwiches aren't nutrients, Valentine. They're fat and salt."

"As am I."

"Anyway, when she went after me yesterday, she

was screaming I 'take the cost away.' That's my Flex, pure, without blowback. Refined, pure 'mancy like mine is – well, it's like waving a red flag. Get a stockpile, she'll have to come after me."

"Does she know you know that?"

"I don't think it'd matter if she did. She's insane."

Valentine fingered her stitches, wincing. "And fucking dangerous, Paul. She killed two hundred and fifty-six people with her last stunt. I came close to being one of them. Her next attack will kill half a thousand. I'm all for the good fight, but... Can we get help?"

Paul wished he could talk to Kit. Kit would make sense of this. But he could stop Anathema; when she showed, he'd backdate warrants to have a hundred cops surrounding her.

It'd have to be cops. No SMASH. He couldn't risk another broach, as he had a feeling Anathema would happily flood New York with buzzsects. Which meant maybe they'd have to lend a hand...

"There's a risk we might get outed as 'mancers," Paul said. "But if we asked–"

The doorbell rang.

"That's not the cops, is it?" Valentine asked.

"That'd be my foot. Would you mind getting it?"

Valentine signed for it, dropping it into his lap with a perplexed expression. "It's a big box. Which they shipped *four days ago*. How did you..."

"I backdated the invoice."

"You can order backwards in *time*?"

"We all have our specialties," Paul shrugged. He unwrapped the box to lift out an artificial leg. The top-of-the-line model he'd had before the buzzsects chewed his old one up. It had cost him as much as a luxury car, draining the last of his savings – but he didn't dare put this claim through Samaritan Mutual, or Kit would track him down. And if he'd lowered the cost, the flux load would have endangered Aliyah.

Getting a leg he *could* have afforded? Minimal 'mancy. Minimal danger.

He plugged it into the wall to charge. "Look, Aliyah. Daddy's got his leg back." He waggled it as if she might move to steal it again.

Aliyah ignored him. She was playing her DS again, as she had since the doctor left.

Was she trying to find her mother in the maze? He shoved the thought away.

"Here's where I need your 'mancy," Paul said. "Normally, fitting a prosthetic leg is a long process. But in videogames, they–"

Valentine snapped her fingers. When Paul shoved his stump into the transtibial cup, there was a drill-like "whrr", a clockwork spasm, and the leg popped on as easily as putting on powered armor in a videogame.

"Three cheers for cross-pollination." She tilted her head to admire the fit. "I wouldn't have thought to do that."

"I wouldn't have thought to revoke my Flex." Paul stood up and almost wept with joy. It shouldn't be *that* big a deal to be ambulatory again. But it was. He felt more competent, more confident, more himself.

He tapped his metal foot on the floor, baiting Aliyah's attention. She didn't look up.

"Okay, Paul," Valentine whispered, hunkering down next to him. "Final Jeopardy time. The answer is, 'What small child should be in the path of a spear-o-mancer?' Remember, all answers must come in the form of a responsible parent."

Paul massaged the bridge of his nose, ignoring the way she mangled the rules of *Jeopardy*. "I know, I know. But if I put Aliyah back in the hospital, Anathema would track her down."

"You're making this sound personal, Paul. She's not–"

"It *is* personal, Valentine. That's the *point*. Do you know why I spent hours filling out every box on every last Samaritan Mutual form? Because if that paperwork wasn't perfect, some vindictive little penny-pincher would use the imperfection as an excuse to refuse the claim. Some poor bastard lost his wife in a car accident, and one incomplete form meant he never got the money. So I dotted all the i's and crossed the t's. For them."

"Paul…"

"Except that was a step *up* from my old job! Back on the force, I'd seen murderers walk because some cop filed the evidence wrong. I didn't get obsessed with paperwork because it was fun, Valentine – I did it because getting it right meant the right people *lived*. Paperwork is how we bend bad organizations to our will. Paperwork is how we twist arms to squeeze assistance from dead-eyed politicians. Humanity stopped being animals once a law became more important than a sword."

She held up her hands, sensing his 'mancy rising up

around him. "Yo, chief, I believe you, I–"

"And *she*. People don't matter to her – Anathema kills hundreds just to make a *point*. She wants to whittle us back down to a 'simpler' time, when women died in childbirth and men died from gangrene!

"So, yeah, Valentine. It's personal. I started my 'mancy to bend the world to make people better. She's using hers to make it worse. Our 'mancies are fire and water – we can't both survive. And she'll go for Aliyah, because hell, you think a born-again *caveman* is bound by a moral code against killing kids?"

"I get that, Paul," Valentine said softly. "I do. But are we the ones to protect her?"

"Who else? The cops haven't stopped her, SMASH hasn't stopped her, Samaritan Mutual hasn't – the only thing that's ever thwarted Anathema is sitting in this room."

Valentine raised an eyebrow over her good eye. "… Me?"

"I stabbed her in the leg. I believe that would make it an 'us.'"

She gave him a slacker's "Yeah, buddy" grin, then held out her hand for a bro-slap. He returned it, with emphasis.

"All right," she said, tucking into a donut. "You've dragged me into your grand life of adventure, Paul. Make the Flex, attract the crazy, save the child."

Paul sighed, looking over at Aliyah. "I wish the child would talk to me."

"…She hasn't?"

"Not since I told her about me."

Valentine held up a "wait there" finger and hunkered down next to Aliyah.

"Hey." Aliyah reacted to Valentine's presence with a full-body wriggle, inching backward, but kept her gaze on the Nintendo.

Valentine yanked it from Aliyah's hands.

"Hey!" Aliyah yelled, infuriated. "Give it back!"

"Why would you want it?" Valentine bank-shot the Nintendo into the trashcan. "A filthy, nasty 'mancer gave you that toy. Why would you want a gift from an ugly, horrible person? Why would you want it from someone you wish was *dead*?"

The look of betrayal on Aliyah's face was the same as when the doctor refused her help.

"You are a selfish, *awful* little girl," Valentine continued in a hateful tone. "I told you how pretty you were when you were scared about looking burned. I brought you games when you feared for your Daddy's life. I snuck past nurses to stay up late with you, sat by your bed until you fell asleep. Then you find out I'm a 'mancer, and none of that matters?"

Aliyah's lip puffed out, sullenly approaching the point of no return. Beating Aliyah up emotionally only backed her into a corner, and once you backed a stubborn kid like Aliyah up, *nothing* got her out.

"Valentine–"

She whirled to face him, her face so furious, Paul flinched into silence.

"Lemme tell you how it is, kid," Valentine continued. "'Mancy? Is like getting burned. You don't become a 'mancer because you want to; you become a 'mancer because the world hurt you badly enough that you had nowhere to go but out the other side. You become a 'mancer because somebody else broke all your happiness, and so you retreat to this fantasy world, and it ought to be great that it's real…

"…but it turns out magic can kill you. And if you don't die, then your mother calls you a freak and says she wishes you'd never been born. Then little girls who you would have given your freaking *life* for tell you they want you dead."

Valentine backed Aliyah against the wall. Aliyah quivered.

"But hey! Maybe I should be dead. Your Daddy? He didn't ask to be a 'mancer, either. But he's done more with that than any other 'mancer I heard of. He's risked his life to save people from the woman who burned you. He's going to do it again, even though most of those people would lock him up if they knew who he was. He's doing it even though his selfish little daughter is having a hissy fit because her Daddy can't help being a 'mancer any more than she can help having seared skin.

"So, yeah. You don't deserve my Nintendo. You don't deserve my friendship. And you especially don't deserve your Daddy."

Valentine pushed herself off the floor, grim-faced. She stepped away as Aliyah burst into tears.

Valentine thumped Paul on the shoulder.

"Bad cop: accomplished," she said. "Go get 'er, good cop."

Paul was about to scream at Valentine for saying such cruel things, when Aliyah held up her arms and begged

Daddy for forgiveness, she didn't mean it, she didn't know about 'mancers, please, Daddy, please.

And there was nothing to do but sweep Aliyah up into his arms and comfort her like the father he desperately wanted to be, telling her it was okay, he loved her, he always *would* love her, and nothing would ever change that. And she clung to him, weeping so violently that he was afraid she might throw up, all those weeks of emotion surging out in one torrent of tears.

As he patted Aliyah's back, trying to soothe her, he saw Valentine, legs hanging over the balcony, lost in thought.

He wondered how much of that speech had been calculation.

He wondered how much he could forgive her.

THIRTY-THREE
Tears of Cold Blue Fire

Aliyah drifted off in his arms. He let her. He didn't know how many days he had left with her. Eventually, SMASH would find him, or he'd overload from his own 'mancy, or maybe he'd find the courage to leave.

So he savored the scent of his daughter's skin – still acrid from the trauma, but her baby-powder scent was creeping back like flowers after a forest fire. The half words she always muttered as she slept, a secret language she either forgot upon waking or refused to tell.

She'd been scared by his 'mancy. Who wouldn't be? But here, as she dreamed, Aliyah clung to him.

He needed no other proof of love.

Eventually, she awoke, blearily looking him over as if to confirm: *That really happened*. She clambered down but did not run. Aliyah had always been an oddly practical little girl; he could see her struggling to try to make sense of these new facts.

He stayed silent. Valentine had toyed with Aliyah's emotions enough. Let her formulate her own questions.

He gave her her prescriptions, Xeroform and ciprofloxacin and methadone – a little bureaucromancy could get prescriptions for anything – and she made faces as she washed it down with orange juice. Then he set up an IV in her arm. The nursing tutorials hadn't prepared him for how small Aliyah's veins were. But she didn't cry out.

All the while, Valentine sat out on the balcony, playing the Nintendo DS. Her whole body was hunched over the tiny screen.

Aliyah touched his hand. "I gotta go," she whispered, not quite seeking permission; seeking approval.

The relationship Valentine and Aliyah had, he realized, moved to a different rhythm from what he and his daughter shared. He had no advice; here, he was clueless as Valentine and instead relied on his daughter's instincts.

So he nodded. And Aliyah let go.

Aliyah approached Valentine carefully, as though sneaking up on a cat who'd scratched her. If Valentine noticed, she gave no sign; she tilted the DS back and forth, playing hard. Aliyah slipped up behind her, holding her breath. Valentine concentrated on the screen for a minute…

Then wordlessly, Valentine handed the Nintendo DS to Aliyah.

Aliyah flung herself into Valentine's arms. Valentine grabbed Aliyah, sobbing her own tears, both whispering apologies to each other.

Paul withdrew, giving them their own time. Aliyah was growing up. This, at least, was a lesson he was glad for her to learn.

• • •

While Valentine taught Aliyah how to beat Mario's cloud level, Paul set up shop.

He set up the card tables Oscar's assistants had brought in, rearranging the Flex equipment in the fashion he was beginning to think of as "his" method: the hematite trays, the copper tubes to distill it, the bingo machine.

And, of course, there were the supplies Oscar didn't know Paul needed, available in any office: fresh pens. Clean paper. Paul found some W-4 tax forms underneath a desk.

He tried to remember he was legendarily good at this. Last time he'd brewed, he'd unleashed havoc. Now he was exploring further uncharted territory... and if it worked, then Anathema would come for him again.

He did not show Aliyah his fear.

"Aliyah," he said. "I want you to go in the bathroom and lock the door."

Aliyah confirmed this with Valentine, who frowned but nodded.

"This is dangerous, sweetie," Valentine explained. "We're – we're good at this. But someone could still get hurt."

"No."

Aliyah gave no screams, no anger, just a quiet dissent that reminded Paul all too well of Aliyah's mother.

"Sweetie," Valentine said, turning Aliyah to face her, "this is 'mancy. It's serious."

"My Daddy does it. He does it for..." Her brow furrowed with concentration, forming the words at the same time she formed the idea. "He does 'mancy for good."

"So?"

"If that's what Daddy is, that's what I watch."

Paul took her by the shoulders. "Are you sure?"

Aliyah nodded.

"All right," Paul said, rising. "Let's brew."

She was scared. Very scared. But Aliyah watched Paul's pen scratch across the paper, his 'mancy wavering whenever he checked in on his daughter. Aliyah stood staunchly near the table, hands balled into fists, straddling the ground wide so she wouldn't be tempted to run.

He was so afraid of hurting her.

The forms shifted underneath his fingers, mutating into hospital discharge papers, federal aid requests, invoices for skin grafts. He wrenched them back to contracts. This batch required agreements literally baked into it. He refocused to think in terms of clauses, restrictions, contingencies, distilling vague notions into hard paragraphs.

Eventually, the 'mancy flowed. It was his comfort, his retreat: the idea the world was predictable. Aliyah seemed to understand this magic was an extension of her father, crawling underneath the slow crumple of expanding paper, wrapping the forms around her shoulders.

Then came the worst part: strangling his love to distill it into drugs. And as Paul squeezed the forms into the alembics, leaving dry husks, he heard Aliyah stifling a cry.

Tears glistened on her scarred cheeks. Oh, yes. She understood the loss.

He allowed a moment of perfect mourning to form between them, sharing this understanding of the beauty and its cost.

Then he squeezed harder, and glowing crystals tumbled from his fingers.

THIRTY-FOUR
Flex Mentallo

Three days later, Oscar arrived on schedule.

Paul was concerned about such a public pickup, though he didn't have much choice – they didn't dare move to a new location. Every time Valentine crept out to get takeout, she brought back papers, and the *only* front-page story was the evil paleomancer who'd driven Paul Tsabo and his injured daughter into hiding.

Of *course* she'd gone after Paul Tsabo, the op-eds and letters to the editor implied; he was the only person in New York who wasn't afraid of 'mancers. People were certain Paul was planning revenge from his Batcave.

Problem was, his hiding hole wasn't a Batcave. It was the first-floor office of a busy downtown building. Thankfully, the wide glass windows had been taped over during construction, but hundreds of commuters still walked by every hour. Hundreds more walked through the lobby, where if a single one pushed their way through the fire doors, they'd find Paul Tsabo and his iconic artificial foot, his very visibly burned daughter, and a shitload of Flex.

Paul wondered how close Kit was to finding him.

He wondered whether Kit would find him before Anathema did.

It had been three days since he'd made the Flex, and Anathema had yet to show. He was hoping she'd attack so he'd never have to come clean on his bargain to Oscar – *Sorry, the rival mage destroyed my supply* – but no. She *should* have attacked. The stockpile of Flex was like a needle shoved in her eye. And Anathema didn't know that *he* knew she could track him.

So, why hadn't she come for him?

It didn't matter. He hid in the back office, cuddling Aliyah, while Valentine – now in full-on Psycho Mantis gas-mask skin – sat with a large sack of Flex on the desk before her. Next to it sat a stack of forms.

Oscar arrived at noon, as instructed, sliding sideways through the door so as not to give onlookers a glimpse. Behind him came three bodyguards, each burlier than the last.

Paul slid his hand over Aliyah's mouth, holding her against him. What a world, where hiding his daughter from a roomful of gun-toting mobsters was the *safest* course of action.

Paul hoped Valentine would remember what he'd told her, and not deviate from the script.

"Mantis." Oscar bowed, then tapped his cane on the floor. "Is that my Flex?"

A hiss from behind the gasmask. Had he been that unsettling? "It is."

Oscar took the sack. "How do I know it is genuine?"

Another hiss. Her claws flexed and unflexed.

Valentine seemed disconcertingly at home in that skin. "What would satisfy you as a test?"

"I wish to see 'mancy. Something startling."

The bodyguards withdrew from Mantis' cold gaze. "…you must decide what 'mancy you want to see."

Oscar nodded, as if he'd expected no less. "Very well. I wish to jump off the second floor and land safely, without a sound."

"Then take the Flex," Valentine/Mantis said, reaching into the sack. She placed a single crystal on the table between them, gloved fingers moving with insectile grace.

"You can't sell Flex! That's bad!" Aliyah cried, loud enough for Oscar to hear. Paul shushed her, but Oscar's gaze rose up to the second-floor office. He knew someone lurked up there. Doubtless that was why his test involved jumping.

The bodyguards chuckled. Oscar examined the glimmering crystal with a jeweler's eye loupe. "Do I… eat it?"

"Plug it in any orifice you see fit."

Oscar gave a thin frown, then tentatively ingested it. And "ingested" was the only way Paul could describe it; Oscar placed it on his tongue without pleasure and swallowed. His bodyguards tensed as Oscar took it down, the pale-eyed glare of tasters watching their king drink wine. When Oscar coughed, they went for their guns.

He waved them off – but didn't gesture for them to put the guns away. "My brother told me it tingled."

"Your brother was wrong about too many things."

Oscar hesitated; he examined Mantis again, sensing some difference, as yet unable to formulate it.

"Is it working?"

"Find out." A psychic gust of wind swept the dust aside, clearing a path up the second-floor stairs.

That wasn't the plan! Paul almost leapt out to yell about terms and conditions. But he didn't dare reveal his position.

Mantis. Mantis was controlling Valentine.

Goddammit... he thought, clutching Aliyah to his chest, formulating plans.

Oscar worked his way up the stairs, leaning heavily on his cane; Paul pulled Aliyah back, noting Oscar's limp was genuine. Had Gunza done that? Oscar crept along the railing, watching his feet, as though he expected to burst apart in a blaze of 'mancy. The concrete floor was twelve feet below, uncarpeted, littered with broken glass.

He paused before the frosted glass of the managerial office, craning his neck to peer into the darkness.

"I believe you wished to jump, not to explore," Mantis hissed.

"I feel no Flex," Oscar replied.

"It's within you," Mantis said. Mantis was not, in fact, lying. Technically.

From here, Paul could see the interplay of emotions on Oscar's face: the recognition that perhaps he should have left this to a bodyguard, the despair as he knew he couldn't leave this to a subordinate, the determination to do something that terrified him, the hatred of knowing that *Mantis* knew how terrified he was.

Then Oscar jumped off, and Paul almost reached out to grab him back.

Paul felt the psychic backwash as Mantis jammed the guards' guns.

Oscar's ankle cracked as he thumped into the concrete floor.

He heard the shouts as the bodyguards rushed Mantis, who smashed their faces into the floor.

Mantis levitated over the desk, absentmindedly snagging the stack of papers, gesturing behind him to call a pen to his hands. He floated towards Oscar; Paul begged, *Please don't kill him, please don't kill him–*

Oscar gritted his teeth, refusing to give Psycho Mantis the satisfaction of a scream. His foot was twisted back to touch his calf in a way that made Paul sick. "You – you will pay – my family will–"

"*Sign here.*" Mantis manipulated the paper and pen so they did a little mocking dance before Oscar.

Oscar breathed out through his nose, a man close to murder. Mantis opened Oscar's clenched fists finger by finger with psychic force, then pushed the pen in. "Sign."

"I will not."

Paul saw himself, chained to radiator: a small, unbowed man refusing to give in.

"That won't work!" he screamed, running to the railing. "He has to sign it willingly!"

Oscar looked up, not at all surprised to find Paul there. Mantis hesitated – how much of Valentine was left?

"Sign the contract voluntarily and the Flex will work," Paul explained before Mantis could do more damage. "The contract activates it. Mantis" – he almost said "I," then choked it back – "has to approve whatever you want to accomplish with his 'mancy. It has to be written out in advance, with no loopholes. In *detail*."

Oscar was beet-red with fury, but there was a relief on his face that Paul understood: he was talking to someone sane. "That was not our deal!"

"The deal is you take what we give you," Mantis purred.

"We don't want anyone hurt," Paul said, smoothing the waters. "We won't interfere with your business. But we don't want anyone killed. Use the Flex for peaceful ends, we'll approve it – which should be good for you. Murders bring cops. But you have to write out what you plan to use it for, in advance. In detail. The Flex works only when you're sticking to the contract."

"Are you mad?" Oscar yelled. "The things I want to do, I'm not *documenting* them!"

"It doesn't have to be your name," Paul urged. "Sign it as 'Peter Parker'. The contracts will know who you are. You can use pseudonyms for anything – call the people you're trying to bamboozle the party of the first part, refer to the building you're breaking into as Sesame Street, it doesn't matter. The details can be obscured. But you have to tell us what you're going to use the 'mancy for before we'll let you have it."

"You only let him do good things with it?" Aliyah asked, thrilled to see her faith in Daddy rewarded, and holy fuck, this was getting out of control. By the time he'd pushed her back into the office, Mantis had summoned a gun from a bodyguard's hand to hold it to Oscar's throat.

"Sign the paper, you useless worm," it hissed.

"*Dammit, get control, Vuh–*" Valentine was fighting for control inside the Mantis construct – but Paul couldn't use her name to help guide her back home. Not in front of Oscar, of all people. "*Sign it*, Oscar! Trust me. Just… trust me."

A stranger couldn't have gotten away with that. But Paul Tsabo, killer of 'mancers, could – and Paul saw Oscar's acknowledgement that he was dealing with someone with a lot of experience in this realm. Oscar bit back his loathing and signed.

The request flooded through Paul's body. He approved it just as Mantis flung a screaming Oscar high into the air, so high, Paul feared Oscar would be smashed against the ceiling.

The Flex kicked in, fulfilling the contract Paul had filled in for him: land safely, without a sound. Oscar landed with a gymnast's grace, his cane clattering to the floor.

He stared, stunned, at his shoes – the fact that they were planted on the ground perfectly, the fact that the impact had set his broken ankle, not healing the bones but shoving things back into optimal healing positions. Mantis, perhaps more under Valentine's control, whipped the cane back into his hands, allowing him to rest his weight.

"This Flex." Oscar's face was suffused with a junkie's wonder. Paul shivered; it was the first time Oscar had resembled his brother. "It is amazing."

"I'm sorry it comes with conditions," Paul apologized. "But your brother taught Mantis how 'mancy could be used against him. And we won't be party to murder."

Someone kicked the door in. *Both* doors. The heavy metal fire doors burst off their hinges, deformed, skidding to a halt at Psycho Mantis' feet.

Beyond it, outlined in the lobby, stood a hulking man wearing only a bright blue banana hammock. He slammed his foot into the floor, causing a tremor that rocked the building – and then posed in the doorframe, flexing biceps that looked like distended, walnut-colored tumors. His tiny head squatted atop a massive body, wide veins squirming between his striated muscle folds.

As he shifted into another position, presenting his biceps as though he were cradling a baby, Paul retched up his donuts. The man radiated wrongness, a fetid swamp-shit stench that smelled like all of New York had died in a hot summer and been left to putrefy in their apartments. He fought for sanity while Oscar, Mantis, and Aliyah all froze in place, their mouths open with awe.

"*Step aside, mortals!*" said the bodybuilder, speaking with the rich resonance of a cartoon superhero. "*I am here to collect your drugs.*"

Paul wondered if this day could get any weirder.

THIRTY-FIVE

It's the End of Paul's World as He Knows it

Oscar's burliest bodyguard scrambled for his gun.

"*Pose!*" the muscleman yelled, and twirled on the balls of his toes to bring his deltoids into view. A visible force wave rippled out from his scalloped shoulder muscles, striking the guard in the forehead. The guard, kneeling, trembled as the bolt shivered through him. He looked at his own herculean physique, then back at the muscleman's…

…and pressed his forehead against the ground in worship.

The muscleman looked both shocked and pleased by this development. "This," he pronounced, "is *awesome*."

Then he advanced across the office floor, striking a new pose with each step. The people behind him in the elevator lobby stood stunned with admiration.

"No fear, citizens," he said, striding towards the table. He touched the two other guards on the foreheads; they shook with adulation. "I am taking only what I need. Some risks are necessary to build a body like mine. I have found the key to a perfect, healthy lifestyle." He winked. "If you're lucky, I may share it with you."

The crowd sighed with happiness. Muscleman bowed, eating up their adulation.

Aliyah breathed shallowly. At first, Paul thought she felt the vomitous sickness the bodybuilder radiated – but then he realized she was mesmerized, her eyes tracking the muscleman's every twitch. Oscar, his bodyguards, the people streaming in from the street; all bowed to this gnarled heap of muscles.

"Get back in the office," Paul told her.

"He's so *beautiful*." She stroked her bed-weakened arms contemplatively. "Could I be strong like that, Daddy?"

Paul gagged on his spittle. The sickness intensified with each bicep Flex–

–*Flex*, he thought, his head whirling. *He's juiced with Anathema's Flex*–

Yet somehow, the muscleman *was* beautiful. In another place, the muscleman'd be a spray-tanned wad of brawn stuffed into an ill-fitting bikini bottom. Yet Paul felt new appreciations opening up inside him – understanding the sweat that went into bulking up those triceps, the fierce dedication to heaving lead weights, the asceticism it took to convert weakness into layers of strength. The muscleman was using Anathema's Flex to force open a window into everyone's soul, showing them his body *as he himself saw it*.

If we could only understand what people loved–

The muscleman took Oscar's sack of Flex. He weighed it in his palm.

"It doesn't look to have nearly the punch of the stuff I just got." He was playing to the crowd, drawing out the moment as if he thought it might never happen again. "But I've had worse. You have to have supplements to get this kind of body, you know. Creatine. Whey shakes. Scoops of glutamine. I spent a lotta time being low man in the gym. There's not much respect for the weak in this world." Businessmen and housewives alike took notes. "So I'll eat *anything* to get ripped!"

He raised the full sack to his mouth, cabled jaws yawning.

Her next attack will kill 512 people, Paul thought. *With Aliyah here…*

Paul hurtled down the stairway, trying to stop the muscleman from gobbling the Flex. Maybe nothing would happen. Unlike this last batch, nothing *could* happen until Paul approved it.

Or maybe the Flex would explode when Anathema's caged 'mancy clashed with his.

"Oh, no," Valentine yelled. "You're not mixing *that* Mentos with my Diet Coke!"

She was still in Mantis' skin, but Valentine was back in charge. She flew across the room and smashed into the muscleman, sending Flex flying up like popcorn. The crowd shrieked at the open display of 'mancy; some fled, but others, outraged at Valentine harming their newly introduced idol, grappled her down.

The muscleman seemed dismayed. "Why would you try to fight me?" he asked, desperate to please. "I'm *strong*! And I'm kind! The strongest *and* kindest!"

He stomped. The building shook. Cracks shot down the walls, racing down from the ceiling to converge underneath his bare heel, rubble tumbling down around him.

"All that muscle gives you is more hit points." Valentine shrugged off the passersby, then force-smashed Muscleman into the wall. Muscleman peeled himself out of the plaster, yanking an iron beam free – which, if you weren't looking too carefully, looked like he ripped it out himself. But, as Paul saw, the beam sheared through at the exact instant the muscleman grabbed for it.

He waggled the beam back and forth, like some obscenely magnified orchestra conductor. Valentine circled him, her feet dangling in mid-air, ready to dodge.

Muscleman didn't swing. He looked deer-in-the-headlights confused, uncertain what to do once people weren't idolizing him, not wanting to hurt even this gas-masked freak.

Then his puglike face lit up with a smile. Sickening 'mancy flooded the room.

The roof collapsed.

Valentine fell sprawling as the roof sagged inward, steel beams shrieking as the fifty floors above them caved in, raining chunks of concrete down on the crowd.

The muscleman stepped in to meet the incoming debris. He raised his hands in a clean-and-jerk to meet the rubble, slapping his palms underneath it–

–and the collapsing ceiling stopped as he heaved upwards.

Muscles trembling, he appeared to hold up the entire building. The ceiling groaned under the strain, a jigsaw mass of rubble interlocking in a fantastic interplay to freeze in place. To anyone but Paul, it appeared the muscleman had shoved the ceiling back into a stable position, as opposed to dashing to where the collapse would have stopped naturally.

Paul wanted to applaud. It was a fake, of course. A dangerous fake. But a magnificent fake.

"*Go!*" Muscleman yelled to Valentine, who lay sprawled – unconscious? – underneath him. Paul realized Muscleman had positioned himself in a Superman pose, interposing himself between certain death and a helpless citizen. "*Save yourself! I'll fix this!*"

This wasn't real 'mancy, Paul realized. Just a sad man juiced with shitload of Flex – which was engineering coincidences to give the muscleman the illusion of superhuman feats.

Feats that required building-crumbling coincidences. Coincidences that were the obvious channel for the muscleman's impending flux.

Paul scooped Aliyah up and weaved through the dazed crowd. They seemed paralyzed, wanting to watch their hero save the day – a significant chunk of the five hundred and twelve who'd die when the building collapsed. But there were louder shrieks from outside, and as Paul blinked in the sunshine, he looked for what had caused the real damage.

A Mack truck had careened out of control, slamming into the building. It had hit the wall when muscleman had stomped down – and caused the walls to crack just in time for him to grab an iron beam. Unlikely, yes, but Anathema's Flex ensured the truck struck the building at its weakest point.

Paul signed in the air, activating his bureaucromancy; the cops arrived as soon as his fingers stopped moving. That, at least, he could do – but could his bureaucromancy stabilize a sagging building?

Another dull *boom* as the building tilted. He told Aliyah to stay here – was that safer? – and rushed inside, hoping against hope to fix this.

Muscleman found the ceiling sagging downward. "Flee!" he yelled again, looking more baffled by the moment. "I'll hold the building until you're safe!" Except he couldn't. The Flex was draining away. When it was gone, Anathema's flux would kill him, along with five hundred and eleven other people.

The muscleman strained against the ceiling, reassuring Valentine he'd set this right – as if all this would make sense if he lifted harder.

Paul felt a horrible pity for the man. He could have used the Flex to crush men's skulls–

–but he'd wanted to be a hero.

Paul understood the temptation. A small man obsessed with being big. But the window the muscleman opened into his soul also showed Paul all the ways Muscleman's body wasn't quite up to snuff – his lats were underdeveloped, his posing too hesitant, his body fat a percentage point higher than it should be. He'd devoted his life to pumping iron and was *still* the mocking boy of the club.

He hadn't given up, though. He'd believed if he just

found the right supplement or technique, he'd break through... and people would admire him.

Those were the people Anathema preyed upon: the wannabes. The people who might have been 'mancers, had they been crazier. The sad bastards who never had a chance and yet never gave up.

He felt certain the ballroom dancers had been killed by some left-footed sad sack. Some innocent person who would have given anything to twirl beneath the stars in top hat and tails.

Anathema had turned their dreams to death. Just like the kid who'd burned his apartment. Just like that nebbish who'd shot up Gunza's thugs. Just like the flux blowback had obliterated all of Anathema's other victims, leaving no witnesses for the people who had no friends.

I'm going to beat you, Anathema, he thought. *And when I do, I'll crush your dreams like you crushed theirs.*

An ominous juddering reminded Paul just who might get crushed.

"Vuh – *Mantis*!" he yelled, shaking Valentine back to consciousness. "Time to give me a hand!"

"Save yourself, citizen!" the muscleman shouted. "I'll–"

"You're going to die." Paul scavenged underneath the desk for forms. "You have been given Flex. Do you know what that is?"

The muscleman's face, dark with blood, drained to a mottled paleness. Of course he knew. Everyone knew what Flex was and how Anathema was using it.

"Right now, you are saturated with flux – with bad luck." Paul patted his pockets for a pen. "*Do not think.*

Keep your mind clear. Pretend you're doing a set of reps. Can you do that?"

"I... I think so... I feel sick..."

"That's the flux." *When that flux pours out, the building will collapse.* "The good news is, you have a lot of Flex to burn." *So much I'm choking back bile.* "You can stabilize this. But you have to..."

Paul concentrated on the forms, trying to think how he'd sign over responsibility. Would it be a lien? A power of attorney? An assumption of debt? He scrawled boxes on the form, debating all the legal ramifications of handing over bad luck.

"...you have to concentrate on *fixing* this," Paul continued. "Not on being a hero. You're trying to impress us – you already have. You didn't kill anyone with your power. That makes you a good guy."

"I *am* a good guy."

"What's your name?"

"Moishe."

"Good, Moishe." He scrawled another name on the contract, which blossomed into typewritten letters. "I need you to sign this."

The muscleman looked up at his quivering biceps, still caught in the illusion of holding up the building. Paul gave him the look he used to give underage kids who thought pushing their beer underneath the seat meant he wouldn't smell it on their breath.

"That's all show. You know that. Now you'll help for real. You're gonna be the first person to *not* trigger Anathema's terror. That's a real hero, Moishe. Let go and sign this."

Moishe lowered his hands slowly, afraid the sagging ceiling would collapse onto him. And the mass of bent lights and rebar *was* creaking, settling, seeking a way to cave in – but five hundred pounds of pressing wouldn't make a difference.

"What will this do?"

Paul took a deep breath, about to belly-flop into the deep end. "It'll transfer your bad luck to me."

Moishe took the pen from Paul's hand to sign the contract. His muscles began to glow a deep green – a jungled hue, like moonlight filtered through tree leaves. Then it rose off him in a wave and arced into Paul.

Paul clamped his hands to his forehead. It squeezed tight, threatening to burst him like a piñata. The pain was like having his still-beating heart shoved into a grinder...

He could not imagine any worst-case scenarios, because once he did, they would happen. And kill them all.

Valentine staggered to her feet. "What do we do, Paul?"

"He's got... enough juice left." Each word was a razor blade cutting his tongue. "Help him stabilize the building. Have everything... collapse so it locks together ..."

"We can do that." Behind her gas mask, Paul saw her real eye narrow. "We can – yeah. All it takes is a fun time. Hey, muscles – ready to play a minigame?"

Bright pulsing circles appeared on the wreckage, irising down into targets. "Hit them hard, and they'll settle this building into a nice, stable configuration."

Moishe cracked his knuckles as Valentine started a timer countdown. Paul ran for the door, knowing he couldn't stay. The slightest doubt would squirm out to solidify, dooming them all.

He staggered out to the street as fire engines pulled up, people flooding out through the doors, the firm hand of state-sponsored guardians stopping the crowd from panicking.

The flux pressed in around him, battering at him. He had to burn this fatal load off in stages – break a leg, lose an eye, chip away incrementally. Otherwise, it'd end his life as he knew it...

Kit clapped a hand on his shoulder.

"*Bubeleh*!" he cried, pulling Paul into an embrace. "I owe you a lifetime's supply of donuts. I've been so worried. I should have known you'd be on the scene..."

He hasn't figured out I'm a 'mancer, has he?

The flux sensed that panic, squirmed through it–

Kit's eyes fell to the contract still clutched in Paul's hand, the one Moishe signed. It glowed with the aftermath of the bargain he'd made. The letters jittered on the paper, finalizing the flux transfer to Paul Tsabo, bureaucromancer.

Kit's arms stiffened around Paul, turning a hug into a grapple. "You," he whispered, voice hoarse with betrayal. "You – you're *sick*."

Oh, yeah, Paul thought. *That'll end my life as I know it.*

THIRTY-SIX
Who's the Leader of the Club?

Kit gripped Paul's shoulders hard enough to leave bruises; hard to believe the old man had that much strength in him. "Are you Anathema?"

"No!"

Kit clutched his head in anguish. "The evidence was before me all the time; I just didn't want to see it – I overlooked something *so obvious* because you were a friend – and *you* told me it was *rats*!"

"I hated lying to you, Kit, I did, but you'd–"

"I can't let this go, boy. *Police! We have a–*"

Things might have gone very badly if Aliyah hadn't shown up.

"*Uncle Kit*!" she yelled, holding her still-burned arms out for Kit to pick her up. Kit glanced toward the cops; Paul could see him asking, *After all she's been through, dare I haul her father off in front of her?*

A little good luck to offset the bad, Paul thought, feeling a swell of love for Aliyah.

"Kit." Paul squeezed Kit's shoulder. "Let's talk."

• • •

Paul's cramped office was not meant for meetings – Kit, Aliyah, the back-in-her-own-skin Valentine, and, of course, Paul. Aliyah propped herself on Paul's desk between keyboard and blotter, hungrily eyeing the tray of donuts Kit had brought in. Paul put his arm protectively around his daughter – and Kit flattened himself against the door, arms crossed, his rumpled tweed hat pulled down over his brow.

Valentine slumped against the filing cabinets, guzzling a Red Bull for energy.

"Whoo, this place *reeks* of 'mancy," she said, wrinkling her nose. "Look, my arm hairs are standing on end."

"Well, it *is* my lair," Paul demurred.

Valentine rolled her eye. "Really, Paul? Your 'lair'? Is there a lever you pull to drop people into a shark tank? Besides, your bureaucromancy's saturated the building. You can feel this in the lobby."

"*When did you start?*" Kit wrung his cap in his hands as though he wished it were Paul's throat. No wonder, Paul thought. The 'mancy had been obvious, and poor Kit felt foolish for not seeing it.

"A month or two ago."

"Oh, Lord." Kit massaged a vein on his forehead. "You've seen what 'mancers do when they get out of control. And you, you... you thought this would be okay? To just... break the world's physics?"

Aliyah looked troubled. Paul squeezed her foot. "Not all the 'mancers I found were bad, Kit. Some wanted to create art. But people get so terrified when they see 'mancy, they push 'mancers to extremes..."

Kit sagged like he'd been punched. "You only turned in the ones you thought were harmful, didn't you? You let them go. Did I even know you at all?"

"'Mancy's not what you think. It's not inherently destructive; it's just... an alternative. A lot of it's beautiful."

"A leopard's beautiful, but you don't keep it in your apartment. Speaking of which, your apartment – was that you, too? Did you – lose control and set something aflame? Did you hurt–"

"*No!*" Aliyah edged away from Paul, Kit's fears feeding hers. "Sweetie, have a donut. It's okay."

"But my nurse said–"

"Today's special. Go nuts." He turned to Kit again. "The fire was Anathema. And Aliyah would have–" Paul couldn't say it out loud. "It would have been very bad if I hadn't been a 'mancer."

Kit craned his neck, picking up on Paul's guilt. "But it wasn't entirely good, either, was it? Something went wrong. You weren't as in control as you thought you were then, and you're not as in control as you think you are now. You need help, boychik. The flux, it always rebounds. It destroys everything you love – then you'll chase it down further, thinking you can fix insanity by pouring more craziness into it. That's the 'mancer's spiral.

"No, Paul. You need to get into the Army. They'll help you."

"You know," Valentine interrupted, "You're talking to the only guy who's stopped Anathema. Twice. I think the Army needs *Paul's* help."

Kit *tch*ed her. "I need no advice from a chocolate kreme donut person. Wasteful. Overloads of sweetness from the messiest donut in the pile. *This* is who you team up with, Paul? Some tattooed freak?"

"I *like* Vallumtime's tattoos!" Aliyah yelped.

Kit ignored her. "When have 'mancers helped *anyone*, Ms DiGriz? I've helped track them down my whole life, and have they ever helped anyone but themselves? No! What do these maniacs care about? Cats. Antique cars. God save me from the Lucasmancers, with their stupid slicey-things. No. They don't want to live here. If a 'mancer cared about making the world better, they wouldn't try so hard to replace It!"

"*I* helped you," Paul said. "Making things better is... it's my 'mancy. And I found a way to *help*. With magic. All I've wanted since this started was to stop Anathema."

"Nobody's debating your intentions, Paul. I'm sure there were good 'mancers in World War II, but... they erred. You need to join the Army, before you lose control. They make 'mancy *safe*."

Valentine spluttered Red Bull. "The way they made Long Island safe? When those fuckers ignited the broach Paul had to clean up?"

Kit scowled, waggling a liver-spotted finger at Valentine. "They didn't start a broach! *You* did, refusing to be arrested for a crime you committed!"

She swatted his finger away. "Okay, yeah, the military's the one to trust. Because World War II was the first war we mass-produced 'mancers. It's not like the military didn't cause the broach that ate *Europe*."

"That was independents! Crazy 'mancers acting on their own volition!"

Paul stepped between them. "Nobody knows what caused the broach there. Nobody survived to tell. Could have been the OSS Extraphysics Detachment or the independent Aryomancers.

"But," Paul continued, "when Europe went up, we lost *centuries* of 'mancer scholarship. Kit, you're a man of learning – you know how little we actually understand about 'mancy. Ever since that tragedy, we've killed or captured every 'mancer on sight. The only people authorized to do studies are black ops SMASH psychologists, and they don't release their findings. Isn't it possible some 'mancers could be motivated to do good?"

Appealing to Kit's intellect was a blatant ploy, which made it no less effective. Kit scrubbed his face with his palm. "Maybe some. That doesn't mean they're not dangerous. Like sweating gelignite."

"Fair," Paul said. "But now you've got dynamite out there with a burning fuse. She's killed five hundred people already. She would have killed another five hundred today. The next time, a thousand. And can you honestly tell me you could have stopped that building collapsing without Valentine and I?"

"...No. You could be useful. But it's not just you, Paul. It's..." Kit couldn't bring himself to look at Aliyah, who was tucking into a Boston Kreme. "If it was just you, then maybe I'd use you and throw you away, painful as that thought is. But you're a *father*, Paul. The flux... we both know where it'll go." He gestured at the fresh mirror-cuts on Aliyah's face. "Will you tell me you can raise your daughter? The way a good man would be satisfied with?"

Paul looked to Valentine for support... and found her questioning him.

"It'd be a tough act, Paul," she muttered. "Not much precedence for well-adjusted 'mancer parents. Most 'mancers, they're kind of... estranged."

"What's 'estranged'?" Aliyah asked, sensing the tension around her.

"Distant." Paul felt wretched about obfuscating the truth yet again. "Weird."

"You're weird. Your 'mancy is weird. It's pretty, *so* pretty, but... it hurts people. It cut me, broke that poor man's ankle. And Uncle Kit says it hurts people, too. I know you wanna stop the bad 'mancer... but after? You need to stop, Daddy. You need to not be a 'mancer."

The sound of Aliyah chewing her donut was the only sound in the office. Kit's face was hooded: *If you can't walk away from Aliyah, Paul*, his expression promised, *I'll call SMASH*.

"Let me find Anathema," Paul pled. "Once I find her, we'll – you'll do what you have to. I won't blame you."

"You saved five hundred lives today," Kit said, softening. "You get full credit for that, my friend. But I don't know what our next move would be..."

"I know how to find her," Paul said.

THIRTY-SEVEN
Time and Space in Relative Dimensions

"How you feeling?" Valentine asked.

Central Park's summery dusk was packed with tourists and students, as always. Paul usually loved the rush and flow of crazy backpack-toting hipsters looking for cheap entertainment, of pudgy middle-aged couples with kids in tow, of grim joggers determined to get the last sunlight run.

Tonight, though, Paul concentrated on the vomit.

He'd thought that sick background vibration was a part of his 'mancy. But no, that was Anathema's influence spreading across the city.

Only one of them could survive.

Focusing on her magic was like pushing his head deeper into a barf bag, but tuning into this violation was necessary. Anathema's next trick would kill a thousand people in one shot. He had to find her before it was too late.

Besides, immersing himself in her queasy spells was better than pondering his future.

He slowed, frowning, talking half steps down different

paths. Anathema's trail was maddeningly faint; he thought of all the times he'd put his phone on vibrate and forgotten where he left it, so Imani called him while he'd wandered around the house, trying to triangulate the softest of buzzes. He and Valentine had wandered all day, wasting time on echoes and false starts, calling Kit with hourly reports that they were closer but unsure how close.

Valentine had hovered two steps behind him all day, reaching out at his every wince, treating him like a wheezing Chihuahua. He hated being treated like an invalid, always had.

"I'm fine," Paul said, biting back irritation. "Hard to focus. Lots of people around tonight."

"They're showing the outdoor film festival tonight. Free movies for everyone."

"You could go, you know." He wished she would.

She shook her head. "Movies are like a videogame cutscene that's twenty times too long. I got the attention span of a—"

Paul looked around for what had distracted her, then frowned. "Very funny."

"No, seriously, I went once. They showed some movie about 2001 – most boring thing ever. My boyfriend got pissed at me when I played my PSP instead of watching the fine cinematography, so I put it away to avoid a fight. I killed time, wondering how it'd be playing *God of War* on an outdoor screen a hundred feet high."

"Was that Raphael?"

She choked, a bitter laugh. "*God*, no. He never took

me anywhere. No, I used to try to have boyfriends, once. You know. Back in the day."

"Back before…" He did a little twirling gesture that somehow signified 'mancy.

"Yeah."

They'd had some amiable silences. This one itched like a wool shirt.

"Let's go," he said.

He shuffled off the path, deeper into the woods, and felt a seething loathing. The forest. The elm trees resented being shackled under asphalt paths, force-fed polluted air and insecticides, wanted to crush the city under root…

Of course she'd holed up in Central Park.

Valentine tugged him back. "Is this a good idea?"

"You got any better ones?"

"Yeah. *Not* heading into the woods to chase a crazy cannibal killer. You're shit at fighting, and we've established she can shut me down. Think she's here? Send in SMASH."

"They didn't find Gunza. They won't find her."

SMASH relied too much on their expensive opals and not enough on detective work. Opals shattered in the presence of active 'mancy but not around unused Flex or clever 'mancers who chose not to cast spells. They'd low-flown their helicopters back and forth across the city, trusting to oversensitive stones to hunt Anathema.

Still, 'mancers weren't common, even Army ones. A hundred SMASH Unimancers – more than most states had total – had been retasked to New York. They had patrolled what they could of Central Park's depths. He imagined a SMASH team's brain-burned 'mancers filing through the woods, concerned with each other in their tiny, incestuous world – then shoved the thought away.

You'll be one of them soon enough.

"They're slow and stupid," Paul snapped. "I've got a GPS that Kit is tracking. If it vanishes, well, he can tell SMASH our last known location. Right now, only I can track her down."

"So, your plan's okay with you dying? That's an acceptable risk?"

He tromped into the woods, not looking back. "I didn't ask you to come along."

She'd been braced for that blow but sounded gut-punched nonetheless. "I *came*," she said angrily, "because that's what friends *do*. And when you start thinking suicide by 'mancer is a better option than taking care of your kid, then you *need* a friend."

"What can I do, Valentine? Keep hurting Aliyah? You've seen SMASH soldiers – you get reduced to a set of orders and an artificially incestuous bond. I'd be better off dead."

"So learn to stop hurting your kid."

"Says the woman who–" He pulled himself from the abyss. Accusing her of getting Raphael killed would accomplish nothing. "You know all my flux will hit her – that's *abuse*, Valentine!"

"Don't you dare educate *me* in abusive fathers, Paul. They wouldn't give a fuck. You do."

"Yeah, well, all my caring doesn't mean a damn when fucking *mirrors* explode in her face!"

"So the solution is suicide or SMASH? You said it

yourself, Paul – we don't know what 'mancers can do. You've done shit I didn't think *could* be done with 'mancy – clear Flex, swapping flux loads, sewing up holes in the universe. If anyone can make parenting with 'mancy work, you can."

"But–"

"*No*. You dragged me into this, Paul. You think I accomplished anything with my 'mancy? No. Kit was right. All I did before I met you was retreat from this world so I could build a cooler one in my closet. But you, Paul – you made me wonder: 'What *good* could I do with this power?' I don't have to fight Anathema, or help you, or help Aliyah – but it's *worthwhile*. I'm melding my fantasy with reality. It makes me stronger. Don't you rob Aliyah of that."

"I'm not robbing her of anything!"

"You're robbing her of all this beautiful shit that we *do*! She cried when she saw you squeeze magic into Flex! She gets it! And you're going to let Kit convince her that this impoverished bundle of physics is all there is?"

She rolled up her sleeves as if preparing for a physical fight. Paul felt shamed, exhausted.

"…I don't wanna fight."

"Then don't be a dick. And yeah. I'm gonna follow you. *I* know why you've spent the last twelve hours hunting down Anathema without so much as a Pepsi break: you're trying to get your heroic blaze of glory over with. Fuck that. I'm in your way. Watch me die first, motherfucker." She spat on the ground. "Also: you're shit in a fight."

Paul's heart was a blender, mixing prickly annoyance and loving gratitude. He spoke gruffly – not the yell he wanted to drive her away, not the embrace he wanted to wrap her in.

"Let's go," he said, feeling better, pushing deeper into the forest's hateful sickness.

When Paul couldn't stop dry-heaving, he knew he'd found Anathema's lair.

"A cave?" Valentine asked, hands on hips in disbelief. "In Central Park?"

"She duh–" Paul retched again. This cave was the most isolated place he could imagine. In the city, he felt surrounded by bureaucracy's support network – the roads that paperwork built, the houses that paperwork bought, the repairmen and road workers and trash collectors that paperwork employed.

Inside that cave was a howling emptiness.

There were no grain silos to get through a harsh winter, no medical books to help the sick – just scrawny Neanderthals chasing deer, killing if they felt like it, no court of appeals except for a knife in the night.

He sensed how Anathema viewed it – men living by cunning alone, men who could make a spear, build a fire, dress a boar, weave a loincloth. A thousand skills civilization had obsoleted. To Anathema, these savages were well-rounded. The people in the skyscrapers were specialized insects living in tiny boxes.

Anathema's humanity involved copious amounts of death. So much so, the stomach acid boiled out of his throat.

He checked the GPS, his phone; no reception. Of course.

Valentine tiptoed around the brush-covered cave opening. "Should we go in?"

"She's not here," Paul said. "I'd feel her presence."

"What are you, Darth Vader?"

"If our GPS signal drops for too long, Kit calls SMASH in to our last known location."

"A fine plan. I like waiting."

"But maybe she's got an alarm, twigs to our intrusion, and destroys the evidence. We should look while we still can."

She sniffed. "It smells like the zoo. Shit and dead meat." She hugged herself, shivering. "I got into videogames because I hated going outdoors, Paul. For me, the sun is this inconvenience I endure while dashing between air-conditioned boxes. This smells like a summer camp where kids kill."

The cave entrance pulsed a dim green, like the aurora borealis. "I'll understand if you want to back out."

"Things glowing is comforting. In my world, things glow to guide you."

"So you wanna go first?"

"Want to? No. But I have yet to see you throw a successful punch, Carter, so I guess Vasquez takes point."

They pushed aside some shrubbery and clambered into the cave entrance, which was just big enough to squeeze through.

"...Now *this* is a lair," Valentine whispered, coming to a halt.

Paul nudged Valentine aside to get a better look, then stood frozen himself. The cave was bigger on the inside than it could have been, should have been – a cavernous ceiling hanging over an amphitheater-sized ring of rock. The ceiling was lost in a night sky – a bold sky free of light pollution, the Milky Way a starry swirl against a stark and engulfing blackness.

"...the flux load," Valentine asked. "How does she live with it? This dimension-warping is vulgar. It should be collapsing – I've tried making my own palaces; they melt like cotton candy in rain..."

Paul crept around the perimeter, afraid to go near the center, where a single bonfire crackled. A small creek trickled through the veldt, providing enough water to live on. This place stank of predators, of death to the unwary... and yet there was something compelling here.

A leopard's beautiful, but you don't keep it in your apartment, Kit had said. He was right. Yet the leopard's devotion to death made its feline grace no less compelling.

This echoing cave was Anathema's idea of beauty.

Yet there was more light than just the bonfire and stars. Chunks of amber crystal were embedded in the stone walls, poking up like weeds, glowing yellowish green.

The crystals had tiny hairs in them, twitching like insects.

–her Flex, he thought. *Of course. She wouldn't use processed hematite; she grows her drugs from the earth.*

"There's so *much*," Valentine said breathlessly. "But it's cloudy, full of flux. And – see that empty chunk over there?"

Paul did, a vast semicircle of shadow in the glowing stone, hinting at a harvest. Something had been left in its place: white-and-brown smudges smeared across the wall.

Cave paintings.

They wriggled, pinned to the wall.

Valentine trotted over, squinting. "That's…" She shook her head. "That's a cave painting of a little girl in a tennis dress. And a tennis court, in front of a mansion. How do I know that's a tennis court, Paul? How can I–"

The paintings shivered and expanded, flowing across the stone to seep into the night sky. He was already tumbling into the paintings, the stick figures and chalk houses growing to swallow him as he was sucked into the story these figures so desperately needed to tell.

INTERLUDE #3
This is Why I Killed Them

The first thing you must understand is that my parents suffocated me. This is why I killed them.

They did not want a daughter; they wanted something pleasant to show at parties. I did not like crowds. Yet crowds of people were what I was shoved in front of – cotillions, ballrooms, conventions to impress my father's clients.

They saw my desire to be alone as a sickness. I was sent to ballet classes, to strangers' birthday parties, to cheerleading clubs, all to train me in the arts of socializing. If I talked to enough people, my parents theorized, I would get good at it.

I didn't.

They saw me crying, so they got me good drugs. Drugs that turned my head into fog. They told me not to tell anyone how disturbed I was; it might make people unhappy. We were a happy family, rich and good-looking. We held parties.

I wasn't good-looking.

It wasn't a big deal, they told me. But they stared at my nose and my lips over and over again, as if my face disappointed them. It wasn't them, they said; don't you feel good about yourself? But now, whenever anyone looked, all I could feel

371

was my bony beak of a nose, my thin and shriveled lips.

I begged them to let me cut my nose. To fill my lips with animal fat. They had a plastic surgeon ready for me. They had a dietician to starve me and a personal trainer to yell at me. They were so eager to hire these people that for a while, I felt blessed my parents were willing to fix a wretch like me.

Then they sent me to boarding school.

They hadn't consulted me. They told me it was about education. But they moved around me as if I wasn't really there, as if they ached to have me gone already. Even after all the nose-cutting and blisters on my feet from dancing and stiff smiles from parties, they hated my awkwardness. How could such sunny, wealthy people have given birth to this lanky, sullen beast?

So I killed them. A knife to each heart. I looked them in the eyes, and they knew why I did it.

It was the only honest moment we ever shared.

The sick thing was that once I killed them, everyone told me I hadn't. People like me didn't kill. So I got a good team of lawyers, and no one wanted to believe a beautiful girl was capable of murder, and my counsel argued until it seemed the cops had done horrible things in attempts to frame me.

So I went free.

Do you understand how insane that is?

As I walked out of the courthouse, I understood what had made me miserable, made my parents miserable, made everyone I knew cradle secret despair:

We weren't meant to live in such numbers.

We're still trembling apes, hardwired to live on the savannah, shoved into crude boxes. We're broken from having to work for money, from being at the mercy of vast economies, from being forced to specialize like insects.

This sickness manifests in obsessions. We gorge ourselves on television, on pills, on sex, on anything that might distract from the truth: we were designed to exist in small tribes.

I have to bring it all down.

I am aware of the irony, yes. Did cavemen have 'mancers? No. How could pyromancers exist in the days of hunting and gathering? No one had time to stare into a fire for hours at a time – who would have subsidized that? No, if you were an able-bodied male, you were raising kids, hunting deer, looking for edible plants. Survival left no time for obsessions.

Some focus in on one relentless thought – usually a consumer need, if you haven't noticed – so much that we sunder the universe with botched desires.

Isn't that proof our society is fatally flawed?

SMASH tries to pluck us out. It won't work. We'll have more 'mancers, more of this poisonous one-note mania. The Internet magnifies this obsession; corporations profit from our addictions. SMASH think sweeping us into brainwash camps will fix us, but no.

There will be more 'mancers. The culture is creating them. Europe burning from the broach? It's amazing we've gotten sixty years without another continent falling to demons. That was just a preview of how the world will unravel.

The only solution is to cut living tissue until the tumors are gone.

As a 'mancer, I'm cure and disease. I'm the planet's way of correcting this madness. I'll kill double every time until nations crumble under the weight of 'mancy, reverting us to a simpler time, one that we can fit into. Billions of unhappy slaves have to die, must die, before we can return to a simpler, cleaner, safer world.

I've tried to bring the end one victim at a time, loading the most poisoned with 'mancy. That time is over. The rulemancer has figured out how to neutralize my pawns. So I'll shift from killing thousands to killing millions.

I killed my parents. I told them why I was killing them. That was honest, and true, and good.

Now I am killing you.

THIRTY-EIGHT
Watered Down

The paintings dumped Valentine and Paul from the sky. Valentine leapt to her feet, flailing her hands.

"Okay, okay, manifesto, I get it. But how does she do *this*? This cave doesn't fit under this hill! The paintings suck us in! This whole thing should have reverted by now – I know! I tried to move into Mario's castle and nearly lost everything!"

Paul knelt by the creek, looking at the mashed and dead Flex fibers Anathema had pounded with a flat stone. The damp husks lay on a woven mat, piled waist-high.

Valentine continued to splutter. "She's talking as though she expects this site to last – like it's a shrine people will make a pilgrimage to! The flux load on the dimensions alone should have killed her, and this whole thing should have dissolved back to a crack in a rock. How is she still wandering around, being evil?"

Paul held up an empty water bottle by way of an answer. Anathema had piled a stack of sodden bottles next to the creek.

"...she's drinking Aquafina?" Valentine asked, puzzled. "That doesn't seem very cavemancy."

"She's changed tactics." Paul bolted for the exit. "She's not going to kill a thousand people."

"Then what'll she do?" Valentine finally noticed the stacks of plastic soda crates Anathema had buried in the dirt.

"She's going to dose a thousand people with Flex to kill a million."

THIRTY-NINE
The Only Living Film in New York

"Get SMASH to Sheep Meadow!" Paul yelled once his cell phone had reception, grateful Aliyah was safe with Kit. "To the film festival. And as many cops as you can. All the cops."

He ran to Central Park's south end, confirming his worst suspicions. The sun had set, and the paths were full of jogging stockbrokers; they eyed him with pity, as if Paul was on some crazy exercise program. A few stragglers, toting picnic baskets, were still on their way, making haste, knowing they were too late to get a good seat.

Paul broke over the hill, seeing the reflected flicker of colored lights as the movie started, projected onto a gigantic screen tied to the grass. Thousands of people – families, lovers, film buffs – had settled into the grass, spread out over the hollows of the moist ground, lying on blankets or leaning back on chairs. They all cast long shadows, turned into faceless penumbrae by the glow of the screen.

The crowd was smaller than usual; Anathema kept people home these days. But these brave souls, half the usual ten thousand who made it out to the festival, had shown up.

Valentine puffed behind him, possibly the only person in Central Park in worse shape than Paul.

"Are you *sure*, Paul?" Kit asked. "The mayor's primed to respond. But if I send SMASH to stop the film festival—"

Paul couldn't get the words out through the fire in his chest. "You're worried she's... going to... strike someplace else?"

"If you're wrong," Kit said, "and someone listening to the police broadband hears she's at the film festival, people will panic. And then we'll have a riot in one place and Anathema in another."

Valentine sweated so hard, her mascara had smeared. "Fuck this," she said, producing an ocarina from her purse. She blew into it, a woodwind triplet melody; one of the police horses bucked off its owner and pranced over to Valentine.

"Fuck running." She boosted Paul up. His artificial foot caught in the stirrup as Valentine spurred the horse into a gallop. Tourists dove out of the way.

"I can feel it now," he told Kit. "Send them in. *Keep Aliyah indoors.*"

And he could feel it. There had been the murmur of several thousand people settling down – the clack of folding chairs being settled into place, the fizz of soda bottles being opened. Now it was deathly quiet, as if the attendees had been muffled. The heat and the silence pressed in around Valentine and Paul like a garbage bag pulled tight over the face; each clop of the horse's hooves felt like a violation of some unspoken pact.

Paul wanted to gag. The stench of Anathema's 'mancy wafted up from the crowd, roiling in the heat, bad magic oozing out of their sweat.

Valentine galloped down the hill's gentle slope – then pulled to a sudden stop by one of the soda vendors.

"Christ, I'm thirsty," she said. "Got any water?"

The vendor slumped forward, as though he was a mannequin with cut strings. Paul thought for a moment the vendor was dead – but no, he was reaching deep into the icebox, leaning far in, up to his shoulders. His face bore no expression as he pushed in deeper, his hands fishing around far beyond where the bottom of the icebox could logically be.

Then he popped up back up, a water bottle in each hand. Valentine lunged for it... and didn't Paul need one, too? It was so hot, the air like a dog breathing in his face, his tongue dry as cardboard, his sweaty shirt sticking to his chest like flypaper. Paul *needed* a drink, his body crying out for it – something moist to splash upon the sponge of his throat...

Valentine moved to guzzle her Aquafina. Amber motes of magic drifted through the water like jellyfish.

She stopped and tilted the bottle.

"I've done *way* too much peyote to see this as normal." She blinked and looked out over the field. Hundreds of bottles glowed firefly green, tucked into drink cozies, tossed by the side of lawn chairs, heaped in the garbage. Paul wasn't sure the glow was only visible to 'mancers, or if Anathema's Flex was activated by moonlight. Regardless, he felt the sick sweep of

Anathema's 'mancy, gaining strength as the moon rose.

The first notes of "Also Sprach Zarathustra" echoed across the field.

On the onyx-black screen, a crescent green slice of earth crept through space. It was shadowed by the moon, the blazing sun rising over it – the classic opening to *2001: A Space Odyssey*.

Paul knew how crowds worked: this is where he'd expect to hear good-natured hoots and hollers hailing the movie's start. Instead, there was burbling confusion as people noticed what their neighbors were doing. Paul heard incoming helicopters, low and too distant.

"What do we do, Paul?" Valentine asked. In the darkness, they saw people staggering to their feet with high, ragged screams – one person at first, then five, then twenty, then hundreds clawing their backs in agony, tearing their clothes as their bodies swelled. Men and women scrambled backwards, knocking over glowing drinks, only to bump into another monstrosity exploding from what had been a fellow filmgoer.

The screen switched away from space to mirror the action below. Cavemen shuffled about on-screen, banging their knuckles against the dry clay floor.

Standing in their center was Anathema, clothed in a dead deer's hide, wielding her deadly spear like a scepter. The camera zoomed in on her as she bared those sharklike teeth at the crowd below.

"*Scatter*," she hissed. "*Kill.*"

The screams coalesced, turning from anguished bellows into a defiant cry of bloodlust. The rest of the crowd began to comprehend what had happened to the people around them; they stampeded in every direction as the newborn cavemen grabbed chairs, wastebaskets, umbrellas, whatever was within grasp, and beat their way through the audience, smashing skulls, stopping occasionally to snap a neck.

Thousands of freshly born savages flooding the streets of New York.

"What do we do, Paul?" Valentine repeated, hauling Paul away from the impending riot. "What do we *do*?"

"Hang on," Paul muttered, clutching his chin in concentration. There was some way to untangle these innocents from Anathema's 'mancy, he was certain—

—the tide of brutes smashed into them.

FORTY
Fragile Skins Torn Away

Paul believed, deep down, that humanity wanted to be rational. Yes, there were killers in our cities, always had been... but deep down, men understood that communal activity was what separated us from the animals. That men and women sought their safety with rational methods. That people inevitably struggled – inefficiently at times, but consistently – toward the light.

Being engulfed in fleeing refugees grabbed that idea by the lapels and shook it until it wept.

A shrieking mother banged headfirst into Paul, bowling him over, not caring where she went as long as it was away from the beasts. The crowd bore him up, pushed him away from Valentine. A black kid in a basketball jersey leapt on top of him in an attempt to climb a lightpost, sending Paul tumbling to the ground. Four college boys trampled him, too terrified to hear Paul yell for help, stepping on his face with gum-sticky sneakers.

I'm being stomped to death, Paul thought as a woman in broken high heels snapped the fingers on his left hand. The crowd fled in any direction, reduced to rabbits in a hunt.

A fat man with a triple bypass scar tripped and fell on him, then grabbed Paul to beg for help. "You need to get off." Someone banged his head with a briefcase. "I can't help until you get off!"

The fat man continued to blubber, unhearing; words were dead weight here. Paul boxed his ears to get his attention. "*Get up!*"

The guy staggered to his feet through the crowd's jostling, stumbling back towards the streets, clutching his chest.

"*Wait!*" Paul said. Someone smashed him in the forehead. A hairy hand yanked him backward.

A savage grinned down at him, the shreds of the tweed jacket he'd worn hanging off his shoulders. His ivory cane was coated with the brains of his friends. His teeth were filed to points, like Anathema.

"*The slow get eaten,*" the savage purred. Paul looked behind him to see the trails of dead bodies – movie-lovers who'd come to the park only to get trampled, beaten bloody, or devoured.

"This isn't how it *works*!" Paul cried, trying to summon up 'mancy, any 'mancy. The savage hauled him up with two clublike hands to bite his throat.

"*Scatter*!" Anathema roared, standing atop the screen, gesticulating wildly with her spear. "Cluster here, and their armies will box you in! Flee down boulevards! Duck into alleys! Break into buildings! Scatter, and feast on those who rely on *others* for protection!"

The savage flinched, hunching from Anathema's terrible power.

"Fight it," Paul whispered. "You're a good man at heart. You don't want to do this..."

The savage peered down at Paul with black eyes, looking through cracked glass-lens.

"*Your words are* nothing." As Paul struggled in his grasp, he laughed and put Paul's neck into his mouth, laughing at Paul's helplessness...

A gunshot.

A spray of warm blood.

Paul tumbled to the ground. Strong arms bore him up.

"...Valentine?" Paul asked, dazed.

It wasn't Valentine. It was a familiar face, the last person he wanted to owe a favor to, a cocky sneer he hadn't seen since he'd been barfing his guts out when SMASH had caught him in Valentine's lab.

"Sweetie, I saved you," Lenny Pirrazzini said, cocky as ever in his NYPD blues. "But that doesn't make me your valentine."

"A girl. Called Valentine. Have you seen her?"

"That's *two* you owe me." Lenny's voice shook with terror. "I saved you from the Refactor, and now I'm saving you from Anathema. For New York's supposed finest 'mancer-hunter, you need a *lot* of help."

Paul would have been irritated by Lenny's scorekeeping, except Paul knew he didn't mean it. Lenny was in shell shock from the tide of savages around him. The cops pushed in over the bodies, firing everywhere, trying to save whoever they could. The savages ignored them, rushing past, disappearing into the alleyways. The cavemen were flooding the streets, vanishing into apartment buildings where they'd murder everyone they could get their hands on...

"You gotta kill that bitch for me, Paul." Lenny held his gun so tight, it quivered. "You knew it. Now New York knows exactly how bad every 'mancer needs a cap in his ass..."

Paul doubted Lenny had ever killed a man in the line of duty, let alone seen a 'mancy-fueled outbreak. He should have been offended by Lenny's remarks, but Lenny was talking trash so he wouldn't crack.

"...Paul?"

Valentine stumbled from the crowd, one of her pigtails torn off. Paul rushed to embrace her.

"At least we saved you and your girlfriend," Lenny said.

"She is not my girlfriend," Paul snapped, just as Valentine yelled, "I am *not* his girlfriend!"

Lenny nodded, too agreeable. "Two saved in a sea of... Christ..." He looked out over the bodies. Cops fired riot gas in vain attempts to disable the Neanderthals. Handfuls of the savages ignored Anathema's commands to go after the remaining cops, cheerfully tearing policemen's limbs off.

It was all so huge, bigger than any one man could solve. Paul could see the thought on Lenny's face: *what can I do?*

"Listen, Lenny. I've got a plan to fix this."

"Paul," Valentine interrupted.

"In a second, Valentine. Lenny, I can undo this. But–"

"*Paul!*"

"Valentine, I have to fix the city. Lenny, you have to help me get to–"

"*Is that the rulemancer, too*?" Anathema's voice echoed across the green as the trio of savages chasing Valentine caught up with her. "*Oh, the rulemancer* and *the illusionmancer in the same place?! Beautiful*\!"

Lenny looked at Paul in betrayal. "Who – is she talking about *you*?"

"*I've always wanted to say this.*" Anathema spoke slowly, relishing the words. "*Minions? Kill.*"

Every savage in Central Park ran toward them.

FORTY-ONE
Power of the People

The three closest savages, still clad in bright muumuu
dresses, barreled towards toward them. "*Zap* them,
Valentine!"

"She shut that shit down," Valentine said. "*Nothing*
works. This whole area is nothing but rocks and fire."

"Gunpowder still works." Lenny fired five times.
Three bullets hit center mass, sending what once had
been three muumuu-clad grandmothers tumbling to
the ground.

Lenny looked down in his gun in astonishment. "I
was best on the range," he muttered. "God damn if I'm
not best in real life, too."

"Lenny," Paul whispered. "I know you hate 'mancers.
And yeah, I am one. But I need to get to Samaritan
Mutual. I can fix this if I get there. And" – he looked at
the other hulking figures sprinting toward them – "I
need to get there in one piece."

Lenny spat on the ground. "Look, buddy. At the
moment, doesn't matter if you're Satan himself. She
wants you dead, I want you alive."

"Not all 'mancers are bad, Lenny – some of us–"

"Quiet." Lenny squeezed off two more shots. "You hid your evil, and you *will* pay. But I believe you 'mancers will kill each other off, just like humans have civil wars. You can serve as my SMASH team today, Paul." He gestured at the incoming. "We'll use you to kill her, and the Order will mop up the rest of your kind."

"The Order?"

"Doesn't matter. For today, and one day only, Paul... I'll count you as a cop. And we *will* get you a ride."

"We?" Valentine asked.

"Fuck, yes." Lenny tapped his badge. "We." And he shouted across the field to the still-standing cops:

"*Attention all officers! New orders! Paul fuckin' Tsabo, killer of 'mancers, needs to get to Samaritan to kill this bitch! I know we're in the shit now, but it's time! Protect and goddamned serve!*"

Two officers tackled the two nearest savages, risking their lives against much burlier opponents. Paul knew why: only Lenny was irresponsible enough to fire gunshots into a crowd like this. Other cops burst from the crowd, intercepting the savages with nightsticks, overmatched as one man but falling upon them in twos and threes, desperate to stop them.

"*No!*" Anathema screamed. Spiked pit traps yawned open underneath them; others fell as clubs appeared in the savages' hands. "*I said kill the papermancer!*" And enough of the brutes smashed past the opposition, forcing back the line.

But Paul felt a thrill. This was the epitome of civilization: underpaid cops with every reason to run, ready to give their lives against impossible odds.

Reinforcements arrived. Fresh officers pushed their way through the chaos to surround Valentine and Paul with clear plastic riot shields, escorting them to the park's edge. They yelled and re-yelled orders, keeping communications up when the radio had failed them. Furious beasts were pushed back with truncheons.

Lenny and the other officers fought their way to the waiting motorcycles. Traffic had stalled, as fleeing drivers had abandoned their vehicles.

The stars went dark. The lights above them flickered out, replaced with an ominous gloom.

"She's coming." Valentine started the engine.

"Get the fuck out and let *men* handle this," Lenny said. Paul felt Anathema's sickening 'mancy washing over them, killing the motor – and then Valentine kicked it back to life.

"You can stop my fighting," she muttered with deep satisfaction. "But *nobody* can stop a good racing game."

"I said *kill them*!"

As they roared off toward Samaritan, Paul saw Lenny in the rearview mirror, bringing his gun up as Anathema and a horde of savages bore down upon them. He stepped into line beside his fellow officers... and then they turned a corner, and Lenny was gone.

FORTY-TWO
Do I Dare Disturb the Universe?

"Tell me you have a plan."

Valentine pulled up next to the Samaritan Mutual building. It was a different world here; the violence hadn't spread out this far yet, but it was coming. Thousands of maniacs were infiltrating New York, killing the softest targets.

"Yeah," Paul said. "Your job is twofold: first, something very bad will happen when I'm done."

"The flux?"

"…yeah." Paul breathed in through his nose, ignoring the stinging in his eyes. "I won't be able to contain it this time. But you will."

Valentine froze.

"I can help you, Paul. We'll work 'mancy together again, split the load…"

"No. This will… I don't even know if it can work. But if it does, the flux load will do almost as much damage as Anathema did. Maybe this building will collapse, maybe a meteor strike will hit New York… something. You've got to ensure my cure isn't as bad as the disease.

There's no 'mancer better equipped for that – you're all about special effects. You could turn a collapsing building into a cutscene. The flux wouldn't be as bad."

"Paul, I told you – you're not allowed to commit suicide–"

"This isn't suicide. It's sacrifice."

Her shoulders slumped. "…what's my second job?"

Paul pinched the bridge of his nose, trying to keep it together. "You told Aliyah Daddy was in the maze. Show her where I am so… so she doesn't look all her life. Give her peace."

Valentine didn't cry; she'd been hurt too many times for that. Her inevitable reaction, Paul realized, was to wad the pain up where no one would see and keep going.

It made him feel better. She'd be all right. He bureaucromanced his apartment, which was oddly calming; no matter how Anathema tried to rip things down to huts and caves, there would always be rents to pay.

"…There. Your name's on the lease. It's rent-controlled. Cheap. It won't stay if you burn it off to flux, but…"

"…you did your best," Valentine finished.

Paul moved to hug her goodbye. Valentine crossed her arms. *She's already walling me off*, he thought, then felt miserable as he realized he was just one more proof the universe had nothing good in store for Valentine DiGriz.

"Do it," she said, turning away from him.

The air was cold in the lobby. Cold as death.

• • •

As he rattled the lock on his door, the papers peeked out of the drawers, playful as puppies. But when they saw him, they crumpled with concern.

"This is it, boys," he said. "You ready?"

They straightened like soldiers, creases flattened.

"Let's go look out the window."

The view from his floor had never been exciting: a sidewalk, a subway entrance, and another skyscraper. But Paul had always liked looking down at the street, the thousands of people making their ways along the sidewalk. He'd always envisioned them going to happy homes, cheerful families, warm meals – a 1950s view of America, he knew, but he also knew there was a lot more love in the city than any news program ever let on.

The papers marched behind him, a funeral procession. SMASH was coming for him even if he survived.

He focused on the street again. The savages hadn't arrived yet. 1010 WINS was knitting isolated reports into a coherent story – but for now, there were still folks headed home after a long workday. He felt affection for them, even love.

He'd need more than love to turn back time.

But he had bent time, hadn't he? He'd called in SMASH forces hours before he'd stepped into Valentine's basement. He'd had his leg sent to a place he hadn't even known existed when the order was placed.

If bureaucromancy couldn't backdate a spell, what could?

He filled his lungs with air – and filled his heart with everything he believed. He believed rules made life better. He believed organizations made humans play fairly. He believed that good records were sometimes all that stood between a well-deserved life and a messy death.

And he thought of the soda stands.

The soda stands in Central Park were licensed sellers, subject to state law, taxes, inspections. He'd read Upton Sinclair's *The Jungle*, knew what the state of food in New York was like before regulations made it safer – spoiled milk mixed with white paint, bread stuffed with sawdust, meat crawling with *E. coli*.

Men had fought shortsighted businessmen seeking a quick buck, and made the world safer.

The soda stands, too, were inspected.

Paul's body vibrated as he reached back, the floating forms turning into a thousand different documents as Paul did the paperwork to find the soda vendors authorized to sell in Central Park tonight. The information was scattered across forms for sales tax, across the W2s filed for the soda jerks, across the filed work schedules. The papers riffled, hunting down what Paul needed.

Within minutes, he knew every route of every soda vendor working that evening.

And here was the tough part:

There should have been inspections.

There *should* have been inspections.

Paul felt the universe Flex as he told it the truth: someone should have been there that evening, particularly in the wake of a series of terrorist attacks, surprise inspections to verify the water was safe. That hadn't happened. But it *should* have.

He clutched his hands into fists, tears streaming down his cheeks, as he battered the universe with nothing but a bullheaded opinion of how things should have gone. There would have been inspectors; Paul culled the names of the finest inspectors in New York City, brought them to the universe's attention, pointed out how fucking reasonable it would have been for these men to be on duty today, *here*, in the wake of all that had happened.

He felt like he'd been shoved twenty fathoms under water. His ears popped, the pressure of What Had Happened so immense, it threatened to crush him.

No, Paul said, his whisper rumbling to a shout. The universe poured in – not just this planet, but all the space between here and the Sun, all of the empty void between this Sun and the next star, every one of trillions and quintillions of solar systems and galaxies and physical matter telling him the past had happened, every atom in the universe had *registered* it happening, and no force in existence could make it rewrite all that work.

Try me, Paul whispered, and his words made the stars shudder.

It fought back, trying to erase what he'd done. He bolstered it by lining up cops, the *best* cops, backdating their schedules so they patrolled the Park with extra special vigilance at the time Anathema was swapping water bottles, ready to call in the Blue Thunder at the slightest sign of 'mancy. He rescheduled the water bottle delivery to delay them, engineering bureaucratic snafus that left no time for Anathema to interfere.

The universe spun underneath him like a spider, frantically trying to reweave time back to its original state. Paul reworked the pay slips and work schedules and invoices, ensuring the most meticulous people were on duty to accept the water, people who'd notice the flecks. He posted security guards who'd notice a swap. He…

…*you cannot do this*, the world screamed, pulling apart at the seams, making Paul's capillaries burst; he sweated blood.

But he'd rebuilt the universe once before, back when the buzzsects had torn its fabric apart.

I said this is what happened! he cried, and the paperwork pinwheeled behind him, showing the elaborate trace of paperwork and vigilant citizens and smart middle management that led to the water being found tainted an hour before the show. There were paramedics, good ones, who'd rescued the handful of sickened people and gotten them to a safe room, where they'd swollen and roared and, once the 'mancy wore off, returned to being functioning humans. There were calm NPR announcers who'd told people to return home, and the furious man who'd tried to tear open his throat in an old and useless world had, in this one, helped three muumuu clad women onto a city-run bus.

He piled detail after detail onto his world, a fever dream of names and records. He pulled a list of

FLEX

everyone who was there from the credit card charges
and subway records, naming person after person and
detailing what they'd done...

...and the universe buckled.

There was a lurch that shook the world, the feeling
the earth's crust had become a thin rubber balloon.
Things *stretched*.

And when they rebounded, the world was Paul's.

He saw Central Park clearly, because he *had* seen it,
but this time, it had the comforting weight of history.
Tainted water, discovered thanks to a series of
discoveries by cautious people. The film festival called
off. Anathema seen by good cops, who had pursued her
into the woods.

The new world fit him like a comfortable pair of
jeans. It fit.

He sighed in relief.

Then the flux hit him in a way he never could have
conceived.

Taking the flux from Moishe had risked death. This
risked obliteration. He had altered time, and as payback,
the universe wanted to expunge him from history,
blank him, strangle him as a sperm. The forms caught
fire, crumbling to ash with papery little cries.

What do you fear? the flux asked, not so much a voice
as a cellular command akin to death.

Paul mentally patted his pockets. He found not one
speck of regret.

...nothing.

It was true. He'd thwarted a killer, saved the park,
saved thousands from being chewed to pieces, and did

it all through other people's strength. Maybe Aliyah would die, maybe he would never have existed, but…

…it was worth it.

He felt a beatific grace. This freedom made it clear how saturated his life was with tiny terrors. It was ephemeral, a soul-cleaning epiphany that couldn't last, but… Paul bathed in the purity of having no regrets.

The flux pushed past Paul's defenses, puzzled. It searched him for the thing that must be set right in order to rebalance the universe.

And when it found no sense of outrage…

…it agreed.

The threads of time solidified around Paul, radiating out from Samaritan Mutual to New York to rocket out to the sky, spreading one thought of humanity to cold galaxies that had never known human life.

The flux dissipated, withdrawing as though it had been embarrassed to even arrive.

Paul reached out after it, confused, then stopped:

The flux isn't a law, he realized, shivering with understanding. *It's a* counterargument. *Magic is a conversation with the universe about how the world should be… and I convinced it.*

He sagged into an office chair, never so glad to be in a cubicle.

Safe.

He'd made the world safe.

FORTY-THREE
Awkward Conversations

Valentine was proof of this new world; her ripped pigtail was still on. The crowd around them moved at an amble, no rush to get to safety. Nobody had stopped to listen to the news bulletins.

Valentine munched on a Ring Ding. "What the hell'd you do, Paul? You look like you're in love."

He was. He floated through a saner world. The magic he loved was no violation of the natural order – it was the natural order's way of evolving. The 'mancy wasn't a flaw in the contract but a hidden clause for bargaining.

His throat swelled shut when he tried to tell her. He hugged her instead.

"You, uh–" She stiffened under his arms, then patted his back awkwardly. "*Ho*-kay, you've had a big day. Stopped the big scheme with a flow of inspecto-mancy."

She gave him a perfunctory squeeze, then stepped out as soon as was marginally polite. "One kiss and I'll fry every neuron in your brain," she told him.

"Aliyah." He felt like he was tugging himself along by hidden strings, a mannequin he piloted by force of will.

"I've done *way* too much peyote to see this as normal," Valentine sighed. "Can your blotter paper dispense LSD? Blink twice for 'yes'."

"No, I… I'll explain later. Too big for words."

"You need little-girl hugs. Let's get you some."

Aliyah was staying at Kit's apartment, which hadn't made Kit too happy. He'd wanted Aliyah back in the burn ward but understood the dangers with Anathema on the loose. As such, he'd offered his home for precisely three days, after which it was time to get the girl professional medical treatment.

Yet the leftover hot cocoa cups piled in Kit's sink, as well as the battered Connect Four set on the coffee table, told Paul Kit still relished playing the loving uncle.

"I see she suckered you," Paul said, feeling life return to normal. Kit's apartment was full of old magazines but never musty; he was an organized pack rat, and his couches were worn but eminently comfortable. The whole place had an elegant design Kit had settled on back when his wife had still been alive, and that hadn't changed since the day she'd passed on.

"You gotta get that girl some help," he groused without any real heat; it was almost like Paul had never revealed himself as a 'mancer to Kit, though he knew *that* fact hadn't been rewritten. "I tried to play games with her. *Real* games. She asked if I had an iPad, then tuned into her Nintendo."

"Her dad was in danger," Valentine said, looking weirded out; if you'd never known Kit's wife, Paul supposed there was an almost mausoleum-like atmosphere to the place. "She heard you coordinating efforts with the cops, hunting Anathema – that's scary. So she takes her mind off by playing videogames."

"I wouldn't mind if it made her happy," Kit shot back. "She looks miserable. I was afraid she'd slip through that screen."

"Where is she now?" Paul asked.

"Sleeping." Kit jerked his chin back to what had once been his wife's bedroom. "Poor thing passed out when she heard the film festival was safe."

It was an act of purest family to have Aliyah stay in that bedroom, Paul knew, because the fact that Kit's wife had withered away in there made it a sacred space. It probably chased away a few ghosts to have a small girl in there.

"I might pass out myself," Paul said. Valentine gave him a pained look – *Please don't leave me alone with this crazy old guy* – but after all Paul had done, he felt he deserved a little selfishness.

"Hey." Kit pushed his hat back on his head. "You... you called in those soda inspections, didn't you? To stop her."

Paul nodded wearily. Kit frowned.

"That was good 'mancy," he finally allowed – not a judgment on Paul's performance but weighing "good" against "evil." "And if I knew – I *knew* – you could do it without the flux, then maybe. Maybe."

It was an apology: *I'm sorry I have to turn you in.* Paul didn't want to think about that. He'd skipped his flux load once, but there were plenty of things he wasn't comfortable changing. Having the government work the way it should to save New York? He felt no guilt for that. But getting a rent-controlled apartment? Looking up someone's voting record? That still felt like cheating... and the next time he 'manced, it'd come with a price tag.

Kit was right: his lifestyle put Aliyah in danger. Maybe SMASH was the right move. But all he wanted was to hug his daughter.

"It's fine." Paul squeezed past Kit to push open the door to Aliyah's room. He heard Valentine trying to make conversation:

"So – where's the donuts?"

"I don't keep them at home," Kit said, vaguely offended. "They're fattening."

Then Paul saw Aliyah.

She snored on a duvet-covered bed, a hand-knitted cover that had kept Kit's wife warm during her final days. The Nintendo rested on her chest, burbling music. Kit had left the window open so a breeze could stir the musty air; the room was cramped with folding tables and cardboard trays of old bills, but there was just enough room to snuggle up on the bed next to her.

He shut the door. A spear point jabbed his spine.

"*Ssshhhh*," Anathema said, her shark's grin obscenely white.

FORTY-FOUR

The Killing Sun

"How did you–"

"*Sshhhh*." She wrenched him back, pulling him onto the tip of her spear; a pinprick of blood blossomed at the base of his spine, the promise of future wounds. "Tell the illusionmancer the girl needs something from the store."

Paul lowered his voice, so as not to wake Aliyah. "What should she get?"

"You know them both better than I. Choose something plausible *he* doesn't have, that *she*'ll have to go out for." She poked, making it clear she could shove the spear through spine and stomach alike. "No tricks."

Paul debated doing some subtle 'mancy – arranging the drinks down at the bodega to send a hidden message? – but if Paul could sense her 'mancy, she'd sense his.

He cracked the door.

"Valentine?" he whispered. She looked up eagerly, a dog chosen at the pound, already stifled in this old-fashioned home. "Could you get Aliyah some animal crackers? She could really use some."

Valentine flung her purse over her shoulder, out the door like a shot.

That left Kit. Who was no match for Anathema.

Neither was Paul, for that matter.

"Lock it." Paul did. Thankfully, Aliyah hadn't woken; she was still curled on the bed. She'd always been a deep sleeper.

Anathema crouched on the windowsill. Why not? The room was small; she could stab Paul from anywhere.

She relaxed, a woman with total mastery of the situation. She wore tattered deerskins drawn with odd insignias; her hair was wild and matted. She nodded, giving Paul a grudging respect, a strange and shared sadness that such an entertaining game was about to end.

"You stopped me today."

"Yes."

"I felt your 'mancy in the park. It knits people together."

"Thank you."

"No. It's like… watching bees covering everything in wax. Those people, they think meat comes from a store. They think bodies vanish into funeral homes. Your 'mancy distances people from truths. Real truths."

"You know I disagree."

"…Yes."

Silence. Aliyah's breathing. Anathema, studying him.

Paul wondered why she hadn't killed him. One spear thrust, and the only person who could thwart her was gone.

Then he realized: *She's lonely, too.* Lonely as Paul had been before he'd found Valentine, lonely as every 'mancer.

She wants to talk shop before she kills me, he thought, amazed.

"You figured it out, didn't you? That this..." She waved her hands at the sky. "...is the way the universe works. Show it a heart lacking fear, and everything realigns. You did that today."

"Yes." Paul should have stayed silent – but he wanted to talk to her, too. She was one of the few who wanted something so badly, she'd willed new rules into existence.

"I didn't think you had that in you." Was that a hint of admiration?

"I couldn't have if you hadn't... won. Everything died in the park. People should be... safe."

"Safe is killing us all." She hunched forward, as if sharing a magnificent secret. "You realize you've already lost, right?"

"Obviously. I can't put a restraining order on your spear."

She gave a grim chuckle. Aliyah began to stir. "The spear will fall, yes. But your birth was my true strike. The deaths? Were the feint. A distraction to slip through the killing thrust. You. *You* were my first knife to the heart. The first of many, rulemancer."

Paul's breath stopped in his throat. What had he done to further her plans? "I don't–"

"I made you. Birthed your 'mancy." She twirled her spear as quick as a magician's trick, thumped him in the chest with the butt of it. "Why would I kill civilians with Flex? That's stupid. You can kick a hive, but the bees will get you. All your SMASH, your army, your policemen... I was guaranteed to fall eventually. Wouldn't waste my life for that."

"Then why *start*?"

She reached out with every sinew, desperate to convince. "Because *we're the rot*. This ability to concentrate on one thing – it's unhealthy, Paul. It's not good to bend the universe to our will. Do it wrong, and the universe breaks. Things leak through. You've seen them."

The buzzsects. "But that's only if we–"

She waved him off. "Yes, yes, a pure heart can change the rules forever – but how many have that? I would raze cities to prove my love, and even I waver. No! The point is, the Internet creates 'mancers. People can craft their own reality, shutting out the facts that make them uncomfortable. They can spend hours, days online, knotting themselves around a single idea, eventually becoming a physics sink that destroys everything around them. More 'mancers are born every day."

"So you'll *kill* people to *stop* them?"

"No." She grinned, and Paul felt her relishing this moment – a secret plan, carried for ages, a thing she'd been dying to share with someone who understood. "I'm accelerating the process. The world needs more 'mancers – hundreds. Thousands. I'll show them a New York filled with magical wars, tears in reality – overloading the land until they *have* to face the problem."

"You didn't create any 'mancers."

"You." She poked him with her spear, a gesture of ownership. "You were born quickly. Others are gestating."

Paul felt like he was arguing from the wrong angle. "You didn't create me!"

"The fire. Your daughter. They forced you to retreat into your obsessions, squeezed magic from your dead soul. We both know no happy man becomes a 'mancer. So I crafted my spells. I figured out ways to let chaos create order, tailoring horrific deaths to make hundreds suffer. Every act of death and destruction I made will rob someone of something they loved. It will cause someone, *many* someones, to retreat into misery. Withdrawal. Obsession. *'Mancy*."

She spoke the last three words as though they were an equation.

"…you did this to seed New York with 'mancers?"

"Yes." She leaned in eagerly, the last secret revealed. Her spear tip rose.

"…Daddy?" Aliyah asked, blinking owlishly.

"But you didn't create me," Paul replied, perplexed. "I found my power months *before* she was hurt."

The spear tip quivered. She shook her head, the tiny rat bones in her dreadlocks rattling. "No. I made you. That's – that's how I planned it…"

Paul continued, feeling strangely guilty for puncturing a fellow 'mancer's dreams. "I believed in bureaucracy for *years*. I'd created the Beast *weeks* before you made your Flex."

"No – you unlocked your power in the flames–"

"Sorry, Anathema," he said, guilt turning to satisfaction. "My 'mancy had nothing to do with the fire. It had nothing to do with *you*. You haven't created a single 'mancer, Anathema. I'm just a coincidence."

"*No!* I *felt* you in the fire! I *felt* new 'mancy! I felt creation when the building burned!"

"*Daddy!*" Aliyah flung herself off the bed to interpose herself between Anathema and her father.

"I was rescuing my daughter," Paul said, straightening. "You've lost, Anathema! You had no long-term schemes. Your rituals were delusions. You're a common mass murderer."

"I'll show you murder!" she cried. "*I'll hack you to bits!*"

She thrust her spear past Aliyah, burying it in Paul's good foot. Paul felt a nauseatingly familiar flow of pain up his leg. Two of his toes tumbled into his shoe's tip.

Blood gushed onto the floor as Paul cried out. *Aliyah, I'm sorry you have to see your father gutted before you…*

"I will cut your limbs off before I *let* you die…" Anathema said, drawing her spear back.

"Don't look, Aliyah…"

But Aliyah was vibrating – some kind of seizure? Her Nintendo DS jittered on the bed. The hairs rose on Paul's neck – a spell; Valentine must have returned to save him–

–but it wasn't Valentine's 'mancy.

"*You – hurt – my – Daddy!*" Aliyah shrieked, her voice thrumming in several dimensions.

She levitated off the floor; Anathema's spear shattered in her hands. Anathema pressed herself against the window, whimpering, a savage fearing the sun.

Aliyah reached into a pocket she had not possessed two seconds ago, pulled out a red-and-white Mario cap too big to fit into the pocket, and placed it on her head.

Flames burned on the cap. They raced down her body, engulfing her in fire. *No!* Paul thought, imagining sizzling flesh – but the flames did not touch her, merely limned her form.

A miniature sun blossomed between Aliyah's palms. She toyed with it, a small girl palming a basketball, except that basketball was hot as a furnace.

Fire Mario, Paul thought.

"*Burn*," Aliyah said – and hurled the sun into Anathema's face.

Anathema's hair went up like a bonfire, her flesh melting, the room filled with the scent of burnt pork. She clawed at her face as she hurled herself out of the window.

"*I said burn!*" Aliyah shrieked. "*'Mancers burn! Bad people burn! All the bad things in the universe burn!*"

Aliyah flung fireball after fireball after Anathema. They impacted the walls in gouts of flames that devoured the wallpaper, raced up the ceiling. Anathema sizzled on the fire escape. The metal grate glowed like a barbecue, cooking the skin from Anathema's bones. She tried to leap away, but Aliyah flung flames at her, caging her, the air wavering with heat…

"…mercy…" Anathema croaked, her melted face an eerie mirror of Aliyah's. "No warrior should die… at the hands of a child…"

"The bad 'mancers," Aliyah informed Anathema in a lofty tone, "*burn.*"

Anathema leapt off of the fire escape in a vain attempt to escape her death – but Aliyah intercepted her in midair with another fireball. Anathema burst apart in a blaze of pyrotechnics, plummeting in a fiery comet down to splatter in a burst of lava and blackened bones.

"Paul?" Kit thumped at the door. The room went up quickly, the air black smoke, the walls lost behind flames. "Paul!"

Aliyah was still on fire. Her tears were like burning gasoline.

"Come on, Aliyah." Paul was afraid to touch her. "We have to get out of here."

Aliyah just cried – and as she wept, the Nintendo DS next to her on the bed caught fire, the flame catching on the padded mattress, which went up instantly. She did not move to meet Paul; instead, she hugged herself and retreated deeper into the fire. A pyre of immolation.

The bad 'mancers burn, Paul thought, and realized with horror what Aliyah intended to do.

What kind of world would drive a small girl to suicide? Paul thought, despairing.

Then: *No. The girl does not understand the world.*

"Sweetie," he said, his hair singeing into acrid smoke. "I know you think 'mancy is... is the worst thing possible. And bad things *can* come of it. But so can beautiful things. Magic reflects what's in your heart.

"I talked to the universe tonight, sweetie. I asked it to do something magnificent for me, and... and it did.

Just like it saved you when you should have died.
'Mancy isn't a bad thing; it's the proof that if you care
enough about things, *the world listens.*

"Which means... it means 'mancers aren't bad.
They're people. And people are good, and bad, and...
you're good. You're my kid. You *have* to stick around,
because the world has so much to hear from you.
Please. Please, Aliyah. *Let it hear you.*"

The mattress smoke had filled the room, filling it with
soot, an impenetrable blackness. Aliyah was in there.
And he would crawl onto the bed if he had to, but...

He held out his arms.

"You're lost in the maze, sweetie," he told her. "It's
scary, but I will come find you. I will *always* find you...

"But you can't stop looking for me."

"*Daddy!*" She flung herself, flaming, into his arms.

Paul caught her. He did not burn.

He opened the door just before Kit chopped it down
with a fire axe. "What happened?" he asked, huffing
with panic. "What did–"

Then he saw Aliyah blazing in Paul's arms, and
slumped. "Oh," he said. "Oh."

It would have been easier if Paul had asked Kit for
help; his "good" foot slipped in blood. He'd never realized
how much of his balance was dependent on toes
gripping the floor. *I'm a cripple now*, Paul thought bitterly,
then heard his artificial foot whir. *Well, more of one.*

But nothing could have compelled him to abandon
his daughter. The apartment complex went up with an
absurd speed, as if eager to erase Anathema. Kit called
911, thumping on doors to rouse people to safety; by

the time Paul struggled down the stairs, fighting streams of neighbors, the place was almost gone.

Aliyah, mercifully, had extinguished herself, just a small and sobbing burn victim.

Valentine rushed up, dropping a grocery bag full of animal crackers and Red Bull. "What happened? What—"

Then she saw Aliyah. Aliyah stopped crying for long enough to meet Valentine's gaze – and Paul felt the residual energy flowing between them, a squirming reaction like two magnets passing each other.

"...oh," Valentine said.

Aliyah cried like a girl who'd lost her soul.

Paul braced himself, searching for flux. He had to cleanse Aliyah of bad luck. Then he realized: her worst nightmare had come true. She was a 'mancer.

This first act of magic came prepaid.

FORTY-FIVE

D is for Denouement

Paul hadn't even known the key to the city was a real thing.

THREE FOR THREE, the headlines read, showcasing a mundane man's triumph over a terrorist 'mancer. Editorials asked whether the government should fund SMASH when a pair of insurance agents could do the job. The banquet the mayor threw in his honor was so full of well-wishers, Paul couldn't keep track.

He wished he could give Aliyah the credit. And he wished his foot didn't hurt. He'd learned a new word: *orthotics*. A special shoe to make up for the toes Anathema had lopped off. Walking was a special kind of memory; his titanium right foot held the regret of the 'mancer he'd killed by mistake, and his lopsided left held the regret of the 'mancer he hadn't killed soon enough.

A couple of good brandies helped dull the pain. And the mayor had hovered by his side, eager for photo ops, his hand resting possessively on Paul's shoulder. It was a nice wrap-up. Paul stayed long after most people had gone home, until the busboys had started to remove the tablecloths from the tables, because why not?

So, he was in a grand mood when his ex-wife Imani and her scheming politician lover David arrived.

"*Paul,*" David said, giving Paul a solid, two-handed pump. "Can you hear that? That's New York City, breathing a sigh of relief."

Paul ignored the blatant back-patting to check Imani, who clutched her purse in both hands. Which made him feel sad; they'd been close, once, and now there was that stiff barrier of *ex-husband and -wife* between them. Or, at least, Imani interposed it between them.

But he was feeling good, so he figured he'd get it over with.

"Great to see you, David," Paul said, relishing the look on David's face as he realized he was being dismissed. "Mind if I talk to my ex-wife?"

David stammered a bit, then skedaddled. Paul was relieved to see Imani could still share one mischievous smile as she watched her boyfriend retreat.

"...So." She looked around at the banners, the empty champagne glasses, the brass key in Paul's lap. "You must be swimming in job offers."

"A few." The mayor had sniffed around, asking if Paul was willing to head up a local 'mancer squad – nothing to compete with SMASH, you know, but the SMASH teams were federal. And, in light of the Long Island Broach, maybe the Feds were a little bit too cowboyish for the mayor's liking. "But more importantly, Aliyah's taken care of."

"You got Samaritan to cave?"

Paul frowned. He was still afraid to use his 'mancy on Samaritan papers – as Kit said, "You don't shit where you eat." And the flux on that might rebound in ways that hurt other patients.

"No," he admitted. "They're tough nuts. But the mayor said there's both federal and state funding to help Anathema's victims – and Aliyah is first in line. She'll get her plastic surgery."

"You believe him?"

"It'll make headlines if she doesn't. So yes."

"That's good." She squeezed her purse. "Listen. I don't want you to think you've done a bad job. Aliyah loves you. But... I'm pressing for exclusive custody."

Paul dropped his brandy, thinking: *She knows*. "What? Why would you..."

"If you'll be chasing 'mancers, then Aliyah will always be at risk. She got burned; she almost got murdered. Twice. So I'm going to take Aliyah somewhere far away. Where she won't be in your splash zone."

Paul felt his stomach unclench. She didn't know about Aliyah. That made it harder.

"I can't let her go," Paul said, wishing he could tell her why: *she's a 'mancer now, Imani. She needs my guidance.*

"I know. So you'll get your lawyers, and I'll get mine, and we'll play tug-of-war. With Aliyah in the middle. Are you sure that's what you want?"

She'd delivered a buried compliment, Paul noted: she didn't ask whether it was what was best *for Aliyah*. She knew, and acknowledged, that what Paul wanted was always what he thought was best for his daughter. And she had come here to tell him face-to-face rather than sneaking it in through a lawyer's summons.

He hugged her. She hugged back, feeling the loss of everything they could have shared; the love could never be recovered, but for one moment they could close their eyes and pretend.

"I have to keep her," Paul said. "I hope you understand."

And he limped away, feeling all the scars of Anathema.

As he walked to his car, a small man in a white suit paced alongside, tapping the floor with a cane, matching Paul's awkward gait. Paul thought it was mockery, until he noticed the man's ankle was in a cast.

"...Oscar?" Paul asked, coming to a befuddled stop. Though he should have expected this meeting, he'd been too caught up in his victory to contemplate hanging threads. He looked around for Oscar's bodyguards, half expecting to see men charging at him, but no one else was in the parking lot, just him and the head of a criminal organization.

"Mister Tsabo," Oscar said politely, removing his hat in a grand sweep. "I congratulate you on your accomplishment. Terrorist 'mancers are never good for business."

"What do you want?"

"The dropping of pretense," Oscar said. "The continued flow of product. We both know what you really are, Mister Tsabo. I'm still owed my three pounds.

And then, perhaps, we can work out some very profitable arrangements for future product. Same guidelines, of course – I wouldn't do anything to upset you. Now that I've seen what you're capable of, I'll sign contracts. Because signing contracts – that means something to you, does it not?"

"Your brother tried this," Paul said through gritted teeth. "He too made a nice offer. I declined. He showed me the iron fist inside the velvet glove."

Oscar flexed his hand, revealing manicured nails. "Then don't make me remove my glove. You and I both know there are parties who'd be interested in hearing what you can do. You and I both know it'd be difficult to stop me if I chose to tell." He spread his hands. "So, why force me? Your medical expenses will pile up. As will your costly flux damage. So, why make an enemy, Mister Tsabo, when you could have a perfectly pleasant arrangement?"

Paul felt, once again, that strange synchronicity that hovered between them. They were both reasonable men in unreasonable situations. And though Oscar Gargunza Ruiz had Paul over a barrel, he wasn't rubbing it in.

"Anything I forbid will shut down my Flex," Paul said. "You know what kind of man I am."

"That leaves a good number of lucky breaks available to me," Oscar agreed.

I'm going to regret this, Paul thought – but then he thought of SMASH hauling him away, then hauling Aliyah away, and had no choice but to extend the hand.

• • •

He met Kit by the burn ward's coffee machine.

"Did you clean it all?" Paul asked.

Kit looked caught between "resentful" and "resigned", mopping his bald pate with a handkerchief. "As much as I could. You got lucky. The muscleman? Was flying high. All he remembers are flying gas-mask albinos and some lawyer making him sign a paper. They've got him in the Refactor, but I doubt he remembers anything worthwhile."

Paul sighed. That was the only real loose end. "That's good."

"Better for you: when that muscleman collapsed the roof, it crushed your Flex-making equipment. And unactivated Flex looks like a lot of other rubble. They let me onto the lot to look over the evidence, and I gathered as much as I could find."

"You find everything?"

"I wish I hadn't." He pushed a sack into Paul's hands. Paul felt his own 'mancy thrumming to life at his touch.

"Thanks."

"Don't you thank me. You're lucky. You should be in the Refactor – except they're running scared because of what you told them. Was that true? Are we... are we in for a flood of new 'mancers?"

"Aliyah, she... she's one point of data. Maybe Anathema was wrong. But given how smart Anathema was... I'm pretty sure we're going to see an uptick in activity. Maybe not the apocalypse but a lot more than we're used to."

Kit crossed himself. "My God."

"What's with the cross? You're Jewish."

"You never heard of insurance?" He hunched over the table. "Look, my friend, I didn't sign up with Samaritan to be your mop-up man. I wanted to put 'mancers away, not cover their tracks. But SMASH is stretched thin, and they're not subtle. So, I've been wrestling: is fostering a little evil all right to prevent a larger one? It's one thing to look the other way – but you're asking me to *help* you lie."

Paul nodded, not interrupting his friend's train of thought. Kit had to make up his own mind on this one.

"I don't know," Kit continued. "You have a little girl to raise, younger than any 'mancer I've ever known–"

"You found nothing on adolescent 'mancers?"

"Europe had records, but that's lost in the broach. The government certainly does. But independent studies? Forbidden. God forbid some unscrupulous country unlocks the secret of 'mancer gestation, creates a 'mancer farm. It's all black-books stuff. So I can't say how your daughter would fare. But…"

"You think SMASH would help?"

He looked troubled. "You, you get sent to SMASH, well… you made the choice to lose yourself in paperwork. Maybe you didn't decide all the way, I see that now, that nobody set out to do this, but… it's still a choice. Enough to make the punishment deserved. But you're not six years old. I can't see them sending her to boot camp, do you?"

"No." Paul warmed his hands by his coffee.

"But more than that. Anathema was just one woman, and she almost took down a whole city. God knows what her progeny will be like – good? Bad? I think they'll all be evil, but that's me, thinking 'mancy corrodes the soul. Maybe they're misguided. Yet I know from experience, Paul – even a misguided 'mancer can do a lot of damage."

Paul couldn't deny that.

"I think, based on the evidence I see before me…" He swallowed. "God help me, I think we'll need a 'mancer to fight a 'mancer."

"*If* we need to fight them," Paul countered. "Maybe some can be trained."

Kit turned around to glance nervously towards Aliyah's room. "That," Kit said, "remains to be seen."

"The training?"

He gave Paul a dour look. "The all-bad."

Paul reached under the table to unlock his briefcase. Dramatically, he pulled out…

…a tray of donuts.

"Would someone out for blood," he asked, "offer you an assortment of your favorite treats?"

Kit pushed himself back to take in the full twenty-four count presented before him. Finally, he chuckled. "…Depends. Let's see which one you go for *this* time, bubeleh."

Paul chose a Boston Kreme – a new taste, far different from his usual cruller. He looked to Kit for approval.

Kit's reluctant smile was like the sun creeping out from behind a storm cloud.

And, finally, Valentine and Aliyah.

One of the good things about all the commotion was that Aliyah now had a private room with a guard stationed by the door to keep out reporters. Not to mention every nurse was all too willing to give Aliyah extra helpings of ice cream.

Valentine hadn't left Aliyah's bedside since Aliyah's readmittance. She slept in a chair next to her bed, never leaving despite Imani's occasional hints for her to go.

Paul knew Valentine's vigil was a sign of love, because Aliyah didn't want the Nintendo DS near her. So Valentine had gone without videogames for days – an act akin to starvation for any normal person.

Aliyah was awake, watching Dora on television. "Hey, sweetie."

"Sssh," Aliyah said, riveted to the screen.

Paul locked the door behind him. He knew things had returned to normal, for his daughter felt free to ignore him. Yet there was something frantic in the way Aliyah watched Dora – a show that was a little young for her. She shouted all the answers at Dora as if she hoped Dora might respond, waved her arms as if she thought she might control Dora's movements by force of will alone...

...and then, as Paul felt a flicker of 'mancy swelling up from his daughter, Aliyah pinched her arms.

"Kill me," Valentine sighed, slumping into the chair. "Dora's all she watches."

Paul pulled up a seat, letting Aliyah yell at the television. He was glad to see that Valentine, tired as she was, had swapped her black eye patch for a glittery rhinestone-encrusted version; she was acclimating herself to her new existence.

"You don't have to stay here. We have a home, Valentine. With a bed. That you've – well, you've mostly assembled it. And you don't seem to mind using your laundry as a pillow…"

She rubbed her forehead. "I know. I just… you know."

"You feel responsible. For her 'mancy."

Valentine gave Paul a hangdog look. "Yeah."

Paul didn't want to ask. "*Are* you?"

Valentine blew a lock of hair out of her eye. "…not consciously. But, you know, miserable girl over there, lack of parenting skills over here… I taught her the way I got through my bad times. And I probably – I probably rubbed off on her."

"Anathema accelerated that."

"She did. But… I catalyzed her." Valentine nibbled a nail guiltily. "I'm sorry, Paul. I didn't mean to… you know. Curse her."

"This isn't a curse."

Valentine glanced over at Aliyah. "*She* thinks it is."

"Yeah, well." He got out the Nintendo DS he'd purchased to replace the one lost in the fire. It was smeared with chocolate from the donuts, but Paul found that fitting.

He slid the Nintendo over to Aliyah.

"No." She pushed it off the bed.

Paul spoke in his best let's-be-reasonable Daddy voice. "You have to learn to control this."

"I'm not a 'mancer," she whispered, and Paul was grateful for that whisper – if she threw a tantrum now, they'd all get Refactored. But Aliyah had always kept her cards close to her chest, and Paul doubted that even her own mother suspected the depths roiling inside her daughter. Some days, he wondered how much *he* knew.

"You're a 'mancer, sweetie. Like Daddy. Is Daddy evil?"

"...no." Her eyes were full of wonder. "All the TVs say how good you are. Mommy's mad at you and even *she* thinks you did a good thing." Aliyah's face, still tight with runnels of half-healed flesh, saddened. "*I'm* the bad guy. *I'm* the burner."

"Oh, sweetie." Paul scooped her into her arms. "The bad 'mancer pushed you into doing that."

"That's why I'm never gonna do that again. I'm gonna squash it. And if I squash it enough, I'll be normal."

Paul double-checked the door was locked and all the curtains drawn – then tossed the Nintendo over to Valentine, who looked at him in guilty puzzlement.

"Show her the rainbow road," he said.

A double take. "...In *here*?"

"We gotta start somewhere."

Aliyah struggled to escape. Paul held her to his chest as Valentine started the Nintendo, took a blissful breath through her nose, and...

The screen peeled off of the Nintendo DS, fluttering to expand into a picture window hovering playfully before Aliyah.

A fresh meadow breeze blew through the portal. The scent of green fields, rubber tires, hot sun on fresh asphalt. The clink of gold coins.

Mario, Peach, and Bowser waved merry hellos. They walked across the multicolored highway to clamber into their cars. Luigi tossed a white circle to Aliyah, who caught it between her hands: a steering wheel.

Aliyah stared, goggle-eyed, down at the invitation to race – then up at the new world beckoning.

"That's the thing, sweetie," he said, holding her close. "You, Aliyah, me – the world was hurting us. And instead of dying inside, or hurting others, we opened up new worlds within us. And this gift... yeah, it's scary. Yeah, it's dangerous. But to leave it unexplored would be to throw the greatest gift anyone ever got right in the garbage."

Valentine had snagged her own wheel from Toad and was clambering into the racetrack, turning into a gloriously abstracted cartoon version of herself. Aliyah hesitated at the threshold, uncertain; she trembled as if she was afraid all this wonder would evaporate the moment she grabbed it.

Paul boosted Aliyah into the raceway. She also transformed into a sleek cartoon version of herself, a joyous black girl running toward a cherry-red coupe with gleaming whitewall tires.

In this new world, Aliyah had no scars.

As they gunned the engines and the racing clock counted down, Paul thought: *How will I teach her something I barely understand?*

And then: *Well, that's all parenting, isn't it?*

ACKNOWLEDGMENTS

steps onto a wide stage
  taps microphone

Testing, testing – this thing on?

This is a weird place to be standing now, man. I was fifteen when I started writing, and as I sit on my couch finishing up my book, it's the week before my forty-fifth birthday. That means, yes, I've struggled for thirty years to publish my first novel. And with each bookless decade that passed, I dreamed of having my own acknowledgements section, like Unca Stevie did. I imagined what kind of pithy things I'd say after y'all finished My Book.

And here you are.

The cardinal sin of acknowledgements is to just list-dump a bunch of names and not tell people what the hell they *did* to help put this book into your hot little hands. So let us discuss the specific ways that people made this book better by reading my early drafts:

Miranda Suri wisely encouraged me to amp up Anathema's personality in the opening scenes so that my Big Bad would be memorable enough to cruise through about 30,000 Anathema-free words before she showed up again.

George Galuschak asked the very vital question, "So why can't Paul just use his own Flex?" which I actually *had* an answer for, but forgot to actually put in the book.

Daniel Starr told me Paul needed more specificity to make his bureaucracy fetish believable.

Mishell Baker was thrown out of the story by almost any off-seeming detail, and so highlighted a bunch of off-character moments I fixed.

E Catherine Tobler had some really good points on Valentine and how to describe her initially. Valentine is carrying a few extra pounds, but how do you tell that to the reader without a) perpetrating the societal hatred that chubby folks like me routinely endure, or b) downplaying the fact that she's a BBW and letting the reader quietly replace the image of a fluffy goth with some generic skinny woman? Elise told me to think, and think wisely.

John Dale Beety didn't like Paul much. Loathed him, actually. His feedback on what he disliked about Paul helped me turn a nebbishy, powerless blue-collar worker into something more sympathetic.

Josh Morrey said that Aliyah's burns didn't seem realistic enough. His medical concerns caused me to seek out my friend...

Cassie Alexander, a nurse and fine fiction writer who has worked in burn wards, who medical-checked my work to ensure its accuracy. If anything is off in the hospitals, well, that's my fault, not hers.

And if we're discussing other writers, well, to quote the great Dante Hicks, I wouldn't even *be* here today without the help of the Clarion Writers' Workshop (2008) and Viable Paradise (2009), both of which completely reforged me as a writer. If you've been toiling in the word-mines, getting nice rejections but never the acceptance level, then either of those workshops will help you level up. Thanks to everyone there who supported me.

Thanks to the creators of the roleplaying game *Unknown Armies*, John Scott Tynes and Greg Stolze, whose amazing magic system is engraved in the DNA of *Flex*. And yes, this book may or may not have been inspired by an offhand comment made during a *Mage* campaign, so thanks to Ian Griffith and Nathan Kossover for putting up with Joder, my pitchfork-wielding, vampire-slaying Amish ninja.

Also much thanks to Angry Robot's very own Michael R Underwood, for handing this book to the right people at the right time. And super-mega-thanks to Amanda Rutter, my editor, for being the person who believed in *Flex* hard enough to persuade the Robots to bring it on board. Check out her services care of *areditorialsolutions.com*.

Now I'll be shuffling off-stage in just another page or two – but remember, it's taken me thirty years to get here, so forgive me for adding in a just few more folks. Thanks to my Mom and Dad, who have proudly supported their weird-ass son all the way in his scribblings (and my Dad even reads my stories!).

Thanks to my special friend Angie, who knows old-school gaming and may or may not have a few habits I put into Valentine. Thanks to my sainted Uncle Tommy and my little spark, Rebecca Meyer; not a day goes by that I don't miss you both. Not a day goes by that I don't hope I'm making you proud.

Thanks to all of you who've read my blog – *www.theferrett.com*, that's two Rs and two Ts. Someone once said that if Edgar Allen Poe were alive today, he'd be a popular blogger with a handful of short story publications. That was me, for a long time; some of you have been reading my essays for over a decade, and I know damn well a lot of you have purchased this book not because you gave a damn about this story, but because you were so fucking thrilled that *Ferrett fucking sold the book* that you ran out and bought it in vicarious triumph.

Ferrett did fucking sell it. Thanks for supporting me. And now that *that* bloom has been knocked off the rose, I really, really hope you like the book as-is, because now? Now I have *no* excuses.

But honestly, if you've read me for a decade, you know who I'm going to end by thanking. There is no other who has been more instrumental in my life. Nobody else could have talked me out of flying home when I bombed out at Clarion and was convinced I could never write again. Nobody else would be willing to read *seven* unpublished novels, watching her husband flail, never being merciful with her feedback because she knew I needed to be punched in the prose and punched hard. Nobody else could have flooded me with such love when failure after failure piled up at my gate, dealing with my depressions, insecurities, and social anxieties.

If I ever seem wise, or well-written, that is an illusion – a glorious illusion perpetrated by the love of my life.

Thank you, Gini.

Arf.

HEY, YOU!

- **Want more** of the best in SF, F, and WTF!?
- **Want the latest** news from your favorite Agitated Androids?
- **Want to be spared**, alone of all your kind, when the robotic armies spill over the world to conquer all weak, fleshy humans?

Well, sign yourself up for the Angry Robot Legion then!

You'll get sneak peaks at upcoming books, special previews, and exclusive giveaways for free Angry Robot books.

Go here, sign up, survive the imminent destruction of all mankind:

angryrobotbooks.com